THE
WARLORD'S
LEGACY

THE WARLORD'S LEGACY

Ari Marmell

BALLANTINE BOOKS

NEW YORK

Copyright © 2011 by Ari Marmell

Published in the United States by Spectra, an imprint of The Random House Publishing Group, a division of Random House, Inc., New York.

Spectra and the portrayal of a boxed "s" are trademarks of Random House, Inc.

Library of Congress Cataloging-in-Publication Data
Marmell, Ari.
The warlord's legacy / Ari Marmell.
p. cm.
Sequel to: The conqueror's shadow.
ISBN 978-0-553-80777-6 (hardcover : alk. paper) — ISBN 978-0-345-52487-4 (ebk.)
I. Title.
PS3613.A7666W37 2011
813'.6—dc22
2010038132

Printed in the United States of America on acid-free paper

www.ballantinebooks.com

2 4 6 8 9 7 5 3 1

First Edition

Book design by Christopher M. Zucker

*For my mother, Carole, who I think owns
a larger library of my work than I do.*

*And with special thanks to George, Naomi, and David,
without whom this book wouldn't be, well, this book.*

IMPHALLION

N

SEA
OF
EMBRAE

TH
S

PELAPHERON

MECEPHEUM

BRAETLYN

ABTH

CADRIEST
MOUNTAINS

THEAGHL
GOHLATCH

SIS

GAR

HOLLECERE

DENATHERE

CEPHIRA

IVIREL

EMDIMIR

RAHARIEM

CHELENSHIRE

DWP
:jmp
2010

TERRAKAS
MOUNTAINS

LEGEND

- ⊛ ~ CAPITAL
- ● ~ CITY
- • ~ TOWN or VILLAGE
- ▲ ~ TAIHEASON'S CROSS
- ■ ~ FORT or CASTLE
- ⋀⋌ ~ MOUNTAINS

- ⊨ ~ PORT
- ~ SWAMP
- ❀ ~ FOREST
- ⋯ ~ HIGHWAY
- ⌒⌒ ~ HILLS
- ⋯ ~ ROAD
- ▤▥ ~ FARMLAND

THE
WARLORD'S
LEGACY

Chapter One

THE EVER-THICKENING SMOKE was more oppressive even than the weight of stone looming above. Black and oily, coughed up by sickly, sputtering torches, it swirled and gathered until it threatened to blot out what little light the flames produced, to transform the passageways once more into a kingdom of the blind.

The stones were old: Dark and made darker by the smoke, they were joined by mortar so ancient it was little more than powder. The corridor, a winding artery of grimy brick, smelled of neglect—or would have, were the air not choked by that selfsame smoke. All along those walls, clad in the sundry hues and tabards and ensigns of half a dozen Guilds and at least as many noble Houses, soldiers stood rigidly at attention, fists wrapped around hafts and hilts, and did their best to glare menacingly at one another. It was an effect somewhat ruined by the constant blinking of reddened eyes and the occasional racking cough.

At the corridor's far end, an ancient wooden door stooped in its frame like a tired old man. Cracks in the wood and gaps where the portal no longer sat flush allowed sounds to pass unimpeded. Yet something within that room seemed to hold most of the thick haze at bay.

It might have been the press of bodies, so tightly crammed together that they had long since transformed this normally chilly chamber into something resembling a baker's oven. It might have been the hot breath of so many mouths jabbering at once, speaking not so much *to* as *at* one another in diatribes laden with accusation and acrimony.

Or it might have been the tension that weighed upon the room more heavily than smoke and stone combined. Perhaps one could, as the aphorism suggests, have cut that tension with a knife, but it wouldn't have been a wise idea. The tension here might very well have fought right back.

Gathered within were the men and women to whom those soldiers in the hall were loyal, and they were doing a far better job than their underlings of glaring their hatreds at one another. Clad in brilliant finery and glittering jewels, the leaders of several of Imphallion's most powerful Guilds stood with haughty, even disdainful expressions, weathering the array of verbal abuse—and occasional emphatic spittle—cast their way. Across the room, separated from them only by a flimsy wooden table whose sagging planks somehow conveyed a desperate wish to be elsewhere, stood a roughly equal number of the kingdom's noble sons and daughters.

Nobles whose anger was certainly justified.

". . . miserable traitors! Ought to be swinging from the nearest gibbets, you foul . . ."

". . . filthy, lowborn miscreants, haven't the slightest idea the damage you've . . ."

". . . bastards! You're nothing but a litter of bastards! Dismiss your guards, I challenge . . . !"

And those were among the more polite harangues against which the Guildmasters were standing fast. Their plan had been to allow the initial fury to wear itself down before they broached the topic for which they'd called this most peculiar assembly, here in an anonymous basement rather than Mecepheum's Hall of Meeting. But the verbal barrage showed no signs of dissipating. If anything, it was growing worse, and the presence of the guards in the hallway no longer seemed sufficient to prevent bloodshed between these entrenched political rivals.

Perhaps sensing that precise possibility, one of the nobles advanced to the very edge of the table and raised a hand. A single voice slowly wound down, then another, until the room reverberated only with the sounds of angry, labored breathing. A red-haired, middle-aged fellow,

Duke Halmon was no longer Imphallion's regent—Imphallion no longer *had* a regent, thanks to those "lowborn miscreants"—but the nobility respected the title he once held.

Leaning forward, two fists on the table, the white-garbed noble spoke to his fellow aristocrats behind him even as his attention remained fixed on the Guildmasters. "My friends," he said deeply, "I feel as you do, you know this. But this is a most unusual gathering, and I'd very much like to hear the Guilds' reasons for arranging it."

"And they better be damn good ones," spat the Duchess Anneth of Orthessis. Behind her arose a muttered chorus of agreement.

Across the room, expressions of condescension turned to frowns of hesitation. Now that it was time, nobody wanted to be the first to speak.

Halmon cleared his throat irritably, and Tovin Annaras—master of the Cartographers' Guild—shuffled forward with little trace of his accustomed athletic step. Smiling shallowly, almost nervously, he took a moment to brush nonexistent dust from his pearl-hued doublet.

"Ah, my lords and ladies," he began, "I realize we've had more than our share of differences of late. I want to thank you for being willing to—"

"Oh, for the gods' sakes, man!" This from Edmund, a grey-haired, slouching fellow who bitterly resented his recent defeat at the hands of middle age. Edmund was Duke of Lutrinthus and a popular hero of the Serpent's War. "Our provinces are starving—not least because of you Guildmasters and your tariffs!—Cephira's massing along the border, and many of us had to travel more than a few leagues to be here. Would you *please* dispense with the false pleasantries and just come to it?"

Again, a rumble of assent from the blue-blooded half of the assemblage.

A lightning strike of emotion flashed across Tovin's face, from consternation to rage, and it was only a soothing word from behind that prevented him from shouting something angry and most likely obscene in the duke's face.

"Calm, my friend." Even whispered, Tovin knew the voice of Brilliss, slender mistress of the rather broadly named Merchants' Guild. "No turning back now."

He nodded. "None of that matters today, m'lords," he said tightly, looking from Edmund to Duke Halmon. "What we must discuss today is of far greater—or at least far more immediate—import."

Scoffs burst from several of the nobles, but Halmon's eyes narrowed in thought. "And what, pray tell, could possibly qualify as more—"

"Lies," Tovin interjected without allowing the question to continue. "Broken promises. Murder. Treason. *Real* treason!" he added, scowling at those who had hurled that word at the Guildmasters mere moments before. "Treachery that threatens us all, Guild and House alike."

It was sufficient to quiet the jeers of disbelief, though more than one noble wore an expression of doubt that was nearly as loud.

"All right," Halmon said, following a quick glance toward Edmund and Anneth, both of whom nodded with greater or lesser reluctance. "We'll hear you out, at the least. Speak."

With obvious relief, Tovin turned toward Brilliss, who moved to stand beside him. A deep breath, perhaps to steady her own nerves . . .

And the room echoed, not with her own slightly nasal tone, but with a shriek from the hallway, a scream of such despair as to bring a sudden chill to the chamber, making even the most irreligious among them contemplate the inevitable fate of his or her own soul.

More screams followed, in more than one voice. The rasping of steel on leather echoed through the hall, weapons leaping free and ready to taste blood, but it was not quite sufficient to drown out the sound of cold bodies striking the colder stone floor.

Edmund, who had stood beside the great Nathaniel Espa while leading the troops of Lutrinthus into battle—who had been present during the near destruction of Mecepheum at the hands of the crazed warlord Audriss—was the first to recover his senses. "Back! Everyone, back away from the door! Halmon! Tovin! Get that table up against it!" It wasn't much of a barricade, but it was what they had. More important, it got the wide-eyed, gape-mouthed aristocrats moving.

Not a man or woman present wore armor, for despite the animosity between Guilds and Houses, none had anticipated bloodshed . . . and besides, that's what the soldiers out in the hall were for. Several did, however, carry swords or daggers, if only for show, and these took up a stance between their unarmed compatriots and the sudden violence outside. Halmon and Tovin retreated from the table and each drew a blade—the duke a short broadsword, the Guildmaster a wicked dirk—and stood side by side, mutual antagonism momentarily buried, though scarcely forgotten.

From beyond the door, battle cries melted into screams of agony, and a cacophony of many voices faded with terrifying swiftness into few. Like the chiming of old and broken bells, blades clattered as they rebounded from armor. A horrifying roar shook the walls until mortar sifted down from the ceiling. The smoke that poured through the cracks in the door grew horribly thick, redolent of roasting flesh.

"Dear gods," Duchess Anneth whispered, dagger clutched in one hand, the linked ivory squares that were the symbol of Panaré Luck-Bringer in the other. "What's *out* there?"

And to her an answer came, though clearly sent by neither Panaré nor any other of Imphallion's pantheon.

A sequence of lines etched themselves across the brittle door, as though it burned from the inside out. For the barest instant the portal split into eight neat sections, each peeling back from the center like a blossoming flower, before the wood gave up the ghost and disintegrated into a thousand glowing embers. Without the door to lean against, the table slumped forward, clattering into the hall to lie atop corpses—and bits of corpses.

More than two score soldiers had stood post in that hall, drawn from the various Guilds and Houses of those who met within this basement chamber. Only one figure stood there now, a hellish portrait framed in the smoldering doorway, a figure that owed fealty to none of the frightened men and women within.

Whimpers rose from what few throats hadn't choked shut in mortal dread, and more than one blade scraped the stone floor where it had fallen from nerveless fingers. For nary a Guildmaster or noble present failed to recognize the man—the *thing*—looming before them.

Plates of steel armor, enameled black as the inside of a closed casket, encased him from head to toe, showing only thin gaps of equally dark mail at the joints. Across the chest, the shoulders, and the greaves were riveted plates of pale white bone. Spines of black iron jutted from the shoulder plates, and from those dangled a worn purple cloak. But it was the helm, a gaping skull bound in iron bands, to which all eyes were drawn.

It was a figure out of nightmare: the nightmare of an entire nation, dreamt first more than two decades ago, and again six years past. A nightmare that should never have been dreamt again.

"You promised us . . ." It was a whisper as first it passed through Duke Edmund's lips, but rose swiftly into a scream of lunatic terror. *"You promised!"*

And the unseen face behind the skull laughed, even as he strode forward to kill.

A VICIOUS CLATTER, a sullen clank, and the grotesquely armored figure stepped through a very different doorway, entering a wood-walled room several streets away from that cellar-turned-abattoir. Soot and crimson spatters marred the armor, as did the occasional scrape where a soldier's blade had landed in vain. Without pause he moved to the room's only chair and slumped into it, oblivious to any damage he did the cheap furniture.

And there he waited, so motionless within his cocoon of bone and metal that the armor might have been vacant. The sun drifted west, its lingering rays worming through the slats in the shutters, sliding up the walls until they vanished into the night. The room grew dark as the armor itself, and still the figure did not move.

A latch clicked, hinges creaked, and the door drifted open and shut in rapid succession. This was followed by a faint thump in the darkness, which was in its turn followed by a sullen cursing from the newcomer and a brief snigger from the armored figure.

"Gods damn it," the new arrival snapped in a voice made wispy with age, "is there some reason you didn't bother to make a light?"

"I'd rather hoped," echoed from within the horrid helm, "that you might trip and break something. Guess I'll have to settle for what sounded like a stubbed toe."

"Light. *Now.*"

"As you demand, O fossil." Fingers twitched, grating slightly against one another as the gauntlet shifted, and a dull glow illuminated the room's center. It revealed the newcomer to be a tall, spindly fellow clad in midnight blues, with an equally dark cloak thrown over bony shoulders. His bald head was covered in more spots than the face of the moon; his beard so delicate that he appeared to be drooling cobwebs; his skin so brittle it threatened to crack and flake away at the joints.

"Better?"

The old man scowled. "Better, *what?*" he demanded in a near screech.

The sigh seemed to come from the armor's feet. "Better, Master Nenavar?"

"Yes," the old man said with a toothy grin. "Yes, it is." He looked around for another seat, spotted none, and apparently decided not to give his servant the satisfaction of asking him to move. "I assume it's done?" he said instead. "You smell like someone set fire to a butcher's shop."

"Nope, not done. Actually, I explained your entire plan to them and led them back here. He's all yours, gentlemen."

Nenavar actually squeaked as he spun, arms raised before him in a futile gesture of resistance—only to find nothing more threatening behind him than cheap paint slowly peeling off the walls.

"I imagine you think you're funny," he growled, crossing his arms so as not to reveal the faint trembling in his hands. The man in the armor was too busy chortling to himself to answer—which, really, was answer enough.

"Of course it's done," he said finally, once he could draw sufficient breath to speak. "They're all dead."

"All?" Nenavar asked, his brow wrinkling.

Another sigh, and somehow the helm conveyed the eye-rolling within. "*Almost* all. A few guards survived. I actually *do* know how to follow a plan, *Master* Nenavar."

"You could've fooled me."

"Very likely."

Nenavar glared. "You stink. Get rid of that thing."

The skull tilted upward, as though the wearer were lost in thought, and then it, and the armor, were simply gone.

Every man, woman, and child in Imphallion had heard the description of that armor, heard the horror stories of the warlord and wizard Corvis Rebaine, who had come so near to conquering the kingdom entire. But the man who sat revealed by the disappearance of the bone and steel—now clad in mundane leathers and a cloak of worn burgundy, his features shadowed in the feeble illumination—appeared far too young to be the infamous conqueror.

"You know what you have to do now, Kaleb?" Nenavar pressed.

"Why, no, Master." Kaleb's expression slackened in confusion, and he somehow managed to unleash a single tendril of drool as his lips gaped open. "Could you tell me again?"

"Damn it, we've gone over it a dozen times! Why can't . . ." Nenavar's fingers curled into fists as he realized he was being mocked. *Again.*

"Well, it appears you were right," Kaleb told him. "I *could* have fooled you."

Nenavar snarled and stomped from the room. Or at least Kaleb *thought* he was stomping; the old man was so slight, he couldn't be positive.

He rose, stretching languorously, and stepped to the window. Pushing the shutters open with one hand, he stared over the cityscape, the winking starlight more than sufficient for his needs.

Yes, he knew what he had to do next. But he also knew that he wasn't expected until after dawn, and that left him plenty of time for a little errand that Nenavar needn't know about.

Whistling a tune just loud and obnoxious enough to wake anyone in the neighboring rooms, Kaleb climbed the inn's rickety stairs and out into the Mecepheum night.

The heat of the day had begun to dissipate, its back broken not merely by the setting of the sun but also by the falling of a faint summer drizzle. Kaleb flipped up the hood of his cloak as he went, more because it was expected than because he was bothered by a bit of rain.

Through the center of town—through the city's best-kept streets—he made his way. Glass-enclosed lanterns gleamed at most intersections, burning cheap scented oil to keep the worst of Mecepheum's odors at bay. The capital of Imphallion was a witch's brew of old stone and new wood, this neighborhood far more the former than the latter.

The roads were evenly cobbled, the rounded stones allowing the rain to pour off into the cracks rather than accumulate along the lanes. All around, wide stairs and ornate columns, some in fashions that had been ancient when Mecepheum itself was new, framed the doorways to edifices that were home and workplace to the rich and powerful — or those rich enough to *appear* powerful.

Despite the hour, Kaleb was far from the only traveler on these streets. The many lanterns illuminated all but the narrowest alleys and deepest doorways, and patrols of mercenaries, hired to police the roads and keep the peace, gave even the most timid citizen sufficient confidence to brave the night.

So it had been for some years now, ever since the Guilds had effectively taken over the city. Tight-fisted they might be, but keeping the shops open and commerce running into the hours of the evening was well worth the expense.

Kaleb kept his head down, sometimes nodding slightly to those he shoved past on the streets or to the occasional patrols, but otherwise ignoring the shifting currents of humanity entirely. And slowly, gradually, the traffic on the roads thinned, the lanterns growing ever farther apart until they were replaced by simple torches on poles, spitting and sputtering in the rain. Gaps appeared in the cobbled streets, missing teeth in the city's smile, and the great stone edifices vanished, edged out by smaller buildings of wood.

On the border between Mecepheum's two separate worlds, Kaleb briefly looked back. Looming high over the inner city, the great Hall of Meeting itself. Here, now, it looked magnificent, untouched by time or trouble. Only in the brightest noon were its recent repairs visible. Despite all the city's greatest craftsmen could do in six years, the new stone matched the old imperfectly, giving the Hall a faintly blotchy façade not unlike the earliest stages of leprosy.

Kaleb smirked his disdain and continued on his way.

Six years . . .

Six years since the armies of Audriss, the Serpent, and Corvis Rebaine, the Terror of the East, had clashed beyond Mecepheum's walls. Six years since Audriss, gone mad with stolen power, had unleashed horrors on Mecepheum in an apocalyptic rampage that had laid waste to scores of city blocks. Six years—more than enough for the Guilds to patch Mecepheum's wounds, if not to heal the scars beneath.

Oh, the citizens had avoided those mangled neighborhoods for a time, repelled by painful memories and superstitious dread. But cheap property near the heart of Imphallion's greatest city was more than enough to attract interest from outside, in turn inspiring Mecepheum's own merchants and aristocrats to bid for the land lest outsiders take it from them. The rebuilding, though slow to commence, was long since complete. An outsider, ignorant of the region's history, might wonder at the abrupt shift from old stone to new wood, from the affluent to the average, but otherwise would never know that anything untoward had ever happened.

The confident footsteps of the richer—and safer—neighborhoods transformed into the rapid tread of pedestrians hoping to reach home before trouble found them, or else the furtive stride of those who *were* trouble. Coarse laughter staggered drunkenly through the doors and windows of various taverns, voices argued behind closed shutters, ladies—and men—of the evening called and cooed from narrow lanes. Still Kaleb ignored it all. Twice, men of rough garb and evil mien emerged from doorways as though prepared to block his path, and twice they blinked abruptly, their faces growing slack and confused, continuing on their way as Kaleb passed them by.

The rain had grown heavier, threatening to mature into a true summer storm, when Kaleb finally reached his destination. It was just another building, large, ungainly; he wasn't even certain as to its purpose. A storehouse, perhaps? It didn't matter. Kaleb hadn't come for what *was*, but for what *had been*.

Ignoring the weather, he lowered his hood and glanced about, his magics granting him sight beyond what the night and the storm permitted anyone else. Even in brightest day, no other would have seen what he did, but there it was: scorched wood and ash, the last remnants of the lot's former edifice, mixed in with the dark soil.

He knelt in the dirt behind the ponderous structure, digging his hands into the earth until he was elbow-deep, first through clinging mud, then drier loam the falling rains had not reached. It smelled of growth and filth, things living and things dying.

Very much like Mecepheum itself, really.

Kaleb tensed in concentration, closing himself off from the world around him. As though he had melted in the downpour, he felt himself—the essence of what he was—pour from his eyes like tears, flow down his skin and meld into the yielding soil. He cast about, blind but hardly unaware, seeking, seeking . . .

There.

He rose, the soil sliding in chunks and muddy rivulets from his arms. He moved several yards to his left and knelt once more. But this time, when his hands plunged into the soil, they did not emerge empty. He carefully examined his prize: a skull, cracked and broken, packed with earth.

Without hesitation or hint of revulsion, Kaleb lifted it to his mouth and drove his tongue deep into a socket, probing through the dirt to taste the essence within. It was not a technique his "master" Nenavar would have recognized. For all the old wizard's skill, there were secrets of which even he remained ignorant.

Six years, but there was just enough left to work with. Just enough for Kaleb to taste, and to know that this was not who he sought.

No surprise, that. The dead from Audriss's rampage, lost amid burned ruins and collapsed buildings—buried by nature, by time, and by the rebuilding—numbered in the hundreds, if not more.

Kaleb, frankly, had no interest in taking the time to search them all.

With a grunt, he planted the skull before him and began to trace symbols in the mud. Twisted they were, complex, unpleasant even to look at, somehow suggesting memories of secrets never known . . .

He was chanting, now, his words no less corrupt than the glyphs accompanying them. Sweat covered his face, a sticky film that clung despite the pounding rain.

Until, audible to none but him, a dreadful wail escaped the empty skull.

"Speak to me," Kaleb demanded in a voice nigh cold enough to freeze the surrounding storm. "Tell me what I need to know, and I'll return you to your rest. Refuse . . . Refuse, and I will bind you to these last of your bones, here to linger until they've decayed to dust."

A moment, as though the risen spirit hadn't heard, or wasn't certain it understood, and then the wailing ceased. It was all the answer Kaleb received, and all he required.

"You did not die alone," he told the skull. "Hundreds perished even as you did, burned by Maukra's fires, drowned in Mimgol's poisons, or crushed as the buildings fell. From here, your ghost made its way to the Halls of the Dead in Vantares's domain. You must have seen the others as well, and it is one of your fellow dead whom I seek."

"A *name* . . ." It was no true sound, a mere wraith of a voice for Kaleb's ears and Kaleb's mind alone. *"His name . . ."*

Kaleb spoke, and the spirit howled as though the worst agonies of Vantares's deepest hell had followed it even into the living realm. But the necromancer would not relent, and finally the skull spoke, told him where he must dig.

And dig he did, in another lot some streets away. Again his senses plumbed the earth, revealing to him the broken bones. Again he drew forth a skull, his tongue flickering out to taste of whom it once had been.

But this time, Kaleb drew no sigils in the mud. He had no use for the spirit that had gone below. From this one, he needed knowledge possessed while living, not sights seen beyond the veil of death.

For hours he sat, fingers and tongue flitting across the interior of the skull, seeking every last trace of lingering thought and dream, every remaining sliver of what had once been a living essence, desperately seeking, desperately hoping . . .

And only as the eastern sky began to lighten, dawn transforming each falling raindrop into a glittering jewel, did Kaleb hurl the skull to shatter against a nearby wall, screaming his frustration to the dying night.

Chapter Two

ALTHOUGH SITUATED ABOUT AS FAR from Mecepheum as Imphallion's borders allowed, Rahariem was one of the nation's more important centers of trade. Grains and hardwoods thrived nearby, and what little trade trickled into Imphallion from Cephira and other neighboring dominions invariably crossed *this* border. Even more significant, however, the local laborers and craftsmen were rather more enthusiastic about working in general, for they kept more of what they earned. Far-eastern Imphallion remained largely under the sway of its hereditary landowners, and while taxes and tariffs weren't precisely low, they were lower than those imposed elsewhere by the reigning Guilds, and handily offset by the high prices Rahariem's merchants could charge the rest of Imphallion for their exotic goods.

Of course, dwelling so far from the centers of power also had its inescapable downsides. This was a lesson taught to Rahariem — in blood — more than twenty-three years ago, at the start of Corvis Rebaine's campaign of conquest.

It was a lesson of which they'd been forcibly reminded two weeks ago.

Today, not only the streets of Rahariem, but also its surrounding fields and gently rolling vales were occupied by thousands of newcomers, and these were not the sorts of traders, travelers, and merchants the region welcomed. They swarmed the city, clad not in silk and velvet but thickly padded doublets, armored cuirasses of boiled leather, and hauberks of chain. At their sides hung not purses filled with discretionary coin, but broadsword and hand-axe, mace and hammer. Like an avalanche, they had rolled over the grossly outnumbered knights and foot soldiers of Rahariem's nobles. What they wanted, they *took*, and woe betide the vendor or shopkeeper who dared raise voice in protest.

Yet for all the terror and violence of their conquest, looting, rape, and other atrocities had been kept to a minimum. Riding their barded chargers throughout the multitudes of soldiers, their crimson banners flying from every government structure in the city, the officers of Cephira kept an iron-fisted command of conquered and conquerors alike. Encased in gleaming plate, tabards sporting the black-on-red gryphon crest of Cephira's throne, the captains and the knights waged a war as disciplined and civilized as war ever got.

And if certain men among the occupied populace—men long frustrated with the nation's bickering factions, furious that the Guilds had not responded to Cephira's act of blatant aggression, disgusted by the lack of discipline in Imphallion's own military—if these men couldn't help but admit a grudging appreciation for the competence of the invading armies and the rigid order imposed by the officers, perhaps they might be excused for such borderline treasonous thoughts.

It was early summer, some weeks yet before the scorching heat of the season would grow fat and harsh. Cooling, cleansing rains remained common, but not so frequent as to thicken the air with oppressive humidity and render sweating its own exercise in futility. And for all of this, the citizens had cause to be grateful, for Cephira's soldiers weren't about to allow such a readily available workforce to go unused.

Overseen by crossbow-wielding sentinels stationed atop buildings and boulders and hillsides, the common folk of Rahariem labored for their new masters. Some constructed fortifications, hauling wood and stone that would ward off the population's potential liberators if and when the Guilds finally ceased dithering. Some razed houses and shops for raw materials, weeping at their loss but never daring to object—for they'd seen the even harsher labors heaped upon the shoulders of those who had. Others labored beyond the city gates, tearing up stumps, hacking through undergrowth, breaking rocks and carting them away: expanding the roads that led east from Rahariem, making them ready for supply wagons and numberless Cephiran reinforcements.

The bite of picks on stone was deafening; the rock dust in the air blinding, choking, a poisonous blizzard. The sun, gentle as it was so early in the season, still beat down between clouds whose shade never lingered long enough to appreciably comfort the workers. Trickles of sweat scribed intricate tattoos into the dirt-caked chests and faces, and though the guards were not stingy with the canteens, the water never soothed.

Leaning upon his heavy spade, one of the workers raised a ragged sleeve to wipe the moist filth from his forehead. Eyes hidden by the gesture, he peered intently at the guards, cataloging, assessing. This soldier was alert, but that one preoccupied; one politely solicitous of the prisoners in his charge, another delighting in any excuse to wield discipline's whip. But today, as every day for the past two weeks, none had what he sought, what he *must have* before he could take his leave of these intolerable circumstances.

He certainly appeared unremarkable. He was a lanky fellow, wiry rather than gaunt, the athletic tone of his limbs sharply contrasting with the crags that creased his weather-beaten face and the grey that had long since annexed his hair and close-cropped beard. He might have been a man just approaching middle age who looked older than his years, or one on the far side of midlife who kept himself rigidly fit; casual observation refused to confirm which.

"Hsst!"

This from the worker beside him, a younger man responsible for cracking the rocks that he himself was supposed to be shoveling. "Whatever you're daydreaming about, Cerris, you'd best shake it off. The guards won't be happy if they see the rubble backing up."

The grey-haired fellow, who was so much more than the moderately successful Rahariem merchant he was known as—so much more, and so much less, no matter how determined he was to think of himself only as "Cerris"—grunted something unintelligible and resumed scooping.

All right, then. He'd given it almost two weeks, and two weeks of hard labor was *more* than enough. It was time to go looking.

———

EVENING NEARED, signaling the workers to queue up under the watchful gaze of the guards. As a dozen crossbows quivered like hounds straining at the leash, a single Cephiran soldier moved down the line, closing manacles around every left ankle. They were simple shackles, these—U-shaped iron cuffs, closed at the back with a stubby rod—but quite sufficient for the job at hand. Following behind him, a second man huffed and sweated as he lugged an enormous length of chain, threading it through hoops in those cuffs.

Watching through tired eyes as they neared, Cerris began to whisper under his breath. His hands opened and closed, the rhythmic stretching serving to hide the subtle twitches of his fingers.

It was a simple enough spell. A shimmer passed over his left leg, so faint and so swift that even Cerris himself, who was not only watching for it but *causing* it, barely noticed. He shifted his posture, standing rigidly, feet together, keeping his real—and now invisible—leg outside the phantom image. Not a comfortable stance, but better that than to have the guard bump a knuckle into something that wasn't supposed to be there.

The guard approached—yawning as he knelt—clasped the manacle around a length of absolutely nothing that looked and felt an awful lot like a human ankle, and continued on his way.

Cerris continued his whispering, new syllables replacing the old. He saw the manacle fall to the dust, but to everyone else, it was invisible, appearing instead to be firmly locked around the equally illusory leg. It was enough to fool the second guard, who passed his length of chain through the nonexistent ring without so much as a heartbeat's hesitation.

Struggling to conceal his smile, Cerris knelt briefly as though massaging a sore foot and slipped the real manacle around his arm so as not to leave any evidence behind. Then, matching his shuffling step to the prisoners who actually *were* chained together, he allowed himself to be led away.

Not far from the road crouched a simple wooden hall of slipshod construction. Thrown together by Cephiran soldiers, it served as bunk for the road workers, far more convenient than herding them back through the city gates every night. Cerris wrinkled his nose as he passed through the wooden doors, the miasma of sweat and fear, waste and watery stew an open-handed slap to the face. It had long since soaked into the wooden walls and the cheap woolen blankets on which the exhausted prisoners slept away their fitful nights. Bowls of that stew, which contained as much gristle as meat, already awaited, one bowl per blanket. Foul as it was, nobody hesitated to down their portion in rapid gulps. While their companions watched from the doorway, two guards moved through the hall, one collecting bowls, the other fastening the end of the long chain to a post that punched through the wooden floor and deep into the unyielding earth. Thus secured, the prisoners could shuffle around the room—clanking and clattering the chain like a chorus of angry ghosts, more than loud enough to be heard from outside—but even if they could somehow force open the door, they wouldn't have sufficient slack to pass through.

It was a simple arrangement, but an efficient one . . . assuming, of course, that the prisoners were actually *fastened* to the chain.

Cerris lay back on his blanket and waited, though he yearned to be up and moving. In a matter of moments, the snores, grunts, and moans of exhausted sleep rose from all around him. He found himself halfway tempted to join them—the accommodations were hardly comfortable, but damn, he was tired!—and it was only sheer force of will that kept him from drifting off.

After what he judged to be about an hour and a half, Cerris was certain that every man in the hall was deep in slumber. Sitting up, he glanced around to confirm, and then rose, wincing at the faint popping of joints that were, despite his fervent demands to the contrary, growing older. Hefting the manacle in one fist, he stepped over the length of chain and crept on silent feet toward the door.

It was slow going indeed, for the room's only illumination was the occasional flicker of the campfires outside, slithering in through tiny gaps in the wood or the handful of six-inch windows that prevented the air within from growing too stale. More than once, Cerris stumbled, and though reflexes born of a violent life kept him upright and silent, he still cursed his own clumsiness.

'*Getting decrepit, old boy. Slow and clumsy. Even just a few years ago, you'd never, have . . .*'

Then he was at the door, the time for bemoaning over, and Cerris gleefully shoved that voice back into its burrow in the depths of his mind. He knew that the door boasted no lock, but was held shut by a heavy wooden bar in an iron bracket. More than secure enough, since even if a prisoner could slip his chain, he had no tools at hand with which to lift that bar.

Except, of course, for the manacle that was *supposed* to be linking Cerris to the others.

For long moments, he listened, struggling to judge the number of guards by the occasional shifting of mail or bored sigh. Possibly only the one, he decided eventually, certainly no more than two. He contemplated a spell to cast his sight out beyond the door, but even after several years of practice, he found clairvoyance disorienting and difficult. He might learn what he needed to know, only to find himself in no shape to take advantage of it.

Ah, well. He'd faced worse odds, in his day.

'*Yeah, but you always had help facing those odds, didn't you, "Cerris"? You never were worth half a damn on your own.*'

He frowned briefly, pressing his lips tight, forcing himself not to respond. It had been *years* since he'd banished the vile thing that had once shared his thoughts, yet *still* he swore he heard that mocking, malevolent voice in his head. And all the more often, these past few months. He must finally be losing his mind.

'*Not that you ever had much of one to lose . . .*'

"Shut up!" he hissed, even though he knew, he *knew* he was berating himself. He forced himself to relax with a steadying breath, then opened the manacle and began working the rod—a length of iron nearly six inches long, and almost as thick around as his thumb—through the gap in the door.

And thank the gods the Cephirans had been in such a hurry to throw this place together! It was tight going, but the narrow rod indeed fit. Cerris slid it upward, slowly, wary of allowing it to screech or grate against the wood. Inch by inch, carefully, carefully . . .

The rod touched the bar with the faintest of thumps. Cerris held his breath, waiting to see if the guard—guards?—had heard. Only when a full minute had passed was he confident enough to continue.

Here we go. All I have to do is lift a heavy wooden bar, with no leverage to speak of, toss it aside, throw the door open, and take out a guard or two before they have time to react. Nothing to it.

He allowed himself another moment to bask, almost to revel, in the insanity of what he was attempting. Then Cerris whispered a few more words of magic, one spell to alleviate a modicum of his exhaustion, another to cast an illusory pall of silence that might grant a few precious seconds. Then, squeezing both hands around the tiny length of metal, he tensed his back, his arms, his legs, and heaved with everything he had.

For a few terrifying, pounding heartbeats, he *knew* he'd failed. The bar had to weigh close to a hundred pounds, and trying to raise it with a few inches of iron felt very much like trying to lift a house by the doorknob. His hands ached where the metal bit into flesh, sweat masked his face, and a gasp escaped his lungs and lips despite his best efforts toward silence.

And then, praise be to the ever-fickle Panaré Luck-Bringer, his problem was solved for him. Something of his struggle—a breath, a twitch, a shiver in the wood—passed through both the door and his phantom shroud of silence. Uncertain of what (if anything) he'd actually heard, unwilling to look the fool in front of his comrades, and thoroughly convinced that the prisoners remained securely chained within, the soldier standing beyond did not signal for help. He did not raise an alarm.

He lifted the bar himself and pulled the door open a scant few inches, just to take a look and reassure himself that all was well.

The iron weight of the manacle—the cuff itself, not the fastening rod—made for a poor weapon, but better than none. Gripping the inner curve of the U, Cerris punched. The prong that broke teeth and tore up the back of the soldier's throat might have left him capable of screaming, if inarticulately. So might the other, even as it crushed an eye to jelly against the back of its socket. But the both together proved too much, and the guard fell with a sodden thump, unconscious if not dead from shock alone.

Glancing around furtively, Cerris stepped through the doorway and slid the bar back into place behind him. Moving as swiftly as he could manage with the awkward load, he dragged the soldier away from the prisoners' bunkhouse, easily avoiding the few wandering patrols that remained awake so late at night. He dropped the body behind a mess tent only after taking the man's own sword and driving it several times through the corpse's face, hiding the true nature of the fatal wound. He couldn't avoid rousing suspicion, not with a dead soldier in the camp, but at least he left nothing behind to point directly at an escaped prisoner.

That bloody business aside, Cerris rose and chanted yet another illusion beneath his breath. The chain hauberk and gryphon-stitched tabard that shimmered into view over his prisoner's tunic wouldn't stand up to close observation, but they would do until he could find another guard—one who, unlike this useless fellow, was near Cerris's own build.

———————

ONCE SAID GUARD HAD BEEN LOCATED, and throttled from behind, the sheer size of the Cephiran occupying force actually proved an advantage. Unable to memorize the face of *every* soldier, secure in the knowledge that the prisoners were under control and that the highway patrols would prevent infiltrators from beyond, the men-at-arms at Rahariem's gates waved Cerris through with scarcely a glance at his uniform.

Within the walls, Rahariem didn't actually look all that different. Crimson pennants flew from flagpoles, yes. Many of the people wandering the streets wore tabards of a similar hue, and atop the walls and makeshift platforms rose an array of engines—mangonels, ballistae, even trebuchets—which had served to aid in the Cephirans' conquest of Rahariem, and served now in its defense. But those streets seemed no less busy, the laughter in the taverns no less raucous. While the bulk of Rahariem's working-aged commoners had been hustled into work camps throughout the city, the young, the old, and the infirm were permitted to continue their daily lives. Shops still fed the local economy, taverns and restaurants provided services to citizens and invaders alike, and of course the officers *definitely* knew better than to deprive their own soldiers by shutting down the brothels or taking the prostitutes off the streets.

Cerris strode casually along those streets, offering distracted nods to his "fellow" soldiers, salutes to the occasional officer, glowers to those citizens who had legitimate business being out after curfew. He made good time, as he knew he would. Intended to facilitate merchant caravans, the city's broad streets were smoothly paved, running in straight lines and recognizable patterns. It was a layout that had served the city well—right up until it facilitated the invading troops just as handily.

'It's astounding these people even have the brains to know which end of themselves to feed. Ants and termites build more defensive communities than this. Serves them right, what happened.'

"They didn't deserve this," Cerris argued with that voice—*his* voice?—under his breath.

'Oh, I see. They only deserved it back when it was you who was—?'

"Shut up!" He barely retained the presence of mind to whisper the admonition rather than shout it to the heavens.

Glass lanterns on posts burned away the darkness, accompanied by stone-ringed bonfires the Cephirans had constructed in the midst of major intersections to illuminate the night more brightly still. Nobody was going to be sneaking around, not on *their* watch.

Nobody lacking a stolen uniform, anyway.

His back quivered with the strain of maintaining a steady walk when every instinct lashed him with whips of adrenaline, demanding he break into a desperate sprint. Every few steps he rubbed the sweat from his palms on his pant legs, and his eyes darted this way and that with such spastic frequency that he was sure he would soon learn what the inside of his skull looked like. Cerris wasn't one to succumb to fear, and frankly being found out and executed as a spy would be a far more pleasant death than many he'd courted, but something about the need to remain so godsdamn *casual* got his dander up.

'Or maybe,' he swore he heard that demonic voice whispering, 'it's *that you still believe, deep down, that they should be afraid of you.*' A moment of blessed silence, then, before 'Even if you and I both know *that there was never any good reason to be. Not without me doing all the heavy lifting. You never were much more than a porter, when you get down to it, were you?*'

Finally, after a few more minutes during which Cerris was certain he'd exuded enough sweat to float a longboat, he neared his destination. The streets grew smoother still; some avenues even had mortar filling in the gaps between the larger cobblestones, to prevent carriages from rattling. The houses here were of a larger breed and stood aloof from one another, boasting sweeping expanses of lawn behind wrought-iron fences or stone walls. Here, in the city's richest quarter, most traces of invasion vanished—except for the guards who stood at the entrance to each gated estate. These were clad in the ubiquitous crimson and boasted the night-hued gryphon, rather than the various colors and ensigns of the noble houses.

Just another example of Cephira's commitment to "civilized warfare"—a concept that, where Cerris was concerned, had about the same legitimacy as "playful torture" or "adorable pustule." The commoners might be pressed into service, but the nobility? Their soldiers and much of their staff were stripped from them, and they were confined to house arrest, but otherwise they remained unharmed and largely unmolested. There they would linger, until either their families offered sufficient ransom to buy their release, or until someone in the Cephiran military command decided that they posed a threat or possessed knowledge the invaders needed.

At which point, all bets were off. Civility only goes so far in war, after all.

"Colonel Ilrik requires information from the baroness," Cerris announced as he advanced up the walk toward one particular estate, dredging from memory a name overheard during the past weeks. "I'm to question her at once."

"What questions?" asked the first guard, a young man whose sparse beard did little to hide either his rotted teeth or his smattering of pockmarks. "What could Colonel Ilrik need with . . . ?"

Cerris halted and slowly, deliberately, turned the full weight of his contempt upon the soldier. Eyes that had seen horrors few could imagine bored into the guard's soul, and the younger man visibly cringed within his armor.

Expression unchanging, Cerris looked the soldier up and down as though examining a rotting, maggot-ridden haunch of beef. "My apologies, Baroness," he said, his tone frosty as a winter morning. "I didn't recognize you in that outfit."

"I . . . Sir, I just thought . . ." The guard glanced helplessly at his companion for support, but the other soldier had the good sense to keep his mouth firmly shut.

"You're still talking," Cerris informed him. "You really ought to have a physician look into that before it affects your health."

The pair moved, as one, to open the gate, the younger even tensing his arm in an abortive salute as Cerris marched past. The guards already forgotten—or at least dismissed as unimportant (he'd never *forget* a potential enemy at his back)—Cerris made his way up the familiar pathway. Around a few small fountains of marble and brass, and through gardens of carefully tended flowers, all of which were actually rather understated where the nobility were concerned, he followed until it culminated at the Lady Irrial's front door . . .

———————————

Cerris paused a moment to scrape the muddy snow from his boots on the stoop, then entered the Lady Irrial's parlor, all beneath the unyielding and disapproving gaze of a butler who probably only owned that one expression—perhaps borrowing others from his employer when the rare occasion required it.

"And is my lady expecting you?" the manservant demanded in

precisely the same tone he might have used to ask *And is there a reason you have just piddled on a priceless carpet?*

For several moments, Cerris couldn't be bothered to answer, instead gazing around to take in the abode of one of his new noble "customers." Where previous houses had practically glowed with polished gold and gleaming silver, brilliantly hued tapestries and gaudy portraits, it appeared that the Baroness Irrial might have more restrained tastes. The chandelier was brass and crystal, but its design was more functional than decorative. A large mirror, framed in brass, stood by the door so that guests might comport themselves for their visit, and a single portrait—the first Duke of Rahariem, grandfather to the current regent and great-uncle to Irrial herself—dominated the far wall above a modest fireplace.

Finally, the butler having stewed long enough that he was probably about ready to be served as an appetizer, Cerris replied, "No, I don't believe so."

"I see. And do I recall correctly that you gave your name as 'Cerris'?"

"I hope you do, since that actually is what I said."

The butler's non-expression grew even more *non.* "Have you any idea at all, Master Cerris, how many people show up here on a daily basis, expecting to meet with the baroness without an appointment?"

"No, but I'd lay odds you're about to tell me."

"None, Master Cerris. Because *most* folk are polite enough, and have sufficient sense of their place, not to arrive unannounced." His lips twitched, and Cerris was certain that he'd have been grinning arrogantly if he'd not long since forgotten how.

"Well, I'm terribly sorry to have upset your notion of the rightness of things. Now please tell my lady that Cerris is here to see her regarding the family's trade arrangements."

"Now, see here—"

"Go. Tell. Her."

"I shall have you thrown out at once!"

"You could do that," Cerris said calmly. "Of course, then you'll have to explain to Lady Irrial why she's the only noble in the city who suddenly can't afford textiles from Mecepheum, or imported fruits, or a thousand other things."

"I . . . You . . ."

"Run along now." He refrained from reaching out to pat the old man's cheek—but only just. Cerris was actually rather surprised that the butler didn't leak a trail of steam from his ears, as he turned and stalked, back rigid, up the burgundy-carpeted stairs.

Only a few moments had gone to their graves before footsteps sounded again on those steps, but the descending figure, clad in a luxurious gown of emerald green girdled in gold, was most assuredly *not* the butler. She looked a decade younger than her years, apparently having faced middle age head-on as it drew near, and beaten it into a submissive pulp with a heavy stick. Her auburn hair, though coiled atop her head, was not so tightly wound as the current style, and her face boasted a veritable constellation of freckles. Most aristocrats would assuredly have tried to hide them with sundry creams and powders, but she seemed to wear them almost aggressively, as a badge of pride.

Cerris, who hadn't really had eyes for a woman since—well, in quite some time—found himself standing just a tad straighter.

"Lady Irrial," he greeted her, executing a passable bow and brushing his lips across her knuckles.

"Why are you bullying poor Rannert, Master Cerris?" she demanded in a husky voice. Her lips were turned downward, but as he rose, her guest could have sworn he saw a flicker of amusement ripple across those freckles.

"Well, I didn't think you'd appreciate me actually knocking him out, my lady, and bribing him just seemed so disrespectful."

Those downturned lips twitched.

"Please be seated, Master Cerris." She swept toward one of several chairs, gown swirling like a mist around her.

"Oh, just Cerris, please," he said, sitting opposite her. Then, "I *do* apologize for just dropping by like this, my lady. I simply thought it best to make sure everyone got to know me, since we're all going to be working together."

"Are we indeed? And why is that, 'just Cerris'?"

"I'm the new owner of Danrien's mercantile interests."

Irrial's jaw went slack. "Danrien sold? *All* of it?"

Cerris nodded.

"I can't believe it. That old coo—ah, that dear old man," she corrected, recovering her manners through her shock, "ate, slept, and breathed commerce. I was certain that, come the day he died—Vantares be patient—his successors would have to pry his ledgers from one hand, and his purse from the other." Her brow furrowed. "To hear Rannert tell it, you're not exactly the most diplomatic individual. How *did* you convince him to sell?"

"Just worked a bit of my own personal magic, my lady," Cerris said blandly.

"I see. I do hope that you're not planning to conduct all your business in the same manner that you dealt with my staff."

"Not unless I have to."

A moment of awkward silence. "You realize, Cerris, that my cousin Duke Halmon actually rules here. The rest of us govern while he sits on the regent's throne in Mecepheum, but we each own only a portion of the city's lands. I can't unilaterally make trade arrangements for all of Rahariem."

"Oh, I understand, my lady. You're not the only noble on my agenda. I just wanted to get to know *each* of you, and to assure you that I won't be taking the opportunity of the changeover to raise prices on goods and transport."

"That's very kind of you, Cerris. And will you be taking Danrien's place in the Merchants' Guild as well?"

"I thought," he said carefully, "that it would be best to deal with the *real* power in Rahariem first, make certain my foundation was solid with you, before—"

Irrial raised a hand. "You wanted to have the nobles backing you before you approached the Guild, so that they'd let you take over Danrien's senior office, rather than starting you at the bottom of the heap as they normally do new members, no matter whose routes they now oversee."

Cerris felt himself flush lightly. "You're quite astute, my lady."

Her eyes narrowed shrewdly. "Then perhaps we ought to discuss a *lowering* of prices, Cerris. Just to make certain that I feel comfortable backing your claim."

For a long moment, he could only stare. Then, "I should have bought out Rahariem's coopers as well. At least that way I could have gotten some work done while you've got me over this barrel."

Irrial laughed—not the genteel titter of an aristocrat, but a full-throated guffaw that would have been at home in any tavern. Cerris couldn't help but smile along with her as they began their negotiations.

⎯⎯⎯⎯⎯ ▶ ◀ ⎯⎯⎯⎯⎯

HE'D VISITED THE ESTATE often in the intervening years—perhaps, though he'd never have admitted it to himself let alone anyone else, more frequently than business strictly mandated—and he knew the layout well. He knew, too, that while his stolen uniform had been necessary to get him through the gate, and indeed across the property, it would stand out dramatically in certain rooms of the main house.

Slipping through the kitchen entrance, he paused, letting his vision adjust to the faint light. He avoided the servants' quarters entirely, for they, as with similar halls throughout Rahariem's estates, were currently serving as billet to a squad of Cephiran troops. The servants who remained, those who hadn't been pressed into work gangs, would instead be bunked three or four to a chamber in the house's guest quarters. In silence born partly of skill and partly of magic—the latter to cover incidental sounds, squeaking stairs, and the occasional pop of aging joints—Cerris crept through those rooms now, and recognized one of the men therein. Sprawled across a sofa, snoring as though Kassek War-Bringer and Oldrei Storm Queen were wrestling in his nostrils, lay the butler Rannert. In all the days since their first meeting, Cerris had never once seen the old man smile, and even in the depths of what must be a worried sleep, his jaw remained fixed in a look of stiff propriety.

The intruder stepped carefully away from the sleeping forms to the wardrobe, slipping on a hanging overcoat he pulled from within and leaving his crimson tabard behind. Back to the kitchen, then, to acquire the necessary props to excuse his presence should anyone awaken and challenge him. Finally, now looking very much the household servant—if, perhaps, a somewhat disheveled one—he trod softly up the stairs and along the hall toward the baroness's chambers.

Decorum demanded that he knock and announce his presence before entering Irrial's boudoir, but prudence demanded with far more conviction that he not risk attracting attention. Working swiftly, Cerris lifted the latch and darted inside, allowing the door to click shut behind him.

It wasn't much of a sound, but the baroness, perhaps troubled at having enemy soldiers in her city and her house, proved a light sleeper. Snapping open a shuttered lantern at her bedside and grasping a long dirk from beneath her pillow, Irrial bolted upright—and stared. Cerris, a tray of steaming tea held aloft in one hand, gaped back at her. Her hair, tousled and tangled with fitful sleep, hung about her shoulders, and the flimsy nightshift she wore to bed was, put politely, neither as formal nor as modest as the gowns Cerris was accustomed to seeing on her.

In a single instant, a dozen apologies and excuses, any one of which might have salvaged the situation with everyone's dignity intact, flashed through Cerris's mind. So of course, what blurted unbidden from his mouth was, "Wow, that really is a *lot* of freckles."

"Cerris!" she protested, flushing hotly. She nearly cut a finger on her dagger as she dropped it, the better to clutch the heavy blankets to her bosom. "What the *hell* . . . ?"

"Oh! Oh, gods, I . . . I'm sorry, I . . ." Stammering like a schoolboy, blushing as darkly as she, Cerris finally had the presence of mind to turn his back, allowing the baroness to haul the concealing blankets up to her chin. It said more for his good fortune, and less for his manual dexterity, that he didn't upend the tray in the process.

"You can turn around," she told him, her tone bewildered and more than a little cold. He did so, to see her sitting upright and utterly concealed, save for her face, beneath the quilts. "Cerris . . ."

I'm *so* sorry, my lady," he told her. "I didn't intend to, ah . . ." He cast about desperately for a way to phrase this. "To startle you like that," he finished lamely.

"Startle. Right." She chewed the inside of her cheek for a moment. "You know, there was a time in Imphallion's history when you'd have had your eyes put out for something like this."

Cerris couldn't help himself. "It might've been worth it," he said, and he was *almost* certain, when she looked down and growled something, that it was to hide that familiar twitch of her lips.

Finally having regained his composure, Cerris approached the nearby wardrobe, selected the first blouse and skirt that looked manageable without the aid of servants, and looked away once more. He could all but hear her pursing her lips at his selection.

"Color-blind, are we?" she asked as she dressed. Once done, she put a gentle hand on his shoulder, guiding him to face her. "What are you doing here, Cerris?" she asked seriously. "If you escaped from your work gang, why in the name of all the gods aren't you miles away by now?"

He stepped aside, poured them each a cup from the teapot he'd brought from the kitchen. "I need your help," he told her softly. "And then we're *both* getting out of here." He seemed surprised even as he said it.

'Oh, please. *Tell me you're just saying that to make sure she helps you,*' his mind taunted in the demon's voice. '*Given the stellar accounting you've made of yourself with women so far, anything else is either delusional or masochistic, wouldn't you say?*'

Cerris found himself grateful that he was already blushing from before, since it hid the shameful flush that newly rose to his cheeks. In any case, it was done, and he focused away from his inner dialogue to listen as Irrial spoke.

". . . commoner might just disappear," she was saying, "but I think if one of the nobility vanishes, they might well come looking, wouldn't you say?"

"Are you afraid of that, my lady?"

"No," she said, and he found he believed her. "I could do a lot more good outside this damn house. But this sort of thing takes preparation, Cerris, and I'm just not—"

Cerris raised an interrupting hand, nearly spilling his tea. "You misunderstand," he said. "I'm not planning on making our escape *tonight*. Actually, in another hour or so, I need to sneak back into the barracks before I'm missed."

Irrial blinked twice, perhaps checking her vision since her *hearing* was obviously faulty. "What are you . . . I don't . . ."

"I need you to help me find something, Irrial," he said, unaware that he'd dropped the proper formal address. "Something that'll give us a vital edge. I can't leave without it."

"What?"

"A weapon. One that would certainly have been claimed by someone of rank. The Cephiran officers meet with the nobles and Guildmasters regularly, don't they? To make sure the city's running to their specifications?"

Irrial nodded. "Twice a week, so far."

"Then you've a better chance of spotting it than I do. It was taken from my home when they attacked, and I want it back."

" 'It'? You're being awfully cryptic. What sort of weapon?"

Cerris sighed. "I don't know."

"Cerris, what are you trying—"

"Have you ever heard," he asked slowly, as though deciding how much to trust her, "of the Kholben Shiar?"

"*What?* You're joking, right? They're a *myth*."

"They're not. I have one. Or I did, anyway."

Maybe it was his eyes, maybe his voice, or maybe the fact that he'd have to be insane to risk escaping—and then *breaking back in*—on a jest. Whatever the case, Irrial obviously chose to believe.

"My gods." She began pacing the length of the bedroom and back. "Rumor has it that Audriss the Serpent and Corvis Rebaine each had one, you know."

"Did they." His voice, flat as an undertaker's slab, made it a statement rather than a question.

"I saw an axe hanging at Rebaine's side, the day he took Rahariem." She was whispering, her expression unfocused. "I don't even know why I noticed it, there was so much else about him . . . Was that it, do you think? The Kholben Shiar?"

Cerris said nothing, and Irrial scarcely seemed to notice his silence. She shook her head as though dragging her thoughts more than twenty years forward, back to today. "If you don't know what form it's taken, how am I supposed to recognize it?"

"It keeps certain traits," he said, hoping now that her memory wasn't *too* precise. "It'll have runes and figures adorning the head, blatant no matter what it looks like. If you stare at them long enough, they'll even seem to move."

She nodded, though her expression remained doubtful. "All right. And if I find out who has it, what then?"

An hour and more they spent in discussion, making arrangements, suggesting adjustments to each other's plans. Night was pregnant with the dawn by the time they'd finished, and Corvis—with a lingering "Thank you" whispered in Irrial's ear—had just enough time to recover his stolen uniform, make his way back through the gates, and sneak into his bunk, where he waited to rise—exhausted but newly determined—with the guards' morning summons.

Chapter Three

TWIN COLUMNS OF HORSEMEN, clad in burnished steel and draped in iron-hued cloths, wound along the highway, a single armored centipede scurrying across rolling coastal hills. Every tabard, every shield, sported the hammer-and-anvil emblem of the Blacksmiths' Guild—as though the sheer quantities of quality armor and mail weren't evidence enough of that particular loyalty. Although they moved at a stately, even staid, pace, the drumming of a hundred hooves shook the earth, melding with the distant waves into a single endless, rolling percussion. The ocean's tang filled every visor, and each soldier knew with a sinking certainty that, though his armor gleamed brilliantly *now*, he would spend many an hour this evening polishing and scraping, lest the coming rust dig too deep.

Between the columns rolled a carriage-and-four, rumbling and thumping over every rut in the road. It, too, was painted iron grey, and it, too, bore the hammer-and-anvil. The driver, a narrow-faced, leather-clad man with sandy hair, held the reins idly in one hand, content to allow the horses to set their own pace. Beneath him, the passengers were concealed from view by curtains of golden cloth.

Another rise, another dip in the road, and the column drew to a halt as the men took stock, their destination finally in view. For most, who had never been so far from Mecepheum, nor come anywhere near the sea, the sight of Braetlyn was an exotic wonder.

Sprawled along several miles of meandering coast, the province consisted primarily of fishing towns. Trade and travel flowed constantly among them, by land and by sea, and those largest communities in the center had begun to meld, early signs of what might one day sprout and blossom into a sizable city. Many a sail fluttered and flapped out atop the waves, nets draped over the sides. The scents of an economy based largely on the fish caught by those nets, day after day, staggered several of the riders like a physical blow.

Above it all, perched atop a low hill, watched a sturdy keep of old stone, surrounded by a palisade of sharpened stakes. From its towers flapped the peculiar ensign of Braetlyn, the crimson fish on a field of blue too dark to accurately portray the sea it was intended to evoke.

The polite thing to do—the *safe* thing to do—would be for the riders to wait, perhaps after announcing themselves with a trumpet blast, for knights of Braetlyn to come and escort them the rest of the way. Instead, after their moment of examination had passed, the soldiers of the Blacksmiths' Guild resumed their march, wending their way into Braetlyn proper.

Citizens poured from their homes, unaccustomed to visitors making so grand, so ostentatious—and indeed, so militant—an entrance. Faces roughened by life in the sun and by the salty spray of the sea stared at the armored forms and the carriage they escorted. On the fishermen, the craftsmen, the carpenters, and the bakers, those faces twisted into expressions of distrust, and occasionally even fear. The local men-at-arms, however, showed little expression at all, despite the caravan's failure to await a proper escort. Some even looked happy to see the new arrivals, and none wore the crimson-and-blue tabard of their supposed home.

Ignoring them completely, the columns followed the road up the final hillside, halting before the drawbridge and the gates—the lowered drawbridge, and the wide-open gates—of Castle Braetlyn.

Here, and only here, a quartet of armored guards wore Braetlyn's ichthyic ensign. Three sets of gauntlets clenched tightly on three gleaming halberds, while the fourth knight approached the newcomers. His salt-and-pepper beard was clearly visible, for he carried his red-plumed helm beneath one arm.

"None may enter Castle Braetlyn under arms," he announced, his voice calm but loud enough to carry over the constant song of the sea.

"Out of the way!" one of the armored horsemen snapped. "We're here to see—"

"I know who you're here to see," the knight replied, offering the mounted soldier a withering glance before returning his attention to the carriage. "There's only one person here *to* see. You still shall not enter under arms."

"You've no right to stop us, you—!"

"Sergeant!" The carriage door drifted open, allowing a sharp, commanding voice to emerge from within. "We are guests here, and we will behave as such."

The horseman grumbled something under his breath, seeming determined to bowl the knight over with the force of his glower alone, but nodded curtly.

The woman who stepped from the carriage was as broad of shoulder as many of the guards ostensibly sent to protect her, and her bare arms were corded with muscle. Her dark hair, wearing just a few streaks of grey, was pulled tightly back in an unflattering bun, and she was clad, not in formal gown or finery, but in a sleeveless tunic of emerald green and leggings of heavy wool. She carried under one arm a small wooden box, latched with an ungainly padlock, and from her thick neck hung an iron pendant: a hammer-and-anvil that did not *quite* form the ensign of the Blacksmiths' Guild nor *quite* the holy icon of Verelian the Smith, but something in between.

"Lady Mavere," the knight of Braetlyn greeted her, and if there was any resentment in the clench of his jaw, he managed to banish it from his voice. "You are, of course, always welcome."

"You are too kind, sir knight." With a gesture, she waved the driver down from atop the carriage. "You needn't fear for your lord's safety," she assured the soldier. "My assistant and I will see him alone. My men will remain outside."

"With the rest of your mercenaries," one of the other gate guards muttered, just loud enough to be overheard. The elder knight, and the emissary of the Blacksmiths' Guild, both pretended not to notice.

"Is my lord Jassion expecting you?" the knight asked instead.

"I'm sure he is, since one of you surely informed him of our presence as soon as we crested the hill."

A scowl was all the response he offered. "Very well. Follow me, please."

"Isn't it astounding," the driver whispered to Lady Mavere as he fell into step behind her, "just how much 'please' sounds like 'bugger right off'?"

In the presence of the elder knight, she was too much the diplomat to grin.

Scattered around the edges of the courtyard, and framing every doorway, stood marble nudes that were either exquisite replicas of Imphallion's classical style, or just perhaps actually dated back to lost antiquity. Impossibly beautiful women reached with beckoning hands, overly muscled men clasped leaf-bladed swords, and all watched the newcomers with empty stone eyes. A few of the statues were not standing at all but lounged supine, draped across the edges of the stairs, leaving just enough room between them to approach the inner keep's doors. Mavere, impressed despite herself, could only wonder just how deep the baron's fascination with Imphallion's lineage and antiquity might run.

Yet the rest of Castle Braetlyn was not so well kept as were those magnificent sculptures. The structure flaunted its infirmity, an aging warrior who knew his best days were long behind him but dared anyone else to tell him to his face. Flaking mortar had been hastily patched, entire bricks replaced, and the brass chandeliers within the entry hall were polished well enough to shine, but not to remove the verdigris and tarnish that had long since set in. It was not the wear of true neglect so much as signs of a slapdash effort by servants who knew that they were hideously outnumbered in their battle against the castle's many years.

Servants in crimson-and-blue livery stepped aside for the knight and his two charges to pass, bobbing their heads in quick respect to the former but glaring from beneath heavy eyelids at the latter. The Lady

Mavere, though she'd expected no warm welcome from the people of Braetlyn, felt her fingers curling into fists despite her best efforts.

Their guide shoved open a hefty wooden portal, and they were there. Before them stretched a sizable room, its stone floor draped in sea-green carpet scuffed paper-thin by years of tromping feet. An enormous fireplace—empty, during these warmer months—occupied most of the far wall, with a marble bust of a warrior's torso mounted above. Tapestries of seascapes and legendary heroics hung from the other walls, as did wooden plaques bearing weapons in modern steel and ancient bronze.

And standing before that fireplace, looking up from an open book in a bored stance quite clearly premeditated to show his guests who was in charge, their host himself: Jassion, Baron of Braetlyn. Not yet thirty years old, his narrow face bore the lines of a man twice his age. Save for a gleaming green ring, he was clad in unrelenting black. Hair the color of newly tilled soil was matched by equally dark eyes—eyes just a touch too wide, as if the man behind them could not tear them from some horror that others could not see.

"Your guests, m'lord," the knight announced, waiting for only the slightest nod before he vanished from the chamber. The door shut behind him with surprising softness, as though afraid to startle anyone remaining within.

"So," Jassion said, shutting the book with a much louder snap and tossing it carelessly into a nearby chair. "Salia Mavere, in my very own home. I'm honored." He apparently couldn't be bothered to even *try* to make it sound genuine.

"Thank you for receiving us, my lord," she replied with a shallow curtsy. He acknowledged with a nod barely more perceptible than that he'd given his knight.

"Do you prefer *Priestess*, Lady Mavere? Or Guildmistress?"

"Just Salia will do, Baron."

Jassion barked out a single incredulous *ha!* "There's nothing *just* about any of you damn Guildmasters. Or anything you've done."

Salia managed, with some small effort, to keep her smile plastered to her face, to show no reaction to the baron's childish outburst. Her companion, however, rolled his eyes dramatically enough for the both of them.

"I'm glad," she bulled on, determined to remain polite, "that you were able to see us without notice like this, my lord. I hope it's not too much of an inconvenience."

Jassion shook his head and took a seat, very deliberately *not* asking his guests to do the same. "I could hardly have been elsewhere, could I, Salia? Your soldiers have been squatting on every road out of here for three years."

"You're not a prisoner, my lord. They're simply meant to ensure your safety, and to accompany you should you need to travel."

Their eyes met in jousting glares, neither under any illusions about Jassion's internal exile. "And do all Imphallion's nobles warrant such *protection*?" he asked.

"Only those who seem liable to attract trouble."

Salia's driver shook his head and slumped into a nearby chair. In response to Jassion's furious glower, he merely offered a friendly wave.

"Why don't you take a seat?" Jassion offered between clenched teeth. Scarcely had Salia done so, placing the box she carried at her feet, than he continued. "Shall we cut the shit, Salia? We both know damn well that I've had nothing to say to the Guilds since you dethroned the regent and sent me on this wonderful sojourn back home. You want something from me, and since you know that I'd sooner sit on a hot poker and then mount a horse than spit on you if you were on fire, I'm honestly at a loss as to what it might be."

"How colorful," the Guildmistress muttered. Then, "First, my lord Jassion, I regret to inform you that I have bad news."

"Oh, *there's* a surprise."

"I fear Vantares has welcomed several of your fellow noblemen into the underworld, Jassion."

That brought him up short. "Who?" he asked in a startled whisper.

"Among quite a few others, Duke Halmon—"

"The regent's dead?"

Salia let that pass, even though both of them knew he'd not held that title for some time. "And Duke Edmund."

Jassion sagged back in his chair, one hand plucking at the cushioned armrest. "I knew Edmund well," he murmured. "We fought together during the Serpent's War."

"I know." And then, her tone suggesting that she might actually have meant it, "I'm sorry."

"Cephira?" he demanded. "I've heard rumors . . ."

"Some of which are true, I'm sure. They've taken several of our border towns, and if we're not formally at war already, I imagine we will be by the time I get back to Mecepheum. But no, they've shown little interest in our territories beyond the borderlands so far, and anyway, this was no Cephiran assassin."

"Then who?"

Salia glanced once at her companion, who shrugged casually, seemingly more interested in picking at something under his nails than involving himself in the conversation.

"There were several survivors among the guards," she said hesitantly, "so most of what we know comes from them. The most helpful of them was a fellow by the name of . . ."

Marlo stood tall, back stiff as a spear, and tried to ignore the chafing of the hauberk across his shoulders, the sting of smoke in his eyes and chest. Many of the others were amusing themselves trying to stare down the other soldiers, but Marlo was new to the ranks of the Cartographers' Guild's men-at-arms, and sufficiently inexperienced—*puffed up* might have been a better term—that he took himself far too seriously for such games. The fact that he'd been chosen to stand guard over a secret summit between select Guildmasters and nobles of the realm wasn't doing his ego any disfavors, either.

Perhaps it was his disdain for the antics of his fellow soldiers, or maybe it was just blind luck, that caused him to look away—to watch aimlessly, so far as the clinging smoke and flickering shadows would permit—down the hall from which they'd all initially arrived. And thus it was Marlo who saw him first.

The young soldier was convinced that he was imagining phantoms in the dark, for how could anyone have followed them down here? Yet the figure refused to dissipate into the shadows; in fact, it was growing quite obviously solid, remarkably fast.

Marlo was reaching for his blade, drawing in a lungful of sooty air to shout warning or challenge, when the new arrival raised a hand. Marlo swore he saw a flash of bloody crimson from the vicinity of the man's chest.

Behind Marlo, half a dozen soldiers screamed, hands flying to their heads as though to hold their skulls atop their necks. Bone shattered, spraying blood and brains from within useless helms, and six men collapsed without ever knowing what had killed them. One of the bodies rocked back on its heels and slid to the floor, spasming muscles holding its hands aloft beside a head that simply wasn't there anymore.

Even as his brain gibbered and his limbs trembled, Marlo was moving, for he alone had seen the danger coming. Broadsword in hand, shouting something he could never later recall, he charged the invader. What part of his mind still functioned, and had not already been overwhelmed with horror, nearly shut down when he recognized the black-and-bone armor, realized who—what—he was facing. But even through a rising tide of terror, brave Marlo knew his duty.

His blade arced downward in a blow that should have cleaved flesh, or at least broken bone, even through that terrible, infamous armor. Should have, but did not, for the warlord parried with a violent backhand that sent the sword scraping harmlessly along the black vambrace.

Marlo felt himself lifted into the air by a hand he never even saw moving. From below that gaping skull came that same red glow, gleaming from an amulet partially concealed by the armor's cuirass. And then Marlo was soaring, briefly, until the passageway's nearest wall ended his flight. He heard his hauberk rattle, heard more than felt the cracking of ribs. He struggled to catch his wind as he slumped to the floor, to breathe around the blood welling up behind his tongue.

Crawling forward on his belly, hand reaching for his fallen sword, Marlo watched in horror as a score of men were torn apart. A vicious axe hung at the armored warrior's side, but the fiend hadn't bothered even to draw it. Fists landed like catapult shot, snapping bones. Flames roared from his open palm, and men crumbled to ash before they could scream. One of the guards slid inside the invader's reach, delivered what should have been a crippling blow to the armor's chest. Instead the dark warrior simply batted the weapon aside, lifted the soldier in a wrestler's hold, and slammed him down upon one of his own armored shoulders. Marlo couldn't tell from where he lay if it had been the spines on that armor, or the brutal impact, that killed the man.

More flames, more blood, and Marlo rose on shaking legs. Struggling through the agony in his chest, sword clapped in both hands to keep it from falling, he moved to strike . . .

The warlord spun, empty sockets gazing into Marlo's terrified face. A black-gauntleted fist rose, and the world went black.

———————

"MARLO WAS ONE OF ONLY THREE SURVIVORS," Salia explained, concluding her recounting. "And the other two accounts pretty well match his. None of the soldiers actually saw what occurred within the meeting chamber itself, but between their stories and the state of the bodies, I think we can draw some firm conclusions. We —"

With an inchoate roar, Jassion was out of his chair and lunging across the room, fingers outstretched for Salia's throat. All semblance of propriety had melted away like so much candle wax, and the veins in his reddened face bulged appallingly.

But Salia Mavere was both Guildmistress of blacksmiths and priestess of their god, her muscles shaped by a lifetime of labor at the forge. A thunderous uppercut snapped Jassion back as though he'd reached the end of a tether. His pupils visibly dilated, and his neck and chin mottled instantly with blood beneath the skin.

And then, though she didn't particularly seem to require his aid, the fellow who was clearly far more than Salia's driver stood between them. Before Jassion had finished staggering, as his legs quivered through the process of deciding whether they were willing to hold him, the other man raised a hand and pushed at the air, as though dismissing some unfunny jest.

Jassion hurtled upward, his feet leaving the carpet, to slam into the wall beside the bust adorning the fireplace. And there he hung, held aloft by unseen magics. His jaw—which must already have ached abominably—fell slack. He shook his head as though to clear it, succeeding only in dislodging bits of dust and mortar that had sifted like dandruff into his hair.

Hand still held aloft, the driver aimed an incredulous gaze at his employer. "Are we *sure* this is the man we want? I've known mad dogs with more sense."

"Salia," Jassion croaked from on high, hands and feet thrashing.

"*Starving* mad dogs," the apparent sorcerer clarified.

"Salia . . ."

"Starving mad dogs in heat."

"Enough," the priestess informed him. She turned a pleasant smile upon the floating baron. "Yes, m'lord Jassion?"

The baron took a deep, calming breath. "I'm all right. I'm calm. Kindly ask your—friend—to put me down."

"You heard my lord," she said sweetly.

The sorcerer shrugged and dropped his arm to his side. Then, staring down at the moaning form that now lay sprawled on the carpet, "Oh. You probably meant lower him *slowly*, didn't you?"

Salia Mavere forced the amused smile to remain plastered across her face, even as her stomach roiled. In a way, she was almost grateful for the baron's outburst, for it provided distraction from her own traitorous emotions.

She didn't fear much, the mistress of the Blacksmiths' Guild. But she knew terror every time she thought of that black-armored bastard— not for what she knew he'd done, but for what he *might* have done.

And she feared, too, what might happen if the other Guildmasters ever came to share her suspicions. *They could take away everything I've worked for . . .*

Jassion rose shakily to his feet, brushing dust from his chest—and, not incidentally, drawing his guest's attention back to what was, rather than what might be. Then, each word strained through clenched teeth, "My sincerest apologies, Salia. That was inexcusable of me. I fear that you've touched on a rather sensitive topic."

You've no idea. Still, she could only raise an eyebrow at that, impressed at Jassion's apparent penchant for understatement. She knew, as did anyone in power in Imphallion, that a young Jassion had been present at the Denathere massacre, when Corvis Rebaine, called the Terror of the East, had ended his campaign in a basement full of corpses. The young baron had watched the warlord disappear with Jassion's older sister, Tyannon, and survived only by lying hidden amid the tangled bodies.

She knew, too, that when Rebaine had resurfaced during the Serpent's War, Jassion had been present at his interrogation. And she knew, though only a few others did, that Rebaine had claimed that not only had he not *slain* his hostage, he had eventually *married* her. At *her* instigation. According to the guards who were present, it had not been a revelation Jassion took particularly well.

So when she said, "I understand," she meant it. "I'll forgive the outburst, Baron Jassion. *This* time."

He nodded curtly. "But I *did* tell you!" he erupted, only barely holding himself in check. "From the day the Serpent died, I warned you that allowing Rebaine to depart in peace was a mistake! We should have hunted him down and killed him when we had the chance!"

"It *was* a mistake," Salia agreed softly. "One I would very much like you to help us rectify." She couldn't help but smile at the stunned disbelief that fell like a veil over his face. "Would you like to reconsider working with us? Or shall I fetch you your hot poker and call for a horse?"

"You want *me* to hunt Corvis Rebaine for you?" He seemed to be having real trouble grasping it.

"I do. The *Guilds* do."

"Why?"

She leaned forward. "Because he couldn't have resurfaced at a more inopportune time. I don't need to tell you that the Houses and the

Guilds are barely speaking to one another, let alone cooperating. Cephira's invaded our borders. We *cannot* afford an internal war on top of all this, Jassion. Our attentions must remain focused on Cephira, and on trying to keep the government running.

"We cannot spare any of our own military forces to pursue Rebaine, not if we wish to check this invasion. In fact, we'll be taking most of *your* soldiers with us when we return to Mecepheum, to join with the massed armies of the other Houses. And I think I'll neither surprise nor offend you when I say that the other Guildmasters aren't willing to put you in the field. You frighten them, for some reason."

"Imagine that," he muttered. Then, "So I'm to hunt down Corvis Rebaine on my own? No men at all?"

"Those few soldiers we *aren't* holding in reserve to deal with Cephira will be needed elsewhere. There's no way we can keep the rumors of Rebaine's return from spreading; might as well try to cage the wind. We'll need troops to keep the peace.

"Besides, any large force accompanying you would be impossible to keep secret, and I doubt a tiny handful of soldiers would be of much use against your quarry."

Jassion couldn't help but smile, then flinched at the pain in his bruised face. "I'm flattered you think so highly of my abilities, Salia, but—"

"I said you'd be without *soldiers*, Jassion, not without *help*." She reached down, lifted the box she'd brought with her. Only an observer far closer than the baron would have noted how her flesh shrank from the touch of the wood. Drawing a key from within her belt, she popped open the lid so Jassion might see.

IT WAS A DRAMATIC GESTURE for something so unimpressive. "A dagger?" Jassion scoffed, his disdain rising like bile in the back of his throat. "I'll need a bit more than . . . than . . ." And then he heard it. His voice failed him as he shuddered at the *whispers* in the back of his mind.

"It was recovered," Mavere told him, her own voice soft, "near where Audriss the Serpent fell. It's been handled only with tools since then, never by hand. Take it."

The Baron of Braetlyn feared little in this world, but his soul shrieked a warning, pleading with his reaching fingers not to close about that simple, innocuous hilt.

Jassion didn't listen. And even as he lifted the weapon, felt it shift and twist and grow within his grasp, the whispers coalesced in the tiny corner of his mind where nightmares dwelt, where a young boy still felt the clammy touch of dead arms and legs pressing against him from all sides. And they spoke to him a name.

Talon.

He blinked, and that eternal instant was over. Jassion held in his fists not a dagger but a great two-handed flamberge, its scalloped blade nearly five feet in length. For Talon was one of the Kholben Shiar, the demon-forged blades who read any wielder and assumed a form best suited to his heart and soul.

"This should even the odds a bit," he said with a smirk.

"You'll also," Mavere said, "be taking him."

Jassion frowned as the other fellow once more offered a cheery wave. "Hello again."

"Salia, I do not—"

"Have any choice in the matter," she interrupted. "Look, my lord, you've already seen some of the magics he has at his disposal. Well, they're now at *yours.* Unless you think you can find *and* fight someone like Corvis Rebaine without such powers."

His scowl deepened further, but he nodded. Though it actually, physically pained him, he extended a hand to the young sorcerer. "I'm sure you'll bring something useful to the journey."

The other looked at the hand, made no move to take it. "One of us has to," he said with a faint sneer.

Jassion ground his teeth. "And what am I to call you, my new companion?"

"Oh, I'm certain you'll be inspired to come up with a great many things to call me.

"But for now, Kaleb will do."

Chapter Four

THE CEPHIRANS WORKED THEMSELVES into a right frenzy upon discovering the two murdered guards, but after a few days of scampering, anthill-like activity, they'd discovered precisely nothing. The bodies were found nowhere near the workers' barracks, and since none of the prisoners had escaped or apparently even freed himself from his shackles, obviously none of them could be the culprit. The soldiers fiercely questioned everyone and doubled patrols in and around the city for more than a week, and stricter curfews made things even more unpleasant for Rahariem's citizens, but the status quo ultimately reasserted itself, as is so often its wont.

Another week or two drifted past; Cerris was starting to lose track. The pervasive but gentle warmth of early summer was steadily building toward its typical midseason inferno, the sun's firm hands curling into pounding fists. Each evening, the forced laborers returned to their barracks weaker, coated in thicker films of a mud consisting of dust and sweat. Listlessly they swallowed cold stew and warm water, then collapsed into exhausted slumber. Cerris began to wonder if he'd have the strength to react to Irrial's signal if and when he spotted it.

On the day he finally did, however, the sudden surge of excitement blew away the worst of his fatigue like a sparrow in a hurricane.

It was nothing remarkable, just a plume of smoke rising from one of the many chimneys of the many houses in Rahariem's richest quarter. Only by scampering up the hillside beside which he was digging the road could Cerris confirm that it came from the Lady Irrial's estate. Just a typical, everyday sight for the manor, since even the reduced staff required a hefty amount of cooking in order to feed them all. Only someone as familiar with the house as Cerris could possibly have known that the chimney smoking *now* led not to any kitchen, but to the large fireplace in the parlor, a fireplace that had no business burning in the midst of the summer heat. When they first came up with this scheme, Cerris had worried that the guards billeted in the manor might ask questions, but Irrial assured him that they rarely returned before mid-evening.

So . . . It was time. Finally. A repetition of his illusions kept Cerris free of the manacles and chains, earning him his freedom once the line of workers had marched back to their stifling, acrid barracks. This time, however, as he'd no intention of sneaking back, Cerris took a rather more direct approach to escaping the billet itself.

Specifically, he set the roof on fire.

It took time—many minutes of intense concentration and chanting eldritch syllables under his breath—but the wood above finally rewarded him with the curling smoke and dancing flame he needed. A few shouts were more than sufficient to wake the others, and their combined uproar brought the guards running. In a frantic rush the length of chain was unlatched from its post and the prisoners shuffled hurriedly outside, there to join the guards in a makeshift bucket brigade.

Cerris, once again cloaked in an illusory uniform, was already moving toward the city, occasionally setting other makeshift structures and canvas tents alight as he went. It should be some hours before the Cephiran soldiers had the opportunity to catch their breaths, take stock, and notice a single prisoner's absence.

It was simplicity itself, in the raging chaos, for the fugitive to find a soldier alone and distracted, and thus to again acquire for himself a tabard and hauberk that would withstand more careful scrutiny. The same two men stood post at Irrial's gate; it was, apparently, their regularly assigned post.

"What's going on out there?" the elder of them asked as Cerris approached, gesturing toward the faint glow beyond the city walls.

"Fire," he said curtly as he passed, scarcely giving them time to haul open the gate. "It's under control, though. Nothing to concern yourself with."

Irrial and her remaining staff were waiting as he slipped through the front door. All were clad in workman's leathers rather than their accustomed finery. The butler Rannert looked particularly put out by the whole affair, but he also hefted a short sword like a man who knew how to use it.

"I'm glad you made it," the baroness told Cerris warmly. Then, without waiting for a reply, "Captain Liveln."

"I . . . what?"

"Captain Liveln. She was wearing a large mace at her side during the last meeting, one with an impressive array of etchings across the flanges."

Cerris smiled coldly. "Is she staying with the others?"

"So far as I know. You never did tell me how you're planning to reach her."

"I thought I'd get her to invite me in, actually. Might I borrow a quill, an inkpot, and some parchment?"

Irrial frowned, but gestured at Rannert. Expression unchanging save for a fluttering eyelid, he delivered the requested items. Cerris took only a moment to scribble a note, and several more to work a taper from a nearby candelabrum. The wax he dripped upon the folded parchment would never pass as any sort of formal seal, but it would suffice to reveal if anyone opened the missive. Cerris stuck the letter through his belt and, even as the baroness drew breath to speak, twisted his neck to stare briefly at every man and woman assembled in the chamber.

"I'm sure you're all faithful to Lady Irrial," he said, voice low, "but be certain. Once this begins, you'll have only a few hours before the Cephirans discover what's happened here, and they will *not* forgive. If anyone's loyalty isn't worth dying over—*and killing over*—tell me now. I'll be happy to knock you out, and you can claim you were never involved. Anyone?"

Several of the staff failed to hold his gaze, but nobody raised a hand.

Cerris nodded curtly and, though he carried the dead soldier's sword at his hip, claimed a dagger from the nearest servant. He looked once more at Irrial who, though her face had grown abnormally pale, nodded in return. "Do it," she told him softly.

Knife clenched in a tight fist, Cerris slipped silently from the chamber, heading for the room in which the billeted soldiers slept.

'Ah, *murdering men in their sleep. That's* the valiant soldier I *remember.*'

When he returned to the others, his hands were crimson. Not one of his victims had awoken long enough to make a sound.

Irrial shuddered, clearly uncomfortable with this side of her friend, however necessary. She and the servants gathered by the front door, ready to cross the lawn and disperse into the streets.

"Remember," Cerris whispered, "groups of no more than two. Once you're away from the estate, *do not run.* Just act casually, behave as though you've every right to be where you are."

'*Easy enough for you,*' the voice taunted. '*You feel like you're supposed to rightfully own everything anyway.*'

It was no more difficult murdering the two gate guards than it had been their sleeping brethren. They knew Cerris—or thought they did—and they expected to see him leaving the house. He approached casually, even offered a friendly smile, and then the younger soldier was crumpling to the earth, clutching uselessly at his slit throat. Stunned, the second man was drawing breath, grasping frantically at his sword, when Cerris drove the dagger up into his chin.

A glance to ensure the street was empty, a wave toward the house, and Irrial and her servants came running. "You remember where to meet us?" she called in a whisper as he stepped away.

He smiled back at her without slowing. "Just make sure you're there waiting for me."

"I'll be there, Cerris," she whispered to his retreating silhouette. Then, with a smile far more confident than she felt, she sent her servants on their way and marched out into the street—arrogant, stubborn, faithful Rannert at her side.

THE ANCESTRAL ESTATE OF DUKE HALMON seemed some-
how off-kilter, standing at the far southwestern edge of the aristocratic
quarter, and indeed the city entire. Haughty and unapproachable,
the first duke of Rahariem had deliberately held his home aloof from
the "lower folk," and while subsequent generations of the line had
softened in their attitudes toward the populace—and vice versa—the
notion of moving and rebuilding their home was never seriously considered.

The property was sprawling, several times larger than the Lady Irrial's, but it was not the rolling lawns or statue-bedecked gardens that
first drew the attention of passersby. The rest of Rahariem's nobles
dwelt in patrician manors—large, luxurious, even imposing, but they
were houses nonetheless. The ducal hall, by contrast, was a sturdy
keep, dating to the days when various lords and vassal states battled for
dominance. The peculiar juxtaposition of a modern and largely ceremonial iron fence surrounding the property, with the looming granite
fortress beyond, gave the estate an unreal, fairy-tale feel.

Today the fortress served as a barracks for Cephiran officers and was
host to many of their strategic and governmental moots.

Still clad as a Cephiran soldier, Cerris approached the front gate
and drew himself upright. Half a dozen guards stood post, and all
looked to be taking their duties rather more seriously than the men
he'd murdered at the baroness's abode.

"I've a vital message," he announced to the nearest, handing over
the sealed parchment. "Captain Liveln's eyes only," he added as the
man made as if to break the blot of wax.

"From whom?" the guard demanded. "There's no seal here."

"I imagine if he wanted that known, he'd have marked it, wouldn't
he?"

The guard swallowed a bitter retort—which apparently wasn't going
down easily—and nodded once. "Deliver this to Captain Liveln," he
instructed one of the others, passing the letter along. A salute, the

sound of jogging feet, and then five guards stood and scrutinized Cerris with various degrees of boredom or hostility. He stared fixedly right back, fighting the urge to fidget. If he'd judged the situation wrong, if Captain Liveln didn't react as he anticipated . . .

'*And a great time it is to be considering that, isn't it, O master tactician?*'

Cerris clenched his teeth and continued waiting.

Finally, after only a few eons, the messenger returned and whispered in the officer's ear. "The captain wishes to see you," he told Cerris. "Immediately." An experienced professional, he *almost* managed to mask his disappointment that he wouldn't be permitted to toss the new arrival out on his rear.

Cerris advanced, refusing even to acknowledge the man, his heart racing. A hundred and one things could still go wrong, and mentally cataloging them all kept him busy, scarcely even noticing the somber stone walls and the occasional bright tapestry he passed along his way. Actually, the artwork seemed remarkably anemic; most likely, the Cephirans had already looted the bulk of it, leaving only these smatterings behind. He stopped only once, to ask directions of a passing servant, and found himself finally before one of any number of identical doors.

A shouted "Get in here!" punched through the door before the echoes of his first knock had faded. Expression neutral, he did just that, casually but firmly shutting the door behind him.

It was a simple enough chamber, a combination bunk and office. Cot, wardrobe, and armor stand against the wall; desk and chair in the room's center. Doubtless identical to every other officer's quarters in the building.

'*I swear, if these people ever had an original thought, they wouldn't know what to do with it. The military mind must be an amazing thing; I hope somebody actually discovers one someday.*'

Standing before the desk was a broad-featured woman, perhaps a decade younger than Cerris himself. Her dark hair was chopped short in a careless military cut, and her tunic and leggings suggested a physique that would be the envy of any warrior her age, gender notwithstanding.

At her side hung a heavy, brutal mace. It tugged at Cerris's mind, but he had no attention to spare it. Even as he entered, a ball of wadded-up parchment struck him in the chest. It fell to his feet with a faint crinkling, blossoming open just enough for him to read the words within. Not that he needed to, since he'd written them.

> *I know about the Kholben Shiar. Let's talk, and maybe your superiors needn't know about it, too.*

"You had damn well better," she growled, "have a very good explanation for this."

"*I* should?" he asked. "Aren't you the one who should have handed it in when you first found it?"

Her flinch was almost invisible, a mere tightening of the lines at the corners of eyes and lips, but it was enough to tell Cerris he'd struck home. "I don't need an enlisted man telling *me* what my responsibilities are!" she hissed at him.

"Look," he said, raising his hands, palms out, "I'm not here to make trouble for you. I'm sure we can come to an, ah, *equitable* arrangement. You keep your toy, I keep my knowledge to myself."

"First things first: I want to know how you even *know* about this."

Here it is. "I recognized it," he lied. "There's more about it that stands out than just the carved figures." Carefully, slowly, he stepped nearer to her side. "Look here," he said, pointing at the mace's head. "Do you see that?"

Furious, paranoid, suspicious, well trained . . . And still, for just that fleeting instant, her eyes left their careful appraisal of this mysterious soldier, flickering to the weapon to see whatever it was he'd indicated.

The first swift blow, his bent knuckles against her throat, wasn't lethal. But as her hands rose of their own accord, grasping at her neck even as she gasped for air, Cerris's other hand dropped swiftly to his waist, then outward. The dagger had already drunk of so much blood that night, but clearly it was not sated. Liquid warmth poured over his hand as he shoved and twisted, wiggling the blade up and around beneath Liveln's ribs until it was only the weapon itself that held her upright.

Cerris let the body fall, carrying the dagger with it, for his hands were already reaching to claim another, far deadlier weapon. Beneath his palm rose a flush of heat like the bare skin of a passionate embrace. He felt the familiar twisting, wriggling in both his fist and his mind as the Kholben Shiar assumed the form of a heavy-bladed axe, whispering in a seductive voice as familiar as his own.

Sunder.

And almost inaudibly amid his torrential thoughts, that *other* voice. *'I'm sure you two will be very happy together.'*

His hands wiped clean on Liveln's tunic, Cerris slipped into the hall—closing the door behind him, of course—and strode casually from the fortress. The guards barely glanced at him as he passed, and if any were keen enough of sight and memory to note that he wore a different weapon than he'd had on the way in, none of them thought anything of it.

AXE HANGING AT HIS SIDE, Cephiran tabard now wadded up beneath one arm, Cerris stepped through the back door of Rond and Elson's, an innocuous shop at one end of Rahariem's central bazaar. He nodded to several men as he passed, recognizing them from Irrial's household, and entered what was clearly a workroom, filled with a multitude of tools and several half-finished barrels.

"A cooper's," he said with a smile, recalling their very first conversation. "Very nice, my lady."

Sitting on a workbench, Irrial smiled brightly. "It seemed appropriate," she said. Then, to her other companion, "Rannert, would you mind?"

The old butler rose and departed without casting so much as a glance Cerris's way.

"You got it?" she asked, rising and stepping toward him.

"I did." He held his breath as her eyes passed over the axe, but while they widened slightly, taking in the sight of the legendary weapon, they showed no recognition. Repressing a sigh of relief, he looked about once more. "This is a good place . . . You own it?"

She nodded. "Rond and Elson rent from me."

"I figured. It's a viable hiding spot, but there's still an awful lot of confusion. This might be our best chance to escape Rahariem, if we—"

"Cerris," Irrial told him softly, reaching out to take his hand. "I'm not leaving Rahariem."

"Um . . . You're not . . . ?"

"Do you remember what I said? I can do more good out here. It's been a month, and neither the Guilds nor the Houses have sent us any troops. We're on our own."

"Well, so far, yes, but—"

"There's an underground forming, Cerris. A resistance against the Cephiran occupiers!" Even in the dim light of the workshop, her eyes shone. "I've been hearing rumors for weeks, but I couldn't do anything trapped in my home. Out here, though? I have resources! Money, people . . . I can contribute. I can help free our home!"

"You can get killed," Cerris protested flatly. "Irrial, there's no way a slapdash underground resistance can stand up to the Cephiran military. Gods and hells, I'm not sure the *Imphallian military* can stand up to the Cephiran military."

"Maybe not, but we have to try. And I'd like you to help us."

Cerris stumbled to the bench and sat hard, Irrial following, still holding his hand.

Is it ever *going to end?* he demanded of no god in particular.

"You're good in a crisis, Cerris. You escaped from the Cephirans, twice! And you can fight, I've seen it. I don't know where you learned how to do what you do, but you could help us. A lot."

He raised his head, and the expression plastered across his face was pained, even haunted. His mouth moved but no sound emerged.

"Just think about it," she asked in a near whisper. "Please."

Cerris offered a wan smile. "I think you're crazy as a snake with hangnails, my lady. But . . . All right. I'll consider it."

'You'll consider it? Really? And you call her *crazy?'*

"Thank you, Cerris." She sat down beside him, her hand rising up his arm, settling gently across his shoulders. "And even though I know it was partly because you needed my help . . . Thank you for coming for me."

She leaned in close, and Cerris paradoxically found himself shivering as he felt the heat of her skin. Her lips brushed his, once, twice, feather-gentle . . . And then hard, almost desperate. He tasted Irrial's mouth, felt her breath in his lungs, and with a final shudder he wrapped his arms about her in return.

And if, behind closed eyes, Cerris saw a face other than hers, a face so slightly younger, gazing at him sadly across a gulf of lost years and broken promises . . . Well, it would never hurt her if she never knew.

Chapter Five

THEY TRAVELED FAR, until Braetlyn was a distant memory and even Mecepheum had fallen behind. Over half the breadth of Imphallion they journeyed, upon the saddled backs of mean, ugly, war-bred mounts from the baron's own stables. Jassion sat his horse stiffly, spine straight, resplendent in chain hauberk—with black-enameled vambraces and greaves—and, as always, the crimson-and-midnight tabard of his barony. His face was sullen, and at irregular intervals his hands reached of their own accord for the terrible sword slung across the saddle behind him, as though afraid that if he ignored it for too long, it might wander away.

For many days, his silence had been a surly one, for Jassion had hoped—despite the discomfort he knew it would entail—to ride forth in full armor, an imposing titan of steel daring the world to deliver its worst. His companion, however, had explained quite resolutely that he did not plan to spend his mornings helping Jassion into his "iron breeches," and since the baron couldn't precisely strap *himself* into his armor, he'd been forced, reluctantly, to settle for mail. Since much time had passed, Kaleb was fairly certain that Jassion couldn't still be angry about so middling an issue, and thus figured that the continued silence was due largely to the fact that the noble was more or less an arrogant, discourteous ass.

Kaleb, who wore no armor but rather a simple leather jerkin and deerskin pants beneath his cloak, took it upon himself, with a malicious relish, to fill the silence with inane chatter. From observations on the weather to the names of sundry flora and fauna, he poured unwanted speech like molten metal into the baron's unwilling ears, and took great delight in watching the fellow quietly seethe.

As the roads grew narrow, however, dwindling into game trails—and as the sparse foliage slowly thickened, the trees towering nearer one another as if seeking comfort from some unseen fear—even the impertinent sorcerer grew serious. Kaleb and Jassion exchanged glances, each beset by a sudden wariness.

A bend in the trail, circling a copse of particularly thick boles, and they saw it rising before them: a wall of green and brown. At that border of branches and brambles, the voices of the wildlife stopped as though the sound itself had been cut by an unseen blade. The sunlight, no matter how it squirmed, failed to wend through the gaps in the leaves, so that nothing but utter darkness regarded the new arrivals from within the foliage.

For several moments they stared at that barrier, each lost in his own thoughts. And only then, as though made abruptly aware of where they were and what waited ahead, the horses reared. Bestial shrieks of terror rattled the trees, startling what few birds and animals had dared draw even this near the looming forest. Eyes rolled madly, and spittle dripped from iron bits.

Even as his mount lurched, Kaleb leapt nimbly from the saddle to land on the thick soil. Jassion, weighted down by his hauberk or perhaps simply less fortunate, fell hard on his back and lay gasping. The baron's mount thundered madly back down the path, and after an instant of wrestling with the reins Kaleb dropped them, allowing his own to follow.

Behind him, the leaves of the impassible wood hissed and rustled in a breeze that neither man could feel, as though chortling their grim amusement.

Kaleb sidled over to Jassion and offered a helping hand, hauling the winded baron to his feet as though he weighed no more than a child's doll.

"Horses . . . ," the nobleman panted between gasps.

Kaleb shrugged. "I can probably call them back once we're through here."

"And . . ." Another wheeze. "If not?"

"Then I guess, my lord, you learn the hard way that your feet are good for more than putting in your mouth or kicking the occasional servant."

Jassion tried to glare, but his gulping breaths—which, Kaleb noted with a snicker, were all too appropriate for a man with a fish emblazoned on his chest—rather ruined the effect.

Remarkably, Kaleb chose to remain silent until the baron had finally recovered. Then, spotting a sudden spark of panic in Jassion's expression, he pointed. "Over there. It fell when you did."

Jassion must have been grateful indeed, for his muttered "Thank you" as he stooped to retrieve the fallen Talon actually sounded heartfelt. He looked taller when he rose, and the lingering traces of pain had faded from his breath.

And again both men stood and scrutinized the wall of trees, like children desperate for any excuse to put off a hated chore.

"Are you certain she's here?" Jassion asked finally.

"What's wrong, my lord? You couldn't possibly be *frightened*, could you?"

"There's precious little in the world that frightens me," Jassion said, still watching the trees. "But I'm not an idiot."

"You—"

"Don't." He paused. "Can't you just cast a spell to find out? Wiggle your fingers and see if she's home?"

"Oh, certainly. Why, I've just been waiting for you to ask. Then, for my *next* trick, I'll gnaw on a steel ingot until I shit broadswords."

"I'll take that as a *no*, then," Jassion muttered.

"You do that."

More staring.

"You must understand," the baron said, "I've heard tales and ghost stories of Theaghl-gohlatch since I was a child. Normally I wouldn't believe a word of them, but then I consider who it is we're looking for. And my understanding is, *very* few who enter Theaghl-gohlatch ever come out again."

"True," Kaleb said. "But Corvis Rebaine was one of them."

Jassion scowled and stalked toward the trees, the smirking sorcerer trailing in his wake.

———————⫂⫃———————

CAREFULLY THEY WORMED THROUGH THE BOLES, pushing and occasionally chopping branches out of their way: Jassion with Talon, Kaleb with a broad-tipped falchion he drew from gods-knew-where. But after fewer than a dozen paces, their progress stalled. The briars and the foliage grew too thick for Kaleb's blade, and while the Kholben Shiar was not so easily ensnarled, the close press of the branches provided Jassion inadequate room to swing.

Branches twisted, contrary to any breeze, to block their path, scraping and tearing at exposed flesh. Thorns pierced leather and wool and even, at times, between links of chain, seeking blood. The air grew thick with pollen and the scents of growing things, cloying and disorienting. Somehow, though they could see the gleaming sunlight behind them, its illumination failed to reach them. They stood surrounded in a pall of darkness as heavy as the plant life.

A distant wolf howled, swiftly drowned out by the flapping of a hundred wings and the chittering of unseen rodents. And when *that* faded away, replaced by dozens of tiny chewing mouths and the whimpering of predator turned prey, even the jaded Jassion blanched, glad now for the shadows that hid his weakness from his companion.

"We should never have come." The baron was shocked to recognize his own voice in that whisper, to feel his lips moving, driven by a fear growing stronger than his will. "Oh, gods . . ."

Kaleb's own face remained as wooden as the trees, and if the same soul-deep terror churned through him, it would have required more than a brighter light to see it. With two fingers, he pushed against the nearest branch, watched as it swiftly sprang back to block his way. He pushed it again, then sniffed carefully at his fingers, apparently oblivious to the panicked whimpering beside him.

He slid the falchion beneath his cloak, back to wherever he'd kept it hidden, and raised both hands before him. He spoke, and though his voice barely rose above a whisper, his words were clearly intended for ears other than Jassion's.

"You brought this on yourself."

From upraised palms poured a sheet of incandescent flame, a torrent of obliteration. It burned a furious blue at its core, leaving spots dancing before Jassion's eyes, but at its edge, where it licked hungrily at tree and leaf and grass, its all-consuming fury was an angry red. On it came, a geyser of fire that seemed to draw strength from the pits of hell itself. And perhaps there *was* something unholy in Kaleb's spell, for the smoke that snaked upward, curled around the trees like a lover's caress, smelled overwhelmingly of brimstone.

Still it continued, until Jassion could see only the blinding light, hear only the furious crackling of the fire. He fell to his knees, hands clasped over his ears, rocking back and forth and praying for it to end. He felt the heat wash back over him, singeing the hairs on his hands, and wondered if his supposed ally were mad enough to incinerate them both.

So overpowering were the reverberations in Jassion's ears, indeed in his *mind*, that when the torrent finally ceased, he took a moment to notice.

Small embers flickered, marking the edges of the clearing that Kaleb had burned into the flesh of Theaghl-gohlatch, though already they were beginning to fade, overwhelmed by the wood's unnatural darkness. Layers of ash coated the soil, and more fell in gentle flurries. Animals wailed from all directions, cries of agony and endless rage, and Jassion was certain he heard words—subtle, alien, unintelligible— intertwined within those calls.

Hands still limned in a cerulean aura, smoke leaking from beneath his nails, Kaleb stepped into the path his fires had gouged. "I can do it again!" he called, and his voice carried far into the forest, passing through the thickest copses without hint of distortion or echo. "And again, and again still! I am no mere traveler for you to consume, and if need be I will burn my entire path, step by step! You cannot halt us, not like this."

And before Jassion's unbelieving gaze, Theaghl-gohlatch replied! Shadows danced at the limits of sight, shadows that should not, *could not* exist in the muted light of the dying flames. Wood and bark creaked in the darkness, accompanied by a low moan that was most assuredly *not* the wind, and Jassion somehow knew that he and Kaleb now stood upon a path that led directly to the heart of this godsforsaken nightmare.

Kaleb gestured for Jassion to rise. The flames around his hands flickered once and were gone, but were swiftly replaced by a steady golden glow hovering in the air just above his head. It wasn't a lot of light, but more than enough to illuminate the path before them.

"How mighty a sorcerer *are* you?" the baron rasped as he rose shakily to his feet, leaning briefly on Talon as though drawing strength from the demonic weapon.

"Enough," Kaleb said simply. "I suggest we move. Theaghl-gohlatch is home to more than just the trees, and not everything is so easily intimidated."

"You find trees easy to intimidate, do you?" Jassion asked wryly as he fell into step beside his companion, and then cursed himself bitterly for providing Kaleb the opening when the man replied with a jaunty "My bite is far worse than their bark."

"This is not the time for jokes, Kaleb!"

"Sure it is. I mean, if I wait until *after* this place kills us horribly, it'll pretty much be too late, won't it?"

It felt strange, striding through that haunted wood, and not merely in a spiritual sense. Beneath the coating of ash, the soil was thick, even spongy. It seemed greedy, reluctant to release their boots, making each step a struggle. Though the trees had apparently cleared their way—Jassion's mind shied away from thinking too long about the implications of *that*—many a branch and root jutted into the path, tripping them, forcing them to duck and edge ahead at awkward angles. They walked within a pocket of sanity that reached only as far as Kaleb's light; beyond, in the dark, lurked trees nourished not on water and sunlight but a palpable, undying hate.

The baron knew, in that moment, that everything he'd ever heard of Theaghl-gohlatch was undeniably, horribly real. And he wondered how anyone, no matter how vile, could stand to make this place their *home*.

Chirping split the dark beyond, a sound very much like a nattering sparrow, and for an instant Jassion began to relax. But the sound continued, never wavering, until the baron felt his muscles quivering, the hair on his neck standing straight—and only then did the woodland song rise to a shrieking laugh. It was a sound no animal, nor any sane man, could have produced, vacillating between a little girl's delight in some new toy, and the gibbering of an old man toying with a new little girl.

Jassion wiped the sweat from his brow with one hand, kept the other firmly wrapped about Talon's hilt—if only to keep it from trembling. He felt a weight pressing on his chest, and he couldn't seem to catch his breath. For a single heartbeat, he was back in the stone cellar of Denathere's great hall, a boy feeling himself slowly crushed beneath a dozen bleeding corpses . . .

No! No, I will not have it! I am the Baron Jassion of Braetlyn! I have faced the worst monster history has ever birthed, and I have proved him nothing more than a man! He shoved past Kaleb, staring into the looming dark, shouting aloud, now, though he never realized he had spoken. "I did not yield to him! I *will not* yield to you!"

Perhaps, just perhaps it was that cry of defiance that saved him, for had Jassion remained behind his ally, his attention locked on his inner struggle, he'd never have seen the shadows gathering, moving *against* Kaleb's light, reaching toward them like questing fingers.

But because he had, when the attack came, Jassion stood ready to meet it.

Rustling, there, in the trees; an explosion of shattering sticks in the foliage beyond. Jassion saw nothing of his assailant, but he felt a gust of movement from the left and dropped into a defensive crouch, taking a blow against his hauberk that would otherwise have gashed open his unprotected hip. A piercing shriek stung his ears as something razor-edged raked across the mail, and though the chain kept his flesh unscarred, the force alone staggered him. Branches and leaves bent inward behind him, the only visible sign of his attacker's passage.

He shifted aside, placing his back to Kaleb's as the forest came alive. From all directions he heard them, though still he saw nothing: footsteps, impossible to pinpoint or to count, circling to a rhythm almost ceremonial, even singsong, in its cadence. The susurrus of brushing leaves blended seamlessly into a choir of incomprehensible whispers. And beyond it, rising to a pitch practically beyond the baron's hearing, that inhuman laughter, never once pausing for breath.

Another flicker of movement, and Jassion swung Talon in a low arc. With a speed seemingly impossible in so large a weapon, the demon-forged blade sliced the air, whistling a war cry of its own. A jolt ran through Jassion's shoulder as *something* intersected Talon's sweep. An impossible, childish voice rose in an abortive scream and died in a liquid gurgle. Milky crimson, like no blood Jassion had ever seen, spattered across the leaves, and he clearly heard the sodden *thump* of something striking the earth near his feet. Yet in the single instant it took him to glance down, something else darted from the undergrowth to claim its prize, leaving no sign of the foe he had slain.

A dozen voices hissed as one, and the mocking laughter died without echo. Even the parchment-like whispers ceased as though the leaves themselves held their breath, perhaps hoping to escape notice.

Refusing to be lulled or distracted, Jassion maintained his crouch, waving Talon before him in wide sweeps, struggling to spy his foe in time to strike. Behind him he thought he heard Kaleb muttering under his breath, but dared not glance around to see what the sorcerer might be doing.

They came as one, from not one side but *every* side. Sound without source, movement without form, they remained unseen—if they were even real at all. Jassion felt the tip of his blade bite into invisible flesh, and then the Kholben Shiar was wrenched from his hand by something that drooled and babbled beside him. He could not help but scream as something punched between the links of his hauberk and into the flesh of his side, searing his nerves like grain alcohol poured across an open blister. Blood welled thickly between the intertwining rings, and though there wasn't enough to suggest an especially deep or gaping wound, Jassion felt the strength drain from his legs. Face beaded with sweat, chewing his lip to distract him from the pain until it, too, bled freely, the nobleman took a step toward his fallen blade, then one step more . . . •

The ground rushed toward his face, an open-palmed slap delivered by the world itself. Jassion tasted soil, felt it filling his nostrils. His hand flopped like a landed fish mere inches from Talon's hilt. Already the pain of his wound was fading, settling into a manageable if constant burn, but Jassion heard the drumming of feet all around him, knew that the seconds he needed to regain his strength were seconds his foes would deny him. Something shifted above, casting a shadow not merely of darkness but of cold across his exposed back, and Jassion all but choked on the bile that surged behind his tongue, the bitterness not of death, but of failure.

The blow never fell, though, for suddenly Kaleb was there. Perhaps driven by whatever magics he had summoned, his limbs moved with speed to rival the forest creatures' own. Jassion twisted onto his side and looked up to see a blur of motion from out of the darkness. And he saw Kaleb step into the assault, his fist closing on an unseen throat and lifting his enemy high with one arm. For a single heartbeat, Jassion thought he could just make out a silhouette, far too lanky and long of limb to be human, flailing as it dangled from the sorcerer's fist. Then Kaleb's hand closed with a vicious crunch, and those limbs fell limp and melted away into the endless night.

Kaleb spun away from his fallen companion, blue flames once more flickering across his fingers. Jassion felt the first burst of searing heat as Kaleb unleashed his magics, and then his wound flared with renewed agony and he felt nothing at all.

THE WORLD WAS BOBBING AROUND HIM. Up, down, up, down, not violently but sufficient to send new throbbing through his aching head, new heaves through a gut that, he was surprised to discover, had already emptied itself. Only with that revelation did he notice that his mouth tasted of bitter residue, and he could only hope that he'd not vomited on anything that wouldn't readily wash.

Jassion pried open eyes that felt gummed shut with the dregs of a tanner's vat, and gazed blearily at the forest slowly marching past him. It must have been drunk, that forest, since it was so hideously out of focus. He snickered at that, a dry, croaking sound that ceased abruptly when he realized just how badly his throat burned.

"And here I was sure you didn't know *how* to laugh, old boy."

The sound of Kaleb's voice was a dash of cold water to the soul, and Jassion's head finally began to clear. He was *walking*, had been so delirious that he hadn't even realized it, and wondered how far they'd come before the slow creep of consciousness had finally reached his brain. Something was tapping him in the back of his head as he walked; he felt back over his shoulder and discovered Talon strapped securely, if not comfortably, to his back.

He was held aloft not by his own strength, but by an iron-rigid grip that Kaleb had looped under Jassion's own arm. His side stung, but it was a dull twinge rather than the roaring agony he'd felt before.

"What . . . ?" he croaked, rather pleased to have gotten even that much out.

"The sidhe," Kaleb told him, jostling the baron painfully as he shrugged, "apparently don't take kindly to intruders in their home. You, my heavy friend, were rather badly poisoned. If the mail hadn't absorbed some of the blow, scraped some of the venom off their claws before it got into your flesh, I might not've been able to save you."

Jassion pushed himself away, standing—wavering and unsteady, but standing—on his own two feet. With a tentative finger, he prodded through the hole in his hauberk. His skin came away covered in some sort of lumpy sludge.

"Spellwork?" he asked dubiously.

"No. My magic is focused primarily in, ah, less *gentle* directions. I'm not much of a healer, and what few restorative incantations I do know wouldn't have been potent enough to help you. I *do*, however, know my herbs. A few particular growths, chewed into a paste, should have counteracted most of the poison. You'll be sore for a time, though, and you'll need to keep the wound clean. It'll be prone to infection."

The baron shuddered at the notion that he owed his life in part to Kaleb's saliva, but nodded his thanks. Kaleb passed him a waterskin from which the parched Jassion drank greedily, rivulets spilling across his chin.

"Careful. We only have so much until we get the horses back," Kaleb warned. Then, "Can you walk on your own?"

"I can." Jassion actually wasn't certain, but he'd *make* himself certain rather than ask the other man to help him again.

"Good. I'm sure this'll come as a surprise, you being an aristocrat and all, but people don't actually *like* carrying you."

Jassion shook his head, then staggered as a new dizziness washed over him, and focused on putting one foot in front of the other.

"Are they gone?" he asked after he'd managed a few score paces on his own.

"Hmm?"

"The sidhe," Jassion said. "Are they gone?"

"Oh, they're around somewhere. But I don't believe they'll be disturbing us any longer." Before Jassion could ask for clarification, the sorcerer continued. "What in the name of Chalsene's darkest orifice was with that speech, anyway? 'I will not yield'? Really? You sounded like a drunken playwright. I could produce more stirring oratory by squeezing a goat."

"Kaleb—"

"An incontinent goat."

"Kaleb, do you really believe I give a damn what the sidhe think of my 'oratory'?"

"Who the hell's talking about the sidhe, old boy? *I* have to be seen with you, you know."

Jassion twisted and reached out a hand, unsteady but enough to stop Kaleb in his tracks. "*My lord*," he snarled.

"Um, what?"

"That's the second time you've called me 'old boy,' and I'll not have it. The proper form of address is 'my lord.'"

"Oh, I'm so terribly sorry. Apologies, my lord Old Boy."

Jassion's eyes flashed, and his hand darted toward Talon's hilt like a striking snake. Clutched it—and froze, without drawing the hellish steel, beneath Kaleb's glower.

"Be very sure," the sorcerer said, his voice low. "You've seen what I can do, *old boy*. You tasted a morsel of it, back at Castle Braetlyn. Even if you *could* take me—which, just to be clear, you can't—you'd be dooming your hunt to failure."

The baron was panting hard with anger, the tendons in his hands creaking with pressure against the Kholben Shiar. "I *will* have your respect!" he demanded.

"No, you won't," Kaleb said. "You'll have my assistance, and that'll just have to do. If it makes you feel any better, it's not you. I really don't have much use for *any* of—well, anyone at all, actually."

"It doesn't."

"Ah. I can't tell you how much that bothers me. Really, I can't."

Jassion took a few deep breaths and, visibly struggling, tore his hand from Talon. He swore he heard a faint wail of disappointment from deep within the blade.

They continued without another word. The world was largely silent, its only sounds the breaking of occasional twigs beneath their boots, or a rustling leaf suggesting that, even if the sidhe would bother them no more, *someone* watched their progress through Theaghl-gohlatch.

Kaleb's mystical light offered little by which to judge the time. Jassion, guessing as best he could, figured that about two hours had passed between his rough awakening and the moment his companion, following gods-knew-what trail, finally led them to their destination.

It wouldn't have looked at all incongruous in most woodlands, that simple hut, but here in the malevolent reaches of Theaghl-gohlatch its presence was nothing shy of miraculous. No trees sprouted within a dozen feet on any side, though their branches intertwined above it, the sensuous fingers of wooden lovers. On three sides of the house, the clearing thus formed was filled with a chaotic admixture of herbs and vegetables, growing in no rows or pattern Jassion could ascertain.

The cottage itself was built of loose stone, though where those rocks could possibly have come from wasn't entirely clear. Ivy crawled across the walls, appearing like veins bulging from a petrified skin, beneath an overhanging roof of bark-coated shakes. The door, too, retained its coating of bark, and somewhere beyond a fire must have burned, for a thin tendril of smoke peeked from behind the rim of the chimney before dashing shyly on its way.

Kaleb pointed at the smoke, waited for Jassion's nod to indicate he'd seen it. "Are you well enough to pretend to be useful in there?" Obviously taking Jassion's murderous glare as a yes, he approached the door and kicked it brutally open, stepping aside so the baron could dart past him, Talon held ready.

An orange ambience emanated from the hearth, though it came from glowing charcoal and ash without visible flame. A teakettle hung from a tripod, keeping itself warm without boiling away, ready to serve at a moment's notice. Plants sprouted everywhere, hanging from rafters, rising from pots, even protruding through the floor.

And sitting on a bed in the far corner, her legs crossed and her eyes shut, was the woman they had braved the haunted wood to find.

Her hair was black as the unnatural night beyond her walls, save for a few glints of earthen brown where the light caressed her locks just so, and her outfit consisted entirely of the same lush browns and vibrant greens as the forest itself. Her face, though lined by many cares, boasted an ageless grace; she might have been just over thirty years old, or approaching sixty, or anywhere between.

Despite the violence of Jassion's entry, the creaking of broken wood and bent hinges as the door twisted slowly in its frame, she did not wake. Her breathing continued, chest rising and falling so softly that the intruders might have thought her dead had they not specifically watched for it.

Jassion stepped forward and slapped the moss-filled mattress with the flat of Talon. No response.

"She's not here," Kaleb said after a moment's concentration.

"Are you daft? She's *right there!*"

"Did you drink much quicksilver as a child, Jassion? I'm starting to wonder how you know which end of a chamber pot to piss in." The sorcerer sighed. "What I mean is, she's not *in* her body just now. Some witches master spells that allow them to briefly inhabit the body of another creature. They use it to pass along messages, or to spy. I imagine she's out seeking the source of the recent disruption in her woods."

"You mean us."

"Why, yes, I do. *Very* good, old boy."

Shashar, grant me tranquility! Aloud, Jassion said, "So how do we call her back?"

"We don't." Kaleb stepped to the witch's side, ran a disturbingly sensuous hand across her face. Jassion shivered and would have moved to stop him, save that he truly didn't know if the man was feeling mere flesh, or the flow of her magics. "It's a shame we don't just want her dead. This would be an excellent opportunity. But no, we wait. She'll be back, sooner or later." He yanked the sheets out from beneath her, letting the empty body tumble aside, and began tearing them into strips. "We *can*, however, make certain that she's in no position to prove, ah, *argumentative* when she awakens."

Jassion's scowl grew even darker at the thought of binding a helpless woman, but he couldn't deny the sense in Kaleb's precautions. The distasteful task accomplished, he left her tied firmly to the headboard and crossed the chamber to wait, his back to witch and sorcerer alike.

Another hour passed, or so Jassion judged by the slowly disintegrating charcoal in the hearth. And then . . .

"Well. If I'd known I was having visitors, I'd have tidied up a bit."

Jassion had to admit, he was impressed. There was almost no trace in her voice of the fear she must be feeling.

Almost.

"And a good evening to you, Seilloah," Kaleb said from beside the bed.

"I don't know you," Seilloah told him. Her attention flickered across the room. "But you, I recognize. Hello, Jassion."

"That's 'my lord' to you, witch!"

Seilloah raised an eyebrow, and Kaleb shrugged. "That seems to be a sore spot with him," he told her casually. "I'm working on it, but he's got a way to go."

"Nobles can be a bit prickly that way," she agreed. Perfunctorily, she tugged on the strips of linen that bound her to the bed. "Are these really necessary, gentlemen? Surely we can discuss whatever brought you here like civilized folk? Perhaps over a meal?"

"I'd hardly call you civilized," Jassion sniffed. "And I know about your dietary predilections, witch. I prefer to be *at* the table come supper, not *on* it."

"I see." Seilloah's lips pursed ever so slightly. "Have you come for vengeance, then, my lord Jassion? Do you fancy yourself my magistrate and executioner?"

"I should," he said, his voice thoughtful despite the rage that quivered behind his teeth. "Your crimes are nearly as monstrous as those of your master.

"But no." He sighed. "We're here to speak with you. Cooperate with us, and you may escape your just sentence for some time yet."

"I see. And what am I to tell you?"

Kaleb and Jassion glanced briefly at each other. "Where," the sorcerer asked her, "might we find Corvis Rebaine?"

Seilloah glanced at the man beside her. "You should know . . . I'm sorry, I don't believe I got your name."

"Kaleb."

"All right. You should know, Kaleb, that I've not seen Corvis in three years. A little longer, actually. I haven't the slightest notion of where he might be these days."

"I don't believe you!" Jassion insisted, stepping forward with fists clenched.

"I'm not the least surprised," she said. "It's true just the same. And even if I did know, it would take far more than you're capable of to make me tell you."

"We'll see about—"

"I *will*, however," she interrupted, "offer you a piece of advice in lieu of the information you seek."

"And what would that be?" he asked, his tone dripping scorn so thickly it nearly splattered across the toes of his boots.

Seilloah offered a beatific smile. "Never attack a witch in her own home, you silly goose."

It hung there for the briefest instant, mocking them. Jassion's eyes grew wide, Kaleb drew breath to shout a warning, his hands already rising.

The torn linens unraveled themselves from Seilloah's wrists and lashed outward, leaving twin welts across Kaleb's face, causing even the proud sorcerer to flinch away. Vines detached from the walls, roots burst through the sides of clay pots, stretching impossibly across the chamber to wrap about Jassion's ankles, his knees, his elbows, his wrists . . . His throat. Gagging and twisting, trying to wrench free even as the foliage dragged him bodily upward, Jassion somehow had the presence of mind to wish bitterly that the world's warlocks and witches had better things to do than lift him off the damn floor.

Seilloah rose to her feet without flexing a muscle, raised by an unseen force. Her arms, her fingers, stretched and twitched as though puppeteering the thrashing vines, and her brown eyes had assumed the hue of Theaghl-gohlatch's leaves, complete with jagged veins of lighter green.

Kaleb hurled fire, but it arced aside before kissing the witch's flesh, pouring into and up the chimney in a burst of thick smoke. The floorboards shattered, flinging splinters to gouge the flesh of all three, as tree roots rose, swaying, enraged serpents of bark and wood. Viciously they tore into the flesh of Kaleb's calves, slapping his legs from under him so he fell hard to the broken floor.

Jassion, who once again lacked the mobility to swing, flexed his aching wrist, sawing at the ivy with Talon's edge. He felt his pulse pounding in his ears. His chest burned, begging for air, and the wound on his side dribbled blood, threatening to reopen as the plants wrenched him back and forth.

But even as Seilloah stepped from the bed to the floor, the smile slipped from her face. Kaleb, spitting syllables nearly unpronounceable by human lips, reached out and grabbed the roots pummeling him. At his touch they halted, bark flaking from beneath his palms as a swift rot consumed them from within. The sorcerer rose to his feet, steady despite the terrible wounds to his legs, and raised his arms once more.

Jassion felt the first of the vines snap beneath Talon's edge. With greater mobility, he went to work next on the ivy that had wrapped itself around his neck.

The witch raised her hands as well, crossed at the wrists, and then she and Kaleb froze, palms perhaps two feet apart, their gazes forming invisible lances in an unseen joust.

The vine around his neck gave way and Jassion dropped to the floor, choking as breath flooded his beleaguered lungs. Even in the midst of his convulsion, however, he couldn't help but gawp at a sorcerers' duel unlike any he'd ever envisioned. No energies flew across the chamber to blast at the stone walls, no fell beasts rose to do their master's bidding, no sounds filled the chamber save his own racking cough and the twitching of the vines. Yet he *felt* the power flowing from the spellcasters, saw the air between them shimmering like a heat mirage, and he understood with a humbling clarity that he would be obliterated in an instant were he foolish enough to step between them.

Sweat bedewed the witch's brow, dripped in a growing torrent down the sides of her lovely face, while Kaleb's triumphant grin grew wider. That his ally would ultimately prove the victor, Jassion didn't doubt. But the vines still writhed, their torn ends reaching for him once more. Smaller plants heaved themselves from their pots, scuttling on tiny roots, and even the teapot on its tripod began to walk with the screech of bending metal. Yes, victory was Kaleb's—*if* his efforts weren't impeded from behind—but even if he won, would he do so in time to prevent the living house from choking out Jassion's own life?

The baron wasn't prepared to wait. Talon clasped in both hands, he approached from the side, careful never to enter the flickering barrier that linked the two combatants, and with a furious cry he swung.

Cloth, flesh, muscle, and bone parted before the Kholben Shiar like a moist pastry, and the floor was awash with blood. Seilloah's fingers clutched at the demonic steel protruding from her gut, fingers leaving bloody artwork across the blade as they spasmed. She craned her neck and, strangely, offered Jassion a knowing smile of crimson-coated teeth.

A rattle of breath, the grating of bone on blade, and the witch of Theaghl-gohlatch slid from Talon to lie in a sodden mass at Jassion's feet.

"I SAID I'M FINE!" Kaleb snapped, hands flexing as though prepared to physically shove the nobleman away.

"Those were some nasty wounds you took," Jassion insisted as they walked, leaving the hut and its wildly thrashing—and now audibly keening—foliage behind. "I'm amazed you can even stand. You told me that your magics weren't much for healing."

"They're not, but they're better when directed at myself than others. I don't need your help."

"The hell you don't. You carried me, Kaleb, and now—"

"If you so much as *try* to put an arm around me, old boy, I'll turn you into something small, stupid, and inclined to lick its own excrement."

Jassion growled something that Kaleb missed (or pretended to miss). Then, as they reached the edge of the clearing and faced the wilds of Theaghl-gohlatch once more, he stuck out an arm to halt the sorcerer in his tracks.

"What did I just—"

"Kaleb," Jassion said, "what now? Seilloah was Rebaine's closest ally, or so I understand. If she didn't know where he is . . ."

The sorcerer nodded. "There's a spell," he said softly, "that I can use to locate people. It—"

"*What?*" Even knowing what Kaleb was capable of, it took all Jassion's limited self-restraint to keep from hurling himself upon the sorcerer, fists flailing. "Then why by all the gods haven't you—"

"Shut up, you yapping pest, and let me finish! First, it requires the blood of a close relative to work. And second, it's easily blocked, at least over any significant distances, and I can guarantee you that Rebaine has any number of spells cast on his person to prevent easy location."

"Oh." Jassion gnawed on the inside of his cheek. "Then why bring it up?"

"Because there's someone else who may know where Rebaine is. I don't know yet where to find her, either, but I *do* have access to one of *her* blood relatives."

"What do you . . . Kaleb, no!" Jassion could feel the blood drain from his face as understanding washed over him. "Gods, no, I will *not* involve her in this!"

"She's already involved, Jassion. She's been involved for twenty-three years."

"No! If you so much as go near her—"

"Do you want Rebaine, or don't you?"

Jassion cursed, vilely, and struck the branches off several nearby trees with the Kholben Shiar. "We talk to her," he said finally, his voice strangely soft, almost child-like, "and *only* talk. If you hurt her, if you threaten her, if you so much as look at her the wrong way, I swear to every god I'll kill you. I don't care how much I need you, or what sort of power you have."

Kaleb just looked at him. "Are you through?"

"If I'm understood, yes."

"Fine. We just talk. Let's get out of this forest before we try it. You're going to be a bit worse for wear after the spell, and I'd rather not chance being attacked by something else while you aren't up to fighting."

"Decided I'm useful, have you?"

"Sure. You make an excellent diversion."

As they resumed their trek, Jassion glanced one final time at the hut they left behind. For an instant, on the clearing's far side, he saw a pair of eyes—a large squirrel, or perhaps a rabbit, the first he'd seen in this wretched place—peering at him, unblinking, from amid the trees. But even as he considered drawing Kaleb's attention to it, the creature was gone, leaving nothing but waving grass in its wake.

Jassion shrugged once, castigating himself for letting his nerves affect him so, and followed Kaleb back into the woods.

Chapter Six

THE WEEKS PASSED in an unending march, and the byways of Rahariem grew ever more crowded. This was, in part, accounted for by the soldiers, extra patrols assigned to the streets since a captive noble-woman and her entire household had vanished into the night, leaving a trail of corpses in their wake.

But only in part. Most of the newcomers were Imphallian, not Cephiran: citizens of the many hamlets and towns that sprouted throughout the region, wild toadstools of expanding civilization. As the invading forces advanced, conquering community after community, it simply made sense to arrange their captives and forced laborers into fewer, larger groups. Thus did Rahariem receive a constant influx of newcomers, prodded along at Cephiran swordpoint.

And with these new arrivals, like camp followers straggling behind, came news and rumors.

Cerris sat in a small office in one of Rahariem's great halls, hunting some of those wild rumors. He wore nondescript tans and greys, and his chin was newly shorn. Without the concealing growth of beard, his cheeks looked hollow, his flesh deeply etched with lines. He looked . . . Well, much as it galled him to acknowledge it, he was start-ing to look old.

Maybe even old enough to justify his presence on the streets, rather than as a laborer in a work gang. So the beard was well lost, no matter how much he missed it.

'Of course you miss it. Never were one for showing your true face to the world, were you, "Cerris"?'

Across from him, a flimsy writing table bowed beneath the weight of heaps of parchment and an array of inkwells. Faint impressions in the old carpeting suggested that a much larger, sturdier desk had stood here not long ago, but it, like so much else of value in Rahariem, was now beautifying the chambers of some Cephiran officer. And behind that desk, chatting on in his infamous drone that could likely have put an erupting volcano to sleep, stood the fellow Cerris had come to see.

". . . fortunate we permitted you entry at all," he was saying, one hand tugging absently at the autumn-red bottlebrush mustache that was his most distinguishing feature—and also the only hair on a head otherwise as bald as a cobblestone. "I almost failed to recognize you without the beard."

"That's sort of the point, Yarrick," Cerris said with a forced grin. "I really don't want a lot of people recognizing me just now."

Yarrick, head of the Rahariem division of Imphallion's Merchants' Guild, nodded sagely. "Yes, I can certainly understand why anonymity might be advantageous under the present circumstances." He sat and offered Cerris a shallow smile, which was about as affable as his expression ever got. "What can I do for you, my friend?"

"Well . . ." Cerris decided to work his way up to it. "First off, I was wondering if you'd heard anything from outside." He frowned, idly tapping his fingers on the armrest. "I know the Cephirans must keep a pretty close watch on you . . ."

Again Yarrick nodded. "On everyone whom they permit to remain active in governing Rahariem. They require our aid to keep the city functioning, but they trust us no more than they must."

"Right, but you're in charge of the largest Guild still operating. You must have some contact with the newcomers they've been herding into the city."

"Some," the bald merchant admitted. "Alas, I've heard nothing to suggest that anyone shall be coming to our aid anytime soon."

The old wood of the armrest cracked as Cerris's grip clenched.

"What the bloody steaming hell is *wrong* with them, Yarrick?" he demanded. "This is a godsdamn *invasion* they're ignoring!"

"If I knew anything for certain," Yarrick said with a shrug, "I would tell you." He leaned forward and lowered his voice. "I'd not even reveal this much, were you not a member in high standing of my own Guild . . ."

"Yes?" Cerris, too, found himself leaning forward.

"A portion of it may, of course, be the standard jockeying for position that's ensnared our government for years now. The Guilds will not commit themselves without consensus, and the nobles are reluctant to relinquish to the Guilds what little authority they have remaining. But it's more than that. I've heard no details, but rumor has it that a number of nobles and Guildmasters were lost recently. I cannot speak to the nature of the attack, or accident, or whatever it may have been, but Imphallion may be facing threats from within as well as without."

"Perfect." Cerris grunted, falling back in his chair. "That's all we need, isn't it?"

'Ah, if only,' that inner voice taunted, *'there was someone in charge who knew what he was doing . . .'*

"Indeed. It almost makes one long for the days of Audriss the Serpent. At least then we understood the threat we faced."

"Not really," Cerris muttered under his breath.

"But surely, Cerris, you've not come to me merely seeking gossip and rumor." Yarrick chewed thoughtfully on the bristles overhanging his lip. "You've your own contacts among Rahariem's merchants and vendors, you could have learned this much on your own."

"Not as quickly. But you're right, there is something else I need." It was Cerris's turn to glance nervously around the room, as though he could somehow spot any prying ears that had so far gone unnoticed. "As part of the Cephiran puppet government—um, no offense . . ."

"None taken. It's an apt enough description."

"Then you must have some insight into their schedules. Specifically, you'd know when their next major supply caravan is due."

Yarrick's expression soured, as though he'd just discovered lemon juice in his mustache. "That's a dangerous question, Cerris. You're not preparing to cause any trouble, are you?"

"I'm trying to *avoid* trouble," Cerris lied. "Frankly, my friend, I'm planning to get the hell out of here—sooner rather than later—and I want to make sure I don't run into a few hundred Cephiran soldiers on the road. A few sentries or a single patrol, I can avoid, but a caravan . . ." He left it hanging, concluding the sentence with a sickly grin and a shrug.

"All right," Yarrick said after a few more moments of mustache chewing. "But if anything goes awry, you didn't hear this from me."

". . . FIVE DAYS FROM NOW," Cerris explained to the crowded, smelly workshop that evening. Irrial stood beside him, pressing close, while the others sat on scattered benches or empty barrels. "It's not coming from Cephira, but from some of the outlying Imphallian villages that they've already taken. Consolidating supplies, that sort of thing. There's no certainty as to what time they'll arrive, but I imagine it'll be early in the day. They'll probably make close camp the night before."

"We're not going to have a lot of options." It was Andevar who spoke, rising and striding toward the front of the room. Ludicrously squat and thickly bearded, he looked rather as though the gods had stuck a lion's head atop an enormous link of sausage and called it life. But he was also the former bodyguard of a local aristocrat who hadn't survived the Cephiran siege. Andevar possessed considerable tactical acumen, and had taken his failure to protect his lord as a personal affront. When Irrial had introduced Cerris to the various leaders of the burgeoning resistance, he'd not been at all surprised to find Andevar among them.

He stopped before Cerris and Irrial, gestured at the parchment map they'd unrolled atop a barrel. "Land's too flat, and the Cephies have cut down too many of the nearby trees. Nowhere to hide there."

"But ambush is our only option," Irrial protested, bolstered by nods and grunts of agreement from the assembly. "We can't possibly take the caravan by main force."

"I think maybe we could," Andevar said thoughtfully, "but even if we did, the losses wouldn't be worth it. No, I agree, it's got to be ambush, and that means it's got to be pretty far out from the city. Here?" he suggested, landing a finger on a tree-bedecked bend in the road toward the very edge of the map, two miles from Rahariem proper.

Cerris cocked his head. "It's not optimal, but I agree it may be our only choice."

"We'll need to figure out how to get our people out of the city and down the highway without being spotted," Irrial pointed out.

Everyone glanced about, hoping someone else would offer a suggestion.

"Look," Cerris said finally, "we've got the schedule, and we've got a few days to figure it out. It's late. Let's call it a night, and work out the details tomorrow."

"All right," Andevar said. "But we should assemble at the alternative site. We've used this one three nights in a row, and it's making me nervous."

With a rumble of slowly receding conversation, the room emptied by ones and twos, the rebels doing their best to move inconspicuously out into the streets, until only Cerris, Irrial, and Rannert remained — and the latter only briefly, for he soon departed to ensure the various doors and windows were latched.

With a dull groan, more of exasperation than exhaustion, Cerris collapsed to the nearest bench. Irrial stepped behind him, running her fingers through his hair. "Thank you again," she told him softly.

"Don't thank me until we've survived this insanity, Irrial. I still think we should be on the road to, oh, *anywhere*."

"Maybe," she said, hands dropping to his shoulders. "But you stayed with me, and that's what counts." She leaned in, kissed the top of his head. "And look at what we've *already* accomplished. They wouldn't have had the weapons to even *consider* something this major without my resources, and without you . . ."

'*Oh, yeah, she's provided just enough weapons for these morons to run out and get themselves neatly diced into small, fleshy cubes. You've done wonders for your cause. Again.*'

"Shut up!" Cerris hissed under his breath. Then, at Irrial's puzzled blinking, "Ah, sorry. Not you. Just . . . Talking to myself. Considering options."

Poor, very poor. Pathetic, even. But what else could he offer her? *Oh, that? I'm just talking to a creature who shared my head for so long that his voice seems to have stayed around even though the bastard's long since gone to hell. Literally.* Somehow, he didn't think that'd go over very well. At best, she'd think him haunted; at worst (and most likely), a lunatic.

Cerris himself wasn't entirely sure which of the two options he preferred. But so long as it—the voice, his apparent madness, whatever it was—caused him no tribulations other than the occasional bout of self-loathing and the need to tell himself to shut up, he could endure.

'Really? Guess I'll have to try harder, then.'

Irrial blinked one last time, then sat on the bench beside him. "You know, you never did mention how you found out when the caravan's due."

"Yarrick."

"*What?*"

Cerris chuckled. "Relax, m'lady. I didn't tell him anything about our plans. He thinks I'm just trying to escape without being caught." He paused. "If this works out, though, we might consider bringing him in. He's got resources and connections you don't, and he's got no reason to love Cephira. They may have left him his office and his Guild, but they're pulling his strings and he knows it."

"Gods, must we? The man's dull as lettuce, Cerris."

"He really, really is. I understand that sheep count *him* when they're lying awake at night." He smiled at Irrial's laughter. "But if he can be useful . . ."

"Oh, all right. If this first operation works out, we'll talk about it." She gave him a smoldering look from beneath her lashes. "But if he starts putting me to sleep, I'm making it your responsibility to figure out new ways to keep me awake."

"Well." Cerris rose to his feet, double-checked to ensure the door was securely bolted, and turned her way once more. "I'd better start practicing, then, hadn't I?"

ASSUMING ALL WENT even remotely to plan, getting back into the city wouldn't be an issue. In addition to all the supplies they could carry, the resistance would find themselves in possession of a whole mess of Cephiran tabards and armor. And since the city's main gates remained open during the day—to allow the labor gangs passage—the rebels need simply hide in the wilderness overnight and then return, by ones and twos, in the same disguise that had served Cerris so well.

No, as Irrial had rightly pointed out, it would be getting *out* through Rahariem's heavily manned western gates that would prove difficult. Suggestion became discussion became argument, and days flew by within the beats of nervously pounding hearts. Only two nights remained before the caravan's scheduled arrival, now, and still every strategy they developed offered more risk than reward.

"I'm starting to think it would be a damn sight easier," Andevar barked in frustration, pacing irritably before the assembled insurgents, "for us to just attack the fucking walls directly."

And following on the heels of that comment, a plan crept fully formed into the forefront of Cerris's mind. For several long moments, as the others continued their fruitless debate, he examined it in horrified disbelief. Yet over the past days, he had spent much time walking the streets, idly examining Rahariem's defenses, seeking inspiration— and despite himself, he had to concede that it might actually work.

'Wow. You really have gone insane, haven't you?'

Every face in the room lit up with elated anticipation when Cerris announced that he had an idea—expressions that swiftly grew hostile when he refused to tell them what it was.

"Look, it's better you don't know," he explained—lamely, he admitted—trying to quell the rising chorus. "It's something I need to handle on my own."

"Cerris, you can't ask us to . . ."

". . . could you possibly do by yourself that we couldn't . . ."

". . . not staking my life on a plan you won't even . . ."

". . . bloody idiot if you think I'm going to trust . . ."

And on, and on, until the individual words lost all meaning, the voices coalescing into a meaningless, angry rumble. But Cerris stood, arms crossed, unrelenting—and struggling fiercely to ignore that wretched voice, needling him, reminding him *'There was a time they wouldn't have questioned you. They wouldn't have* dared. *Gods, you've grown soft in your old age. Or maybe it's old in your soft age. But soft and old, regardless.'*

Finally, the verbal floodwaters subsided enough that he might make himself heard over the din. Perhaps "Everyone shut the hell *up!*" wasn't the most politic way he might have made his case, but it bought a moment of astonished silence.

'That's a little more like it. Still needs work, though.'

"Perhaps," he said more quietly, "I'll be able to explain later. I *can't* now. It was you," he said, meeting Andevar's glare, "who chose the supply caravan as our target. And you"—now directing a somewhat gentler expression toward Irrial—"who begged for my help. Well, I've helped, and I'll continue to help, but I'll do it *my way.* I remind you that we no longer have the time for debate. I need you . . ." His gaze swept every man and woman present before ending, once more, on the baroness. ". . . to trust me," he finished gently.

Nobody left the meeting happy that night, and the new suspicion in Irrial's eyes sunk painfully into his gut like a steel-shod hoof, but at the last they had agreed. What else, ultimately, could they do?

CERRIS SLIPPED FROM THE HIDDEN chamber several hours before dusk. Despite the mask of confidence he'd worn to reassure his allies, he knew damn well his plan was fraught with hazards. It was not these that caused him to chew nervously at his lips and cheeks, however, or to wipe a constant sheen of sweat from his palms. No, instead it was the thought of the magics he must invoke . . .

An intricate, ancient spell whose prior use had cost him everything he treasured, and delivered precious little of what it promised.

Streets and alleys, homes and storefronts, citizens and soldiers passed by all unnoticed, for Cerris's attentions were turned inward.

He'd long since committed the incantations and tendon-contorting gestures to memory. He hadn't dared keep the original writings on his person, for this was the last surviving spell of the Archmage Selakrian, a page torn from his ancient tome before the spellbook perished in flame. To keep such a terrible prize was to invite the attention, if not the enmity, of Imphallion's small but potent community of sorcerers.

But even with his iron will and a mind as sharp as the Kholben Shiar, he had difficulty retaining such arcane formulae, for this was a complex spell indeed, well beyond Cerris's normal proficiency. He had cast the invocation several times before—most recently a few years back, on a particularly stubborn Rahariem merchant—and he recited it over and over on his walk, lips moving and twisting until they were numb, but still he remained only half convinced that he'd properly re-called it.

Evening's advance scouts were peering over the horizon, perhaps hoping to see where the sun would hide himself tonight. A cool breeze wrestled with the lingering heat of the day when Cerris neared his des-tination, many blocks from the western gates. Swiftly he ducked into a nearby alley, changing into the Cephiran hauberk and tabard he'd kept from his escape. By now his combination of military walk and sporadic illusions came naturally, and nobody offered him a second glance—in most cases, not even a first one—as he strode boldly toward the nearest cluster of Cephiran defenses.

For many minutes he wandered, head high and shoulders straight, as if he knew precisely where he was going, but constantly watching, cataloging, timing. It took only a short while to track the movements of various servants and low-ranking soldiers who brought missives and water to those who manned the gates, those who patrolled atop the walls . . .

And those who crewed the Cephiran siege engines.

It took an even shorter while for Cerris to corner one of the servants alone and to take his place, disposing of the body down a nearby cistern.

Lugging a sloshing bucket, Cerris climbed the narrow stone steps toward the nearest of half a dozen platforms the Cephirans had erected along the ramparts. Drawn upward as if hooked by some divine fisherman, his gaze rose, taking in the awesome power of the wooden monstrosity above. Dozens of feet high, equipped with a counterweight heavier than many houses, it seemed to exude a living malevolence. Cerris had seen more than one trebuchet in action, and held nearly as much awe for their power as he did for the magics of the Kholben Shiar, but he hadn't the slightest notion of how to operate it.

That was all right, though. Operating the infernal machine wasn't his job.

Over the following hour, Cerris acquired the tiniest piece of each member of the trebuchet's crew. From the first, a rag with which he'd blotted the worst of the evening's sweat from his face; from the second, a dollop of spittle collected after he hawked something up onto the floor; a few strands of hair from the third, when Cerris brushed a nonexistent wasp from his shoulder; and so forth.

And then he was gone, back down the stairs and out into the streets, as casually and unobtrusively as he had come.

Privacy was actually harder to come by than anything else he'd required, but he finally found a home, broken and abandoned during the Cephiran siege and never reoccupied. He scrambled over piles of rubble, cringing from walls that rained dust and seemed to be waiting only for the right time to crumble inward and squash him into a delectable pâté, but he found two of the inner chambers standing, and that was one more than he needed.

Pushing aside bits of broken brick, he cleared a spot to sit that was, if not comfortable, at least not actively painful, and lowered himself to the floor. First he laid Sunder beside him, in easy reach. Next he carefully spread out the various bits and dollops and goo before him, placing each just so, *this* far from the others, *that* far from him. And for the next several hours, his voice steady but low, mouthing impossible syllables until his tongue felt like taffy and his throat as though he'd been gargling eggshells, Cerris struggled to invoke what just might have been the most potent spell in Imphallion.

Chapter Seven

A SIZABLE PROPORTION of the nation's citizenry firmly believed
that Duke Meddiras, the middle-aged governor of Denathere, was
paranoid. The so-called Jewel of Imphallion, Denathere was second in
importance only to Mecepheum itself. Yes, it was geographically and
conceptually the heart of Imphallion, where the major highways that
were the veins carrying Imphallion's lifeblood converged. And yes,
more than half the Guilds kept their greatest halls and highest offices
within its borders.

But surely Meddiras—or "Mad-diras," as some called him—went
rather to extremes. Since he'd assumed the title of duke almost six years
ago, he'd tripled the size of the city's standing militias. From the old
city walls, new layers of stone had been layered upward and outward,
until most of Denathere was surrounded by a rampart larger than that
of Mecepheum, or of border cities under far greater risk of siege. What
few stretches of the outer wall had not yet been sufficiently reinforced
were bandaged in great wooden scaffolds, swarming with both paid laborers and petty criminals sentenced to indentured servitude. Meddiras had even attempted to institute more thorough entry requirements,
demanding that the guards search *every* visitor and *every* wagon from
top to bottom. He'd relented only when the merchants had threat-

ened everything shy of open revolt. Men and women in hauberks or breastplates marched atop the walls in groups of five or more, and various engines—from small ballistae to great catapults as large as Cephira's trebuchets—lurked every few hundred feet, eager to hurl death upon any foe who might dare approach.

Yes, nearly everyone thought Duke Meddiras paranoid—but nearly everyone, even those most inconvenienced by Denathere's slow transformation into a military city—also had to admit that the man had his reasons.

Twenty-three years ago, the city had fallen to the armies of the Terror of the East, at the end of his fearsome campaign. And here, almost seven years ago, Denathere had fallen once more to the forces of Audriss the Serpent, at the *start* of his own.

Meddiras, who inherited the dukedom when his aunt perished at the hands of the Serpent's soldiers, would sooner have ripped out his own fingernails with his teeth than allow history to record him as the third duke in a row to see Denathere conquered.

And that paranoia had saved his life once already. For Duke Meddiras, and several of Denathere's Guildmasters, had some weeks ago been invited to Mecepheum, to participate in a meeting of great import, a dialogue between the nobility and the Guilds to discuss some means of reconciliation.

Or so the message had stated. Meddiras and Denathere's Guildmasters, in a show of unprecedented unity, had refused to leave their city while the murderous dawn of war threatened from beyond the eastern horizon. They had dispatched emissaries in their stead—emissaries who, like everyone else present in that meeting chamber, were now purported dead at the hands of Corvis Rebaine.

That rumor, unconfirmed though it might be, sent Meddiras and his court into a frenzy, and his captains and military advisers ran themselves ragged following his assorted orders. The gates to Denathere were now so choked with guards that it was challenging even to drive a cart through them, and those gates shut firmly more than an hour before dusk no matter how many travelers sought admittance. Every noble manor and keep, every governmental office and Guild hall, was surrounded by vassal soldiers and hired mercenaries, and the street patrols were redoubled yet again. It looked very much as though Denathere had been flooded by a pounding rain of swords and armor.

In the end—for the Guildmasters and for Meddiras himself, if not for his city—it was, every last bit of it, a wasted effort.

In an inner room of a large stone house, a faint breeze kicked up where no breeze could possibly blow. The dust and dead beetles accumulated over years of neglect danced across the carpet, fetching up against the walls, and the flimsy wooden door whistled in its uneven frame. Had anyone been present within the room, and had he possessed a *remarkably* acute nose, he might have noted the faintest humid odor, rather akin to mildewed parchment.

The impossible wind ceased as swiftly as it appeared, and then there *was* someone in the room, standing at the heart of the miniature storm. One hand clutching the bridge of his nose, the other outstretched to prop himself against the nearest wall, the wizard Nenavar took deep, deliberate breaths, trying to allay the quivering of his muscles.

Teleportation was so much easier when I was younger . . .

It would pass quickly enough; it always did. While he waited, he placed his back against the wall and allowed himself to slide. There he sat on his haunches, the overly large sleeves of his fine tunic dragging in the dust. He found himself, for lack of anything better to do, staring at the floor.

"I really must remember," he muttered to himself, "to hire someone to tidy up while I'm away."

After a few moments, Nenavar felt his strength (such as it was) returning, and he rose. Night had fallen outside, and no lamps burned within the house, but the old man had little trouble finding his way. This was but one of several abodes he owned throughout Imphallion's major cities, and all had been built to his specifications, identical to one another in every particular. Such intimate familiarity with one's destination made teleportation easier—not to mention rather less prone to catastrophic accident—and exhausting as it was, Nenavar far preferred it to weeks on horseback.

He felt a few startled glances from neighborhood folk who knew the house to be empty, but otherwise attracted little attention as he shut the door behind him and stepped into Denathere's streets. The throng bustled around him, jostling and deafening even at this hour, and he felt himself cringing, his skin threatening to unwrap itself from his body and go hide in a corner. Gods, he hated being touched!

Or spoken to. Or looked at. It was one of the reasons he'd taken up his studies in the first place: lots and lots of blessedly peaceful solitude.

Nenavar gritted his teeth into a cage to imprison the various snarls, imprecations, and occasional pestilential spells that sought to hurl themselves from his throat at anyone who drew too near, and continued on his way.

There was, at least, no danger of becoming lost. He'd made certain he could *always* find the man he now sought before he first let him out of his sight.

The unseen path led him, after twenty minutes that weren't doing his elderly knees any good, to a house not much larger—though certainly far nicer—than that in which he'd appeared. Two stories overlooked a modest property, complete with flower garden and a stable large enough for only a single horse. Despite his confidence in his magics, Nenavar couldn't help but wonder if he'd come to the right place. He'd expected—well, more.

Then he spotted a quartet of burly figures loitering in the street nearby, laughable in their efforts to remain inconspicuous, and he recognized the sentries for what they were. This was, indeed, the right place.

Nenavar mumbled into his beard as he approached, tongue and cracked lips forming sounds that scarcely qualified as words. He walked right past the guards and up the path toward the house, and none made so much as a move in his direction. He wasn't invisible, precisely; the spell simply rendered him unworthy of attention. One of the men even nodded politely in his direction before dismissing him as a random passerby and forgetting his presence entirely.

The wizard swallowed a delighted cackle, shaking his head at the feebleness of the average mind, and pushed through the entryway.

And practically toppled backward, overpowered by the scent that had lurked in ambush behind that door. Heavy smoke in the air stung his eyes, and he gagged on the metallic miasma of blood and other humors. He gulped twice, fighting the urge to spit and clear what felt like a clinging film on his tongue and throat.

The interior of the house had been transformed into the fever dream of a demented cannibal. Corpses and bits of corpses formed a layer of carpeting. Mail rings lay scattered across the floor, and several bodiless hands still clutched weapons. So widely strewn were the remains, Nenavar couldn't guess how many guards had actually stood post within the house.

Grimacing, he picked his way carefully through the carnage, his steps mincing as he focused on keeping the worst of the sludge from his shoes. The room's far door revealed a dining nook, and here the scene was even worse. What had once been a woman—a serving girl, to judge by what remained of her clothes—lay facedown in the fireplace; fluids leaking through blackened skin had smothered the last burning embers. Beside her, an old cook hung from the wall, held by a torch sconce protruding all the way through muscle and bone. Around the table—some slumped forward in their chairs, others sprawled on the floor—were half a dozen more, their bodies in various stages of mangling or incineration.

And sitting in one of those chairs—*atop* a fallen corpse, the weight of his armor slowly crushing the body beneath him—was Kaleb. He had removed the skull helm that completed his disguise, and kicked his feet up on the table. He waved Nenavar over with one hand, the other clutching a chicken leg from which he was taking great, tearing mouthfuls.

"How in the gods' names can you *eat?*" the wizard choked as he entered.

Kaleb shrugged. "It's good. You want some?"

"I'll pass."

"So will the chicken, once you've eaten it."

For some time, Nenavar just glared. Then, "Was all this truly necessary, Kaleb?"

"You wanted it, *Master*. You wanted horror, and fear, and panic. Well, here are the seeds. Now we just let them grow."

The wizard sighed, but nodded. "The guards outside?"

"Didn't hear a thing. They'll be my witnesses. I'm planning to make a suitably dramatic exit, make sure they all see 'Rebaine,' maybe even kill a few before I disappear." Kaleb grinned. "I already got Duke Meddiras and his people in the keep. This was my second stop. Three Guildmasters and their families. They were here because one of their assistants was throwing a dinner to celebrate his daughter's coming out next week." He gestured with the greasy drumstick at the headless corpse of a teenage girl.

Nenavar swallowed the vomit rising in his gullet.

"Don't go soft on me now," Kaleb said. "You knew what you were getting us into, and you know what's at stake."

"I . . . Yes, I know. Don't think you have to lecture *me*!"

"I don't have to. I just like to."

"I want you to do Braetlyn next. Say, five nights from now."

Kaleb tossed the remains of the chicken leg to the floor, where they landed with a wet squelch, and rose, stretching. "That's a bit fruitless, isn't it? We sort of know Jassion's not there."

"I know. But I want to keep driving him, keep him too furious to think of anything else. Do his staff and servants. It'll take a bit of time for the news to catch up to you, but sooner or later he'll hear rumors of it in some town or other."

"I think you're wasting my time. He's already committed."

"Perhaps. But never forget, Kaleb, that your time is mine to waste."

Nenavar spun on his heel, heading once more for the door, again muttering the incantation to keep the guards from noticing him. He didn't particularly care to be present to witness Kaleb's "dramatic exit."

THE TUMULT THAT SHOOK the council chambers of Mecepheum's grand Hall of Meeting *probably* wasn't as deafening as an earthquake's birthing pains, but it wouldn't have been a safe bet. Eddies of hot breath whirled, flinging angry words hither and yon, threatening to fill the room until surely either the walls, or the people within, must burst.

Above them, disapproving eyes stared down from the many carvings, paintings, and reliefs that adorned almost every inch of ceiling—an array of symbols to be found not only here, but also in the lesser meeting halls throughout the city, duplicated over and over as a sign of Guild unity. Heroes of legend and mighty archangels made up the bulk, but some boasted the symbols, or even the stylized faces, of the divine: Ulan the Judge, Daltheos the Maker, and so many others. Only in one shadowed corner was the stone rough and pitted, vacant of embellishment. Once the terrible visages of Maukra and Mimgol, the Children of Apocalypse, had loomed within, but after the events of six years prior, those images had been chiseled away.

From the great horseshoe-shaped table at the head of the room, Salia Mavere, priestess of Verelian and current Speaker for the Blacksmiths' Guild, could only roll her own eyes upward toward those remaining stony countenances, and wish she possessed their patience.

One of her neighbors at the table, a spindly scarecrow representing the Tanners' Guild, leaned toward her—the acrid scent of his trade washing over her, making her tear up a bit—and shouted in her ear to be heard over the tumult. "Are you going to do something about this?"

Salia, saving her breath, just shrugged. Still gazing at the images above, she remembered similar meetings during the Serpent's War, recalled how the sorceress Rheah Vhoune had easily silenced the screaming factions. She wished now that her own priestly studies included the *practice* of magic, rather than merely its philosophies and histories.

For minutes the shouting and arguments continued, until Salia had to acknowledge that her companion had a point. She reached behind, striking a small hammer on the hanging gong, calling the chamber to order. And then again, harder. But if any of the shrieking nobles, Guildmasters, priests, and other leading citizens heard, they didn't seem inclined to obey.

Grinning without mirth, Salia rose, unfastened the brass circle from its hooks, and hurled it like a discus over the heads of the assembly. Startled gasps presaged the sudden press of bodies struggling to clear out as it fell, and every face in the crowd had donned an expression of anger.

But it was, for the moment, a *silent* anger, and that made all the difference.

"Ladies and gentlemen, this cannot continue. We're all exhausted . . ."

This understatement was being met with a chorus of derisive snorts. Custom dictated that these meetings end by sundown, but just as they had every night for the past few weeks, they'd already progressed well into the nighttime hours.

"We're all exhausted," she said again, "and there's still much work ahead of us. My tenure as Overseer ends in two nights, and I'd like to have accomplished *something* during my week with the hammer. So perhaps whoever follows me will put up with this, but I won't any longer. The next time you choose to ignore the gong—and Erland, would you be kind enough to bring it back up here? Thank you—the next time you choose to ignore the gong, I'll be throwing it *at* you, not *over* you, and anyone who has a problem with that is welcome to seek satisfaction."

An array of murderous glares threatened to knock her clean over, but everyone present knew her reputation, could plainly see the large hammer hanging at her side—far larger and more brutal than the ceremonial mallet that marked her status as current assembly Overseer— and none of those glares transformed into spoken protest.

"Good. Then the issue up for vote . . ." *As it has been every night since before I took the damn hammer,* she added silently, though everyone heard it anyway, ". . . is one of military command. To wit, are we agreed to unite the various armies of Imphallion under a single command in order to—"

"No!" This from Sathan, the young and newly ascended Duke of Orthessis, dressed in mourning black for his mother, the Duchess Anneth. "We'll not be handing any more of our power over to you!"

"Then you'll soon not have it at all!" Caryna, Assistant Guildmaster of the Masons' Guild, yelled back. "Cephira's already taken most of our eastern territories!" She pointed to one of several empty chairs, ceremonially left vacant to account for those nobles and Guildmasters who could not attend, or those who had died and whose successors had not yet been named. "How long before they advance farther, Your Grace? We've invaders *on Imphallian soil,* and your damn muleheadedness has prevented us—"

"*My* mule-headedness? We—"

"It's not mule-headedness, it's self-preservation!" The third speaker—third shouter, really—was Bennek III, Earl of Prace. "If Rebaine's slaughtering us one by one, I'm sure as Vantares's deepest hell not putting all my men under someone else's command!"

The tanner beside Salia stood, leaning over the table. "Only a unified force can stand against either Cephira *or* Rebaine! Did we learn *nothing* from the Serpent? Have we all so quickly forgotten our inability to cooperate *then*?"

"Audriss was one of us!" Duke Sathan reminded him. "He's precisely the reason we *cannot* turn over complete command of our forces to anyone we don't implicitly trust!"

"And do you not trust the Guilds?"

His snort was answer enough. "We *can* repulse Cephira, but we'll do it with our own forces, not by giving them to you!"

"Cephira's forces are too large and too disciplined. If we go in piecemeal, we'll be slaughtered!"

"If we don't stop Rebaine," Bennek muttered, "Cephira won't *need* to slaughter us."

"Why has Rebaine returned *now*?" Salia couldn't see who spoke; someone toward the rear of the chamber. "Perhaps he's trying to take advantage of the Cephiran attack."

"Do we even know he's not *cooperating* with Cephira?" Caryna asked.

"We—"

"*Enough!*" Salia rose and struck the gong, not with her ceremonial mallet but with the brutal hammer at her waist. The chime was surprisingly quiet—primarily because the blow cracked the gong straight down the center—but it shut everyone up.

"I called for a vote," she reminded them darkly. "And that means no debate or argument until the vote is *cast.* So . . . All in favor of uniting our forces, that we may repel the threats both at and within our borders?" A pause. "All opposed?"

She sighed, slumping back in her chair. She didn't need the chamberlain's official tally to know the vote had split exactly as it had each previous night. The bulk of the Guildmasters wanted unification, as did a few younger nobles whose predecessors were recently slain. The majority of the aristocracy did not, at least not unless the overseer was another noble rather than a Guild appointee; a concession the Guilds — presumably fearful of losing their stranglehold over the aristocracy — were unwilling to make.

And so, for another night, what had once been the greatest nation on the continent huddled impotently, allowing the Cephiran invaders to dig in more deeply, and the murderer of nobles and Guildmasters to advance his current scheme, whatever it might be.

It was, indeed, an unpleasant, dream-like echo of the Serpent's War.

The Guildmasters *almost* had enough votes to carry the necessary majority — thanks be, though she felt ashamed to admit it, to the recent spate of murders, which had claimed more nobles than Guildmasters. Almost, but not quite. And even if they had, would the nobles accede as the law required, or would the Guilds be compelled to take their armies by force? Salia shivered at the realization that the problems they faced might only be leading them to the brink of *civil* war.

Furrowing her brow against an incipient headache, Salia Mavere called a recess until the following day and dejectedly trudged from the assembly chamber, praying that she had the strength to see everything through, to do what must be done.

And that, in the end, it would all prove worthwhile.

BESIDE A SMALL COPSE OF TREES, abutting the slope of a rocky hill, a stone-lined pit held grey ash and bits of charcoal that were the cadaver of a cooking fire. A faint breeze wafted through the night, rustling branches and cooling the skin of the man who lay slumbering by the fire pit, twisting and muttering in the grasp of rapacious dreams.

Much as it had in the center of Nenavar's house in Denathere, the wind picked up, lifting loose leaves skyward, clashing and swirling against the natural currents in the air. Sticks crunched into the soil as a massive weight appeared atop them, and then Corvis Rebaine, the Terror of the East, stood beside the sleeping Baron of Braetlyn, the blood of Jassion's servants dripping from his gauntlets.

Or at least Rebaine's armor did.

The image wavered, and then that armor—and the blood—were gone. Kaleb stood in their place, clad in his mundane cloak and leathers. A quick look around, just to ensure that nothing had disturbed the camp in his absence, and then he knelt beside his supposed ally. Without ever quite touching him, Kaleb ran a hand over Jassion's face, removing a phantom film of magic that had kept the man in deep slumber. Jassion snored once and rolled over, unaware that anything was amiss.

Exactly how Kaleb wanted him. Suppressing a grin, he reached out and shook Jassion's shoulder, waking him for his turn on watch.

Chapter Eight

THE ROYAL SOLDIERS of the Black Gryphon of Cephira never did learn precisely what happened on that muggy summer night. Or rather, they ascertained most of what happened, but never *why*.

The blush of dawn hadn't fully covered the face of the eastern sky, and the nighttime breezes had faded into sputtering, wheezing breaths. Pre-morning dew was swiftly coalescing on the grasses, the leaves, and the eaves of Rahariem's homes, courteously making room in the air for the new day's coming humidity. The soldiers on night duty stifled their yawns, struggling to keep alert or maintain proper cadence, grateful that the rising sun would soon signal the end of shift and the opportunity to get breakfast, get drunk, and get to bed—*probably* in that order.

Until a scream of inchoate rage shattered the calm, a rock rudely hurled through the brittle glass of silence. From atop one of the engine platforms, a Cephiran guard leapt upon a passing patrol, naked sword in hand. Maddened spittle spattered the shocked soldiers, followed immediately by the warm blood of their commanding officer. The crazed attacker was already lunging at his next target before the officer's head fetched up against a wall, and two more men were down before the remainder had so much as pulled steel.

Drawn to the hideous shrieks and the clash of battle, soldiers from neighboring posts came running, ready to aid their brethren against any attack, stunned briefly into immobility when they realized just what form that attack had taken. The murderous warrior seemed driven by a fury not even so much "berserk" as "utterly inhuman." Blades rebounded from mail, bruising flesh to the bone, yet he barely staggered before launching a blistering counterattack, more raw fury than training or skill. The tips of swords dug into thighs and arms protected only by leather-backed padding, and still he remained oblivious to their efforts. One soldier, already wounded, ducked under his guard and ran her broadsword across the back of his knee; only then, as tendon separated and his leg buckled, did he finally slow. Staggering in a tight circle, dragging his now useless leg, he fought on until the limp and the blood loss finally took their toll. Face paling, he wavered, his body quivering, and a Cephiran morningstar crushed the life from his skull.

And it was then that the Cephiran soldiers—panting hard, bleeding, horrified at their maddened brother—discovered that the entire affair had been only a terrible diversion. For it was then, when the tumult of battle and the groans of the dying had faded, that they heard the ominous creaking of wood and hemp from above.

All unnoticed in the tumult, the rest of the man's squad had heaved a three-hundred-pound block of masonry from their ammunition stores into the trebuchet's great sling. Far too late to take any action save an openmouthed gape, the troops below could only watch as the massive weapon ratcheted into position and heaved its monstrous payload.

End over end the missile tumbled, a child's block hurled in a divine tantrum. In a perfect arc, calculated by a skilled team of operators, it sailed over the roofs of Rahariem for more than two hundred yards . . .

And finally plummeted to crash, in a cloud of dust and timber and debris that blotted the moon and every star from the sky, upon the city's western gate.

Against such a massive assault—had it come from *without*—the thickest of the city's walls might have held fast. Against the gates themselves, from the direction opposite that which they were braced to hold, the boulder might as well have been punching through bread crust.

Wood and stone exploded. The walls of neighboring structures cracked beneath the shrapnel, or merely from the shuddering of the earth. Panicked citizens clogged the streets, fleeing the devastation raining from above. The guards—save those at the gate itself, who formed a trail of broken bodies in the tumbling masonry's wake—dived for cover, emerging only long minutes later when the dust began to settle and it was clear no further projectiles were inbound.

The first soldiers to reach the platform found the trebuchet's crew lying dead, scattered near the base of the engine. All had weapons in their hands and protruding from their bodies; they appeared to have murdered one another in a savage rampage of shared insanity. Strewn around were charts of the city and its surroundings, inked by the invaders when they'd first set up their defenses. Carefully indicating angles and distances, those charts ensured that the engine crews were practically incapable of missing any attacking forces—or, as they'd just proved, any targets within Rahariem itself. Physicians and alchemists examined the corpses, their food, their water, and found no signs of drug or poison that might explain their behavior. In the end, though it satisfied no one at all, the officers of the Royal Soldiers were forced to conclude that these men had gone mad for reasons unknown, and unleashed their terrible weapon upon the city before turning on themselves and their fellow Cephirans.

That the entire sequence of events might have been orchestrated purely so a band of insurgents could depart the city via the shattered gates, during the few precious moments when the soldiers were cowering against further attack, was a notion that wouldn't occur to anyone for quite some while.

———————————

ON THE FLOOR OF THAT same broken house, Cerris lay shaking. The remains of everything he'd eaten that day pooled across the room, congealing into a harsh, pungent sludge, and still his stomach lurched, distending his jaw in dry heaves. His head pounded as though last night's dreams sought to batter their way free, and his entire body shivered beneath a sheen of feverish sweat.

Only once before had his body been so terribly ravaged by the casting of that ancient spell, on the day he'd arrived in Mecepheum—well disguised—to ensure the election of Duke Halmon to the regent's throne. Then, he'd scarcely escaped the Hall of Meeting before the illness overcame him, rendering him naught but a quivering, agonized wreck for a day and a half. That time, he'd extended his mystical influence over a score of men and women, a strain that he truly believed had come close to killing him. He wasn't remotely powerful enough a sorcerer to be fiddling with such magics, and well he knew it. Tonight, he'd needed to command only six, but forcing them to betray their nation, to slay their friends and even themselves, had taken more effort than he'd anticipated. This was only the fourth time he'd ever used the spell—and only the second time on more than a single individual— and he couldn't help but idly wonder if a fifth attempt would finish him off entirely.

And he hoped, to the extent he was capable of hoping for *anything* other than for the pounding and the nausea to stop, that he'd never need find out.

Cerris was never certain how long he lay there before he finally recovered the strength to raise his head and even *consider* lifting himself off the floor. The sun was high enough for its light to creep through the ill-fitting doors and shutters, to transform the room into something akin to a small kiln. The stench of slowly baking vomit made his eyes water, but Cerris appreciated the heat. The sweat he shed now felt somehow cleaner than the film it was washing away.

Leaning on Sunder he rose, pleased to discover that his legs, though wobbly, were willing to support him. He'd be weak for some time, but this was the weakness of simple fatigue, no longer the sick helplessness it had been.

Again his stolen tabard served him, for so great was the throng of activity around the shattered gates that nobody noticed another soldier in their midst. Cerris lifted a chunk of rubble (a small one was all he could manage just yet), carried it through the open wall, and disappeared behind the growing heap of broken stone accumulating on the roadside. As there was no tree line this near Rahariem, he moved at a diagonal, struggling to keep the refuse pile between himself and casual observation until he'd passed some distance from the walls. He tried to maintain a steady jog, but his exhaustion—'*Are you sure it's not your age?*' the inner voice taunted—held him to a rapid walk. He prayed that his departure had attracted no attention; at his current pace, and with the trail of perspiration he was sure he'd dripped into the grass behind him, a toddler could probably run him to ground.

But at least, as he drew nearer the copse that marked the ambush point, he felt as though he were getting his second wind.

'*Or your third, or your fourth . . .*'

And he felt, as well, that he was likely to need it.

He sensed something wrong before he rounded the bend in the road, though he wasn't initially certain what. From ahead echoed the clash of steel, the shouts and grunts and screams of battle. That was to be expected. He'd known the caravan might pass at any time, that the ambush might launch before he arrived. But something about the sounds—he could not, just yet, put his finger on precisely what—was off, made his hackles rise and his fingers tighten about Sunder's haft.

And then, as he drew near, he found himself recalling the many battles and sieges of his life, and he knew. The calls from ahead were too measured, too disciplined, too clear. These were the shouts of trained soldiers, not the eager, passionate cries of a diverse resistance.

Cerris dropped to his belly, worming through the dirt and twigs until he could just poke his head beyond the copse's undergrowth. He grimaced, biting back a vicious oath at what he saw.

Four horse-drawn wagons lined the roadside, the tarps that had once covered their contents lying crumpled beside the wheels. But those tarps had apparently revealed no cargo, for the wagons now stood empty. Corpses littered the crimson-stained earth, and most were the bodies of men and women Cerris had known. The Cephiran soldiers were gathered in groups, battling the last pockets of opposition or moving to chase those who had fled. Even from his limited vantage point, the tired old warrior couldn't help but note that there were far more soldiers than should have been assigned to a supply caravan moving across Cephiran-controlled territory.

He knew, then, what—or rather *who*—had lain beneath those tarps. *The whole damn caravan* had been a trap.

He'd worry later how they'd known, who must answer for this treachery. Now, through a haze of sudden panic, Cerris scanned the wagons, the road, the ongoing skirmishes, and yes, even the corpses, for a head of auburn hair . . .

There! Amid a knot of Cephirans, a trio of insurgents struggled to survive. One was old Rannert, his short sword a bolt of steel lightning as it darted in and out, keeping the soldiers on the defensive, but even from a distance Cerris could see the old man tiring, his shoulders drooping, his arms beginning to quiver. Cerris couldn't recall the name of the second fellow, younger but wilder, whose wide slashes with a woodsman's axe would leave him open any minute to an enemy thrust.

With them, wielding a narrow blade longer than her arm, was the Lady Irrial. And if her stance, parries, ripostes were perhaps a touch stiff—the result of formal training without hint of genuine experience— then at least that training was comprehensive, and the baroness a fast learner. For the nonce, she held her own.

But for all their valor and all their efforts, they were merely three, facing an experienced band of thrice that number, with reinforcements close at hand. They would fight well—they might take several of the enemy with them—but they would lose. Of that, even a blind man could have little doubt.

His rudimentary disguise would not hold, not here, for these soldiers were a unit and knew one another by sight. Still, as Cerris rose and sprinted from the copse, his tabard bought him precious seconds before the enemy recognized him as an outsider, seconds that would have to suffice.

He stumbled on weakened legs, and his side ached as though a Cephiran blade had already punched through his hauberk, but Cerris dared not stop. He nearly collided with the first of the wagons, his chest heaving, and shattered a wheel with the Kholben Shiar. On he ran, crippling the second vehicle, then the third, while soldiers closed from all sides. At the fourth, he took his blade not to the wheel but to the harness, and clambered awkwardly atop the horse he'd freed. The beast glanced back at him curiously, but if it was not a trained warhorse per se, it had seen sufficient combat that it shouldn't readily panic.

The first soldier reached him, stabbing with a short-hafted spear. Cerris kicked it aside and brought Sunder down upon the man's helm. It was an awkward blow, made more so by the lack of saddle and stirrups, but still the Kholben Shiar cleaved steel and bone. Cerris hauled on the reins, kicking the body toward another of the onrushing enemy as he guided the horse about. A Cephiran broadsword swung as the beast moved, drawing a thin line of blood across a tan-mottled flank. The horse whinnied and leapt away from the sudden pain, and only three fingers curled in a death grip through its mane kept Cerris from tumbling off the rear end.

Kicks, tugs, shouts, and possibly even a few vicious threats finally brought the beast under control; and indeed, it was already heading where he needed it to go. Sunder held aloft, hollering to draw attention away from Irrial, Cerris charged the cluster of crimson tabards surrounding her.

The outermost soldiers scattered, unsure at first what sort of menace thundered their way. Two of the men nearest the sore-pressed insurrectionists split their attentions just a heartbeat too long and dropped, bleeding, to the earth.

Drawing nearer, horse surging beneath him, Cerris saw that the man whose name he'd failed to recall had fallen, leaving Irrial and Rannert to face the Cephirans alone. Sunder whirled in an underhanded arc, catching an approaching soldier from the side, lifting him briefly off his feet before shearing through him. More of the warriors who'd leapt from the charging mount's path were up and converging once more, and Cerris could only curse, wondering if he'd could reach Irrial's side in time.

And then Rannert—stiff, staid old Rannert—broke past the nearest soldier facing him, ignoring what must have been an agonizing blow to the ribs, and hurled himself at the wall of Cephirans separating the baroness from her would-be savior. Sword and fists, feet and even teeth pounded flesh or glanced from armor. Cephiran blades pierced aged skin, broke weakened bone, but the faithful servant steadfastly refused to fall. Not now, just a moment more . . .

Cerris gawked, awed, at the venerable butler as the horse galloped on, and damn if he couldn't have sworn that, for the first and last time,

Rannert smiled at him. Then he was past, slipping clean through the corridor Rannert's wild assault had opened in the Cephiran ranks. Cerris tossed Sunder to his left hand, reaching to catch Irrial's arm with his right. With a grunt of sudden pain—Cerris never was certain which of them it had come from—she was off the ground, swinging awkwardly up and around behind him.

In an instant they were gone, leaving the Cephirans far behind, though Cerris knew better than to slow down lest a swift-thinking soldier free another of the horses and pursue. He felt her hands clasp tight about his chest, her face pressed against his neck, the wet touch of tears trickling down his skin.

But with his own fingers wrapped tight about Sunder's haft and the horse's reins, his voice trampled beneath the pounding thud of the hooves, Cerris couldn't even try to comfort her.

"THERE'S ALMOST NO ONE LEFT," she told him softly as evening neared, the first words she'd spoken since the disastrous battle. "A few ran, but I don't know if they got away."

Cerris had driven the poor horse mercilessly, running it ragged across uneven grasses far from the highway. Finally the panting, lathered beast had snapped its leg in some animal's burrow. Irrial, eyes encircled in red, had looked away as Cerris and Sunder ended its pain.

But the horse had done them proud before the end, carrying them in a wide circle behind the Cephiran wagons, almost back to Rahariem, before it fell. The fugitives had once more blended with the scurrying workforce of citizens and soldiers, still hauling rubble after all these hours, then vanished into the city. They huddled now in the cooper's workshop where the stillborn resistance had been conceived.

Cerris, limbs aching, his entire body limp with exhaustion, forced himself to sit upright, to place what he hoped was a comforting hand on Irrial's arm.

"They knew we were coming, Cerris," she said. "There were so many soldiers waiting in those wagons, they *must* have been expecting trouble."

"It was a trap," he agreed. "I just wish I knew who . . ." His shoulders bunched in a sad shrug.

"Someone in the resistance?" Irrial asked. "Is it safe for us to be here?"

"I think it should be." Cerris rose and began slowly to pace, the mindless repetition helping his fatigue-swaddled mind to think even as it sent new complaints through sore calves. "If someone in the group had betrayed us, the Cephirans wouldn't have *needed* to set a trap. They could have hit us during any one of our meetings." He jerked to a halt as a thought struck him across the face like a gauntlet. "Is Andevar . . . ?"

Irrial shook her head sadly. "He led the ambush, Cerris, and he tried to hold them off so we could run when he realized what was happening. He was one of the first to fall."

"Damn. *Damn.* I liked him."

"Me, too."

Silence, save for Cerris's pacing steps. And again he halted abruptly, brought up short this time by Irrial's sudden intensity.

"Yarrick," she spat. "It had to be!"

"I don't know, Irrial. I told you before, he has no real reason to love Cephira. They—"

"They could have paid him off! Or made him gods-know-what promises. But who else could it be? Nobody outside the resistance knew we were going to hit that caravan!"

"*Yarrick* didn't know we were going to—"

"But he knew you were asking about it. If they knew an underground was forming, and that you hadn't fled town after your escape . . . Well, it wouldn't be hard to figure out the *real* reason you were asking, would it?"

"It doesn't sound right," he protested, but it sounded weak even to his own ears.

No, that wasn't true at all. He just didn't *want* it to sound right. Because if Yarrick was a collaborator, that meant Cerris himself tipped them off. It was *his* fault those men and women, Rannert and Andevar, were dead.

'*It was your fault the moment you agreed to support this stupid insurgency. You're only feeling guilty about it because they* failed. *But then, you've always looked smashing in that particular shade of hypocrisy.*'

"That's not true!" he hissed, ashamed that he was once more arguing with himself, grateful that Irrial hadn't heard him—and terrified that, just maybe, that mocking tone spoke truth.

Irrial stared at the floor, Cerris at the far wall. Neither provided them with any answers.

TOO MANY OF THE CEPHIRANS had seen them this time, Cerris reluctantly decided as Rahariem bedded down beneath its blanket of night. Even if the names *Baroness Irrial* and *Cerris the Merchant* weren't known through the ranks of the soldiers, the *descriptions* of those who had escaped their trap would surely be making the rounds. Someone might even have sketched them. They couldn't be seen out and about any longer, but neither could they indefinitely sit in the back of Rond and Elson's shop. For one thing, they had to know if anyone else had escaped, if there remained any ashes of the resistance from which a phoenix might arise.

And so, with no other options available, Cerris admitted to Irrial just how he'd escaped from his work gang and his Cephiran overseers. On any other day, Irrial might have reacted to the revelation that he was a wizard on top of everything else—even one of only middling talent— with no small degree of amazement. Tonight she said only, "I wish it had been more help."

Cerris began to wonder if something more than the loss of their companions, devastating as that might be, was eating away at her.

She brightened a little, though, when he explained that those same magics might enable them to hunt for other survivors. "Though I'm not saying it'll be *easy*," he warned her. "I'm tired as a succubus with a quota, my spells aren't very potent at the best of times, and I've never tried maintaining one of these phantasms on someone else at any great distance. We can't afford to rely on them for more than a few hours, and you need to avoid speaking with anyone who knows you well. There's a good chance they'll see through it."

"I understand. Do it."

Moments later, a man and a woman who only somewhat resembled Cerris and Irrial departed the cooper's workshop.

The better to avoid running into anyone whose familiarity might prove troublesome, Irrial headed toward the late-night taverns she'd never frequented in her prior life as an aristocrat, while Cerris donned the Cephiran tabard that was starting to feel as familiar—and as much in need of a warm bath—as his own skin, and took to the streets.

As the moon flounced through the sky, leaving a wake of broken-hearted stars, Cerris meandered from block to block, chatting with guards standing post, off-duty squads working on a friendly drunk, even an officer for whom he offered to carry a crate of charts and records (aggravating his back in the process). Most had heard only third- or fourth-hand accounts of the engagement, in which the size of the attacking force and the valor of the Cephiran warriors were both obscenely exaggerated. All accounts agreed, however, that only a very few insurgents had survived, and most of those were held under heavy guard, awaiting brutal interrogation. Cerris felt as though his heart had sunk so low he was in danger of digesting it, and he held precious little hope that anyone but Irrial and he remained.

By the time he returned to the cooper's, it was all he could do to drag his feet across the cobblestone streets, and his neck ached abysmally from the strain of supporting a head stuffed with sand. It had been a *very* long day, filled with exertions physical, emotional, and mystical, and Cerris was frankly surprised that he hadn't simply collapsed like a sack of grain—very, very *tired* grain—hours ago.

Irrial, apparently having taken his warnings to heart, was already back, waiting for him on the workbench.

"I'm afraid," he said, dropping hauberk and tabard in an untidy heap by the door, "that I didn't—Irrial! What's wrong?"

For he'd seen, finally, that the gaze she'd turned his way was harrowed, her face so terribly pale that her freckles stood out like blotches of rust, the dark circles beneath her eyes as gaping sockets.

"I think my cousin's dead, Cerris," she told him softly.

"What—Duke Halmon?" He'd meant to go to her, to comfort her, but found himself sitting down hard, all but falling, on a barrel across from the bench. "How . . . ?"

"They're just rumors," she admitted, chewing the ends of her hair, "but so many . . .

"I spoke to friends and family of half the resistance," she said after a moment, regaining some measure of composure. "But nobody's heard from anyone. Either everyone left is hiding *very* quietly, or . . ." There was no need to finish. They both knew what *or* meant.

"It was while I was in the taverns," she continued, "that I heard the rumors. Some of the people the Cephirans have rounded up from other towns say that there's a reason beyond the normal squabbling that's keeping the Guilds and the nobility from responding to the invasion. They say a lot of Guildmasters and nobles have died recently. Including—including Halmon."

"I heard a little something about that," he said, deciding that now wasn't the time to mention precisely who had told him. "But I never heard anyone named, or I'd have told you. And they didn't say exactly what—"

"Murdered," she told him intently. "By Corvis Rebaine."

The barrel tilted beneath him. Cerris's legs twitched, his arms flailing as he struggled to keep his balance against what felt like a physical blow. "Wh-what did you say?"

She shook her head incredulously, misinterpreting the cause of his shock. "I know. Of all the times for *that* godsdamn bastard to crawl back out of his hole. If it's true, no wonder the nobles are so hesitant to give up their soldiers. And no wonder the Guilds are that much more determined to have them. This is all we bloody needed, isn't it?" Then, more softly, "Hasn't he hurt us enough?"

Cerris actually trembled, just a bit, his jaw hanging mute.

"Oh, Cerris, I'm sorry." Casting her own grief aside, she rose and laid a gentle arm about his shoulders. "You must be *exhausted*. Come, we've got some cots back here that'll do for the night. We can decide what to do tomorrow."

Numbly, he allowed the baroness to lead him across the room, to tuck the blankets around him as though he were a child. But despite a weariness so deep it pressed upon his soul, Cerris found sleep an elusive quarry for many hours to come.

———————

"My sincerest apologies, good sir." The speaker had a greying beard and heavily lined face, but though his physique was running to fat, the peculiar rippling of his flesh suggested a powerful musculature beneath. He wore a leather apron scorched a dozen times over, and smelled strongly of smoke. "I didn't rightly expect it t' take me so long."

"Quite all right," the younger fellow replied as the blacksmith led him past the forge and into the workroom beyond. "I knew it was an unusual commission from the start." He grinned without much mirth. "I'd have to have been crazy not to, really."

The blacksmith wisely chose not to respond to that. "I know we've been over this," he said instead, "but I have t' ask once more. Are you certain this is what you want? You'll find no better armor'n mine, but those spikes you asked for ... Someone strikes 'em at the wrong angle, they'll guide the blade right to you when it might've missed."

"I'm willing to take that chance. May I see it, please?"

A callused hand yanked away a heavy cotton blanket. Both men stood rigid, a faint chill running up both spines even though the younger had designed the abomination before them, and the elder had forged it.

Even unoccupied, it *loomed*, straining forward on the rack as though ready to wrap metal fingers around exposed throats. Black steel, white bone, spines sharp enough to skewer anyone who so much as looked at them wrong ...

But it was the helm to which they were irresistibly drawn, rats staring up at a swaying serpent.

"If nothin' else," the old man offered with a forced chuckle, "nobody who sees you in this monstrosity's goin' to forget you anytime soon."

"That," the other said, "is *entirely* the point."

The gaping sockets of the iron-banded skull looked into their souls, and the jawbone laughed in silence.

———————————

CERRIS AWOKE, blinking away the dream and the afterimages of that blasted skull, to find the blankets twisted into a veritable rope around his body. Obviously, his fatigue notwithstanding, he'd not experienced the most restful sleep.

'Why, it's almost as though you had something weighing on your mind.'

Disentangling himself and tossing the blankets to the floor, he sat up and peered blearily about. The light gleaming through the high windows and the sounds of the street outside suggested that he'd slept away not only the morning, but part of the afternoon as well. No surprise, that. As the various shocks and disappointments of the past days filtered slowly into his brain from wherever memories hid at night, he rolled off the cot, made quick use of the copper pan currently serving as a chamber pot, and stumbled halfway across the workroom. Then—limping on a newly aching toe and loudly cursing the leg of the workbench, but substantially more awake—he crossed the rest of the chamber, dipped a mug into a barrel of lukewarm water, and washed some of the nighttime grit from his mouth and throat.

And it was only then that his mind caught up with his senses, and he realized he was alone.

"Irrial?" And a bit more loudly, making a slow circuit of the room as though she might've been hiding behind a barrel. "Irrial? Are you here?"

Nothing.

All right, no reason to worry. She could be elsewhere in the shop, perhaps arranging with Elson or Rond to acquire some food. She might even have darted out for supplies, or to find out what was happening in the city, though he wished she'd waited for him to cloak her in another illusion. Or perhaps—

He stumbled to a halt at the far wall, where a polished sheet of brass hung as a makeshift mirror. A large pair of shears lay open on the floor, amid a scattered heap of auburn tresses. Cerris nudged it with his bare feet, seemingly unable to comprehend its presence. Despite the poking and prodding, the hair revealed nothing new.

Now, perhaps, it was time to start worrying. Obviously, whatever she was doing, she'd taken rudimentary steps to keep from being recognized, and that assuredly meant it was something Cerris didn't want her doing alone. He dressed swiftly, ready to go hunting for her, scooping up Sunder and reaching for—

The Cephiran hauberk and tabard were gone.

"Oh, gods . . ." Cerris burst through the door and pounded into the street, legs pumping, only just remembering to cloak himself in an illusory disguise. And if it proved insufficient, if any of the "Royal Soldiers" made to stop him, he'd cut them down. By pairs, by squads—it didn't matter.

Because he knew, as surely as if she'd tattooed a map into his flesh, *exactly* where Irrial was going.

'*Ah, you're just pissed that she has the stones to do what you should have . . .*'

Maybe he'd been blessed with an extra dollop of Panaré's fortune that morning, or perhaps, after the past few days, the sight of a crimson-clad soldier racing pell-mell through the streets didn't draw much attention. Whatever the case, while he received more than his share of startled glances, nobody made any effort to stop him as he pounded across the cobblestones, twisting around or even leaping the occasional vendor's stall, until he finally arrived at Rahariem's Merchants' Guild.

He blew past the clerk at the desk—who may well have shouted a protest, but Cerris never heard it—and hurled doors from his path, sometimes hard enough to crack wood against an adjacent wall. A hired guard stepped into his path, more likely to ask his business than to stop him, but Cerris drove a knee into the man's groin and two fingers into his sternum, and was off and running once more before the man finished crumpling to the floor. Stairs flashed by beneath his feet, three, even four at a time, until he'd reached the highest floor. Around the corner, down the hall, praying he wasn't too late . . .

Irrial spun, sword outstretched, as he burst through the final door, and for an endless breath they didn't know each other. Her hair was chopped short in crude imitation of a military cut, and the hauberk weighed heavily on her shoulders, but her arm was steady. Blood dripped from the blade, adding to a larger pool of crimson that spread across the carpet from the body of Guildmaster Yarrick.

Sunder fell slowly, as though wilting, to Cerris's side. "Gods, what have you done?"

"What *had* to be done," she said flatly, daring him to argue.

He accepted, slamming the door behind him. "*Damn it*, Irrial. We *needed* him! We needed to know why, who else was involved—"

"I'm not an idiot, Cerris. I tried! But he came at me, I didn't have—"

"Don't you *dare*! You *had* a choice, all right. You could have asked me to come with you! We could have taken him without *killing* him."

"I thought—"

"You *didn't* think! You were angry, and you acted blindly. So how did you enjoy murder, Irrial? Is it everything you'd hoped?"

The baroness staggered as though he'd slapped her, nearly tripping as her heel struck the corpse by her feet. Her jaw worked soundlessly, and the sword fell unnoticed to the gore-soaked carpet. Even within the heavy hauberk, her shoulders quivered visibly, and she seemed unable to pull her gaze from her open hands.

"Cerris . . ." It was not the voice of an adult, but the call of a distraught child. "Oh, gods . . ."

Cerris understood, then, just as clearly as he'd understood where to find her. Taking a deep breath, he shoved his own anger aside and crossed the room, holding Irrial as her entire body shook with racking sobs.

He said nothing, for there was nothing to say. Both of them knew what she'd lost; knew for what she'd grieved, all unknowing, since the attack on the caravan. And they both knew that her tears, no matter how many she shed, would never wash the stain of blood from her hands.

Just as they had the prior evening, Cerris and Irrial took the long way home, avoiding streets on which he might have earlier been seen. And just as they had the prior evening, they made the trip in silence.

Cerris helped her from the tabard and—as gently as the awkward mail allowed—the hauberk, dropping both in the corner near the scattered strands of hair. The rest of her clothes followed, not out of any romantic ardor but because they were spattered with Yarrick's blood. The normally modest baroness seemed disturbingly unaware of, or indifferent to, her nakedness. He handed her the nearest tunic and trousers; she climbed into them stiffly, mechanically.

Cerris, who could scarcely recall the years before he'd first learned to kill, found himself utterly at a loss. He didn't know what to say, or how to comfort her.

And gods damn him, more than a small part of him just wanted to shake her, to demand she get over it. To insist that they had larger worries than guilt.

'Well, finally! Now you're thinking like yourself again!'

He ruthlessly smothered those feelings, but every now and then he'd glance her way and feel not sympathy, but a flickering ember of irritation.

Some minutes later, she apparently came to the same conclusion. With a literal shake of her head, as though she could shed the crush of emotions like so much water, she took a deep breath and faced him. "What now, Cerris?"

"Now? Now we get the hell out of this damn town."

"What? But—"

"Irrial," he said, perhaps more sharply than he'd intended, "there's nothing more we can do here. The resistance is over. The Cephirans know our faces. Dying for a hopeless cause may *sound* noble, but I've come damn close to doing it myself, and it's really not as much fun as you'd think."

"I know," she admitted. "But I can't just abandon my people."

"You want to help Rahariem? The way to do it is out there." He gestured vaguely in what he was pretty sure was a westerly direction. "Find out what's keeping the Guilds and the nobles from reacting to this invasion, and fix it. I promise you, the armies of Imphallion have a much better chance of driving the Cephirans out than you do."

'*Oh, right.*' Gods, he wished that inner voice would just shut up, but it kept right on yammering. '*Like* that's *the reason you want to be out there. You couldn't care less about Rahariem. You want to find out about—*'

"We already know part of the problem, don't we?" she asked. "It's Rebaine."

'*Yeah. That.*'

"It's *not* him, actually," Cerris said carefully. "Someone's lying, or—or something."

Irrial blinked twice. "What would make you think that? It's not as though he hasn't done this sort of thing before."

"I just—I just don't think it sounds right."

"Why not?"

"Look, it doesn't matter—"

"Cerris." She rose, stepping toward him, and there was something he didn't recognize, and didn't like, behind her expression. Her gaze flickered to his face, to Sunder, and back again, and while they still showed no sign of recognition, he could swear he saw the first gathering clouds of a terrible notion in the depths of her eyes. "*Why not?*"

He was utterly exhausted, his last reserves drained. He was worried, even terrified, at the repercussions of those rumors. He was furious at having been betrayed by Yarrick, at whoever or whatever was behind the falsehoods spreading through Imphallion. And maybe, just maybe, he was falling in love for only the third time in his life.

And even though he knew it was a mistake from the moment the words passed over his lips, a part of him exulted in freedom as Cerris spoke the truth he hadn't uttered to another living soul in years.

"Because *I'm* Corvis Rebaine, Irrial."

Irrial's features went so utterly slack that he wondered briefly if she'd passed out, even died, on her feet. It was the clenching of her fists, the slow flushing of her cheeks, that convinced him otherwise—and convinced him, as well, that it never once occurred to her to doubt his word.

After all, what halfway rational man would *lie* about such a thing?

"You bastard . . ." It wasn't even a whisper, barely a wisp of breath.

"Irrial, I—"

"You *bastard!*" No whisper, now, but a shriek of such fury that it almost, *almost*, hid the agonized heartbreak beneath it.

He never saw it coming. One instant he was standing, reaching for her with a pleading hand, and the next he was on the floor, his jaw throbbing, blood trickling from where his lips had split against his teeth.

Irrial stood over him, fists shaking, and he truly believed in that moment that had she held a weapon, Yarrick would not have been the only man to die at her hands that day.

"Irrial, please. I'm not the same man I—"

"Not the same man? Not the man who conquered Rahariem? Not the same man who slaughtered more people in *one day* than the Cephirans have killed in the last month? Not *that* man, *Cerris?*"

"Not anymore," he insisted, propping himself up on his elbows. "You've known me for three years! Do you really think those were all a lie? How about the past weeks? Were *those?*"

She glared, mouth twitching around two or three possible answers.

"Irrial, I don't even think of *myself* as 'Corvis' anymore. It was so long ago . . ."

"*Long?* Not so long that I don't still have nightmares. Not long enough to un-kill all the people—some of them my friends, my family!—that you butchered. No, *Cerris*, it hasn't been that long at all."

"Irrial, I'm sorry. I truly am. I lo—"

"If you say it," she hissed, "I swear to every god that I'll slit your damn throat!"

"Fine!" He surged to his feet, shoving her aside, anger rising to reflect her own. "Then how about the fact that I saved your damn life? How about the fact that you need me to save your precious city?" He stopped, breathing heavily, struggling to rein himself in. "Irrial, whatever happened in the past, whoever I am and whatever you think of me, Rahariem needs us *both. Imphallion* needs us both. And we need each other."

She glared up at him, he down at her. "You're right," she said, shoulders slumping and head bowing, a marionette with its strings gone slack. "We do . . . for now.

"But make absolutely no mistake," she added, stiffening once more. "We're allied in this because I want what's best for my city and my people. But that's *all* we are: temporary allies. Nothing more, not now, not ever."

"Irrial . . ."

"That's *Lady Irrial*," she corrected, turning away with her head held high.

And Corvis Rebaine, the Terror of the East, could only stand and watch as she stalked from the room, leaving him to make his own preparations for the long journey ahead.

Chapter Nine

"IT'S . . . JUST AN ORDINARY HOUSE."

Kaleb looked askance at the fellow beside him. "You were expecting a palace? A mansion? Maybe a warren of some sort?"

"I'm not sure," Jassion admitted, fingers fiddling with the links of his mail sleeve. "I guess I just expected . . . I don't know. *More.*"

The sorcerer's spell had guided them across dozens of leagues, from the terrible forest at Imphallion's outskirts to the city of Abtheum, crouching like a hunting cat beside a major highway. They'd had little difficulty entering, for this far from the borders (and lacking the paranoia of certain other rulers), the Earl of Abtheum hadn't done much in the way of increasing security. Jassion had packed away his tabard, since the last thing they needed was the attention of an official welcome and state visit, and they'd instead passed themselves off as traveling tradesmen. The guards at the gate gave them a glance that would have had to linger even to qualify as cursory, and permitted them passage.

A somewhat more modern city than Mecepheum or Denathere, Abtheum was built as much of wood as stone. Its streets—some cobbled, others hard-packed dirt—were mostly aligned to a prearranged plan, rather than twisting every which way in a more natural growth. Roofs sloped sharply to high peaks, their overhanging eaves casting narrower streets in perpetual dusk, and the air was surprisingly pleasant. Abtheum, apparently, had benefited from the relatively new innovation of underground sewers.

Through sundry neighborhoods they'd walked, Jassion growing ever more pensive, following a trail only Kaleb could sense. And finally that trail had led them here, to a neighborhood of vendors and artisans, neither affluent nor impoverished. Just . . . comfortable.

Ordinary.

The house, clearly of recent construction, wouldn't have looked out of place in a village a fraction of Abtheum's size. Its walls and surrounding fence were whitewashed, and most of the grounds were occupied by vegetable gardens, each plant clearly marked and arranged in orderly rows.

Jassion stood immobile in the street, gawping as though it were the maw of hell.

"If you don't move eventually," Kaleb finally said, "you're going to get run over by a cart. Either that or they'll put a plaque at your feet and dedicate you to somebody."

"I can't, Kaleb." The sorcerer actually had to lean in, so quiet was that voice. "I can't go in there."

"All right, then," he said with a shrug. "I'll talk to them by myself."

It was, as he'd obviously intended, precisely the right thing to say to spur Jassion into motion.

Dirt and pebbles crunched underfoot, Jassion starting with each sound until they'd finally reached the door. The hand he raised to knock was visibly shaking.

The door drifted open, accompanied by a slightly nasal "Yes?" Staring up at them was a sandy-haired boy with startling green eyes and a poor complexion, probably just entering his teens.

"I . . ." Jassion's tongue cleaved to the roof of his mouth, smothering whatever words might have emerged.

"We need to speak with your mother," Kaleb interjected, though not before perceptibly rolling his eyes at Jassion's unease. "Is she here?"

"*Mom!*" Even Kaleb started back a step as the boy turned and unleashed a shout that implied his father might, in fact, have been some sort of trumpet. *"Someone's here to see you!"* Then, far more softly and with a careless shrug, "She'll be here in a minute, I'm sure."

Indeed it was rather less than a minute before they heard an inner door—or perhaps the back door into the garden—slamming shut, the pitter-pat of soft footsteps approaching. "Lilander," a feminine voice admonished from an unseen hall, "what have I told you about shouting . . ."

Jassion couldn't hear the rest of it. The blood pounding in his ears was as the hammering of Verelian, or the charge of Kassek War-Bringer. Had the street behind him been consumed in a volcano, he'd probably never have noticed.

She appeared before him, clad in a sea-green tunic, wiping the garden dirt from her hands. Her chestnut hair—darker than he remembered, and shorter—was tied in a haphazard tail, and her face showed the lines and cares of decades. But hovering about her like a haunting ghost, Jassion saw the teenage girl he'd known, the sister who'd given herself to evil's own avatar to keep her baby brother safe.

"I'm so sorry," she said with a gentle smile. "I've asked him to mind his manners around guests, but—"

"Tyannon?"

She blinked once. "I'm sorry, have we—"

And then she looked, *really* looked, at this stranger on her porch. "Oh, my gods . . ." It was her hand, now, that shook as she slowly reached for him, the other held tight to her lips. "Jass?"

The Baron of Braetlyn crumpled to his knees, arms wrapping of their own volition about his sister's waist, and wept.

THE KITCHEN WAS JUST AS PLAIN as the rest of the house, and smelled faintly of wood smoke. A hearth with a cauldron, and a relatively new wood-burning stove, occupied one wall, leaving the bulk of the room for an oak table and thinly upholstered chairs.

Jassion sat hunched over the table, as small as he could make himself, his hands wrapped tight around his second flagon of mead.

Tyannon, across from him, kept reaching out and pulling back. Lilander hovered beside her, puzzled, worried gaze flitting between his mother and this strange, frightening man who, so he'd just been told, was an uncle he'd never met. Clearly, he was trying to decide whether he believed a word of it, and wondering what the hell to do about it once he'd made up his mind either way.

But Kaleb, who'd pulled two chairs back from the table before slouching into one and propping his feet on the other, paid them little mind. No, his attention appeared fixed on the most recent member of the gathering who stood, arms sullenly crossed, beside the kitchen door.

Hair darker than either her mother's or brother's was cut just below her chin in a "just be done with it" sort of style. Her eyes, too, were dark, the green of the deep seas off Braetlyn's shore. Her features were sharp and angular—clearly she favored her father more than she did Tyannon—making her, although not at all beautiful in the most classical sense, certainly striking, even exotic.

Or maybe that was just the irritated scowl that had staked a claim on her face. Regardless, throughout the conversation, Kaleb's attentions would flicker between Jassion and the baron's niece, and once or twice he gave a shallow nod, as though in sudden understanding.

Finally, after an uncomfortable interval for everyone involved—save possibly Kaleb—Jassion looked up from his drink. "I'm sorry," he said, his voice steady though his cheeks flushed with shame. "I didn't mean to . . . Well, that wasn't the first impression I'd have chosen to make."

"It's all right, Jass," Tyannon told him. "I understand. We all do." Her eyes had not, in truth, remained entirely free of tears, either.

He nodded and stood, then bowed toward the young woman at the door. She returned a stiff curtsy.

"I'm delighted," he said, and behind the formal tone he might even have meant it, "to meet you both." He extended a hand to Lilander, and his lips even twitched in a brief smile at the boy's deeply sincere expression as he took it.

"It's nice to meet you, Uncle Jassion," his niece told him, though her attention was fixed mostly on her mother. Her voice carried a surprising weight, given her slight frame. "Even if it should have happened much sooner."

"Mellorin!" Tyannon snapped at her.

"It's all right," Jassion said. "Perhaps I should have looked for you before—"

"It's not you, Jass," his sister told him. "Don't worry about it. Just an—old family squabble."

Mellorin rolled her eyes, and Kaleb coughed into a fist—probably to keep from snickering at the lot of them.

But Jassion's stare had gone flinty as he began to understand Mellorin's meaning. "She may have a point there, too, Tyannon."

"Jass—"

"You never came back."

"Jass, please—"

"You *never came back!*" Mead sloshed over the edge of the mug. Jassion glanced down, as though it had moved on its own, then once more at Tyannon. "*Twenty-three years!* How *could* you? How could you stay with that *creature*? How—"

Tyannon shot to her feet, chair toppling out from beneath her. "You didn't *know* him, Jassion. There was so much more to him, I really believed . . ." She sighed, brushing her hair from her face. "I loved him, Jassion."

"*No!*" He, too, was standing now, leaning over the table as though preparing to scramble over it.

"Mom?" Lilander whispered. His eyes were wide, but he stepped forward, putting his spindly, twelve-year-old frame between Tyannon and his uncle.

And in those eyes, Jassion saw reflected a figure in black armor snatching his sister away. He swallowed once, hard, and sat down, intertwining his fingers to keep his hands from shaking.

"Don't say that to me," he demanded, though far more softly. "Not ever. Not about—"

"Cerris," Tyannon interrupted, with perhaps the slightest emphasis on the name, "was not the man you think he was."

Jassion frowned, puzzled, failing for a moment to understand the fear, the *pleading,* in his sister's voice.

But only for a moment.

The children didn't know.

And Jassion would *not* be the one to tear their innocence from them. "Perhaps," he conceded, "we ought to speak alone."

"Lilander, go play outside." Her tone hadn't changed, but her shoulders slumped in obvious relief.

"I don't—"

"Please don't argue with me, Lilander. Not now. Mellorin, go keep an eye on him."

"Mother, come *on*! I'm not stupid, I—"

"Mom, I don't need—"

"I said *don't argue with me*! Please," she added softly, putting a hand on Lilander's face, turning her own face toward her daughter. "Please."

With that sigh of aggravation known to teens all over creation, Mellorin stomped from the room. Lilander trailed after, watching over his shoulder until the door shut behind them.

"Well," Kaleb said brightly, "that ought to keep the neighbors in gossip for a few more days."

The glares cast his way pretty well cemented the family resemblance.

"Thank you," Tyannon said, sitting across from her brother once more.

"I wasn't about to do that to them. Everyone deserves a childhood." The accusation was unmistakable.

"I did it to save *you*!"

"I know why you *went* with him, Tyannon. But you *stayed* with him. You weren't a prisoner, not after a while, anyway. He told me. You could have left anytime you wanted."

"Oh, he told you, did he? Would that have been when you had him chained up and beaten like a dog? Is *that* who I saved, Jassion? A monster who tortures helpless victims?"

"He *was* a dog, and I did what I had to do." The baron's face was flushed, his teeth grinding. "I should have *killed* him!"

"He saved us, Jass. He beat Audriss, and he saved us all."

"It doesn't excuse what else he did. And you, you . . ." He literally sputtered, unable to put words to her betrayal.

"I loved him," she said simply. And again, even as he flinched away, "I loved him. I saw more in him than you ever did. I saw the man he *could* be, and I helped him get there."

"You left me alone to do it," Jassion whispered. "And for what? Where's your 'new Corvis' now, Tyannon?"

This time, it was she who looked away.

"He's not here," Jassion said. "From the looks of things, he hasn't been for a while."

"He's never been in this house," she admitted, voice catching. "We left him a long time ago."

"Because you knew he hadn't changed after all, didn't you? You saw it when he came back from the Serpent's War."

"Oh, Jassion, I thought . . . I really thought he . . ."

He sat, staring at his hands while his sister cried, and wished he dared comfort her.

"I hate to interrupt this little family moment," Kaleb said in a tone that fooled nobody at all, "but the reason we're here . . . ?"

Jassion nodded, took a deep breath. "Tyannon, it's not over."

She nodded, dashing away her tears with the back of her hand. "I've heard rumors. I think everyone has. Duke Halmon?"

"Among many others. He has to be stopped. For good."

"I don't understand." She was mumbling, face turned toward the table. "Even at his worst . . . He always believed he was doing what was best for Imphallion. Why would he do this?"

Jassion's body tensed at her words, but he only shook his head. "I don't know. And it doesn't really matter, does it? If we don't deal with him—and fast, before Cephira advances any farther—there may not *be* much of an Imphallion left."

"I think . . ." Tyannon shuddered as the implications of her words overcame her, but she forged ahead. "I think I'd help you, if I could."

The air vanished from Jassion's lungs. "*If* you . . . ?"

"We used to live in Chelenshire, but I don't think he's there anymore." She sighed, reached out a hand to take his. "I'm sorry, Jassion. I know you've come all this way, and finding us couldn't have been easy. But I can't help you. I truly don't know where he is."

Kaleb muttered an ugly curse while Jassion stared down at the fingers that overlay his own, saying nothing at all.

———————————

THEY REMAINED FOR SOME HOURS, Jassion and Tyannon telling each other—haltingly, and without much detail—of the years they'd spent apart, while Kaleb sat across the room and fidgeted. But all too soon, or perhaps not soon enough, neither had anything left to say.

"We have to go," Jassion told her finally, rising from his chair. "Even if you can't help, we have to find him."

"I understand. Jass?"

"Hmm?"

"I know how you feel about him, and maybe you're right. But . . . Take him alive, if you can? For me?"

The baron's lips pressed tight, but he nodded. "If I can, Tyannon." Then, haltingly, "And perhaps, when this is over . . . Maybe you and the children might come to Braetlyn? I know you've no interest in being baroness, and I wouldn't foist it on you, but . . . It'd be nice not to be alone."

"I don't know, Jass. I'll think on it."

And that—along with a timid, tentative hug and the soft thud of a closing door—was that. Jassion stood on the walkway outside, staring out over the vegetable garden, and for once Kaleb was wise enough to hold his comments.

It was Jassion himself who finally broke the silence. "What now? We didn't really have a backup plan."

"Now? We wait. It'll be dark in a few hours. They'll all be asleep by then."

Jassion stiffened. "So?"

"So Lilander's too young to put up a fight. We can take him without much of a fuss, and with his blood—"

"*Have you lost your godsdamn mind?*"

"No, but if you keep shouting like that, I may lose my godsdamn hearing." He actually stuck a finger in his ear, wiggled it about a bit. "What's your problem?"

In a slightly lower voice, "Do you truly believe, for one single instant, that I'm going to let you abduct my nephew?"

"I won't hurt him, old boy. We just need—"

"No. Absolutely not. I told you, I don't care what sort of magic you have—"

"Yes, yes, you'll find some way to kill me. I've heard it before."

"You may not be around to hear it again. Besides, you said you couldn't find Rebaine even with familial blood, that he had spells to block you."

"From a distance, yes. But his magics aren't that powerful. If I can get near enough, I can break through his defenses. *If* I have a relative's blood. It's not much, but it's far better than nothing. You know, nothing? Like what we have now?"

They faced off in the middle of the yard, two men each as unyielding as oaks.

"Don't you have other means?" Jassion asked eventually. "Other magics we might use?"

"Oh, plenty. There are a dozen spells I could use to try to locate Rebaine."

"Then why—?"

"Because none of them would work. Even *his* magics are potent enough to completely block most lesser divinations. Neither of us has seen him personally in the past few months, and we don't have any of his hair or skin, so that rules out the more powerful options."

"Tyannon might have something."

"Oh, sure. She abandoned him with kids in tow because he'd betrayed everything she thought he was, but she kept a tuft of his beard as a keepsake."

Jassion grumbled something under his breath.

"Look, it's the only way—"

"No." The baron glared at Kaleb once more, but he wasn't seeing the sorcerer. Again he saw the black armor dragging his sister from him, again he saw the guards approaching, felt the warm blood and the flopping limbs as the corpses piled up around him. He saw, in his mind's eye, the pimply face of his nephew twisted in sudden fear.

And in that moment, he swore to himself: *I will do almost anything to stop Rebaine—but I will not become him to do it.*

Perhaps Kaleb saw some of that in Jassion's expression, because he simply nodded and turned to go, wandering back down the walk toward the posts at which they'd tied their mounts. Startled by his abrupt acquiescence, but unwilling to broach the subject further, Jassion scurried after.

For more than an hour they rode in silence, passing once more through Abtheum's gate and back onto the open highway. The *clop-clop* of the hooves seemed to tick away not merely distance but time itself.

"So what," Jassion asked again when it grew too heavy to bear, "do we do now?"

"We wait."

"It seems to me that we've had this conversation before. What, exactly, are we waiting for this time?"

"For our other option." Kaleb grinned smugly, steadfastly refusing to elaborate.

That option caught up with them in the early evening, moments after they'd made their nightly camp. Jassion stood by a tree off in the shadows, checking the tethers on the horses, while Kaleb crouched by a crackling fire he'd lit without benefit of flint or tinder, preparing a haunch of heavily salted beef they'd acquired in Abtheum's market. Both looked up as one, heads cocked at the soft whinny and faint jingling of an approaching mount.

"Right on schedule," Kaleb muttered, dusting his hands off and rising to his feet. Jassion's hand strayed toward Talon's hilt as he moved to join his companion, but the sorcerer shook his head. "That won't be necessary, O master swordsman."

A small palfrey rounded the bend, clearly a beast of burden rather than war. The slender figure atop the saddle wore undyed tunic and leggings. Face and chest were concealed by a hooded cloak that might have been described as "pearl" if it were of higher quality but, as it was, could only be called "off-white."

Horse and rider drew to a halt, faces turned to study the men by the fire. Small hands lifted the hood, dropped it back, revealing slim features and dark hair.

"Good evening, Mellorin," Kaleb said.

Jassion just cursed. A lot.

The daughter of Corvis Rebaine slid from her saddle, landing softly on her feet and striding toward them as though she had every right and expectation of being there. As she approached, Jassion whispered to Kaleb, "How did you know?"

"I saw a rather familiar look on her face during our conversation."

"Familiar?"

"Just like one of yours, actually. The one you get when you're about to be idiotically pigheaded about something. I've seen it a *lot*, actually."

"Gentlemen," she greeted them, halting some feet away. Her voice was steady, confident, but the flickering of her eyes in the firelight betrayed an underlying unease.

"What are you doing here, Mellorin?" Jassion asked. "Is something wrong?" A sudden twitch of fear touched his face. "Did something happen back home?"

Kaleb sighed and rolled his eyes in a gesture that was becoming as familiar as breath. "Nothing happened, you jackass. She wants to come with us. Don't you, Mellorin?"

She nodded. "I know you're looking for my father. I need—I want to find him, myself."

"Absolutely not!" The baron advanced, hand outstretched to clutch her shoulder. "There's no way I'm letting you—"

Boots etching a crescent in the dust, Mellorin spun. Her right shoulder connected with Jassion's chest, throwing him off his stride, while her left hand closed about his wrist. She continued, feet crossing, and Jassion, already off-balance, found himself yanked forward. He slammed to the earth, landing hard on his back and kicking up a cloud of dirt around him.

One more cross-step and Mellorin ended her spin nose-to-nose with Kaleb. A truly ugly knife, short but broad of blade and serrated down one side, protruded from her fist in an underhanded grip and pressed—gently but unmistakably—against the sorcerer's throat.

"I don't like being touched," she told them softly. "And I can take care of myself. I'm not asking to just 'tag along.' I can help you."

"Feisty, aren't you?" Kaleb asked with a grin.

Mellorin's expression grew frosty. "I was—attacked once, when I was just a child. My dear father saved me, but just because the danger was gone didn't make me any less terrified, and he couldn't be bothered to wait around afterward and make sure I was all right."

"So you learned to take care of yourself." It was not a question.

"Anywhere I could."

"I admire the spirit, Mellorin, but there's a big difference between street fighting and what we do out here. Look behind you."

Scowling in distrust, she glanced down. Jassion, without rising from the dust, had twisted around and drawn Talon, leveling the tip, steady and unwavering, mere inches from the small of her back. Only after a long moment, once he was content that she understood, did he withdraw the blade and rise to his feet.

"And your uncle will tell you," Kaleb continued, "that the instant you decided to talk to me rather than just slit my throat and be done with it, you gave me all the time I needed to kill you, if that's what *I'd* wanted."

The blade disappeared up Mellorin's sleeve and she stepped away, flushing brightly in the firelight. "You don't understand," she protested, sounding now more like a child than the young woman she'd so recently become. "I *have* to go with you. I have to know. Please . . ."

"Know what?" Jassion asked carefully, twisting awkwardly to brush his back clean.

"How my father could do what he did. How he could . . . How he could choose his damn crusade over his family."

Kaleb and Jassion glanced at each other, then at Mellorin, both sharing a comical expression of uncertainty.

"I know," she told them softly, sitting on a small log that Jassion had earlier dragged to the camp for use as a chair. "Mother never told us, and Lilander's too young to question, but . . . I know when he left, and *everyone* knows about the Serpent's War. It wasn't hard to figure it out. Just because Mother thinks I'm an idiot," she spat bitterly, "doesn't make me one."

"Don't you dare—" Jassion began hotly, but Kaleb was already kneeling at Mellorin's side.

"Your mother thinks no such thing," he told her gently, *almost* putting a hand on hers, recoiling at the last moment as he recalled her earlier words. "She was trying to *protect* you. And I think you know that, Mellorin."

She sniffed once, cleared her throat, offered the sorcerer a shallow shrug. "It doesn't matter. I have to know who he was. I have to ask him why."

"All right," he said, standing, smiling softly. "You can join us."

Even as Mellorin's face broke into an astonished smile, Kaleb could actually *hear* Jassion stiffening up behind him.

"Kaleb?" The baron's mouth barely moved, so tightly was his jaw clenched. "Can I speak with you over by the horses for a moment?"

The sorcerer frowned thoughtfully. "No, I don't think so. Mellorin's not a child, Jassion, no matter how much you treat her like one. The least you can do is respect her enough to say whatever you have to say to her face."

Mellorin actually beamed.

Jassion reached out, snagging the clasp of Kaleb's cloak—looking very much like he'd prefer it had been the man's *throat* beneath his fingers—and dragged him across the campsite. His niece glared after them but remained where she was, apparently deciding not to press the issue.

"Do that again," Kaleb said, knocking the baron's hand aside, "and we're going to have a disagreement."

"Did we not *just* discuss this?" Jassion demanded, so near that Kaleb felt the spittle on which those words rode. "Did you not understand me this afternoon?"

"We're not kidnapping anyone. She *wants* to join us, old boy. And she can take care of herself. You saw that."

"Pfft. She's a brawler, Kaleb, nothing more. *You* said as much."

"But she's good. We can teach her. Besides, I don't think even Rebaine would hurt his own daughter."

"I'm not so sure. Besides, there are other dangers—"

"And anything we can't teach her to handle, we can protect her from. I have several wards I can cast over her, just for an added bit of protection. Would you permit that, Mellorin?" he called so that she could hear. "Let me cast some defensive spells over you as we travel, to mollify your uncle?"

She blinked, then shrugged. "If that's what it takes."

"We need her," Kaleb continued, his voice hushed once more, "and you know it. Besides," he added, glancing again over Jassion's shoulder at the object of their discussion, "she'd probably just keep following us."

"You said the blood wouldn't help us much," Jassion protested, but his tone and even his posture were weakening.

"I said not unless he was nearby. But 'near' is a relative thing where magic's concerned. Suppose we manage to track him to the right city, then what? You plan to knock on doors at random? We've a *far* better chance with her than without her."

Jassion turned reluctantly to study his niece. She, sensing his attention, glared back defiantly.

"If anything happens to her, Kaleb . . ."

"Don't fret, old boy. If it makes you feel any better, I'm a lot more likely to protect her than I am you."

Jassion snarled and went to tell his niece the "good" news. Unseen behind him, Kaleb couldn't quite repress a secret smile. That there was more to Mellorin's motives than she'd admitted, he was absolutely certain, as certain as he was of his own name. But he had time, plenty of time to draw out the truth.

It might prove almost as useful as the girl herself.

Chapter Ten

Rahariem had fallen.

From beyond its walls they'd come, a swarm of mercenaries both Imphallian and foreign, and if their armor, their weapons, and their war cries were all different, still they fought as a unified force.

Alongside them had marched warriors of far more fearsome mien. Horned, cyclopean ogres ripped soldiers and horses and siege engines apart with great serrated blades and bare hands. Twisted, creeping gnomes crawled from the earth, cloaked in gloom, to murder soldier and citizen alike. The grounds surrounding Rahariem had become a swamp, made clinging mud by the shedding of so much blood. The shadow of flapping wings and the squawking of uncounted crows were an endless storm in the skies.

Yet the horrors of battle had paled before the horrors to come.

The courtyard of the Ducal Estate was crammed to bursting, its grasses and flowers trampled by the crush of so many feet. Rahariem's citizens milled aimlessly, aristocrat with pauper. Whimpers of terror rose as a single breath from the throng, and frightened eyes could not settle in any safe direction. From the fences surrounding the property, from the lampposts on the streets beyond, even from the flagpoles of the great keep, rancid bodies dangled, decanting vile fluids across the ground below. Thanks to the crows and creeping vermin, most were unrecognizable, and this, gruesome though it might have been, was a blessing—for each surviving face was known and loved by someone in the crowd.

Surrounding them—prodding with swords and spears; keeping the sheep from stampeding—were the invaders, human and otherwise. So long as the citizens held themselves in check and made no attempt to cause trouble or to escape, the soldiers left them largely unmolested. Any disruption, however, drew immediate and brutal response.

Nobody made a nuisance of themselves twice—because nobody survived the first time.

The keep's massive doors swung wide, and there he stood, framed within. The black steel of his armor faded into the darkness of the hall beyond, so that the plates of bone and the terrible skull seemed to hover, phantasmal and disembodied. For a long moment, precisely calculated for maximum effect, he waited, making no move save to rake that empty gaze across the assembly, examining every face and every soul, and disapproving of what he found. Then and only then did the monster who called himself Corvis Rebaine step into full view. Despite themselves, the crowd cowered away. Several began to weep.

"You've had the time I promised," he told them, and his voice was no less hollow than the empty sockets of the helm. "It is time to choose."

The people of Rahariem turned to one another, tearfully begging for understanding, for forgiveness. And they chose.

Many nobles and Guildmasters had escaped the city's fall, abandoning their offices and estates to hide among the populace. And now that populace grabbed them, exposed them, hauling them into the open to suffer Rebaine's judgment, for they knew what he would do to them otherwise.

He'd told them, after all, and they need only look at the dangling bodies to know he spoke the truth.

Most of them, aristocrats and Guildmasters both, screamed as they were dragged from amid their fellows, pleading for secrecy, for sanctuary. But some few stepped forward on their own, heads held high, unwilling to force their brethren into making such a terrible decision.

Sir Wyrrim, respected baron and landed knight, revered as highly in Rahariem as the duke himself, was the first to come forward. He faced the crowd around him, and to each of them he offered a gentle smile.

He felt a small hand take his own, and looking down saw his distant cousin, a young noblewoman of Rahariem. Her face was pallid with terror, a sheen of sweat across her brow, but she forced her lips into a matching smile.

Ignoring the weeping from all sides, the flapping of the fleshy banners above, Sir Wyrrim and the Lady Irrial joined their fellow prisoners, following Rebaine's soldiers toward whatever fate awaited in the dungeons below.

DROWNING IN THE TIDE OF MEMORIES she had fought so long to escape, Irrial sat upon a knotty tree root and glared across the embers of the dying fire at the blanket-wrapped figure. Her bloodless lips were pressed together, her hands clasped tight about the hilt of her stolen sword. It would be so simple, the work of an instant, and so many years of unspeakable suffering would find some tiny measure of justice. No murder, this, but legitimate execution; perhaps even the putting down of a wild beast.

"If you're going to try to kill me," Corvis said without opening his eyes, "could you go ahead and get it over with? Clichés to the contrary, a man can't *actually* sleep with one eye open, so you're sort of keeping me up."

"You're *really* pushing me, Rebaine."

"Am I?" He sat, allowing the blankets to fall from his shoulders and finally opening his eyes. "Look, Irrial—my lady," he corrected at her expression, "we need each other. You accepted that when we left

Rahariem. You're just making yourself miserable thinking the way you are now."

"I'm *so* sorry that my revulsion at your crimes is disturbing you."

Corvis sighed. "Just tell me that you'll wait until after this is all said and done before you decide to try anything stupid, all right?"

"Fine. But only for Rahariem and Imphallion."

"I don't really care *why*." He lay down once more, hauling the blanket up to his chin.

"That's it?" she asked after a moment, curious despite herself. "You trust me just like that?"

"I've trusted you for years," he told her. "Nothing's changed for me, even if you think it has for you. But if it'll make you feel better, you can swear an oath to one of the gods. That's how I made it work last time."

Another pause. "Last time?"

"Somehow, my lady, I doubt you'd be surprised to learn that I've had other traveling companions who wanted to kill me."

"Rebaine, I'd be surprised if you had any that *didn't*."

"Funny."

"I wasn't joking," she insisted.

"I know." Corvis yawned once, loudly. "Wake me when it's my watch. Irrial?"

"What?"

"It's *very* simple to set up a spell to wake me if anyone comes too close. I really do trust you, but I'm not an idiot."

He was snoring softly before she could come up with a viable answer to that one.

THEIR FIRST DAYS ON THE ROAD had been more than a little harrowing. Travel was a nervous affair, as they remained alert for approaching soldiers, ready to scurry into whatever cover might make itself available. Once they'd ambushed a small patrol—obtaining mounts, supplies, and a replacement weapon for Irrial—they moved a bit faster, but it was only after they'd passed beyond Cephiran-held territory, and the highways began to boast Imphallian travelers, that they breathed easy. Corvis felt his shoulders and back relaxing, and the next morning was the first in a week that he'd awakened without a headache crawling up the back of his neck.

Not that they'd escaped the invasion's shadow; far from it. Long stretches of road were packed with refugees, making their slow and sad way westward. Some rode mounts with saddlebags stuffed to bursting, others drove wagons laden with the pitiful remnants of homes and lives, and many carried only what they could hoist on their backs. Un-counted plodding feet kicked up the dirt of the highways, tromped flat the grasses alongside, all accompanied by muffled sobs, whispered re-assurances, and tear-streaked prayers. Sweat perfumed the air—sweat and, somehow, the stink of despair. It turned the stomach, this stench of slowly rotting hope.

Corvis, though it shamed him, found himself grateful for their pres-ence. They offered plenty of cover for Irrial and him to hide, should any Cephiran scouts range this far; and they held the baroness's attentions, so conversation—and acrimony, and accusation—remained scarce.

'Well, we always knew the masses had to be good for something, right?'

After some days, however, the bulk of the refugees turned aside. The road passed by the city of Emdimir, the informal line of demarcation between central and eastern Imphallion. Already the city was so crowded the stone walls threatened to bulge, like the distended belly of a starving man, and every moment more people arrived. The air above the city wavered with the heat, and Corvis was sure he could actually see pestilence lurking within the clouds above. But the people had, for the most part, no strength to travel farther, and Emdimir's government hadn't yet hardened their hearts enough to begin turning them away.

Once past that city, Corvis and Irrial made excellent time, thanks to the horses and the highways—and a good thing it was, for the journey remained remarkably unpleasant, even without the sorrowful throng. The sun seemed utterly determined to cook them into some sort of stew, its heat letting up only for the occasional summer squall—which, in turn, summoned up mosquitoes by the bushel. After the second such shower, Corvis had scratched himself bloody and was fairly convinced that he'd prefer a dagger in a vital organ over one more bite.

Irrial promptly offered hers, and Corvis decided to keep his future complaints to himself.

Nor were these the only bites he had to endure. The Cephiran warhorse he'd acquired was a nasty, ill-tempered brute who still wasn't entirely sold on his new master. The beast was more than cooperative while Corvis was riding—its training saw to that—but it constantly tugged at the reins when they walked, balked while he was trying to lead. It had bitten him thrice already, once drawing blood as he tethered it up for the night, and had even once kicked at him, a blow that would assuredly have broken bone had it landed.

Corvis, sick to the death of the whole thing, had cuffed the horse hard across the nose. Apparently he'd gotten some of the message across, because the kicking had ceased, though the biting continued unabated. Also, he had to endure an extra-intensive glare from Irrial for a day and a half after he struck "that helpless creature."

For the first time in years, Corvis found himself desperately missing Rascal. He'd been such a good horse; the poor thing just, after trying so hard for so long, hadn't proved up to being *Corvis Rebaine's* horse.

And then there was Irrial herself, who spoke with him as infrequently as feasible. The prior discussion on whether or not to murder Corvis in his sleep was perhaps the longest exchange they'd shared since Rahariem.

'*Have you considered cuffing* her *across the nose?*'

"Shut up." Corvis actually found himself hoping, for an instant, that the voice in his head was genuine; he didn't like the idea that such a thought came from him, crazy or not.

But as summer entered its downward slope—not that one could tell by the stifling heat—and they drew ever nearer their destination, passing by larger towns and ever more numerous travelers, Irrial's curiosity apparently overcame her hostility. As they made camp that evening, she moved to sit across the fire from him, rather than taking her meal to the far side of the campsite as had been her wont. He tilted his head, his expression puzzled, and maybe just a little pleased.

"Where, exactly, are we going?" she asked him, one hand clutching a sharp stick from which hung a greasy haunch of rabbit.

"We're heading to Mecepheum. I told you that."

"Yes, but you never explained why."

"That," Corvis told her, "is because you didn't want to know. Told me to 'do whatever needed to be done,' and then stomped away in a huff."

"Corvis . . ."

"It was a very *nice* huff, if that matters at all. Skillful. Easily one of the best I've seen."

Irrial scowled, but she looked as embarrassed as she did angry. "All right, maybe so. But now I want to know."

"It's all pretty simple," he said, pulling his own skewered rabbit from the flames and blowing on it before taking a healthy bite. "Lessh looka whawno."

"What?"

Corvis swallowed and tried again. "Let's look at what we know. We're facing a full-on Cephiran invasion. Even if they don't advance any farther than the eastern territories, they've come farther than any prior skirmish. Imphallion can't just let that pass."

"Except that so far, we have," she reminded him.

"Exactly. Now, the Guilds and the nobility are really good at letting their differences stop them from accomplishing anything. I've seen it myself—decades ago, and again during the Serpent's War—and things have just gotten worse in the past few years. So it's *possible*—even after the lesson they should've learned from Audriss—that they'd rather argue with one another while Cephira pulls the walls down around their ears.

"What's *not* possible—or what I'd have *thought* to be impossible, anyway—is for them to completely ignore the situation like they have been. Even if they can't agree on a unified response, many dukes, barons, and Guildmasters would've responded on their own. We should've seen at least a few armies by now—mobilizing near the border, if not attacking outright."

Irrial nodded thoughtfully. "But the only soldiers we've seen have been guarding the cities and estates we've passed along the road. So something's keeping them not only from unifying, but from mobilizing entirely." She frowned. "Part of it, of course, is those murders."

"Which we both know I didn't commit." Then, at her expression,

"Oh, come on, Irrial! No matter how much you might distrust me now, you were *there*."

"I don't actually know how much magic you have, Rebaine."

"If I could just whisk myself from city to city, do you think I'd be pounding my rear end raw on that saddle? Besides," he added, "you pretty much knew where I was every *minute*, didn't you?"

Irrial actually wrapped her arms around herself. "Don't remind me."

'*Me, either.*'

"The point," Corvis continued, pretending not to be stung by the revulsion in her tone, "is that my supposed reappearance is awfully convenient. Either whoever's impersonating me is in league with Cephira, or they're using the Cephiran invasion as a distraction from something else. In either case, while I can see the return of Corvis Rebaine causing quite a stir, I don't know if it's enough to keep *every* noble and Guild in check. So we have to find out not only who's pretending to be me, but what *else* is going on in the halls of power. And that means going to, well, the halls of power."

"And how, pray tell, do you plan to get anyone to *tell* you what's going on? Or convince them you're not responsible for the attacks?"

"As to the latter, I'm working on that. And as to the former . . ." Corvis grinned. "Let's just say that I still have a certain amount of influence."

"What sort of influence?" she asked suspiciously.

"Why, my lady, the same sort that inspires a Cephiran siege team to attack their own people."

Irrial had further questions—he could see it in her face—but her rising from the campfire and walking away was sufficient indication that, for tonight, she'd heard enough.

———————————◖▪▪▪◗ ◖▪▪▪◗———————————

It was a modest celebration by any standard, attended by a scant two dozen souls—and if most had known the happy couple for less than a year, that made them ignorant, not blind. So when the groom vanished from the hall of that small wooden temple, someone was bound to notice, but for the moment he just didn't much care.

Outside in the courtyard, he strode through the sparse spring precipitation, feeling the water drip down the back of his fancy (albeit secondhand) doublet, watched the petals of the brightly colored flowers bend and rebound against the rain. Finding a marble bench that was likely older, and certainly sturdier, than the temple itself, he lowered himself to the stone. The accumulated rain that instantly soaked through the seat of his pants was a small price to pay for getting off his feet for a bit. *Precisely what sadistic inquisitor,* he wondered sourly to himself, *had come up with what modern society laughably called "formal shoes"?*

"You know," a gentle voice said from behind, "you're supposed to get cold feet *before* the wedding. Fleeing afterward doesn't really do any good."

He smiled and raised a hand to cover the smaller fingers on his shoulder. "I was actually just thinking about feet," he answered. "Aren't we supposed to be married longer than an hour before you start reading my mind?"

Tyannon, absolutely resplendent in a borrowed gown of whites and greens—and utterly oblivious to what the rain was doing to the fine materials, or the elaborate coiffure that had taken hours to arrange just so—stepped around the bench and took a seat beside him. "What is it?" she asked, her tone far more serious.

"It's just . . . Cerris."

She blinked, and he knew it wasn't because of the water. "What?"

"Cerris. Tyannon, the priest called me 'Cerris.'"

"Well, yes. That's what we told him your name was. It's not as though we could have—"

"I know. But . . ." He waved helplessly, sending a spray of water arcing over the flowers, perpendicular to the rain. "Can we build a marriage—" he asked in a whisper, "can we build a *life*—on a lie?"

"No! Not a lie." She slid from the bench, dropping to her knees before him, allowing the gown to soak in the rivulets of water and mud as she clasped both his hands in her own. "Cerris? The man you are now? He's a good man, and he's *not* the man you were. How can it be a lie for me to be married to Cerris, when that's who you are?"

Corvis—Cerris—stared down at his new bride, and gave thanks for the gentle shower that washed away his tears.

———————————————

AND THEN TYANNON WAS CALLING his name, her voice low but harsh. Except it *wasn't* Tyannon, as his bleary eyes opened, but Irrial standing opposite the embers of the dead fire, waking him for his turn at watch. She nodded brusquely as he awoke and returned to her own blanket without another word.

He was grateful, then, that the second woman Corvis had stolen from Cerris's arms fell swiftly asleep, for today no rain fell to hide his tears.

———————————————

THE LAST FEW LEAGUES OF ROADWAY GREW somewhat more crowded again, not with refugees—a few had come this far, true, but *only* a few—but with more traditional travelers: farmers and merchants, laborers and couriers.

And soldiers.

Not nearly enough, as Irrial had hoped when first spotting them, to suggest that Imphallion was finally mobilizing. No, these were sporadic patrols of a dozen or fewer, less concerned with advancing eastward than in carefully scouring those coming west. After their third time being stopped and questioned without explanation, Corvis realized that these sentinels must have been assigned to ensure that none of the fugitives come from the border were actually Cephiran agents in disguise.

As if there were any way to tell. "Damn fools," he grumbled to himself, his words lost to the tromping of the warhorse's hooves. "Even when they decide to do *something*, it's a bloody waste of effort."

'*Sort of like leading an untrained resistance against the Cephiran army on behalf of a woman who'd now sooner behead you than bed you, Corvis?*'

If this is just all in my mind, Corvis bemoaned silently, *I must really hate myself.*

Thanks to some quick shopping in towns along the way, the travelers who finally arrived at the towering gates of Mecepheum were not entirely the same pair who had fled Rahariem. Irrial wore a fine green cloak, lined in velvet, over a startlingly white tunic and thick riding trousers. The fellow accompanying her was clad in the formal but practical outfit of a household servant, and sported a few weeks' worth of neatly trimmed beard.

He also, due rather less to new clothes than to judicious use of subtle illusions, didn't especially resemble Corvis Rebaine. It had been a long time, but there were too many among the capital's elite who might recognize him.

When Irrial had asked how he could make use of his local contacts when he didn't resemble himself, he'd merely wiggled his fingers and said "Maaaaagic."

She hadn't spoken to him since.

Although it required standing in line for upward of an hour, they entered the city with little hassle or fanfare, stopping just inside the gates to take a long look. After occupied Rahariem, Mecepheum was an alien land. The streets were bustling—one might even say "flooded"—with people and horses, carts and wagons, all shoving their way through walls of sweaty flesh. The tumult was nigh overwhelming, but it was the typical rumble of daily life, with nary a sob of despair or a barked command to be heard. The absence of shattered homes and piles of rubble seemed somehow improper, as though Mecepheum were rudely refusing to acknowledge the troubles of its distant sister.

Which wasn't all that inaccurate, really.

Though many blocks separated the gates from the political offices in and around the Hall of Meeting, the travelers chose to make the trip on foot rather than trying to ram their horses through the throng. A nearby inn provided quality stabling at only slightly hair-raising prices, and Corvis also acquired a couple of rooms before they braved the streets again. This time, Irrial walked with the slightest trace of a limp and leaned on what looked to be a plain but expertly carved cane. Corvis wore her Cephiran sword at his waist; Sunder was nowhere to be seen.

The baroness, who'd not been to Mecepheum in many years, gawped like a yokel, not taken by the capital's finery so much as by the sharp delineations between the poorer and richer quarters, as well as the obviously new repairs to the ancient structures. As the apparent age of those repairs finally sank in, she cast a suspicious glance at her supposed "servant," trailing a few steps behind.

"Audriss," he said defensively. "Not me."

Irrial didn't look convinced.

They mounted the steps to the Hall of Meeting, noses held high as though they not only had every right to be there, but questioned everyone *else's* presence. Recognizing the arrogant mien of the nobility—and the servant thereof, which was frankly even worse—the clerk positioned near the entrance didn't even bother to ask their business.

Unfortunately, stopping to ask him directions might have ruined the effect, and Corvis hadn't the slightest idea where they were going. Running through a mental list of Guildmasters and nobles over whom he still held "influence," he stepped up the pace a bit and whispered "Mubarris. Cartwrights' and Carpenters' Guild."

Irrial's hair barely twitched, so shallow was her nod, but clearly she'd heard. As they rounded a corner, their footsteps muffled by the thick carpeting—which, if ubiquitous throughout the Hall, must have cost enough to buy a small village—she raised a hand to stop the next passerby. "Tell me, good sir," she asked, voice distant but stiffly polite, "where might I find the office of Guildmaster Mubarris?"

The fellow they accosted sported immaculately curled blond locks and was clad in the blue-and-white livery of one of Mecepheum's numerous aristocratic Houses. "And what, do pray tell," he asked with a disparaging sneer, "would a highborn lady such as yourself need with one of those *merchants*?" It might have been the most foul, blasphemous epithet the way he choked it out, and Corvis groaned inwardly.

Things were obviously even worse between the Guilds and the nobility than he'd thought.

That, or the guy was just a jackass.

'You're such a pessimist. Why can't it be both?'

Irrial's expression grew so cold and so stony, it might well have convinced an angry basilisk not to waste its time. "That would be between me and the Guildmaster, wouldn't it? Now kindly tell us where to find him."

"So you can make more concessions? Give away more of our power?" The pugnacious fellow was on a tear; apparently having found a target for his frustrations, he wasn't about to surrender it without a fight. "You're not from Mecepheum, my lady, I can see that right off. So why don't you go back wherever you came from and leave the *real* politics to the people who know what they're doing?"

Corvis sucked in a breath between his teeth and began to step forward, but Irrial raised a hand to stop him. Her voice, when she spoke, had gone completely calm. "You, dear fellow, will answer my question."

"Oh? And why is that?"

"Because if you don't, my servant here is going to find the nearest blunt object and play your head like a drum until your eyes switch sides."

"I—you . . . !"

"I still remember some great military cadences," Corvis told him. "Very impressive. *Lots* of percussion."

"You can't lay a finger on me!" the aristocrat whined, though he took a hesitant step back.

"I'll swear blind that you raised a hand to me first," Irrial said. "My servant was just defending me."

"Third floor." It was a surly mutter, scarcely audible. "Fourth hall to the left of the stairs, third door on the right."

"My thanks, good sir. You're a credit to your kennel."

They were gone, Irrial leading the way in a billowing flurry of cloak, before he could cease gawking long enough to formulate a response.

"Where," Corvis asked, voice quivering with suppressed laughter, "did you learn to do *that*?"

"That's all politics is really about, Reb—Cerris," she corrected swiftly, lest anyone overhear. "Finding some way to get the last word." For just an instant, her lips twitched in that smile Corvis hadn't seen in weeks.

"I think I'm rubbing off on you," he said—and right away, even before her smile vanished and her face hardened once more, he knew it was exactly the wrong thing to say.

'How's that foot tasting, Corvis? Have you really gotten this stupid, or are you just trying to prove something?'

They climbed numerous stairs, traversed numerous halls. It was easy enough to see which doors led to the offices of anyone remotely important: Those were the doors flanked by mail-clad guards. They were armed with broad-bladed short swords, brutal thrusting weapons well suited to the tight confines of the corridors, and loaded crossbows leaned against the walls at their feet.

"You'd think they were afraid of something," Corvis whispered. This time, Irrial didn't smile at all.

Without pause, she approached the mercenaries standing outside the room to which they'd been reluctantly directed. "Would you be so good as to inform Guildmaster Mubarris that the Baroness Irrial of Rahariem requires an audience?"

In a practiced maneuver, one of the guards moved to block her way while the other opened the door just wide enough to ask whether or not they were to be admitted. The one whose attentions remained fixed on the newcomers gestured over Irrial's shoulder with his chin. "Your man all right, m'lady?"

She glanced back and was startled to see Corvis's face—well, the face he was currently wearing—furrowed in concentration, beaded slightly with sweat.

"He's fine," she answered with far more conviction than she felt. "It's just been a long journey."

"I understand." Then, "Is it as bad as we've heard out there?"

"I don't know what you've heard, but it's bad enough. We've basically lost the border towns entirely."

That brought a fearsome scowl. Apparently, not everyone here was thrilled with the government's failure to act. "I'm glad you got out, m'lady," he added politely.

The second warrior turned back from the door. "The Guildmaster will see you."

Irrial began to step forward. "Thank you so—"

"Uh, I'm sorry, m'lady," the first guard interrupted with a nervous smile. "But nobody's permitted into a Guildmaster's or noble's chambers under arms. Nervous times, you understand."

"Of course." She waved a finger at Corvis, who dutifully detached the sword from his belt and handed it over. When the soldiers looked her way, she shrugged, leaning on her cane. "I'm unarmed. That's what I keep *him* around for."

The guards glanced at the cane, which could have functioned as a makeshift club—but then, so could the chairs inside the room. With a mutual shrug, they stepped aside.

Irrial swept between them and offered a shallow curtsy to the fleshy, balding fellow behind the desk. Corvis followed, shutting the door behind him.

The Guildmaster rose and bowed, his movements slightly stilted. His expression was just the tiniest bit unfocused, something she'd never have noticed had he not looked directly at her. He looked—*preoccupied* wasn't quite the right word, but she could think of none better.

Brow furrowed, Corvis appeared at Irrial's side. "Hello, Mubarris."

"Hello."

Irrial nodded in understanding. "You weren't joking, were you?"

"About using magic? No."

"I didn't see you casting any spells."

"You're about six years late for that."

The baroness frowned and opened her mouth to ask a question, but Corvis shook his head. "Later." He took a seat, gestured for Irrial to do the same.

For more than an hour they talked, Corvis and Irrial asking questions, Mubarris providing answers in that same "not entirely there" tone of voice, but those answers were proving relatively unhelpful.

He confirmed for them the murders committed by "Corvis Rebaine," not only in Mecepheum but later in Denathere, and a purported few in other cities as well. He provided a list of the dead, and though she'd already known, Irrial lowered her head when her cousin's name passed his lips.

Corvis, ever suspicious, chewed at the inside of his cheek and wondered if it was simple chance that so many of the dead—not all, not even most, but more than he'd easily accept as coincidence—were men and women over whom he'd long ago cast Selakrian's spell.

What Mubarris could *not* offer was any hint as to who might be behind the false Rebaine. He did not, in fact, even have reason to disbelieve the rumors himself, given his ignorance of the magics under which he currently labored—or who had cast them.

Nor could he offer any reasons beyond the obvious as to why the Guilds and the nobles were proving *so* stubborn, so mulish, that nobody had taken action.

"We're all scared," he admitted. "Nobody wants to be without protection—and lots of it—in case Rebaine comes for us next. And you know that the Guildmasters and the nobles haven't agreed on much of anything since the Guilds dethroned the regent."

Corvis and Irrial nodded in unison.

"But it does seem," he continued, "as though there's some added pressure. As if the leaders on both sides are demanding concessions and promises that they *know* the other side won't accept. I couldn't say for sure, though, or tell you where that pressure's coming from. I'm not really part of the inner circles anymore. Haven't been for a few years; I guess nobody thinks the Cartwrights' and Carpenters' Guild is important anymore." His heavy sigh dragged an anchor of self-pity along behind it. "Or maybe it's just me."

The visitors made their excuses, Corvis delivering a final command to forget the conversation—or at least never to speak of it to anyone, since he wasn't sure if the spell *could* compel Mubarris to forget—and departed. He reclaimed his sword from the guards, then requested directions to another room.

Over the course of the afternoon, Irrial and Corvis visited two more

Guildmasters, and two nobles with offices in the Hall. All were among
the surviving number of Corvis's "contacts," and all told the same story
as Mubarris. All confirmed what he had confirmed, suspected what he
had suspected; and none knew any more than he, for each and every
one had found him- or herself excluded from the pinnacles of power in
Mecepheum. The nobles lacked much real authority, now that the
Guilds had firmly taken over, and the Guildmasters, again like Mubarris, had been carefully shuffled to the periphery.

Corvis was finding it harder and harder to accept this as coincidence. He'd *known* that his puppets had to have lost some of their
power when Imphallion failed to sail the various courses charted by
Duke Halmon—or occasionally by Corvis himself, *through* Halmon.
He'd known that several of the Guildmasters he'd beguiled had even
lost their positions. But to see it before him like this, so deliberate and
precise . . .

"What now?" Irrial asked, interrupting his musings.

He shrugged, running through the names of every Guildmaster he
could recall, disliking the direction his thoughts were taking.

"Now," he said finally, reluctantly, "we talk with someone I *know* is
in a position to tell us more about what the hell's going on."

And we hope, he added silently, *that she's willing to tell us, because
over her, I hold no influence at all.*

THE HALLS GREW ever more crowded as they progressed. No surprise, that. The higher one climbed in the Hall of Meeting, the more
important were the inhabitants of its chambers; and the more important the inhabitants, the greater the quantity of rugged mercenaries
and minor functionaries.

Corvis hung back as Irrial approached the door, and the no fewer
than six guards posted beside it, and was momentarily grateful to be
masquerading as a servant. The deference expected of his role would
do well to cover his genuine unease. He disliked the notion of coming
here, of exposing himself—even disguised—to a Guildmaster over

whom he lacked any control. And if anyone here was likely to have the knowledge, the discipline, and the presence of mind to discover him, it was she. But he knew that, now as when he'd last seen her more than half a decade gone by, she was highly regarded by the other Guildmasters. If *anyone* was in a position to see the whole picture, to understand what was happening here in Mecepheum—and what wasn't happening, and why—it was she.

"The Baroness Irrial of Rahariem," his companion announced to the guards as she halted before them, cane thumping dully against the carpeted floor, "to see Salia Mavere."

As before, one of the guards slipped through the door while the others maintained their positions, and Corvis struggled not to hold his breath. Odds were good that Mavere would want to speak with Irrial, to learn what was happening on the eastern front, but . . .

He couldn't quite suppress a sigh of relief when the guard returned and announced, "The Guildmistress will see you."

Also as before, Corvis handed his sword over to the soldiers before entering, then followed Irrial as meekly as he could manage.

The priestess of Verelian and leader of the Blacksmiths' Guild offered the baroness something oddly between a bow and a curtsy, which Irrial politely returned. "I was heartened to hear your name," Mavere said as she offered chairs and then drinks to her guests—the former of which they gratefully accepted, the latter politely declined. "It's been difficult getting any reliable news from the east, but we'd heard that most of the elite were being held."

Elite. A very useful word, Corvis couldn't help but note, for the nobility and the Guilds both. If there was anything on which the two sides could agree, after all, it was that they were certainly superior to everyone else.

'*Someone ought to show them otherwise, don't you think?*'

"Most of us are," Irrial said, adjusting her skirts across the chair. "I managed to escape with some outside help." Very briefly, and leaving out a number of salient details—such as, just for instance, the true name of the man who'd assisted her—the baroness recounted the tale of her escape and her abortive attempt at resistance.

"You're a very fortunate woman," Mavere told her finally, one powerful hand fiddling idly with the combination ensign and holy symbol hanging about her neck. "The gods were surely watching over you."

"Surely," Irrial agreed. Only someone who'd known her as well as Corvis would have detected the bitterness in her tone.

"And I can certainly understand why you fled Rahariem with all haste," the Guildmistress continued. "But I have to admit to some puzzlement as to why you'd travel all the way here, my lady."

She wasn't puzzled at all, of course, and everyone in the room knew it. She just wanted to make her guests broach the topic.

"Why?" Irrial's response was, perhaps, hotter than she'd intended. "Because, Mavere, I would very much like to know why you people have allowed a hostile kingdom to conquer eastern Imphallion without lifting so much as a finger in response!"

"My lady, as you well know, there's been a great deal of strife between the Guilds and the nobility as of late . . ."

"Yes, ever since the Guilds combined their influence to illegally force my cousin to abdicate as regent."

Mavere's face twitched, but she revealed no other sign of her irritation. "For the good of Imphallion. The old ways weren't working."

"And we're doing so much better now, are we?"

The Guildmistress sighed, and there actually appeared a touch of genuine sorrow in her demeanor. "I'm afraid the nobles have proved more resistant to change than we'd hoped. They're making demands and insisting on concessions that we cannot possibly afford, and until they cooperate, our ability to govern their lands—or field their armies—is limited."

"It was my understanding," Irrial said, carefully modulating her voice, "that *both* sides were making unreasonable demands."

"Yes, well, the nobles *would* claim that in order to justify their intransigence, wouldn't they?"

Corvis wondered briefly if he'd need to put himself between them, and fast, but Irrial showed substantially more restraint than he would have in her position. She frowned but otherwise made no move at all.

"Perhaps," she said instead, "I can convince the assembly to put aside some of their differences, at least temporarily. I've come from Rahariem, I've seen how thoroughly Cephira's digging in. A firsthand account might sway some votes."

"It might," Mavere said, though she clearly didn't believe it. "But I fear that there are other issues not so easily dealt with."

"Rebaine." It was not a question.

"Rebaine, yes." Then, again with apparent sincerity, "I'm sorry about your cousin, my lady. We might have had very different ideas on how to govern Imphallion, but he was a good man. His loss diminishes us all."

She allowed a moment of respectful silence before continuing, "We've no idea what Rebaine's up to, but with that . . . that *creature* running around and slaughtering nobles and Guildmembers alike, we're finding it very difficult to convince *anyone* to give over command of their vassals. They fear being left without protection. Some of them"—she leaned forward—"those who know the truth, fear having their own soldiers turned against them."

"The truth?" Irrial asked, confused. Corvis felt his stomach drop to his toes.

"It took us some time to figure it out," Mavere said, "but when he was here last, Rebaine cast some sort of enchantment on many of us."

Lower than his toes, now; he was pretty sure he could actually feel his guts squishing around inside his boots.

"You don't say," Irrial said darkly.

"It was remarkably subtle. Very unlike him."

'Got you pegged, doesn't she?'

"Even after many of the nobles and Guildmasters began acting strangely—sometimes so much so that we had to replace them—we didn't understand." Her voice quivered, just once, with what might, or might not, have been fury. "But I'm a priestess as well as a smith, my lady, and I've studied more in my life than many scholars. I may not know magic, but I know much *of* magic. I finally recognized the effects for what they were, though only on a few of my colleagues. To this day, I've no idea how many more might be compromised."

Not enough, Corvis thought bitterly.

"I told my most trusted fellow Guildmasters, of course, and I've reason to suspect that some nobles know as well. We've told few others, for fear of causing a panic. But in any case, it's made his reappearance even that much more disruptive."

So why is she willing to tell us? Corvis couldn't help but worry.

"I see," Irrial said. "What if I told you," she continued slowly, "that Corvis Rebaine was *not* behind the recent murders. Do you think that, combined with my accounts of Rahariem, might convince the assembly to act?"

It was all Corvis could do to keep his chair. *What is she doing?*

'How quickly can you kill them both?'

Mavere leaned back, raising an eyebrow. "You'd have to offer some fairly convincing proof. What in the gods' names makes you think this?"

"I've reason to know that Rebaine was, in fact, present in the occupied territories during some of the murders," she answered evasively.

"Do you, now? Even if that's true, my lady, Rebaine has all sorts of mystical capabilities. For all we know, he could have transported himself across Imphallion with a snap of his fingers."

Irrial fidgeted, almost cast a glance at Corvis and caught herself, clearly trying to decide how much more to reveal.

Too late, Corvis seethed.

But Mavere seemed disinclined to allow her to continue. "No, my lady, I think that even if you know Rebaine was in the east—and I'm going to want an explanation as to *how* you know that—it wouldn't convince anyone of anything. Some might even think it evidence that he's in league with Cephira."

"At least let me address the assembly, Mavere. Then I can—"

"No, Baroness, I think not. You've been remarkably unwilling to share the specific details of your so-called escape."

"*So-called*—" she protested, but the Guildmistress kept going.

"You, and you alone, have fled Cephiran-held territory—and you're sitting in my office with a servant cloaked in illusion. I told you," she added as Irrial and Corvis glanced in shock at each other, "that I know much of magic. I cannot penetrate the illusion, but I can sense it—and I know that such spells cannot be maintained indefinitely.

"No, Irrial, I worry that you've been turned, that Cephira *allowed* you to escape, to muddy the waters here even further. And there's no way in hell I'm letting you anywhere near the assembly."

Irrial rose, leaning heavily on her cane. "That's the most asinine thing I've ever—"

"If I'm wrong," Mavere told her, pulling a lever on the underside of her desk, "you'll have every opportunity to convince me, I promise. But I cannot risk it."

The door opened with a resounding crash, revealing all six guards, crossbows leveled.

"You will both be escorted to secure quarters—pleasant ones, as befits your status, my lady—until you're willing to tell me *everything* about what occurred, and to provide corroborating evidence. And until *you*," she added, pointing at Corvis, "are willing to reveal your true face. A Cephiran face, I expect. Guards?"

Corvis and Irrial allowed themselves to be escorted from the chamber. With half a dozen bolts chomping at the bit to punch through flesh and bone, there was precious little else they could do.

Chapter Eleven

KALEB STOOD stripped to the waist and so glistening with sweat that he shone like his opponent's blade. As he twisted on one knee, hands rising in swift parry, his skin rippled with an array of muscles startling on so slender a frame; he could have been one of Jassion's classic marble statues made flesh. The heavy branch he wielded thrummed with the impact of his own falchion, now clasped in someone else's hands.

"No," he insisted, friendly but firm. "You're not putting enough muscle into it."

The young woman, whose only concession to the baking sun had been to leave her cloak folded atop a saddlebag, just stared at him as though she hadn't heard a word.

"Mellorin? Are you listening, or just ogling?"

"I—!" It wasn't much of a protest; more a squeak, really. Her face reddened with far more than the summer heat.

"I thought," she said after a moment to compose herself, "that the idea was to keep control. Wild swings leave you open."

"They do," Kaleb acknowledged. "But you're taking it too far. A sword's more than just a big knife. You can't treat them the same way."

"I should know this already!" she spat with sudden venom. "*He* should have been there to teach me!"

"But if you already knew," Kaleb said, his voice soothing, "this wouldn't be nearly as much fun."

She couldn't help but smile. "This is harder than I expected," she admitted as he approached, trying without much success to keep her gaze above shoulder level.

"You're doing fine, Mellorin. A falchion's a clumsy sort of blade to be learning with, but until Baron Creepy Uncle gets back, it's all we've got."

"Is he always like this?" she asked, ruminating over the past few days together on the road.

"You mean rude, brooding, utterly humorless, and short-tempered as a badger with piles?"

"I'll take that as a yes, then."

"He's a challenge," the sorcerer agreed. "And honestly, not the most entertaining traveling companion. I've held more stimulating conversations with spoons."

Mellorin giggled.

"Good man in a fight, though. And smarter than he looks, on those rare occasions he bothers to think."

It was, in fact, an idea of Jassion's that brought them here today. The five of them—Mellorin, Kaleb, and three horses—whiled away the hours in a camp half a mile from Orthessis, while the baron wandered through town on his own. Corvis, he'd recalled, had made use of a great many mercenary companies during his war against Audriss the Serpent. While rumor suggested that they'd not parted on the best of terms, Jassion reasoned that some of those mercenaries might possess knowledge that could prove useful in their search. Thus, upon leaving Abtheum, they'd made a beeline for its sister city, where Jassion's political and military contacts might point them in the right direction.

Kaleb felt it was something of a long shot—but then, for the time being, long shots were all they had. Besides, it allowed him the opportunity to spend some time in far more charming company.

"Let's work a bit on your stance," he said, sidling around beside the warlord's daughter. He reached out, resting an arm on hers, taking her hand in his. "You need—oh!" He retreated a pace at the shiver in her skin. "I'm sorry. You don't like to be touched."

"No . . . it's all right," she told him. "You just—startled me."

Kaleb, moving as slowly as if he approached wild game, took her wrist once more. Behind her head he smiled, pretending not to notice that she wouldn't meet his gaze.

JASSION SWEPT INTO CAMP some hours later, a raging tempest wrapped in mail. Clearly having kept himself pent up all the way from Orthessis, he now flew wholly out of control. Talon's wave-edged blade sheared through branches—and even whole saplings—sending leaves spinning and splinters flying, and the curses he howled at the uncaring sky were sharper still. Mellorin stepped back, astonished, while Kaleb could only—as was so often his response to the hot-blooded baron— roll his eyes.

Or so it was until Jassion, clearly overcome and devoid of rational thought, turned toward the first of the nervous and fidgeting horses, Kholben Shiar held high. Kaleb thrust out a hand, and just as within Castle Braetlyn, Jassion found himself graced, albeit briefly, with the miracle of flight.

He ripped through a cluster of boughs that seemed to scrape deliberately at his exposed skin, perhaps in retribution for their slaughtered brethren, and finally slammed to a halt against a broad trunk. There he hung, spitting profanity and saliva in equal measure.

"Have you ever considered meditation?" Kaleb asked lightly, once the tirade had finally run its course. "Or perhaps shackling yourself to something heavy?"

"You seem to do that just fine," Jassion groused, thumping an elbow into the tree. "Please let me down, Kaleb."

The sorcerer blinked, so startled he allowed Jassion to fall halfway to earth before recovering his concentration and lowering him gently the rest of the way.

Did Jassion really say "Please"?

The instant his feet touched soil, Jassion bowed toward his niece. "I seem," he said softly, "to be making a habit of embarrassing myself in front of my family. I'm sorry, Mellorin."

"That's—that's all right," she offered.

"I'm going to assume," Kaleb said, "that something untoward happened in Orthessis?"

"More word of Rebaine," Jassion spat. "He attacked Braetlyn! He butchered the castle staff, and I wasn't even there!" His hands trembled so violently that Talon shook in his grasp, but he maintained a fingernail-grip on his temper. "There was no *need*, Kaleb. No reason! So many of my people . . . My friends . . ."

"I'm sorry, Jassion," Kaleb said with apparent sincerity. Mellorin darted forward long enough to give her startled uncle a stiff, awkward hug before withdrawing once more. Her face was blank—not *lacking* emotion, but rather processing so many at once that it couldn't settle on any single expression.

"I'm afraid I forgot to purchase you a sword," Jassion told her. "But we've got to pass back through Orthessis on our way, so we can pick one out for you then."

"Our way?" asked Kaleb. "So you *did* learn something? Useful, I mean."

Jassion seemed to consider taking offense at that, but shrugged it off instead. "Yes. Some of my friends in the ducal militia were very helpful. It seems a great many mercenary companies are camped out— either near the Cephiran lines, or near Imphallion's major cities—just waiting for the Guilds to come down with a sudden case of balls-and-brains, and start moving against Cephira. And it seems that a few baronies have already decided to move, Guilds be damned, and are preparing to mobilize. At either point, there'll be a lot of demand for warriors, and the companies want to be ready."

"And?" the sorcerer prodded.

"And it happens that a certain captain by the name of Losalis is camped just east of Pelapheron. If we push the horses, it shouldn't take us too long to get there."

"Aren't you glad, then?" Mellorin asked as they moved to saddle up their mounts.

"Glad of what?"

"That Kaleb stopped your tantrum before you filleted your horse like he was that silly fish on your tabard."

Kaleb could only snicker at Jassion's expression, one that spoke as clearly as words, and far more loudly. *Mellorin*, it seemed to growl, *could stand to take just a little less after her father.*

ON SHE RAN, AND ON, though so very many miles still lay ahead. Twigs and stones gouged raw, bloodied feet. Summer air burned in heaving lungs. She couldn't remember the last time she'd been so exhausted, so agonizingly *weak*, so desperate to lie down and sleep.

And still she ran, through a haze of confusion and fatigue—and yes, she'd admit in her more honest moments of self-reflection, of fear. Only rarely did she stop, to gulp a few mouthfuls of water from stream or puddle, to chase down a morsel of prey, or to reorient herself, pausing to feel the tug of someone else's magic that she'd made her own. Once, not so long ago, it would have been a matter of moments, simplicity itself, to sense that spell-wrought trail. But now? Now her head pounded, the blood roared in her ears, and she almost sobbed with frustration at the effort.

But again she groped about until she felt it, and again she ran. She *had* to find him, to reach him.

Corvis had to know, before it was too late. Before what time remained to her was gone.

Before she died—again.

PERHAPS BY MERE CHANCE, perhaps by the will of an irritated god, the summer rains had managed to miss Pelapheron entirely. The city's surrounding fields were sparse and wilting; dry grasses crunched loudly underfoot. So far, the situation hadn't deteriorated to the point of drought or famine, but supplies were growing scarce—and expensive. It was, frankly, not a particularly wise location for an army, no matter how small, to make camp.

Which was, paradoxically—one might even say perversely—why Losalis had picked it. Yes, rations and equipment for his men would prove costly, but they would also be the only mercenary company here, and that meant they could name their own price once the local high-and-mighty shook off their pall of stupidity and recognized the need to act.

Or that, at least, was the explanation Jassion's contacts had provided him, and that he in turn had offered Kaleb and Mellorin, when they wondered aloud what the hell could have inspired the mercenary captain to roost in such wretched terrain. And from what Jassion knew of Losalis himself, he could believe it: The man who had once been Corvis Rebaine's lieutenant was a big believer in standing out from the pack.

Unfortunately, as the trio of travelers had just learned, Losalis only wanted certain *kinds* of attention.

"I told you," Jassion growled, struggling to keep his voice in check, "this is important."

"And I tol' you," said one of several gruff, dirty, but very heavily armed men who blocked the meandering deer trail on which they'd been riding, "the captain don't want to see nobody 'cept potential employers."

"How do you know we're not?" Mellorin asked from atop her palfrey, less in challenge than honest curiosity.

"'Cuz anyone makin' a serious offer'd know enough to bring a whole heap o' coin as down payment. And you three ain't got the bags to carry it. 'Nless"—he leered up at her—"they're thinkin' o' offerin' you. You're a bit skinny, but—"

Kaleb opened his mouth and advanced, but Mellorin was faster. She dropped gracefully from her horse, hand flying to the hilt of her new blade.

The mercenary looked down at the gleaming metal, the stiff and unmarred leather of the scabbard, and snorted. "Ain't that cute? Baby's first sword. You named it yet, sweetheart?"

"I have." Her face was pale, but her voice and her hand remained steady. "Eunuch-Maker."

The mercenary's grin slid from his face as Kaleb, Jassion, and even a few of the man's comrades chuckled.

"Now, see here . . . ," he began, hand reaching for her wrist before she could draw. And just as swiftly he froze, for while the sword hadn't budged an inch, the knife concealed in Mellorin's *left* hand poked abruptly against his groin.

"Look, friends," Kaleb interjected, *hopefully* before things got any worse. "There's no need for unpleasantness, is there? No, we're not looking to hire your company—but we *do* need to speak with Captain Losalis, and there might be *some* degree of payment involved if he can help us out."

"Not interested," the mercenary grunted, his attention glued to the ugly blade.

"Really? Losalis must put a *lot* of faith in you, my friend. Letting you make decisions like that, considering how much gold and how many contracts it could cost him? *And* the rest of your men? Well, so be it. I'm sure that when he hears about this, he'll be grateful you kept his best interests at heart."

It took the bulky fellow a few moments to work through that, but he eventually arrived at the point the sorcerer was trying to make. His lips curled in a sneer, but he nodded. "All right. Tell the girl to put her knife away, an' I'll take you to him."

Mellorin's blade vanished as abruptly as it had appeared.

"You see that?" Kaleb asked as he and his companions gathered up the reins and followed the grumbling fellow. "I knew he'd see reason eventually. I'm sure it just took him a while to recognize it, since I doubt it's very familiar to him."

"Could you possibly refrain from insulting the heavily armed men aloud while we're in the midst of their camp?" Jassion asked as the mercenary glared back over his shoulder.

Kaleb cocked his head, apparently considering it. Then, "Probably not."

Following their reluctant guide, they picked their way through clusters of tents, fire pits, and other components of an encampment only halfway organized. Losalis was known for maintaining an unusual level of discipline, but these were still mercenaries, and there were still limits.

They halted before a tent that, though larger than average, otherwise had little to distinguish it. A small throng of warriors had pressed close, curious to see what their visitors had to offer—and how their captain might react if said offer proved insufficient—while their guide stuck his head through the canvas flap.

Moments passed, mercenaries whispered and jested, the summer breeze died to nothing as even the winds decided the weather was just too damn hot for all this running around. Jassion tapped a foot and drummed his fingers on his thigh, Mellorin looked about in rapt fascination, and Kaleb just waited.

Finally, the canvas flipped open and the mercenary returned, followed by two more men. One was huge, the other even bigger.

Losalis was a dark-skinned giant, a foot taller than Jassion's own six feet and muscled enough to crack small rocks like chestnuts. The eyes peering over a thick growth of beard were of two different hues, and he wore a triangular, razor-edged shield bolted to his armor in place of his missing left hand.

His lieutenant—a moment's quick reminiscence provided Jassion with the name *Ulfgai*—was only slightly smaller, but otherwise his captain's polar opposite. The barbarian from the frozen south was pale practically to albinism, and his long blond locks and beard were wildly tangled.

They'd killed enough people in their careers, between the two of them, to qualify as a plague in their own right, and neither looked particularly thrilled at being yanked away from whatever discussion they'd been having. Jassion and Mellorin both suppressed the urge to recoil, or grab for their blades.

"All right, my lord," Losalis said in a surprisingly soft voice, nodding first to Jassion, then Mellorin. "Reng here tells me that you need to speak with me, and that you seem to have difficulty with the word *no*. You don't want to hire my company—you don't have enough gold with you, and besides, you're obviously not here on behalf of Pelapheron. So would you care to explain why you're wasting my time—while I'm in a good mood?"

Kaleb's mouth began to open, but Mellorin swiftly stepped on his foot.

"It's a simple enough arrangement, Captain," Jassion told him.

"I want some information and advice from you, and I'm willing to offer coin in return."

"Do we look like sages to you?" Ulfgai grunted from behind Losalis.

The sorcerer threw Mellorin a glance, all but begging for permission to comment. She shook her head, struggling to stifle a grin and failing miserably.

Jassion, perhaps inspired by the presence of so many unfriendly mercenaries, kept a lid on his temper. "Not a lot of people might know what I need to know."

"Go on," Losalis said, raising a finger to silence his lieutenant.

"We're hunting," the baron told him, "for Corvis Rebaine."

Every nearby face darkened with anger.

"I know," he continued, "that you've little cause to bear him any affection. Rumor has it that he abandoned the lot of you after the Battle of Mecepheum. Help us find him, and we'll *all* enjoy some measure of justice."

"What makes you think, after six years, that I know anything useful about that traitorous rodent?" Losalis asked them.

"You were his lieutenant," Jassion pressed. "You led his armies while he was imprisoned."

"By you, as I remember it. Which means *you* let him escape."

Again, the baron kept his calm, and again it required more of an effort than anyone would ever know. "My point, Captain Losalis, is that even if you don't know where he is, you can help us. Knowledge of his habits, how he thinks, anything he might have revealed to you about his plans and objectives beyond defeating Audriss. *Anything* would prove helpful, and you'll be paid for all of it."

Losalis stood for long moments, ignoring the impatient shuffling of not only his "guests" but his own mercenaries as well. Until, finally, "No."

Jassion—and, to judge by his expression, Ulfgai as well—couldn't have been more thunderstruck if Losalis had dropped his trousers and given birth to a unicorn.

"*No?*" The baron's voice almost squeaked.

"Captain," Ulfgai protested, "maybe we should hear what he's—"

"No," Losalis said again. "Gods know I'd like to see you succeed in your hunt, but even if I knew anything useful—which I don't believe I do—I wouldn't tell you."

"But—"

"It's taken me a long time to get where I am, my lord. Me, my company, we've got a reputation as the best, and we get *paid* the best. And part of how I keep my reputation as a man worth hiring is that I don't blab the secrets of my employers, even after I'm done working for them. I'll fight a man I've worked for in the past, but I won't *betray* him."

Ulfgai looked as though he'd swallowed something venomous, with many wriggling legs, but he nodded in agreement with his captain.

"I've heard it said," Kaleb interjected, "that Rebaine *didn't* actually hire you, though. That he reneged on payment when he abandoned you."

The southern barbarian snarled something ugly, but Losalis's own expression never wavered. "Rumors only. I can't stake my reputation on people believing a rumor's true, can I? There would always be *some* folk certain that I'd violated my code. No, my lord, I'm sorry to disappoint, but it's time for you and your friends to be off."

And Jassion, fists clenched and jaw quivering, began to turn away.

No. Kaleb scowled internally, though his face remained impassive. *No, this won't do.*

Largely unnoticed, save for his single interjection, the sorcerer hung back by the horses, watching the proceedings. So Losalis wouldn't or couldn't help them; the sorcerer found no surprise there. But now the mercenary posed something of a problem.

Losalis knew, now, that Jassion was seeking out Rebaine's old minions. He knew, too, that Mellorin was accompanying them—by face, if not by name. So far he'd not noted the family resemblance, but if he gave it any real thought, or if someone were to ask . . .

And since Jassion *wasn't* an employer, there was nothing to stop Losalis from revealing all this to anyone who made him an enticing offer.

No, this simply wouldn't do at all. Something would have to be done.

And that, Kaleb abruptly decided with a hidden smile, was a *good* thing. It meant Losalis could yet prove useful after all.

Two quick spells, in rapid succession. He saw Mellorin shiver as the first washed over her, and then he tensed, ready to act as his carefully crafted illusion began to form . . .

JASSION SPUN, Talon leaping free of its scabbard, as one of the mercenaries burst from the throng, his own blade raised to attack. The Kholben Shiar swung, hewing armor and flesh with equal ease. Jassion, who had expected far greater resistance, stumbled as his momentum carried him full circle, but if he thought about it at all, he attributed the ease with which he'd cleaved a man nearly in twain to the power of his demon-forged weapon.

For less than a heartbeat he paused in a half crouch. Losalis was actually recoiling, a look of stunned horror on his face, mirrored on Ulfgai's own.

Clearly, they'd anticipated a different result from their cowardly attack. Jassion leapt, Talon held high, and allowed his ever-burning fury to flare bright. Before him, before the Kholben Shiar, men and women fell. Their blades were as twigs, their shields as parchment. Blood flew, bones shattered, and the Baron of Braetlyn rejoiced.

MELLORIN STAGGERED BACK from the unprovoked assault, footing unsteady as she fought to remain standing against a pressing tide of terror. *Gods, what was I thinking?* She wasn't ready for this, not nearly! A few street fights, squabbles picked as much for the practice as anything else, that was one thing, but *this* . . .

Despite her terror, or maybe because of it, she moved faster than ever before. Kaleb's falchion protruded from one fist, her ugly dagger from the other, and she couldn't remember drawing either. She watched

Jassion plow into the assembled warriors like a whirlwind of razors, saw the mercenaries lunging to protect their captain, to punish these interlopers who dared raise steel against them. And though everything in her head screamed at her to run, Mellorin moved to meet them.

No, wait. Not *everything*. In the back of her mind, behind her thoughts and memories and dreams, a voice spoke to her. She heard it in her soul, calm, steady, and she trusted it without hesitation.

And when it warned her, she listened.

Whether it was real or imagination, Mellorin never knew. What she *did* know was that, though a fast learner, she'd not had anywhere near sufficient training to stand toe-to-toe with even one of Losalis's men, let alone the many who were closing—and yet, she did just that. Guided by that voice, she wielded falchion and dagger in twisting parries, deflecting swords that should have split her skull. She stepped and whirled as though in the midst of a formal ball, and blows rained harmlessly in her wake. She struck, falchion opening holes in her enemies' guard so her dagger could open holes in their flesh.

Blood washed over her hands, and Mellorin felt sick. She gritted her teeth, swallowed hard against the bile that threatened to choke her, and continued to dodge, and to parry, and to kill.

KALEB LIFTED BOTH HANDS above his head, but this was clearly no surrender. Flames blossomed from his palms, not in a sweeping wave as in the depths of Theaghl-gohlatch, but pouring in torrents to the earth. They swirled away to either side, sweeping across the soil and igniting sunbaked grass. A wall of roaring fire sketched a rough circle around the center of the camp, preventing the bulk of the company from entering the melee. One or two attempted to leap through the crackling barrier, assuming they could pass with only a painful singeing—and were reduced to blackened bones by the heat and hunger of the unnatural conflagration. Roasting flesh, burning grasses, and a faint whiff of brimstone combined in a choking miasma that rose more slowly and more stately than the screams of the dying.

Satisfied that the barrier would hold so long as he maintained his concentration, Kaleb glanced about him. Jassion was cutting a swath through the soldiers, reaping them like wheat, though a few rents in his hauberk and trails of blood leaking down his sides served as ample evidence that this particular crop had blades of their own. Mellorin largely held her own, though the sheer press of enemies was forcing her slowly back, step by step. The sorcerer was impressed, despite himself. He'd known the girl had the potential to be good, had cast his spell so she might survive long enough to reach that potential—but the ease with which she'd acclimated to his magics suggested a budding *greatness*.

It was something else about her worth cultivating, definitely. Time to see how that cultivation was progressing.

This next bit—Kaleb braced himself—*could hurt if I'm wrong.*

The torrent of fire still cascading from his hands, feeding the blazing wall, Kaleb took a step nearer Mellorin and aimed a blast of flame over her head. The mercenaries fell back, shrieking as hair and beards ignited, and the young woman smiled her thanks.

A smile that fell from her face as though it, too, had melted. For when Kaleb hurled fire her way, a gap had opened briefly in the fiery bastion. The footsteps of a mercenary pounded across the earth behind him, but he pretended not to hear. He saw Mellorin tense, begin to move his way, and only then did he look behind . . .

THE LAST OF THE INTERVENING WARRIORS slumped at Jassion's feet, and the baron stood face-to-face with Captain Losalis. The one gripped Talon rock-steady in both hands; the other had produced a crescent-shaped saber and raised the knife-edged shield before him.

"My lord," Losalis began, "stop! I swear I didn't—"

But Jassion was already lunging, and though he *heard* the words, the pounding in his ears and the fire in his mind had long since rendered him incapable of *listening*.

With nigh supernatural grace, Losalis ducked beneath the first slash and swung the saber in a brutal cross-cut. Jassion's chain took the blow without parting, and the blade left only a light scoring on the steel, but the impact doubled the baron over, ribs aching, struggling for breath. Losalis raised his shield-hand high and brought it brutally down, an axe as deadly as any executioner's, but Jassion allowed himself to tumble left, turning his pained collapse into an awkward roll. He staggered upright and parried another slash as Losalis pressed his attack, refusing Jassion the moment he needed to recover.

Losalis was better than he; of that, even in the midst of his murderous fury, Jassion had no doubt. But he held Talon, and that would have to make the difference.

Again he parried, and again—first saber, then shield. Only the unnatural speed of the Kholben Shiar allowed him to bring the massive blade in line, and even so he found himself retreating. Gradually, he allowed his parries to rise ever higher, leaving himself open for another slash. Mentally he braced, girding himself against the pain to come.

Maybe Losalis recognized the trap for what it was, or perhaps he simply knew that his saber couldn't penetrate his foe's armor. Rather than delivering another bruising blow to Jassion's ribs, as the baron had hoped, the mercenary swung at his legs.

Desperate, Jassion dropped to his knees lest he find himself crippled. The blade indeed rang against chain and Jassion brought his right elbow down, briefly pinning the saber to his side. That was as he planned; being on his knees rather than his feet, as Losalis raised the shield overhead once more, was not.

Swiftly as he could given the awkward posture, Jassion swung the Kholben Shiar upward even as Losalis brought his brutal shield down. And indeed, Talon's infernal magics made all the difference. With the hideous squeal of rending metal, the shield—and a small portion of the flesh to which it was strapped—pinwheeled away to land in the dust.

Losalis screamed in agony. Jassion fell sideways and rolled across the earth, taking the mercenary's saber with him. He kicked at the ground, spinning on his back, whipping Talon around him.

Leather, flesh, and bone parted before the Kholben Shiar and Losalis, now silent as his body convulsed in shock, tumbled to his back, both feet severed at the ankles.

The baron staggered up once more, ignoring the pounding agony in his chest, raised Talon one last time—and Losalis, former lieutenant of the Terror of the East, suffered no more.

———————————

"KALEB!" MELLORIN SHRIEKED, SPRINGING toward him even as she recognized that she couldn't possibly reach him in time.

The sorcerer was fast, spinning to meet the man who had burst through his faltering flame. He *almost* dodged, so that what would have been a murderous thrust through his chest instead sliced along one arm, spraying drops of blood to boil away in the roaring fire. Again he shifted the angle of his magics, and the warrior who'd dared attack him fell to earth in a burning heap of human wreckage.

But that distraction allowed Ulfgai to close. He'd crept around the edges of the battle, drawing ever nearer the man who was holding their reinforcements at bay. Tears clouded the vicious barbarian's eyes as Losalis fell, and his entire body twitched in apparent desire to hurl himself at Jassion, but no. Clearly he knew that, with the sorcerer down, he and his men could overwhelm the enemy, and *then* he would have his vengeance.

The southerner raised a wedge-shaped axe, prepared to dash Kaleb's brains across the earth . . .

And shuddered with the impact of Mellorin's falchion. Fur-lined leathers absorbed most of the blow, and Ulfgai was already turning to swat aside this nuisance when she drove the point of her dagger into his gut.

Ulfgai coughed, staining his beard with blood, and Mellorin forced herself to twist the knife in the wound. The fingers clasping that axe trembled but did not drop the weapon.

Whether he would have had the strength left to kill her, Mellorin never knew. Kaleb appeared behind the mercenary, and his hands were now empty of fire. They closed, instead, upon Ulfgai's shoulder, and shoved the weakened southerner back into the flames.

"I can open us a path," he said tiredly to his companions. "And with the grasses burning, it should be a few moments before the rest of them realize that they're just facing normal flames, now, not magic. We'd best be gone by then."

Mellorin helped her uncle, who couldn't seem to stand upright, to mount his horse, and then the wounded sorcerer to do the same. She wondered, briefly, why the beasts hadn't panicked, whether this was more of Kaleb's magic or simply that the ring of fire permitted them nowhere to run.

Kaleb unleashed one last burst of flame through the grassfire, hoping to scatter—if not to slay—any mercenaries on the other side. Then, suppressing the flame as easily as he'd summoned it, he carved them a path to freedom. The pounding of hooves was lost in the roar of the fire, and the frustrated screams of the warriors beyond.

THEY MADE A COLD CAMP, far from the roadside. Hours of hard and painful riding had probably averted pursuit, but they weren't about to take that for granted.

Jassion, his ribs wrapped tight, muttered and grumbled as he struggled to find a position in which he might sleep. Kaleb, arm neatly bandaged, crossed the camp to kneel before the young woman, who was sitting on a stump and gazing off into the distance.

"Mellorin?" he asked gently.

"I didn't . . . Kaleb, I've never . . ."

Carefully—giving her every opportunity to pull away, to ask him to stop—the sorcerer took her hand. "I know," he told her. "You know what else you did?"

She stared blankly.

"You saved my life." He turned her hand over, brushed a light kiss across her knuckles. "Thank you, Mellorin." Then, hesitantly, he leaned in and placed another soft kiss on her cheek. He smiled at her as he rose, pretending not to notice the sudden flutter of her pulse in her neck, and returned to his own blankets.

Yes, he decided with a grin that absolutely did not mean what Mellorin doubtless thought it did. *That worked out just fine.*

Chapter Twelve

THE CORRIDORS OF THE HALL of Meeting felt a lot more claustrophobic than they had mere minutes prior. Irrial could have sworn the walls were actually closing in, the doors transforming into prison bars. Not even the carpet muffled the tread of the soldiers who pressed in from all sides, reverberating in unison, the inexorable march of time itself.

She knew the plan—such as it was—for they'd both acknowledged the possibility of capture, but damn it all, if Corvis didn't act soon, she wasn't going to wait for him!

Two guards strode before her, broad shoulders and hauberks blocking her view of the hallway, while the other four marched behind. Irrial didn't need to look, for she could feel their looming presence, and the skin between her shoulder blades twinged nervously at the thought of those brutal crossbows.

Corvis walked beside her in a peculiar slouch, shoulders slumped and head hanging. He lurked at the corners of her vision, where detail blurred like moist watercolor, and she thought she saw his lips moving.

Almost time, then.

Her hand grew clammy, her breathing tight. "When it starts," he'd told her, "all I need is for you to keep them off me." A simple enough proposition, in theory. But what if—?

Corvis waited until they drew even with a branching passageway, the intersection providing a bit more room to maneuver than the narrow halls, and then he collapsed. With a pained, sepulchral groan, he struck the floor, limp as a boned trout. He landed facing away from Irrial and guards alike, and the noblewoman could only trust that he was maintaining his near-silent concentration.

Not being utter imbeciles, the soldiers reacted swiftly, calmly. The two in front knelt beside the fallen prisoner, one checking for pulse or fever, the other keeping tight grip on the hilt of his sword in case this should prove some feeble ruse. The remaining four clustered around Irrial, blocking any possible escape with their bodies while keeping their arbalests trained on Corvis.

The thought that the freckle-faced baroness might prove the greater threat had clearly never crossed their minds.

Irrial took her cane in both hands and yanked. For an instant, the walking stick seemed to come smoothly apart, before the illusion that Corvis had wrapped around it—subtle, static, far harder to detect than that which cloaked his own features—unraveled. In her left hand, Irrial clutched two thin strips of wood, wrapped in a leather thong to form a makeshift scabbard; in her right, a narrow, long-bladed sword, the weapon of a duelist rather than a soldier.

A sword whose blade was etched from tip to hilt with spidery runes and wavering figures. Even surrounded by enemies on all sides, it was all she could do to keep her focus off the whispers and urges that crawled through her mind, weevils hatched from the demonic spirit of the *thing* in her hand.

The baroness struck in both directions at once. The crude scabbard slammed one guard across the bridge of his nose, cracking wood and cartilage alike, while Sunder cleaved through a second mercenary's crossbow, rendering it so much junk. Dropping the shattered wood, she drove her knee into the groin of the man whose weapon she'd just obliterated. He doubled over in an awkward bow and Irrial thrust Sunder over his head, stabbing into the shoulder of yet a third guard. She prayed it would be enough to keep him out of the fight . . .

The last of the four drew his own blade and thrust brutally at her chest. Irrial leapt aside, sweeping Sunder in a desperate parry, awkward but impossibly swift. She heard the creak of leather and mail as the pair behind her rose from Corvis's side, but could not spare a moment to glance their way. She could only keep moving and hope that they'd recognize the distinct possibility of skewering their fellow guards before pulling the triggers on those crossbows.

Apparently they did, for no bolts flew. Instead she sensed a presence looming behind, twisted, then stabbed Sunder down into the thigh of the approaching man. He screamed, clutching at the gaping wound.

But the second soldier hurled himself bodily at Irrial's legs, knocking them out from under her. She fell hard, and only the thick carpeting saved her from a cracked skull. A broad-shouldered man, nose battered and bleeding, knelt painfully on Irrial's left arm, while the fellow she'd kneed stomped brutally on her other wrist. Despite herself she cried out, and felt Sunder slide from her spasming fingers.

"Cerris!" she cried out, trying desperately to peer past the shapes gathered around and atop her. No help there, she noted gravely; he lay on the carpet where he'd fallen. The guard who'd nearly gutted her now stood over him, sword held to his throat. Footsteps sounded in the hall, and another dozen guards appeared from around the corners and through various doors, drawn by the commotion.

Well, Irrial thought bitterly, *that could have gone better.* They were in worse trouble now than they'd been, without the slightest indication that Corvis's plan had even—

More footsteps, again from both sides. Guards and prisoners alike strained their necks first this way then that, desperate to see.

What they saw were Guildmasters and barons, knights and earls— perhaps eight or nine in total. Some wielded swords, some daggers, some chair legs or other makeshift clubs, but *all* wore that subtle, preoccupied look Irrial had seen upon so many faces earlier that day. And in the lead, bludgeon held high, was Mubarris, master of the Cartwrights' and Carpenters' Guild.

They were a rockslide of living, panting, *foolish-looking* flesh, ready to dash themselves to bloody bits against the bulwark of the assembled mercenaries. Stronger, more numerous, better equipped, and *far* better trained, the soldiers could have slaughtered the lot without breaking a sweat.

But these were their employers, men and women they'd been hired to *protect*. Confusion stayed the warriors' hands for a precious instant before self-preservation usurped control, and in that time the blades and bludgeons landed. Blood seeped into the formerly expensive carpeting, and the first soldier fell without having raised a finger.

The shock of the unprovoked assault faded, and the remaining mercenaries responded as mercenaries do. Crossbows thrummed, blades swung, and bodies toppled.

Irrial felt the pressure on her arms ease up as the guards holding her rose to deal with this new threat. She surged to her feet, reaching for Sunder.

Corvis, who had rolled from beneath his captor in his own moment of distraction, got there first.

The blade shifted like living clay from dueling sword to brutal axe, and the aging warlord began to kill. Irrial flinched from the butchery, the deaths of men and women who had committed no evil, but were simply doing the job for which they'd been hired. But when Corvis stopped for an instant at her side, extending, hilt-first, the sword he'd yanked from a mercenary's hand even as he'd ripped Sunder from the fellow's chest, she sighed and accepted the blade. And when Corvis waded into the thick of the melee, chopping down soldiers like saplings, she was at his back, stabbing and lunging. She would survive, she would escape, no matter what it took.

For Rahariem's sake, perhaps for all Imphallion's.

She had no choice.

———————◗ ◖———————

THEY RACED ALONG THE HIGHWAY, kicking up a cloud of dust as thick as a desert sandstorm. For more than an hour they'd galloped, Corvis desperately casting a handful of spells to keep the horses fresh.

Alas, he had no similar spells to protect his aching rump from the punishment of their grueling pace.

They left behind a capitol in chaos. Over two dozen guards, and perhaps four or five aristocrats and Guildmasters, lay butchered throughout the Hall of Meeting. Nobody seemed sure precisely how it had happened, for Corvis's surviving "minions" had once more been mystically coerced never to speak of what had occurred, and none of the soldiers who'd been present had survived. The former warlord had every reason to hope it would be some time before anyone in authority even knew for certain that they had escaped—and even longer until they could mount any sort of pursuit.

None of which was even remotely enough to convince him to slow down, no matter that his entire body throbbed like one big saddle sore.

Eventually, however, they reached the limits of Corvis's modest magics. The horses began to tire, their sides lathered, and though he'd have liked to cover a few additional miles, Corvis reluctantly reined in his mount and guided the laboring beast off the road. For only a few moments more they continued, until they found themselves on the cracked banks of what, during cooler months, would have been a stream. A few puddles of muddy water remained, and the horses gratefully submerged their noses as though planning to dive in and float away.

Irrial wilted from the saddle with an extended groan.

"You're starting to remind me of bagpipes," Corvis joked weakly as he, too, flopped to the dirt. He knew she must be exhausted when she couldn't even muster a glare.

"I'm sorry," he wheezed at her, taking a huge gulp from his waterskin. "But it's not just foot pursuit I'm worried about. I don't know what sorts of sorcerers the Guilds might have access to these days. Our best defense really is distance at this point. And—"

"I didn't ask," she told him flatly. And that, throughout the sweltering summer night and into the next morning, was the end of the conversation.

"So why don't you do that more often?" she asked while they saddled the horses, after a cold breakfast of salted venison and dried fruits.

"Do . . . ?"

"That spell." She hauled herself into the saddle, wincing at the pains in her back and thighs that hadn't faded overnight. "The one you cast on the horses. Don't misunderstand, I've no interest in enduring that on a regular basis, but it would save us a *lot* of time."

"Dangerous," he told her, standing beside his own roan, one hand resting idly in the stirrup. "It's far too easy to kill the horses—either by pushing them too hard, or just from the strain of the spell itself. If we hadn't been so damn desperate yesterday, I'd never have risked it." Still he stood, idly tapping a finger on the leather, and made no move to mount.

"Problem?" she asked.

"Maybe . . ." He frowned.

"Don't tell me: You have no idea what to do next?"

"Oh, I have some thoughts. It's just . . ." He sighed, and his expression became even more dour. Much as he'd have liked to hide it, any observer—let alone one who knew him as well as Irrial—would probably have suspected that he was *frightened* of something.

"I didn't really *expect* we'd find all our answers in Mecepheum," he admitted, "but I'd *hoped.* If we're to go chasing leads all over Daltheos's creation, there's someone I have to see first."

"Someone you think has answers?"

"Someone I think has questions."

"Um . . . All right," she said finally. "So where are we going?"

"Give me a minute." Then, at her expression, "I don't actually know, Irrial. Ever since my first campaign, I've cast a particular spell on my lieutenants. It lets me locate them far more easily than I could with any traditional divination."

Irrial shook her head. "I can't *imagine* why anyone could ever mistrust you. So we're looking for one of your lieutenants, then?"

"Ah, no." Corvis was clearly hedging now. "I, uh, I've also cast that spell on . . . On someone else I thought I might need to find."

"Fine. So get to—whatever it is you need to get to, already."

Corvis leaned against the stirrup, lost in deliberation. Distance, direction . . . He spread a mental map of Imphallion across his vision, and if they'd come roughly as far from Mecepheum as he thought they had, then that meant . . .

He couldn't quite repress a groan. They'd *been there*! They'd passed through on their way to Mecepheum! She'd been so near, if he'd only known to look!

Could that, come to think of it, have been what his dream had been trying to tell him?

"Where to?" Irrial asked again.

"Abtheum. We're going back to Abtheum."

***

CORVIS LEANED BACK IN HIS CHAIR, the shredded remnants of egg and pork sitting on the table before him, and idly ran a whetstone along an edge of steel. The metal rasped and screeched through the common room of Whatever The Hell This Latest Roadside Inn Was Called. The barkeep scowled from across the counter, but because there were few paying customers this early in the day—just Corvis himself and a few bleary fellows who'd drunkenly slept the night away in that very room—he didn't *quite* seem willing to object.

"It's not going to get any sharper if I do it outside," Corvis said casually. The man began fussing with something behind the bar. Corvis continued to work, and the steel continued to shriek.

Sunder, of course, never needed sharpening, but the same couldn't be said for Irrial's sword. He'd shown the baroness the proper way to hone the blade, but he trusted his technique more than hers.

Rasp, shriek. Shriek, rasp.

"How did you get that?" a familiar voice demanded.

He looked up as Irrial dropped into the seat across from him. "I'm sneaky."

"Apparently. You stay the hell out of my room."

"Yes, my lady."

Shriek, rasp.

He'd hoped her mood might have improved at least a little this morning. During the previous day's travels, they'd passed several de-tachments of infantry. Men and women, their faces grim—clad in padded armor, pikes resting on shoulders—marched east beneath the banners of four different noble Houses. One unit had been led by a team of steel-encased knights on horseback; another time, they'd seen an entire squad of knights, and their squires, upon the property of a vast estate, making ready for war. It seemed that, even without the backing of the Guilds, at least a *few* of Imphallion's nobles were finally prepar-ing to mobilize against the invaders.

It was the most hopeful sign they'd yet seen, but Irrial seemed to draw no hope from it. "They'll all be killed," she'd said simply when Corvis raised the topic last night, and given their numbers, he'd been unable to argue the point.

She was clearly no more cheerful today.

"Shouldn't we be getting on the road?" she asked him.

"You haven't breakfasted."

"I'm not hungry."

"You will be. I'll wait."

Rasp, shriek.

"You're nervous!" It was uttered with the reverence of revelation.

"No, I . . ." Corvis finally ceased his efforts, much to the barkeep's patent relief. "Maybe," he admitted grudgingly. "There's a lot left un-said between us."

"I'll just bet." Then, more softly, "Rebaine? *Why?*"

He winced at the use of his real name, but a quick glance sug-gested that nobody had overheard. "Why was there a lot left unsaid between—?"

"No."

"Ah." Well, he'd known it had to come eventually.

Corvis propped the sword against the chair and craned his neck back as though reading the past in the dust and cobwebs along the ceil-ing. "Would any answer I could give make any difference, Irrial?"

"Probably not. Try anyway."

"Because Imphallion was dying—*is* dying. Slowly rotting away, while a few parasites grow fat off its diseased wounds. The cities grow corrupt and stagnant, while small villages starve. The Guilds want only to make themselves rich, and the nobility are too weak, and often too selfish, to stand up to them.

"I wanted to change that. I wanted to make Imphallion great again. Not just for me, but for everyone."

"And if you had to kill a few thousand people to do it, well, that was just fair trade, was it?" Clearly she didn't believe a word of it. "Was it worth those lives? The lives of my friends and my family?"

"Yes," he told her without hesitation. "If it had worked out the way that I'd planned, absolutely." Then, more softly, "I'm just . . . not sure anymore that it *would* have. Even if I'd won."

Irrial rose, swept up her sword, and disappeared back up the stairs, leaving the former conqueror alone with his thoughts.

"HELLO, CERRIS."

Through the open door, Corvis stared through time, listened to a voice carried from the past on a gentle breath. He knew she must have changed in five years, but damn if he could see it. Only the faint circles under her eyes were new.

"Hello, Tyannon."

Silence, for a while. Then, "I hate the beard. It makes you look old."

"No, the fact that I'm getting old makes me look old. The beard just makes me look hairy." He watched, expectant, but the smile he'd hoped to elicit never appeared. "You don't seem surprised to see me," he added finally.

"I'm not." Tyannon stepped back from the door. "You'd better come in, both of you." She punched the word *both* perhaps a bit harder than she'd needed to.

"Ah. Tyannon, this is the Baroness Irrial, of Rahariem. Lady Irrial, Tyannon. My wi—my former wife."

"My lady." Tyannon somehow managed to curtsy without breaking stride.

"Tyannon."

They were in the dining room, now, though Corvis had no memory of taking a single step. Habit, rather than courtesy, kept him on his feet until the women were seated—habit, and perhaps more than a touch of confusion. He finally selected a chair beside Irrial and across from Tyannon, and couldn't help but wonder if he'd chosen properly.

"The children?" he asked softly.

"They're fine," she said, voice tight.

"Could I—?"

"No, that's not a good idea. Anyway, they're not here."

Corvis found himself scowling. "Damn it, Tyannon, I'm not going to hurt them. I just want to see—"

"You've *already* hurt them more than enough, thanks."

"Gods damn it, *you're* the one who left! You . . ." He stopped at the pain shooting through his hands, startled to find himself pounding the edge of the table without even realizing it. Corvis examined his fist, as though unsure what it was. Tyannon watched him. Irrial watched them both, her face unreadable.

"But they're all right?" Corvis asked finally, rather than retort to the voice only he could hear. "You're all doing well?"

"As well as can be expected. Cerris, why are you here?"

Tyannon, he couldn't help but note, hadn't even bothered to ask how he'd found her. Either she had a pretty good guess, or she didn't want to know.

Or both.

'*You should tell her anyway,*' the ugly inner voice suggested. '*Don't you think she'd love to know about your spell? About how much you actually trusted her? Come on, it'll be funny!*'

"I suppose you've heard the rumors?"

She nodded brusquely. "From some fairly reliable sources."

"I didn't do it, Tyannon. I've been in Rahariem until just recently. I haven't murdered anyone."

'*Oh? Those Cephiran soldiers, and the guards in Mecepheum, they just dropped dead on their own, did they?*'

"You came all this way just to tell me that?" She sounded—not *doubtful*, exactly, just vaguely astonished. "Why?"

"I just . . . needed you to know."

"And I'm supposed to believe you?"

Corvis felt as though he'd been slapped; the chair literally rocked back beneath him as he flinched. "You—I . . . Tyannon, I've never lied to—"

"Don't you *dare*!" Even Irrial, off to the side, cringed from the venom in Tyannon's voice.

"I didn't," Corvis insisted, his own tone pleading. "I promised you an end to it, and I meant it! It wasn't the same—"

"Magic? Charms? *Mind control*, Cerris? It's *exactly* the same thing! It—"

"No, I—"

Irrial coughed, deliberately, just once. It cut through the argument like an assassin's dagger.

"I'm sorry," she said, "and I truly don't wish to be rude. But I have to guess that this particular disagreement is one you've had before, and I don't think we've the time to try to settle it now."

The glares Tyannon and Corvis hurled her way were identical, a tiny indication of how close they'd once been.

"She's right, you know," Corvis admitted grudgingly.

"Probably. Are you two—together?"

"Absolutely not!"

Irrial's vehement denial, though painful, saved Corvis the trouble of coming up with his own, far more complicated answer. He was, at the very least, heartened to note a swift flash of what might just have been relief cross Tyannon's expression.

'You're a fool. You know that you're a fool, right? I'm sure I must have mentioned it a time or two . . .'

"But I can assure you," the baroness continued, far more calmly, "that he's telling you the truth. Cerris was in Rahariem, aiding our fight against the Cephiran occupiers. He's not behind these murders."

Tyannon nodded slowly. "I owe you an apology, Cerris. I'm sorry.

"And I'm sorry for your loss," she said to Irrial, perhaps having abruptly made the family connection with Duke Halmon.

"Thank you."

Again the trio sat, none quite looking directly at any other, silent save for the constant commentary in Corvis's head.

"What's happening in Mecepheum?" Tyannon asked finally.

He shrugged. "Same as always. Everyone's running around like a two-assed dog chasing both tails, and nothing's getting done."

She took a deep breath, steeling herself. "What happened, Cerris? Why didn't it work?"

Why did you throw your family away on a gambit that failed?

Corvis sighed, absently fidgeting with the finger that once wore a ring. "Those damn Guilds . . . I knew they'd fight, but I had no idea they'd . . .

"I pushed too hard, too fast," he acknowledged finally. "I thought that once I had my people near the top, once I'd arranged for the ascension of a regent who'd make the right decisions, held the right beliefs—"

Irrial inhaled sharply but chose not to interrupt.

"—I thought that'd be it."

Tyannon grimaced. "But the Guilds didn't bend, did they?"

"No. I thought with the amount of pressure I was putting on them, from the nobles and from some of their own members, they'd have no choice. I never thought they could replace so many of their own people, so quickly. I *certainly* never thought they'd use their economic influence to force Halmon to abdicate." He grinned, a rictus without a trace of mirth, a sickly echo of the helm he'd once worn. "I always thought of the Guilds as weak. I guess, when it came to defending themselves, I underestimated them."

Irrial apparently couldn't keep silent any longer. "*You* arranged for my cousin to become regent? How much power did you *have?*"

Corvis shrugged. "Not enough, obviously."

'There's no such thing. You should have learned that long ago.'

"I don't understand. If you hate the Guilds so much, what were you doing as 'Cerris the Merchant'?"

"I couldn't just leave things the way they were," he told her. "Imphallion was in worse shape than ever, and part of that was my fault. But another military campaign wasn't an option. I'm getting too old for that, and besides . . ." Here he glanced sidelong across the table. "I gave Tyannon my word that the Terror of the East was dead. Maybe she doesn't believe me, but it's a promise I intend to keep."

His heart skipped a beat as, clearly despite herself, Tyannon smiled.

"So I thought," he continued, "that maybe I could change things from within. There were too many people who might recognize me in Mecepheum, but Rahariem was far enough away while still being economically important. I figured if I could gain power in the Merchants' Guild there, maybe I could use that influence to steer the Guilds."

"But how could you be sure you'd—?" Understanding finally dawned, and Irrial's face purpled. "You *forced* Danrien to sell you his businesses! You used that same damn spell, didn't you?"

"He got a fair price," Corvis protested.

The women shook their heads in unison.

"So what now?" Tyannon asked.

"Now we find out who's been murdering people in my name," he said simply. "Maybe then we can figure out a way to get the government moving while there's still an Imphallion left to defend."

Tyannon chewed the inside of her cheek, clearly struggling with some decision. "Jassion's hunting you," she said finally.

"*What?*"

"He was here, looking for you, just a few weeks ago."

Corvis shivered. Despite the intervening years, despite the mystical healing that had dragged him between death's jaws, he occasionally ached where bones had broken, still felt the chafe of manacles on his wrists.

No, he'd sooner die than allow the Baron of Braetlyn to take him alive a second time.

'*Pansy.*'

"What did you tell him, Tyannon?"

"What *could* I tell him? I might have helped if I could—I thought you were running around murdering people, remember?—but I didn't know anything."

"How many men does he have?"

"He—just one, I think. His name's Kaleb."

It meant nothing to Corvis. "Well," he said, trying for a lightness he didn't feel, "we'll just have to avoid him, won't we? It's a big kingdom, shouldn't be too hard."

Unsure of what else to say, he rose to his feet. Irrial and Tyannon followed.

"Tyannon, I . . ." He shook his head. "You won't even tell the kids I was here, will you?"

"No," she said softly. "I don't think so."

"If you change your mind . . ." His voice cracked, and he swallowed hard. The room was starting to blur. "If you change your mind, tell them I love them. And tell them—tell them I really thought I was making the world better for them."

He spun, chair clattering to the floor in his wake, and was gone.

———

TYANNON WATCHED the man she'd loved—or the man she'd thought had become a man she could love—flee the room. The house quivered as he threw the front door open. The other woman, Irrial, bowed swiftly, offered what Tyannon assumed was meant to be a kindly smile, and followed.

Only when she heard the door click shut did Tyannon collapse to the table. Her entire body shook, her shoulders heaved, but now that she finally needed them, the tears wouldn't come.

She'd trained them too well, these past five years.

"Mom?"

She jolted upright. Lilander stood beside her, one hand reaching out as though he didn't really know what to do with it.

"I thought I told you to wait in your room," she said without much weight. She couldn't bring herself to be angry, not now, not with him.

"I couldn't." He sat beside her, not even trying to dissemble—truly a strange state of affairs for a boy his age. "It was all I could do not to come in, Mom. But I had to listen. I had to hear his voice again."

Tyannon's brow creased in worry. Eventually, he'd ask about what he heard, and she'd need an explanation. Eventually—but not now.

"Why didn't you tell him about Mellorin? Maybe he could have gone looking for her."

"That wouldn't have been a good idea, sweetheart."

"Why?"

Because I know damn well she's gone with my brother. And as long as she's with him, I don't want Jassion and your father anywhere near each other.

Tyannon took her son's hands in hers, squeezing as though she'd never let go, and said nothing at all.

———

IT TOOK IRRIAL TWO BLOCKS to catch up with Corvis, who moved with a stiff-legged pace that chewed up distance at a startling rate. Clearly he wanted nothing more than to leave that house behind.

"We could have stayed," she told him, dodging a small cluster of workmen in the street and falling into step beside him. "At least long enough for you to see your children."

"They weren't there." He refused to look at her. "And Tyannon wouldn't have let me stay until they got back."

"I think maybe they were," Irrial argued. "Did you notice she always called you *Cerris?*"

He shrugged. "Doesn't mean anything. She called me that as often as she did Corvis. And especially now . . ." Another shrug.

Irrial's expression clouded. Clearly she wasn't sure she believed him—but just as clearly, she knew that now wasn't the time to press it. "I'm sorry," she told him gently, and anyone watching would have been hard pressed to decide which of them looked more surprised that she'd said it.

Through the day's moderate traffic, and the occasional squad of soldiers moving to join the eastern nobles' haphazard mobilization, they wound their way, each lost in very different thoughts. And so they might have continued, had it not been for a soft, high-pitched cry from off to the left.

"Corvis!"

He froze in the center of the road, and his neck ached as he fought the panicked instinct to glance about him. Nobody here should have known to call him by that name! If he'd been recognized, it was only a matter of instants before . . .

But no. A few people glared at him for blocking traffic, but it appeared nobody else had heard the call. Even Irrial, who'd continued several steps before noticing that he'd stopped, seemed bewildered.

"Corvis! Over here!"

He focused on a narrow gap between a winery and a baker's. Irrial must have heard it, too, this time, for she was peering intently the same way.

"Trap?" she whispered.

"Maybe, but I think we'd better find out."

They approached warily, hands on hilt and haft. Their eyes watered and noses stung at the miasma of uncontrolled and unintended fermentation, an indication that both neighboring establishments thought nothing of dumping their dregs in the alley. Beetles, roaches, and rats scurried through the detritus. One particularly large, mangy rat approached them with a peculiar stagger, and Corvis almost chuckled, wondering if it had gotten itself drunk on the rotting sludge.

Then the rat looked up at him and said, "Hello, Corvis," in that same high tone, and he started to wonder if *he* was the one who'd somehow gotten accidentally drunk.

Irrial gulped loudly beside him, her jaw hanging open, and Corvis actually felt better. It meant he wasn't going insane.

'*Not about that, anyway.*'

On the heels of that realization, a second swiftly followed, and he knew, with an abrupt certainty, what was happening. An enormous grin split his beard as he knelt to meet the rodent's beady eyes.

"Why, hello, Seilloah."

The rat blinked and appeared to notice Irrial for the first time. Whiskers and tail twitched in agitation. "So, uh, *Cerris* . . ." it—she—began nervously.

"It's all right, Seilloah. She knows pretty much everything."

Another blink. "Was that wise?"

Corvis shrugged. "I'll let you know. Seilloah, this is Baroness Irrial. Irrial, Seilloah."

"Charmed," the rat said.

"She's a rat" was Irrial's brilliant reply.

"She's a witch, actually," Corvis told her. "She's just *inhabiting* a rat."

"But it's talking. How can she make it talk?"

He couldn't help but smile, remembering the first time he and Seil-loah had held a similar conversation. Echoing what she'd told him then, he asked, "Are you telling me that you've no problem accepting the fact that she can mind-control a rat, but it bothers you that she can make it speak?"

Seilloah snickered. Irrial just shook her head. "I don't think I'll ever really understand magic."

"That's why it's magic." Corvis turned back to his smaller companion. "Not that I'm not glad to see you, Seilloah, but surely there was an easier way. Where are you actually . . . ?" Without really thinking about it, he focused, casting his mind along the mystic tethers he'd fastened to all his lieutenants, the same spell he'd used to keep track of Tyannon. And he found . . .

Nothing.

"Um, Seilloah? I'm not getting any sense of—um, of you."

Somehow, she twisted the tiny snout into an approximation of a sad smile. "That's because this is all that's left of me, Corvis. I'm—well, I'm dead."

Corvis felt the alleyway tilting. He fell back against the wall, slid to sit in a sludgy heap of refuse. "My gods, Seilloah. What . . . ?"

"Jassion came to Theaghl-gohlatch."

"I'll kill him." Corvis felt blood pounding in his temples, saw the bricks of the opposite wall waver in and out. He'd lost friends, lost family, but Seilloah? He'd always thought of the graceful witch as eternal. "I don't bloody *care* whose brother he is, I'll gods damn kill him!"

"Well, I should certainly *expect* so," Seilloah said primly.

"Corvis," Irrial said, kneeling at his side, "keep it down." She tilted her head toward the street. "So far, we're just getting the occasional odd look for sitting in this filthy alley, but if you start raving . . ."

Fists clenched, he rose to his feet, pausing just long enough to lift the rat from the ground—and this close, the creature looked sickly indeed—and place it on his shoulder. Lips pressed tight, he stepped from the alley, glaring at anyone who looked his way, daring them to say a word.

"THE SPELL WAS NEVER MEANT TO WORK this way," Seilloah explained some time later, as they sat huddled in a cramped, dusty room on the second floor of an inn so cheap that even the bedbugs were obviously slumming. On the way, they'd explained to the witch everything they knew about what was happening, what *wasn't* happening, and why. Once they'd arrived, Irrial had claimed the room's only chair, brushing aside the cobwebs before she sat, while Corvis perched on the edge of the sagging mattress. The witch herself was holding court from the center of a rickety table.

"But I was desperate," she continued. "I didn't know what else to do, and I had to warn you."

"Thank you," he told her, his voice rough with repressed emotion. "How long . . . ?"

"I don't know, Corvis. It's so hard . . . My mind keeps drifting. And these poor creatures, they can't contain a human soul for long. This is my—I don't know, I've lost count. At *least* my sixth or seventh body since I left Theaghl-gohlatch, and I can feel it dying. Sooner or later, one of them will die around me, and I won't have the strength to move on." The tip of her tail twitched, drawing patterns on the dusty tabletop. "But I'll stay with you for as long as I have left, Corvis. And I'll help where I can."

He nodded, swallowing hard. "Can you work your magics?"

"It's harder than it was, sometimes a lot. But yes. That's how I found you, actually. I just traced back the spell you'd cast on me."

"But that spell was cast on your body. If it's—you're—dead, how . . . ?"

"I'm a better magician than you are." Again she managed a faint smile. "Even as a rat."

"I can't believe we're having this conversation," Irrial muttered. Then, "Who's Jassion? You never gave me the chance to ask when Tyannon mentioned him."

"The baron of a seaside province called Braetlyn," he told her, biting each word in two as it emerged. "He's a cruel-minded, vicious bastard with a piss-boiling temper and a chip on his shoulder the size of hell's own gate. Which is where I should have sent him a long bloody time ago."

'Finally! We agree on something.'

"Corvis," the witch said seriously, "have you horribly irritated any powerful wizards lately?"

"Not that I know of. Why?"

"Jassion's companion. Kaleb."

Irrial and Corvis exchanged glances. "We've heard the name," he told her, "but I don't know him."

"Well, he knows you. And he's a bad one. Maybe even as strong as Rheah Vhoune was."

Corvis pursed his lips, remembering the woman who'd been one of his most potent foes before the threat of Audriss the Serpent had forced them into an uneasy alliance. "There aren't supposed to *be* any sorcerers that powerful anymore. Well, not in Imphallion, anyway."

"Somebody should have told Kaleb that."

"Maybe he's not Imphallian," Irrial suggested, determined to contribute despite understanding only half the conversation. "Could he be Cephiran?"

"He didn't have a Cephiran accent," Seilloah said thoughtfully, "but that doesn't prove anything. Hell, he could be Tharsuuli for all I know." She paused, snout tilting as she examined Corvis. "Could he be?" she asked. "After what happened to you up north, could the Dragon Kings have sent him?"

Corvis shuddered. "Gods, I hope not. That's all we need." Then, at Irrial's puzzled expression, "Before I came to Rahariem. It's a long story, for some other time."

She frowned, but nodded. "Isn't this all a bit academic, anyway?" she asked. "Shouldn't we be more worried about what we're going to *do* about this Kaleb? We can figure out where he's from later."

"She has a point," Seilloah squeaked. "You're a better caster than you used to be, Corvis, but I'm not telling you anything you don't know when I say you're still not all *that* impressive. And I couldn't match Kaleb at my best, let alone now."

"I see that being a rodent has done wonders for your sunny disposition," he grumbled.

She inhaled deeply, hesitantly, a truly peculiar image in her current form. Then, tentatively, "Pekatherosh?"

Corvis's face went hard. "No. Absolutely not, under no circumstances."

'For once, old boy, we are in complete *agreement. You leave that pompous pustule* right *where he is.'*

"We may need that sort of power, Corvis."

"Because it worked out so well last time? No, not a chance."

"I don't suppose one of you would care to let me in on this?" Irrial demanded sharply.

"Corvis . . ."

"She's a part of all this, Seilloah. She deserves to know." He faced the baroness. "When I was . . ." He cast about for a tactful description.

"Butchering your way across Imphallion on the backs of a thousand innocents?" she interjected helpfully.

"Um, right. The magics at my disposal weren't limited to my own. I had an amulet, a charm if you will. It made me the equal of any true sorcerer, if not stronger.

"It was also inhabited by a demon, who gave it its power. A truly loathsome creature called Khanda." He braced internally when he spoke the name, ready for a withering barrage of commentary from the voice that was either his memory of the demon, or some tiny remnant sliver of Khanda himself. But for a change, he seemed to be alone in his mind.

Irrial scowled. "Every time I think you can't sink any lower . . ."

"The point"—he bulled ahead, refusing to be sidetracked—"is that Audriss had a demon of his own, imprisoned in a ring. Pekatherosh. At the end of the Serpent's War, I banished Khanda back to hell, but I'd gotten hold of Pekatherosh as well. I didn't know if I'd need that sort of power again, so I entombed the ring in a cave atop Mount Molleya, in the Terrakas Mountains."

"And now that you *do* need him," Seilloah said, "you're not going to retrieve him?"

"I've learned a lot since then," Corvis said quietly. "About who and what I am. And I won't have my life resting in the hands of a demon again. Not ever."

"That's all very well and good," Irrial said after a moment of silence.

"I might even admit to being a *little bit* impressed that you really do seem to be trying to put the Terror of the East behind you."

Corvis smiled, startled. "Well, thank y—"

"But it doesn't," she continued, the rickety chair creaking alarmingly as she leaned forward, "help us much in deciding what to do next."

To that, neither the former witch nor the former warlord had an answer.

Chapter Thirteen

SALIA MAVERE SAT in her office and fumed, her smoldering temper threatening to ignite the parchments scattered across the massive desk. How could things possibly have gone so wrong, so quickly? If she'd only known, only taken the proper precautions, just maybe they—

She practically leapt from her chair (and her skin) as the door slammed open, her hand dropping to the hammer at her waist. So powerful was the blow that the brass knob gouged a small chip from the wall. Powdered stone cascaded in a gentle shower to the carpet.

She'd heard muffled conversation in the hallway beyond, but the guards were under strict orders to admit absolutely nobody.

Kaleb stomped through the doorway, his body rigid, radiating a violent fury held at bay by only the thinnest emotional leash. Nenavar followed a step or two behind, muttering, and Salia wondered if the older wizard's presence was all that kept Kaleb in line.

The guards in the hall still stood their posts, motionless as sculptures, staring at what must have been a particularly fascinating vista of absolutely nothing.

"What in the name of Maukra's searing arsehole is wrong with you?"

She'd never seen Kaleb like this, so near losing control. Her widening eyes flickered to Nenavar, who could only shrug a silent protest.

I'm trying!

Kaleb checked his advance only when the desk intruded itself between them, and even then he leaned forward as though ready to leap the obstacle or casually toss it aside. "Have you totally lost what passes for your mind, Mavere? You *had* him, and you let him go!"

"Kaleb, that's enough," the old wizard ordered, perhaps less forcefully than he'd have hoped. "You'll show some respect!"

"I'll show some respect when someone earns it, *Master*. So far, that's not looking likely."

Her own temper heating steadily, not unlike the forge over which she so loved to labor, Salia rose, matching Kaleb's stare. "What the hell are you two doing here?" she hissed. "If anyone sees you here—"

"Nobody will know we were here, Lady Mavere," Nenavar protested. "Few locals even know who we are, and once I release the spell on your guards, they won't remember a thing."

"Right," Kaleb added. "It's *astonishing* how weak everyone's mind is in this building."

Salia very deliberately took two deep breaths, struggling for control. Then, "Sit," she offered—or perhaps ordered—doing the same herself. First Nenavar, after closing the door, and then finally Kaleb complied.

"If you'd had the old man—sorry, *Master Nenavar*—summon me immediately, I could have dealt with him," Kaleb growled. "This could have all been over."

"I contacted Nenavar as soon as we learned it was Rebaine," the Guildmistress protested, trying hard not to sound as though she was whining. Just the thought that he'd been here, *right here*, had been enough to give her genuine nightmares. *I'm not sure how much longer I can stand not knowing* . . . "By then, it was too late."

"You didn't *know*?"

"All I knew, Kaleb, was that Baroness Irrial was accompanied by a servant cloaked in an illusion."

"And that didn't ring any alarm bells, Mavere? Do you keep your brains in that damn hammer?"

"Kaleb . . . ," Nenavar warned. "I won't tell you again to behave yourself."

"Oh, good. Because frankly, I'm getting a little sick of hearing it. If I—"

The sorcerer's jaw continued to work, but nothing emerged save a rasping sigh. Sweat broke out across his brow, down his arms; a line of spittle dangled from the corner of his mouth. His body quivered, every muscle tensing and pulling against every other.

"And I," Nenavar said, rising to his feet, "am more than a little sick of your disobedience. You call me 'Master' as though it were a joke, Kaleb, and I tolerate it. But do not *ever* forget that it is *true.*"

Salia watched her guests engaged in a battle of—what? Power? Will? For all her studies into the ways of magic, she didn't really understand the dynamic, the relationship, between them. At that moment, she knew only that she regretted involving herself with either.

Nenavar unclenched his fist and Kaleb doubled over with a pained gasp, breathing heavily. When he finally straightened, his pallid face wore a subdued expression, though he couldn't quite keep the resentment from his voice. "My apologies," he offered breathlessly—whether to her, to Nenavar, or both, Salia couldn't tell.

She decided, however, to accept it, if only to keep the fragile peace. "Of course I suspected something was wrong," she said. "But why in Verelian's name would I have assumed Lady Irrial would be keeping company with *Corvis Rebaine*? I figured that either she'd been turned and the man with her was a Cephiran spy—"

"Lady Mavere," Kaleb protested, "you know very well the Cephirans don't *need* to spy on us."

"I know that General Rhykus is aware of that," she said, again choosing to take no offense at the interruption. "But most of his officers are ignorant of the true situation, just as most of ours are. Any of them could have put something like this in motion."

Kaleb nodded, conceding the point.

"Or," she continued, "it might have been some move against the Guilds by the nobility. A House spy, a hired assassin . . . *Those* are the threats I've reason to anticipate here. It wasn't until I heard the details of their escape that I realized who we were dealing with, and by the time I was able to get word to Nenavar, they were long gone."

"I thought," the old wizard said, "that I heard none of the guards survived."

"They didn't. But a few folk in the hall had the courage to stick their heads out of their offices to see what the fuss was about. Some of them saw the axe, and we all know *its* description by heart, don't we?"

"I could try divining for them," Kaleb offered thoughtfully.

Nenavar shook his head. "I tried that before coming to fetch you. They moved fast—unnaturally fast—and Rebaine has a great many defensive spells in place." He frowned irritably. "The man's not much of a sorcerer, but he's made a pretty thorough study of such spells."

"I can't imagine why."

"It doesn't help," Nenavar continued, "that nobody here saw him without his illusory disguise. If they had—or if I myself knew more of this Lady Irrial, whom Lady Mavere *did* see clearly—I might use that familiarity as the basis for more potent divinations. But as it stands, we'll have to continue with our search the hard way."

"By which you mean, *I'll* have to continue with it," Kaleb said. "Then may I ask," he continued, far more politely than before, "precisely what I'm doing here? Jassion and Mellorin won't be waking up anytime soon—I saw to that—but still, the longer I'm gone . . ."

"You're here," Mavere told him neutrally, "because our witnesses also identified several of Corvis's helpers among the aristocracy, some of whom I hadn't realized he had under his influence. So we're going to feather two bucks with one arrow by having 'the Terror of the East' do something hideous to them."

"Why, my dear Lady Mavere, I'm always happy to oblige."

She couldn't help but recoil from his crocodilian grin, and once more cursed herself, wondering if she was irrevocably damned for consorting with the likes of these warlocks.

Not for the first time since that horrible day, Mellorin awoke, screaming, in the dark of night. The sheets were twisted around her, soaked with sweat, and she'd thrown her pillow clear to the window.

Almost before the echo faded, a figure filled the open doorway. To the girl's terrified imaginings, her mother, hair and nightshift illuminated from behind, appeared an angel of the gods. From behind the folds of that thin fabric, little Lilander peered with frightened eyes.

Tyannon swept into the room, wrapping her weeping daughter in an embrace as tight as the womb. "Oh, my baby," she cooed, gently rocking the girl, one hand caressing her hair.

"Mommy . . ." It was barely audible, amid Mellorin's sobs. She'd not called Tyannon anything but "Mother" for several years now.

As though scaling the highest peak, Lilander hauled himself up the side of the bed and put his head on his sister's knee. "Don't be sad, Mel." He couldn't have understood, then, why she only burst into fresh tears.

Mellorin knew her mother was worried, knew she wanted her to speak of the dream. But how could she? She had to stifle a scream just *thinking* of it!

Again she lay sprawled in the wood, head aching from that awful blow. She felt the crunch of leaves and the skittering of insects in the dirt, the sticky patch of drying blood on her scalp. Again she heard those vile men with their harsh voices and cruel laughter, debating her fate like she was nothing, like she wasn't even there. And again she heard and understood enough, just enough, to know that those who argued for murdering her outright were offering the *kinder* option.

She waited, the part of her that knew she was dreaming, for what was to come next. She waited for the bushes to part, for the sound of that gods-sent voice, for her father to save her. That was, after all, how it had happened.

But in the dream, the men closed around her, filling her nose and mouth and lungs with the tang of sour sweat, and her father never came.

SUMMER WAS FINALLY PACKING UP to depart, a guest who'd only belatedly gotten the hint, while autumn stood behind, arms crossed and foot tapping. Through most of Imphallion, the breeze assumed just a tiny hint of the cool scents to come. Most of Imphallion, but not here. At the periphery of the great swamp, the heat lingered, conducted and spread by the oppressive humidity, transforming the world into a simmering stew. Mosquitoes flew, or perhaps swam, through that syrupy air in such quantities that inhaling squirming mouthfuls of the damn things was as great a hazard as contracting some horrible pestilence from their bites. Kaleb had prepared an herbal paste, bolstered by a touch of magic, to repel them, and the constant buzz had taken on an angry, almost frustrated tone.

Some few dozen yards from the shallowest reaches of the marsh, Mellorin sat cross-legged within the shade of scraggly, sun-blasted trees. She studiously watched the thick grasses at her feet so she needn't look into the face of her companion.

"Mother told me, over and over," she said to the ground, "that he'd gone to make sure the 'bad men' never hurt me again. She never—*neither* of them ever understood. I was only a child, Kaleb. It didn't matter to me if there were bad guys *out there*. There were bad guys *here*—well, you know what I mean, at home—and that's where I needed him." Her voice shook; with pain, yes, of course, but also with a smoldering rage that threatened to set her alight from within.

He blotted the light from her vision as he knelt in the grass beside her. She said nothing, refused to look up, but a shiver ran through her skin as his hand—hot and clammy in the heat, but no less welcome—took hers. "I'm so sorry, Mellorin."

Then she did look up at him, for something in his tone rang ever so faintly false. Not that she thought his sympathy a lie, for the softness in his face looked genuine enough. Rather, he seemed not entirely to *understand*.

Over his shoulder, way out in the swamp, a few sporadic and leafless trees formed tiny cracks crawling up from the western horizon. The marsh might have marked the edge of the world, its filthy waters leaking out through that broken sky.

Despite herself, she smiled. "You've never really been afraid of anything, have you?"

Kaleb shifted so he was sitting, rather than kneeling, beside her. "I—

not really," he admitted. "Anyone with the patience and the will can learn *some* magic, but some people are just born to it more than others."

She nodded.

"I was born to it. I've had more power than I've really known what to do with for my entire life. When you have that, it's hard to take fear seriously."

"You're not even afraid of my father? Not even a little bit?"

"Hm." Kaleb frowned thoughtfully. "I respect what he's capable of. I acknowledge that he's dangerous. But fear, like you're talking about? I certainly don't *think* so. But maybe I wouldn't know it if I were."

"And here," she told him, her smile growing, "I thought you knew *everything*."

"Not yet," he said pompously. Then he, too, grinned.

"Kaleb," she asked, partially out of a sudden need to say *something*, "why are you here?"

"Well, when a mommy wizard and a daddy wizard love each other *very* much—"

"Stop that," she ordered, punching him in the arm even as she battled a case of the giggles. "I mean it," she said, regaining control. "I've told you why I had to come along. And we both know why Uncle Jassion hates my father."

"Anyone with ears who's ever been within ten miles of Jassion knows that."

"And maybe a few without them. But why are *you* here? And *don't* try to tell me it's just a job you were hired for, either."

"Well, that's partly what it *is*," he answered.

"Yes. *Partly.*"

"Just because I've never really been afraid," Kaleb told her seriously, "doesn't mean I can't be hurt. Your father's hurt a *lot* of people." Her face went stony, her teeth grinding, and she nodded. "He wouldn't know me to look at me," the sorcerer continued, "but I was one of them. Maybe, when we find him, I'll remind him of it."

She wanted to ask, to know, but she wouldn't push him. Not on this, not now. Her free hand rose, seemingly of its own accord, to his face. "I'm sorry, Kaleb. I'm sorry he did that to you. I don't know who he is, anymore. I guess I never did."

She felt his other hand on her shoulder. "It's not your fault, Mellorin."

"I know, but I—"

"Shhh." He was leaning forward, now. She felt the heat of his breath on her lips, could all but taste it on her tongue, and she was certain he must be able to hear her heart pounding. Closer, almost touching . . .

"Kaleb!"

Mellorin could not have jumped any faster had she been manacled to a catapult. She gawked at Jassion, who stood with arms crossed at the edge of the copse, and nearly choked as a whole battlefield of warring emotions squeezed through her chest, leaving little room for breath. Cheeks flaming, she rose and fled beyond the trees.

KALEB WATCHED MELLORIN GO, chewing on the inside of his lip. Languidly he stood, and the expression he directed at the newcomer was utterly bland. "What's your problem, old boy?"

Three steps forward, and Jassion stood as close as Mellorin had been. "I've warned you before about hurting her. Don't think I'm not on to you."

"Damn," the sorcerer said. "You've seen through my clever attempt to not hide anything. I haven't tried to deceive you, Jassion. Does it look like I've any interest in *hurting* her?"

"There are many kinds of injury, Kaleb, and I'm not choosy. You hurt her, and I'll—"

"Kill me, yes. Possibly by boring me to death by repeating the same threat over and over. Was there a reason you came back? Other than to embarrass me and your niece, I mean."

"There was, actually," the baron said, apparently having decided he'd made his point. "I've found one of them."

WHILE THE VOICE IN HER HEAD that warned of pending danger had faded after the battle with Losalis's men, Mellorin's own natural talent allowed her to retain much of the instinct Kaleb's spell had imparted. She'd been hoping, once Jassion returned from his scouting efforts, for the opportunity to practice them. (Had anyone actually used the phrase *showing off*, she'd have been mortally insulted.) So the young woman was rather disappointed when Kaleb informed her that she and Jassion would serve primarily as a diversion.

That was, until she finally got a good look at her first ogre.

For some time they'd slunk through the edges of the marsh, following Jassion's lead, and every step was an endeavor. So far as Mellorin could tell, the swamp had no true "bottom," just a point at which the filthy mix of mud and water coagulated enough to support their weight. It clung to her ankles like a terrified child, seeped through the seams in her leather boots to caress her skin with sticky, lukewarm tendrils. Kaleb swore that his herbal paste would survive immersion long enough for them to finish what they were doing, but still she flinched, fearing some terrible sting or venomous fangs each time something hidden in the murk brushed against her legs.

Cypresses and other gnarled, bony trees protruded now and again from the swamp. Mellorin's imagination transformed them into the desperate fingers of drowning giants, their bodies sunken in the muck. The stench of slow decay scratched at her lungs with dirty, ragged nails, and she struggled to remind herself that what she smelled was the natural odor of the bog, and *not* the remnants of those lost titans.

And so it went in all directions, save back the way they'd come: an endless expanse of stagnant water, creeping mildew, and the rotting, ravenous earth that lurked below. Were this *truly* the edge of the world, it couldn't have been any more disturbing, any more oppressive.

So caught up was Mellorin in her surroundings, it required a quick "Hsst!" from Jassion before she spotted the distant figure. A sentry, no doubt, watching the borders of ogre territory.

Though little more than a distant silhouette, he showed arms and legs—or at least, portions of those legs above the waterline—blatantly corded with muscle. His proportions were just a bit skewed from human, and she could clearly make out the single horn protruding from his skull. Fearsome, certainly, but at this first glimpse he didn't seem all *that* impressive; dangerous, but not some nightmarish legend.

Then he leaned back against a trunk of a jagged cypress that Mellorin had thought was much farther away into the swamp, and her cheeks went pale. "My gods . . ."

Kaleb's lips curved in a faint smile. "He's a big boy, isn't he?"

"If that tree's anywhere near as high as . . . Kaleb, he's got to be ten feet tall!"

"Probably closer to twelve," the sorcerer said speculatively, as though he were looking to *buy* the damn ogre. "Plus the horn, of course."

"Oh, of course." Mellorin was trying to wrap her mind around the notion of a creature twice Jassion's height. "We wouldn't want to forget that. Wouldn't be polite."

"If you two are quite through," Jassion growled, "I'd very much like to get this done *before* he spots us skulking out here, thanks. Do you remember the plan?"

"Yes, old boy." Kaleb sighed. "*Some* of us aren't complete idiots." Mellorin, for her part, rolled her eyes in perfect imitation of Kaleb's traditional expression.

The sorcerer hunkered down in the muck, practically vanishing, while the others advanced on their target, spreading out slowly as they walked. The hilts of her sword and dagger felt somehow sticky and slippery at the same time. Mellorin chose to attribute it to the humidity of the swamp, and not to the fearful sweating of her palms.

With a deliberate calm, the creature turned toward them as they neared, its single eye darting from one to the other. Rather than move to meet them, it remained where it stood, dropping into a shallow crouch with the cypress at its back. At the ogre's waist, positioned for a one-handed draw, hung a sword longer even than Jassion's demon-forged flamberge, and the beast clutched a leaf-bladed spear that could have spitted a warhorse lengthwise, with plenty of room to spare.

Despite the humidity, Mellorin felt her lips go dry, her tongue swell to fill her mouth. She felt like a child wielding toy blades against a very angry parent. Her legs ached as she slogged through the mud, and she knew that any fancy footwork would accomplish little more than to drive her even deeper into the sludge. If it actually came to fighting this monster, the only question was whether she or Jassion would die first.

She could see the ogre's leather armor, now, cut from alligator hide.

Opposite his sword hung an iron-banded horn on a leather thong, but he'd made no effort to lift it to his lips. No sense alarming the whole tribe, Mellorin assumed, when it was just a couple of humans either too stupid or suicidal to live.

That, of course, had been the entire point of this little charade, but the warlord's daughter was beginning to question the wisdom of "the plan."

And her own, for that matter.

Nearer still, and the beast sidled to one side, keeping its back to the tree. It could watch Mellorin's approach from the corner of its eye, but clearly it had determined Jassion to be the greater threat. Mellorin, despite her recent "influx" of skill and the days of practice since, had to admit it was probably right, and she couldn't keep a sigh of relief pent up in her chest as it turned its attention away.

A few more steps, and Jassion would come within range of that impossibly long spear. Mellorin felt a flutter of panic. *Kaleb, now would be a* really *good time!*

She didn't *actually* believe the sorcerer was listening in on her thoughts, but at that moment he might as well have been.

Her hair blew across her face as *something* passed with impossible speed overhead. She glimpsed nothing more than a ripple in the air itself, the faintest wisp of steam or mist, wadded into a ball like so much discarded parchment. Had she not been looking right at it, indeed *expecting* something very much like it, she'd never have known it was there.

The swamp erupted. The murky water was the blood of the earth, gushing from the wound inflicted by Kaleb's invisible hammer. A ferocious tide slammed into her, threatening to knock her from her feet, and for the first time she was actually *grateful* for the tight grip of the muck below. Mud, bits of plant matter—even a smattering of dead frogs and snakes—rained across the bog, blinding Mellorin to anything, everything, else. Her ears rang with a deafening crack, followed by a second enormous splash. Spray spattered her face, the surface of the swamp roiled against her legs, and even without sight she knew the cypress had fallen.

Mellorin finally managed to wipe the worst of the gunk from her face—remembering, first, to sheathe the dagger she'd held in that hand—and gawped at the carnage Kaleb had wrought.

The tree was indeed gone, snapped unevenly just above the waterline. Only that jagged stump, and a few branches long enough to break the surface where it had fallen, suggested it had ever existed. The ogre lay facedown, limbs sprawled every which way—including a few in which they weren't at all supposed to bend—and the sorcerer himself was struggling to flip the fallen giant onto its back before it drowned.

Jassion, who'd been closer than Mellorin, was only now picking himself up out of the swamp. Water sluiced through the rings in his hauberk, matted his short hair into stubby clumps, and dribbled from his lips as he emptied his lungs with a racking, body-shaking cough. Filth streaked his face, clinging stubbornly despite the sudden bath, and Mellorin thought some of it might be blood.

They reached Kaleb's side at roughly the same time, helped him in flipping the ogre. Jassion, wincing with pain, dug into his pack and removed a coil of waterlogged rope, but the sorcerer shook his head.

"Not necessary. Now that he's out, I can keep him unconscious as long as we need." With a grunt, he manhandled the ogre to slump against the broken stump, ensuring that he'd neither float away nor sink beneath the swamp.

Only once that was done did Jassion give Kaleb a fearsome shove. It wasn't *quite* enough to send the sorcerer splashing back into the water, but his awkward flailing was satisfaction enough.

"*What?*" Kaleb demanded, struggling to recapture some measure of dignity.

"What the hell was *that*, Kaleb?" Bits of swamp water from the baron's hair splashed Kaleb's face as he shouted. "By the gods, were you *trying* to kill us?"

"Certainly not Mellorin," Kaleb answered calmly. Then, as Jassion's face reddened, "Oh, calm down. I *had* to hit him hard enough to make sure he was out. If I was trying to *kill* anyone, I'd have hit him—or you—with the spell *directly*, rather than casting it *nearby*."

"You mean to tell me that was a *miss*?" Mellorin gasped, horrified.

"Well, not *really*. I hit what I was trying to hit, didn't I?"

"I . . . ," Mellorin began.

"You . . . ," was Jassion's contribution.

"Nobody's dead," the sorcerer insisted. "I'm sorry if I scared you—"

"I wasn't—" the baron protested, but Kaleb wasn't about to let him finish.

"—but you *had* to be close. I had to make sure he was too distracted to see the blast coming. It's not *entirely* invisible—" Here Mellorin nodded. "—and if he'd dodged it, if he'd realized he was facing a wizard, he'd probably have sounded that damn horn, and we'd be dealing with the entire tribe.

"So," he continued, driving a finger into Jassion's sternum, "why don't you assume that I know what I'm doing, try something brand new just for a change, and *quit flapping your lips for half a bloody minute!*"

Jassion's face couldn't actually go any redder, but it certainly made its best effort. Mellorin was a bit surprised that she couldn't actually feel the breeze from his twitching eyelid.

"I, uh, don't want you to think that *I* assume you don't know what you're doing," she said hesitantly, "but couldn't you have just put the ogre to sleep or something? Was it really necessary to drop a phantom anvil on him?"

Kaleb chuckled. "Poetic. No, I'm afraid I couldn't. *Keeping* someone asleep is easy. Putting them out in the first place? That's rather more like mesmerism. It requires a few moments of contact, and a relatively unwary mind. You think the ogre would've been willing to sit down for a nice long chat with us? I'd say it's about as likely as your uncle over there founding the Braetlyn chapter of the Corvis Rebaine Appreciation Society and Knitting Circle."

"Kaleb . . . ," Jassion warned darkly.

"You're right," the sorcerer said apologetically. "I should have just had the ogre talk to you. You'd have put him to sleep in a minute flat."

"Can we just get on with this?" Jassion sounded almost plaintive. "You dragged us all the way out to this hellish place just so we could find an ogre. Great, we've found one. So let's be done with it, shall we?"

"Fine." Kaleb knelt in the muck beside the cyclopean giant, placed a hand on the creature's neck, and began to chant.

Unwilling to interrupt, Mellorin sidled over to her glowering uncle. "You want to tell me what we're doing, exactly? When Kaleb first talked about coming to this wretched swamp, he said tracking down an ogre would help us, but he didn't tell me how."

Jassion shrugged. "Not much to it. Kaleb can use the blood of someone's relative to find that person, as long as they're not protected. One of your father's old lieutenants was an ogre. They're all an extended tribe, so pretty much *any* ogre can lead us to him. Or that's the hope, anyway."

"Kavro?" Mellorin offered, wracking her memories for half-heard tales of the wars.

"Davro, but yes, him."

They watched, both standing with arms crossed.

"Is that why you let me come?" she demanded eventually. "To use my blood to find my father?"

"At first," Kaleb admitted, rising from his crouch. "Corvis is protected, but the spell might prove useful anyway.

"But," he added, voice and features softening, "that's not the only reason anymore."

Her expression remained unreadable.

"Have we got it?" Jassion asked him.

"Yes. As long as he doesn't decide to go sightseeing before we get there, I can take us right to him."

"Good. Then we don't need *this* any longer."

Mellorin gasped and started forward, hand outstretched, but there was nothing she could do. Jassion whipped Talon over his shoulder and down in a brutal stroke. The waters reddened, and the ogre's head bounced once off the stump before floating gently away across the swamp.

The baron stepped back from his somber duty and promptly toppled once more into the waters as his niece violently shoved him. He stared upward, spitting and gasping, too shocked even to be angry.

"You didn't have to *do* that!" she screamed down at him. "He wasn't any danger to us! We could have just walked away."

"Mellorin—"

"My father's not the only monster I've got to deal with, is he?"

"Mellorin, it was an *ogre*." And then, apparently bewildered that his explanation wasn't sufficient, he could only blink as she unleashed a low growl and stalked away as rigidly as the marsh would allow.

Kaleb, too, watched her go, brow furrowed in thought, and made no move to aid Jassion out of the muck.

Chapter Fourteen

BOISTEROUS CACOPHONY and stifling heat battled for the right to claim possession of the Third Sheet's common room, while a thick miasma of alcohol and body odor waited in the wings to challenge the victor. Shutters and the front door gaped wide, propped open by sticks or stones, but the gentle breeze that wafted through, stirring sawdust across the floor and hair across many heads, was no match for the roasting temperature within. Press so many bodies together, fill the air with the hot breath of laughter and conversation, add just a pinch of smoke from the kitchen fires, and the result was a refuge where summer lingered long after the rest of the city had kicked it out.

Given its halfway clever name, Corvis had hoped for more from the Third Sheet, but it was just another tavern. Tables and chairs stretched unevenly across the room. Laborers and craftsmen—some as uneven as the furniture—sat scattered around those tables or along a bar formed of a single tremendous log. Barmaids with harried faces and pinch-bruised bottoms wended through the throng, delivering drinks and plates of roast something-or-other on orders from a bearded bartender with an equally harried face (though, one might assume, a less battered rear).

A number of the larger men, and no small handful of women, carried themselves with the posture of professional soldiers. Even half drunk, clustered around a table and trading jests coarse enough to send a sailor diving overboard, they kept watch on the door, and on occasion a particularly startling sound inspired a few to drop their hands toward their waists.

Corvis, clad in the scruffiest traveling leathers he possessed—which was saying something—had seated himself a few tables away. He nursed a tankard of more foam than ale, and tried his best to make sure they noticed him watching them, all while appearing as though he was trying to be inconspicuous.

Harder, by far, than it sounds.

Eventually, however, one of the women met his gaze once too often. Scowling, she elbowed the fellow beside her and whispered, pointing Corvis's way with a chin so pronounced it was practically belligerent. Her companion, in turn, said something to the man beside *him*, and a moment later Corvis found his table surrounded by five tipsy soldiers.

This plan made a lot more sense before I actually put it in motion, he thought grimly.

'*Don't most of them?*'

"You got a problem?" the woman who'd first noticed him demanded, leaning across the table on her knuckles.

"I do," Corvis told her, deliberately keeping his hands well away from Sunder. "But not with you. Actually, it occurs to me you might be able to *help* me." He offered up what he hoped was a friendly grin. "Join me for a round?"

"You buyin'?" one of the others rasped.

"Wouldn't be a very polite invitation if I wasn't."

Amazing what the promise of free drink did for their attitudes. As Corvis waved over the nearest barmaid, he found himself suddenly surrounded by his best friends in the world.

More of them, he realized with a quick head count, than had actually come to threaten him in the first place.

"So," he said, once everyone was settled with tankard, mug, horn, or flagon in hand, "it seems to me that you folk have the look of fighting men. And women," he added, with what he hoped was a respectful— and perhaps just *slightly* appraising—glance at the sharp-featured soldier. She smirked and raised her mug. "And I'm thinking, with you being here *in* the city, and rumor telling me that the various House and mercenary companies are assembling *outside* the cities, that at least some of you must be city guards. Right so far?"

Nods and assenting grunts proved adequate, if not eloquent, response.

Corvis took a deliberately messy swig of his own beverage, wiping foam from his mustache. "So would I also be right in guessing, then, that some of you could tell me a bit about those murders that happened here recently?"

The table went dangerously silent, smiles flipping over and inside out into aggressive glowers. "Some of us lost friends that night," one man muttered darkly. "What makes you think that we'd want to talk to you about it?"

"Look," Corvis said, leaning inward, "I think we've all heard who was responsible, right? Well, there's an *awfully* large price on his head because of it. I don't pretend my odds of finding him are all that good, but I'm looking to collect on it. A man could retire on what they're offering, and the gods haven't yet answered my prayers about getting younger."

"You're a bounty hunter?" the women to his left asked.

"I am." Then, after an almost imperceptible pause, "Evislan Kade, at your service."

"We don't need any help from your kind," the first fellow grumbled.

"I don't doubt that," Corvis said lightly. "But you're stuck here. If You-Know-Who is still in Denathere, fine, you'll get him, and gods help him when you do. But you think he *is* still in Denathere? He's killed folk from here to Mecepheum, and if he's moved on, wouldn't you want to see him get what's coming to him? Even if you can't do it yourselves?"

The guards glanced and mumbled at one another, working through the logic in what "Evislan" said. While they considered, Corvis took the opportunity to order them all a second round, wincing only slightly at the tab he was racking up.

It did the trick, though. "All right," the woman said to him, hostility once more gone from her voice. "What is it you want to know?"

———————— ▌⋯⋯▷ ◁⋯⋯▐ ————————

THE CLOUDS HUNG LOW AND PREGNANT over Denathere, overripe fruit seemingly ready to burst. The scent of autumn rains perfumed the air, but the mischievous sky would only tease, withholding the cleansing showers it promised.

Corvis took it all in as he walked the streets: the shuffle and clatter of passersby, the looming faces of edifices nearly as old as Mecepheum's, the occasional flicker as beggars and urchins earned a few coppers by lighting the street lamps in advance of evening.

And he hated it, loathed every last inch of it with a burning passion that startled him after so many years. This damn city represented everything that had gone wrong in his life. Here, his first campaign had ground to a halt in bitter failure. Here, though he'd not recognized it at the time, he'd left behind sufficient clues to alert not one mortal foe, but *two*, to the nature of the wondrous prize he'd sought. And here, Audriss the Serpent had reignited the slow-burning embers of his own conquest into a roaring conflagration that had dragged Corvis from his family and ultimately cost him everything he'd loved.

There *were* places he'd want to be even less than the city of Denathere—but not many.

It had been Seilloah's idea to come here. "Maybe it's from spending several days as a dog on my way to find you," she'd said, "but it seems to me that if you're looking to track someone, you start where the trail started."

Corvis hadn't been able to argue with her, as much as he desperately wanted to. They *had* to examine the murder scenes, maybe find some clues there they'd not unearth anywhere else. He couldn't safely return to Mecepheum, and since the only other "Rebaine murders" that they knew were more than idle rumor had occurred *here*, they'd had precious little choice.

So here they'd come. Corvis scoured the taverns of Denathere, leaving Irrial to ask questions of the more affluent and influential, and with every moment he seethed beneath the fury, the hatred, and the burning shame the city cast on him from all sides.

Wrapped in a smothering cocoon of self-pitying anger, Corvis didn't realize he'd stormed clear through the small bazaar of vendors' stalls and open carts where he and Irrial had agreed to rendezvous.

Only when he felt a hand on his shoulder and spun, fists rising, did he comprehend where he was. He recognized Irrial—in time, thankfully, to arrest his punch—and the scents of roast meats, smoked fish, and sweet fruits finally penetrated the thick fog blanketing his mind.

'Aw, you should've hit her. When else are you going to have the chance to pretend it was an accident?'

"Damn it!" As swiftly as he'd returned to his senses, he seemed to forget that it was he who'd left their meeting point behind, forcing her to chase him down. "Don't sneak up on me like that. I—Irrial, what's wrong?"

"Come with me. Quickly."

She launched into a barely restrained pace that threatened to break into a run at every step, and Corvis fell into lockstep behind. Again he was utterly oblivious to the hawking shouts and brightly fluttering pennants of the marketplace, though now his vision was obscured and his gut churned with worry rather than anger.

They cut across one corner of the bazaar, and the baroness finally led him to a halt directly in front of . . .

"Another alley?" Corvis complained. "Isn't there anywhere—"

He staggered as Irrial bodily shoved him into the narrow walkway, caught himself just in time to avoid tripping over his feet, and found himself staring downward.

"Oh, gods. Seilloah . . ."

It had happened before, twice, on their way to Denathere. But then the witch had slunk away in secret, on her own, returning in a new form when it was all over. Never before had Corvis *seen* it.

The arm-length lizard that was her current shell lay on its side, body heaving as it struggled to breathe. Limbs spasmed; its jaw hung open and drooled a thin, blood-tinted soup. Even as they watched, scales sloughed from its hide, exposing open sores and necrotic skin beneath.

Corvis dropped to one knee with a dull splash, scattering the slimy refuse of the alley. A finger reached out, stroked the creature's squamous crest. "What can I do?"

She twisted her head his way, and Corvis gagged as a faint ooze trickled from beneath one eye. The jaw twitched, just once. The lizard emitted the faintest squawk, a sound that might, just might, have been "Cor . . ."

And then, with a final shudder, lay still.

"Seilloah?" It was a whisper, at first, then a cry almost loud enough to be heard beyond the alley. "Seilloah!" He searched frantically, actually digging through the garbage as though some other animal might lie hidden therein. "Seilloah!"

It couldn't end this way! Not for her . . .

"I'm here, Corvis." The voice was weak, her breath ragged and gasping. "I'm all right."

From atop a fence, a tortoiseshell alley cat bounded to the ground, stumbling slightly. Corvis frowned at the awkward landing, and wondered if the patches of mange on the creature's fur had been there moments before.

"Don't scare me like that, Seilloah," he said, slumping against the wall.

"Scare *you?*" It was peculiar, more so even than listening to it speak, to hear a cat laugh. But then, more seriously, "I'm not sure how many more times I can do that."

"What about a person?" Irrial interjected. Corvis jumped a bit. He'd all but forgotten she was there.

"What *about* a person?" he asked.

"Seilloah, I mean. Wouldn't a human body last longer, since it's meant to house a human soul?"

Four eyes, two human, two feline, widened in shock.

'Say, that's not a bad idea. The lady may not be entirely hopeless after all.'

"Oh, for the gods' sakes . . . I'm not *advocating* it. You two haven't *completely* corrupted me. I'm just wondering *why* you don't do it."

"Can't be done," Seilloah said. "Not by any magics *I* practice, anyway. It's *because* of the soul. I can't impose mine on a body that already has one, and I can't ride anything that's already dead."

Irrial nodded. "I guess that makes sense."

"I hope so. I'm too tired to explain it any further."

Corvis reached a hand toward the cat. "I can carry you, for a bit."

"That might be nice." She sniffed and recoiled as he hefted her in his arms. "Corvis, are you drunk?"

He couldn't help but chuckle. "No, I'm not drunk. I had just enough ale to make them think I was getting sloshed along with them."

"Well," Irrial muttered impatiently, "I hope you learned more than I did. Nobody I spoke with wanted to say much. Thought it an *unseemly* topic. Might drive away customers."

"A bit," Corvis said as they moved back into the crowded streets. Seilloah climbed from his arms and draped herself across his left shoulder. "It seems—Seilloah, must you?"

She froze, claws half extended, in the midst of kneading his chest. "I'm sorry, Corvis. Instinct, I suppose. I'll try to pay more attention."

"I'd sure appreciate it." He turned back to Irrial. "So it seems the killings occurred in two separate locations: the ducal keep, which is probably crawling with more soldiers than a brothel offering free samples, and a home belonging to the majordomo of one of the Guildmasters. I'm thinking that'll be the easier one to get into."

To get into, perhaps, but not necessarily to *find*. While Corvis had wormed the house's general vicinity from the soldiers in the Third Sheet, he felt he'd have been pressing his luck trying to pin them down to specific directions. For long hours he and Irrial wandered the streets of one of Denathere's fancier neighborhoods, nodding politely to passersby in colorful bloused tunics, gleaming brocades, and whatever other foolishness the aristocracy could foist off under the guise of "style." They dodged horse-drawn carriages trundling over cobblestones, squinted at homes whitewashed to a blinding sheen, gagged at the cloying aroma of flower gardens that had survived the sweltering summer, and found nothing at all out of the ordinary.

Yes, Corvis had anticipated that any obvious signs of violence would have long since been swept away, but he'd figured on spotting *some* indication—a house with a boarded-up window or a newly replaced door, a property that pedestrians crossed the street to avoid, *something.*

"That one." Seilloah, whom Corvis had thought to be sound asleep on his shoulder, raised her muzzle at a modest house they'd passed twice already—when the witch actually *had* been asleep.

"Are you sure?"

"I smell old blood."

Corvis shrugged at Irrial, drawing a sharp yelp of protest from his passenger. "I guess that makes sense."

"As much as any of this does," the baroness replied.

As casually as they could, they lingered, watching. Now that they were focused on it, they did indeed note that the locals quickened their pace just a bit as they went by, as though fearful of being spotted by someone within.

"All right," Corvis said finally to Irrial. "I think we wait for evening, and then you keep watch on the road while I take a look inside."

"Maybe I should go. If there's trouble, it's likely to be outside, right?"

He shook his head. "I'm not looking to get into a fight with the guard, Irrial. Besides, you don't know what to look for. If anyone shows up who you can't distract or dissuade, I'll give them my bounty hunter story."

"I'm not sure that'll justify you being inside the house."

"It's a better excuse than you could—"

"Or," Seilloah interrupted, "you could, you know, send the person who won't draw any attention or suspicion at all since she happens to be a *cat* just now."

Corvis turned away, so embarrassed that he was certain even his beard must be blushing. "Say, I've got a thought," he told them a moment later. "Why don't we send Seilloah?"

The tip of the witch's tail flicked against the back of Corvis's neck. "What a remarkable idea," she said.

SILENT AND INEXORABLE as an embarrassing memory, Seilloah padded across the yard. A frightened sparrow took off in a flutter of feathers, while a handful of insects and what sounded like a squirrel skittered away through the garden, but otherwise no one and nothing marked her passage. She remained fixed on her objective, ignoring both the vague urge to chase after those fleeing creatures, and the hot, infected ache of lesions forming beneath her matted fur as feline body and human soul seared each other.

The violence hadn't been limited to the house. She could smell where the blood had seeped into the soil, run between the stones of the walkway. This near to the earth she saw scratches in the cobblestones and pebbles, perhaps where weapons were dropped or armored bodies fell. If the murderer had battled someone outside, there might be witnesses; she made a mental note to mention it to Corvis.

Corvis. Seilloah felt a surge of uncharacteristic anger, and though she squelched it with a will so strong it had already defied death, she could not wholly forget it. Twenty-three years ago, six years ago, it didn't matter; she'd joined him willingly, stood by his side committing horrors scarcely less foul than his own. She'd well understood there might one day be a price to pay, and it had never stopped her. And it had been the Baron of Braetlyn's blade, not the Terror of the East's, that had cut her down.

Yet she could not entirely shrug off the chilling knowledge that she was already dead save for the formalities, wasting away her last days in a sequence of diseased, agonizing bodies—and that it was, in part, because of Corvis Rebaine.

Seilloah leapt from the grass to land atop a windowsill and wormed her tiny form between the wobbly shutters. Again the scent of death wafted over her, and she directed her attentions to the task at hand.

She wouldn't blame Corvis, at least not much—and certainly no more than he would himself. And if the witch required any small vengeance on the friend she'd followed unto death, his own guilt would surely suffice.

***

THE HOUSE HAD BEEN CLEANED, at least to an extent. The worst of the blood and other humors had been washed away, the tattered bodies and mangled clothes removed, the shattered furniture discarded. Still, senses far less acute than those Seilloah currently enjoyed would have detected lingering signs of murder. The carpet looked diseased, showing stains of a deep, brittle brown. Several walls were badly scorched, and a few corners retained bits of splintered wood. The stench was overwhelming to her feline nose, and even if she were to go utterly blind, she'd have easily pinpointed the precise locations where death had come.

Between the distractions of her new form and the agonies of her current condition, Seilloah could perhaps be forgiven for initially failing to discover anything of import. Yes, some of the victims had died by fire and some by blade, some by magic and some brute force, but this they already knew. And yes, she could, if asked, have provided a precise count of the slain, but she couldn't imagine what possible value such information might have.

Dining room, kitchen, back to the living room, occasionally stopping to lick bits of dried carnage from her paws, and Seilloah grew ever more irritated. They were wasting their time; there was nothing here, nothing of use . . .

Nearing the front door, she froze, save for the slight twitch of her tail and the quickened flare of her nostrils. Most of the room was nothing but an empty abattoir, specific details obscured by the remnants of half a dozen lives running together in a single stain beneath the carpeting and between the floorboards. But off to one side, a single man—probably a bodyguard, perhaps a servant—had died just a few steps from the others, far enough that the scents and stains of his death weren't mixed with the general filth.

She sniffed where he'd stood, where he'd stumbled back as he died. She saw the faint remnants of a soap-scrubbed stain, scented the edges of the blood, the bone, and the brain that had splattered themselves across the wall.

And Seilloah's own blood ran cold, her tiny heart fluttering like a hummingbird's wings, as she recognized the evidence before her.

She'd seen it last in Mecepheum, when Audriss the Serpent had wielded the power of not one demon, but *two*, against the assembled aristocracy. She'd seen it far more often in Corvis's campaign, over two decades past, when he'd allowed Khanda to feast upon the souls the demon needed to maintain his power.

She'd watched the victims hemorrhage, from eyes and nose, ears and mouth, before the skull itself, unable to bear the pressures that consumed the soul from within, simply blew itself apart.

It was certainly a *disturbing* death to witness, and it wasn't precisely a secret. Many had seen it happen during the Terror's conquest, for Corvis had wielded Khanda as a bludgeon, hoping to cow the nation into surrender. But few knew the *purpose* of that peculiar method of killing, knew enough to associate it with the demon-spawned magics the warlord wielded.

That whoever was framing Corvis now had thought to include such a means of death—regardless of what magics they actually used to imitate it—suggested at the very *least* a deliberate attention to the details of all his past crimes.

And just possibly a greater knowledge of his methods than any random murderer, however potent, should possess.

Frowning as far as her snout would permit, uncomfortable with any of the myriad directions her thoughts were taking, Seilloah bounded back through the window and toward her waiting companions.

"... WISH I COULD HELP YOU," the guard was apologizing, though he didn't really sound like he cared much one way or the other. "Kassek knows I'd like to see the bastard brought down. But I'm just not authorized to allow *anyone* into the duke's quarters. His family doesn't want people poking around in there."

Corvis—or rather, so far as the soldier knew, Evislan Kade the bounty hunter—stood in the lee of the great keep, watching the flickering of torches dance across its dark stone wall, and could only nod his understanding. Perhaps he might sneak in under illusion, or slip Seilloah past the soldiers at the gate, but honestly, he didn't really think he *needed* to see the second murder scene.

He was already well and truly disturbed by what they'd found at the first.

But that didn't mean there was nothing else left to learn. "I understand," he said affably. "And I certainly wouldn't want to cause the grieving family any more hassle." He offered a disingenuous grin. "People tend to forget to pay when they're upset."

The guard grunted something.

"I also understand," Corvis continued, dropping to a conspiratorial murmur, "that some of your fellow guardsmen actually *fought* the bastard outside the Guildsman's house? I'd sure love to speak to one of them, see if he can tell me anything new. And of course, I'd be more than generous with whoever pointed me the right way."

That brought an uncertain frown. "I don't think," the soldier said slowly, "that that's the sort of stuff I ought to be blabbing, you know? I mean, giving guards' names to strangers . . ."

Corvis sighed and reached into a leather pouch at his belt, muttering under his breath. Then, with a sequence of individual clanks, he methodically dropped ten gold coins into the palms of the slack-jawed fellow before him.

"Ask around for Corporal Tiviam," the guard whispered breathlessly. "He lives in the barracks within the keep, so you wouldn't be permitted access, but he likes to drink at the Three Sheets."

Of course he does. Corvis shook his head, wondering when the gods might finally have had enough entertainment at his expense.

'*Not for a while yet, I'm sure. I'm certainly still laughing at you.*'

"You should have no difficulty finding him there," the young sentinel continued. "He's been there a *lot* since that day, and his arm's still in a sling."

Corvis nodded in quick thanks and strode away. He wanted to be long gone before the muttered illusion faded, and the "gold" coins transformed once more to brass.

". . . might have talked his way out of it," Borinder was saying, struggling to keep a straight face. "But then . . ." A chuckle forced its way through his lips, painting his face red as it passed.

"Yeah . . . ?" Tiviam pressed, amused yet frustrated by his companion's jocularity. The man had some great stories, but he was utterly *miserable* at telling them.

"Then," Borinder finally managed to sputter, "he left for his shift that morning, and—and he left her a handful of coins on the nightstand!"

The rest of the squad burst into peals of laughter, Tiviam guffawing louder than any of them. Even as he struggled for breath, wiped tears from his cheeks, he worried briefly they might be revealing their presence, but no. Nothing suspicious about a group of workmen enjoying a bit of fun after a hard day's work, was there?

And besides, the captain of whom Borinder spoke was a splinter in the heel of everyone present, and indeed most of the guard as a whole. Not a man or woman at arms in Denathere would waste a single second in sympathy for him.

"Considerin' where Captain Lorkin spends most o' his nights," Arral chimed in, "not to mention most o' his pay, his wife's lucky that a few coins is *all* he gave her. I'm stunned that neither o' 'em's come down wit' a good, blisterin' case o'—"

All four glanced up, across the yard and the winding walk, as the door to the house drifted slowly open. Tiviam expected a few silk-clad folk within, perhaps guests leaving early, or one of the uniformed guards making a quick inspection of the property.

What he saw, instead, was a glimpse of hell.

Blood and flesh were strewn about the foyer, soaking into the carpet, coating the walls. He couldn't see the faces of the dead, but then he didn't need to, for he knew the names of everyone within.

For a span of several gasping breaths, four trained, experienced members of Denathere's guard couldn't move a muscle, their souls staked to the earth with coffin nails.

It isn't possible! Tiviam could have sworn he heard the words shouted, loud enough to echo from the rooftops; only later would he realize it was all in his mind. *We'd have* heard *something! We* must *have heard something!*

As abruptly as it had been revealed, the carnage was obscured, for the hell that lay beyond that door birthed a devil of its own. It didn't seem to step into the doorway so much as it was simply, suddenly *there:* a looming figure of naked bone and darkness filed to a jagged edge. Blood ran in rivulets from the grotesque axe in its hand, far more than should ever have clung to the blade.

Tiviam *knew;* knew how a houseful of people could be slaughtered without sound, knew how so many guards could fall before a single foe.

Knew who it was he faced.

And Tiviam, in the bravest act of his career—an act that would later win him a commendation and a medal that he left to rust on Borinder's grave—screamed at his men to charge.

The Terror of the East emerged to meet them, and shrieks of panic erupted along the street. Passersby, their attention drawn by Tiviam's cry, shoved and tripped over one another, desperate to flee the horror they all recognized. Some would tell later how a band of courageous civilians—Tiviam's men were, after all, dressed in workman's clothes—had hurled themselves at the walking nightmare, bought everyone else the time to flee. It was the only thought that kept Tiviam sane in the months to come.

Borinder, long-legged and fleet of foot, was the first to reach the Terror of the East. Tiviam couldn't even tell precisely what happened; he knew only that he saw a blur of blades, and the jovial soldier's sword was shattered. A second flash, equally swift, and Borinder himself lay in pieces on the lawn.

The Terror raised his hands, palms out, and a gout of liquid flame the envy of any volcano arced through the air. Nassan lacked even time to scream as half his body liquefied, sloughing from his bones. Arral, hurling himself desperately aside, proved more fortunate. Though a portion of his leg sizzled away like so much frying grease—though he would never again walk without a crutch—he would live. The gods were even kind enough to allow him to pass out, that he might dwell for a time in the realm of Shashar Dream-Singer, rather than in the agony of his own ruined flesh.

And that left Tiviam, standing alone before the man who'd inflicted crippling scars upon an entire culture. He was dead; he knew he was dead. But in that, Tiviam was wrong.

He approached in a desperate lunge, broadsword leveled to punch through armor and into the bastard's black and putrid heart. But the Terror of the East *moved,* far faster than any man, and the guardsman saw a haunting crimson glow emanating from beneath the warlord's breastplate. The broadsword passed harmlessly, and the black-armored arm slammed downward, trapping Tiviam's elbow in a grip of unyielding steel.

A twist, a barely perceptible flex, and Tiviam convulsed in agony. The sword fell to the grass as his arm flapped uselessly, the bones within broken, the elbow separated at the joint.

Empty sockets stared into frightened eyes. Tiviam trembled beneath the weight of death's own regard, and hoped only that it would bring an end to the pain.

And then he was falling, all support gone. For the Terror of the East had simply disappeared.

LOCATING CORPORAL TIVIAM had been just as easy as the guard had suggested. Corvis and the others set themselves up in the Three Sheets, and it was only the second evening when a broad-shouldered fellow with cropped hair and his left arm in a leather sling showed up and began drinking as though to douse a fire in his gut. In fact, Corvis realized upon seeing him enter, the man had been present the other day, sitting off alone in a corner and guzzling mead. He'd been right there, had Corvis known to talk to him.

Coaxing the story from him had proved somewhat more challenging. Corvis loosened his tongue with multiple rounds, and left a small but gleaming heap of coins on the counter before him — real, this time, in case the whole escapade should take too long for an illusion to hold. And still, in the end, it was not Corvis at all, but Irrial, who got what they came for. In her huskiest voice, her auburn locks falling across her face, she fawned over the "courageous warrior." Her breath came in sympathetic gasps over his mangled arm, and her eyes grew moist at the account of his fallen companions.

And only when she — and Corvis, sitting rapt at the next table, hanging on every word — had heard it all, did they depart, leaving Captain Tiviam to his efforts at washing the memories away. When last they saw him, his head was slumped over a drinking horn, empty save for a tiny puddle sloshing around the bottom. Into that vessel, over and over, he repeated again the last words he'd said to Irrial.

"He could have vanished at any time. He didn't have to kill them at all . . ."

Corvis and Irrial pushed through the crowded market, weaving around last-minute shoppers hoping to do a final bit of business before the vendors closed up for the night. This late into the evening, the sounds of Denathere had grown muted but otherwise remained unchanged. Corvis had to fight the urge to stick a finger in each ear and waggle them about, trying to clear an obstruction that he knew was purely imaginary.

It was, for a few minutes, preferable to actually thinking.

Mindlessly, he allowed Irrial to guide him back to their quarters. The rooms stood on the third floor of an establishment far nicer than the Three Sheets (it'd been the baroness who acquired them, and it showed), but truth be told Corvis was so distracted that, if his life had depended on it, he never could have recalled its name. Only when they were settled in one of the two bedchambers—replete with chairs upholstered in cherry red, down-stuffed mattresses lined with clean linen sheets, even a brass lamp with jasmine-scented oil—did he reluctantly crawl from his comfortable mental quilts and direct his thoughts toward the tale they'd been told.

"I think we have to assume," he said without preamble, "that whoever's behind this has a *much* more detailed knowledge of me and my methods than we'd suspected." Even saying it aloud made him uncomfortable, and he could only hope his voice was steady. The last time someone had popped up with excess information about Corvis's past, he'd thrown the entire nation into shambles and nearly obliterated Mecepheum itself.

To say nothing of Corvis's family . . .

Seilloah leapt up to the tabletop, sniffed unhappily at the glittering lamp, and then nodded perfunctorily before proceeding to chew at something stuck between her claws. "Probably a safe assumption," she agreed.

Irrial, however, sounded less convinced. "Why? What about the corporal's story worries you—other than the thought that someone might be even more vile than you were?"

"It's a combination of things," Corvis said, vaguely disturbed by the cat-witch's behavior and, for the nonce, oblivious to Irrial's verbal dig. "The men who died in that house by what's been made to look like Khanda's soul-consumption, the red glow Tiviam described . . ." He tapped his fingers idly on the edge of the table, stopping immediately as Seilloah glared at him. "It's all the little details, and they're all *right*."

"What *about* that glow?" the baroness asked.

"Khanda. I usually wore the pendant on a chain, and it hung beneath the armor. Only someone very close when I used my magics—*his* magics—would have seen it. So, yeah, *maybe* someone who saw me fight in the past was just astoundingly observant, and remembers *every* detail, but I'd say the odds are pretty heavily against it. Plus, they wouldn't necessarily understand the *significance* of what they saw."

'But it's nice to be noticed. An artist is never appreciated in his own time, you know?'

Corvis felt his fingers curling into fists. "Would you *stop?*" He was never certain if he'd only thought it, or whispered aloud.

'See? That's exactly what I mean. You never appreciated me, Corvis. I bet you don't remember my birthday, either.'

He allowed his eyes to squeeze as tightly shut as his fists, hoping the others would attribute it to his exhaustion.

"No," he continued finally, "I think we'd better prepare ourselves for the notion that we're dealing with someone who knew me personally, or who's spoken in depth with someone who did."

"At least it's a short list," Seilloah remarked around a mouthful of fur. Then, "I hate to bring this up, but Jassion *did* go to see Tyannon . . ."

"No. No chance."

"Corvis—"

"No. I'm not saying it's impossible that she'd have helped him to find me, under the right circumstances, but even if she remembered details, why would she tell him? They wouldn't do him any good in hunting me down. We're looking for someone else."

Seilloah and Irrial exchanged skeptical glances, but neither pressed the issue.

"So yes," he said, "it's a small list. And the first step is to find them."

Corvis looked deeply into the lamp's burning light, focusing past his fatigue. *And gods, the last few days shouldn't have been so exhausting! I should never have agreed to getting old . . .*

"Davro first." Corvis felt the faint tug of his spell, gazed off in its direction even though there was little to see but a dull beige wall. Wading through sluggish thoughts, he translated the strength of the pull into a sense of distance, and that distance into a line on his mental map of Imphallion . . .

"Still in that bucolic valley of his, I think." Corvis couldn't help grinning, remembering his response upon first learning what had become of the fearsome ogre.

"I'm not sure that means anything," Seilloah warned. "He was *really* unhappy with you."

"True. But he also doesn't want anyone knowing where he lives. I doubt he'd risk drawing attention to himself. Still, we'll follow up if we need to."

Again he concentrated, using the flickering flame as a focus. But this time, there was . . .

"Nothing." He rocked back in his chair, blinking rapidly. "Losalis is gone, Seilloah."

"Are you sure? Maybe someone just broke the spell."

"Maybe." But he didn't sound at all convinced, and for long moments he refused to speak any further.

"Losalis was a good man," he said finally, answering the question embedded in their silence. "Or at least he was a loyal one. I just hope, if he *is* dead, that it was nothing I did that got him killed."

"Right," Irrial spat with surprising rancor. "Because that's *so much* worse than the thousands of good men that you killed *deliberately*."

"Let it go," Seilloah commanded, even as Corvis, his face growing hot, opened his mouth to retort. He glared, nodded, and turned again toward the lamp.

'What, she doesn't even get a "Shut up"? If I'd said that, I'd have gotten a "Shut up."'

"Shut up," Corvis whispered.

One last time, one more soul who had served at his side during the Serpent's War, one more to whom he'd attached his invisible tethers of magic. Again the tug, again the mental struggle to translate that amorphous sensation into real distance.

A peculiar gurgle bubbled from his throat, the result of hysterical laughter and a frustrated sob slamming into each other deep in his chest. And he wondered, even as he delivered the news, just how often he would have to retrace his own steps before this was finished.

"*Emdimir?*" He'd never heard Irrial's voice reach quite such a pitch as he did in that disbelieving squawk. "After all this, why would you want us to go back *east?*"

He shrugged. "Near as I can tell, that's where she is."

"Well . . ." Irrial frowned. "At least it's not all the way back to Rahariem. I'm not sure I could face . . . What?" she demanded at the sudden chagrin, almost schoolboy-like, on Corvis's face.

"I, uh . . . I wasn't sure how to tell you, or, well, even *if*, but . . ."

"Yes?" It was, perhaps, the most venomous *yes* Corvis had ever heard.

"Emdimir's fallen, Irrial."

Her freckles appeared rich as ink, so pale did the baroness's face become. "What?"

"A couple of weeks ago, according to the mercenary talk I overheard at the Three Sheets."

"And nobody's done anything? *Still* nobody's done anything?" Her voice was rising so fast, it threatened to take wing. "What's *wrong* with everyone? What's wrong with the damn Guilds?"

"Irrial, we should really be more qui—"

"What's wrong with *me?*" She reached a final, undignified screech, and then slumped in her chair, her tone following suit. "Gods, they keep coming, farther and farther, and I haven't done *anything* . . . We'll never free Rahariem now, we—"

"Irrial!" It was Seilloah, not Corvis, who barked that name—a peculiar sound indeed, coming from a feline mouth. "You *are* working for Rahariem. It's what you've *been* doing. Don't forget it."

"Right. Sure I have."

"And besides," Corvis added, "you've seen the soldiers. *Some* of the noble Houses are mobilizing. Yeah, I know, it's not enough, but if the others start to follow their example . . ."

"Horseshit. They're bloody useless, the whole lot of them are going to die, and you know it." Her hair fell around her face and hung limp for a moment, until she'd finally regained her composure. "All right," she said, looking up once more. "Emdimir, then. For, what was her name? Ellowaine?"

"Ellowaine," he confirmed.

"What," Seilloah asked slowly, "makes you think she's the one?"

Corvis smiled grimly. "Because Ellowaine's a mercenary, Seilloah. And since Emdimir's occupied just now, her being there almost certainly means she's either a prisoner, or . . ."

He let it dangle, and Seilloah understood.

"Or she's working for Cephira."

Chapter Fifteen

SHELTÉRED FROM THE WORST of last season's malice by the gentle shade of surrounding slopes, the valleys of the Cadriest Mountains had long since shed their verdant summer garb, wrapping themselves in coats of scarlet and gold for the autumn to come. The air, though still, was refreshingly cool and smelled of tomorrow's gentle fog. After the distant swamp's oppressive breath—and the strenuous journey over many a hillside trail, down forest paths, and on the King's Highway—the vales were a paradise unto themselves.

But if so, it was a paradise only the horses bothered to notice.

Jassion, as always, saw nothing but the distance stretching before them, separating him from the man he hated more than anything in this world. It seemed, at times, as though the baron's obsession was a tangible barrier he carried around him, one that hemmed him off from the rest of the world.

But for the ignoble nobleman, Kaleb cared little. No, he would reserve his concern, and devote attentions that might otherwise have noted the surrounding beauty, to Mellorin.

The young woman had drawn inward since their encounter with the ogre. Her cloak had become a cocoon, a rampart, a security blanket; her horse an island amid an otherwise empty sea. She spoke to her companions only when she must, and even then, despite her obvious anger at him, directed her queries and comments to her uncle. She'd barely met Kaleb's eyes during those many days, though she often snuck quick glimpses when she thought his focus lay elsewhere.

And Kaleb, after many nights of considered deliberation, finally had to admit that he hadn't any idea of how to deal with her. He was a man of many talents, of substantial knowledge—more than either of his companions suspected—but the eccentricities of young women lay beyond his ken.

He dropped back, ostensibly permitting his mount to crop a few mouthfuls of the deep green grass that sprouted in the shade of far more colorful trees, and allowed Jassion to move some distance ahead. Then, startling the horse with an abrupt yank on the reins, he fell into step beside Mellorin's palfrey.

Still, she would not look at him.

"It's beautiful here, isn't it?" he asked, gesturing as though she'd somehow missed the hills that rolled like playful toddlers around the feet of their mountain parents. "A man could certainly understand why even an ogre would make a home here."

Silence, save for the call of circling birds, the bleating of some distant beast.

"Mellorin," he said, far more softly, "are you ever going to speak to me?"

She offered only a soft sniff, and Kaleb had already tensed to tug at the reins and move away, a scowl forming on his lips, before he recognized it as a sound, not of disdain, but muffled grief.

"Would you truly weep for an ogre?" Only the tenderness in his tone prevented the question from becoming accusation.

Finally, finally, she turned her face his way from within the folds of her hood.

"I don't understand," he told her. "I watched you fight, when Losalis's men attacked us."

She nodded. "And it's the fact you and my uncle see no difference that bothers me. Oh, gods . . ." He watched her clasp hands to her stomach, as though she would physically restrain the emotions threatening to overwhelm her. "Gods, Kaleb, is *everyone* in this world like *him*? Is my father just more honest about who he is?"

For a few moments, the sorcerer struggled to form a reply, for he knew what the wrong answer might cost him. "Mellorin," he said, "do you know what happened to your uncle at Rebaine's hands?"

"I know he was a child when Denathere fell. I know he saw my father disappear with my mother."

"Your father's men didn't flee when he did. First, they slaughtered everyone in the Hall of Meeting. Nobles, commoners, men, women . . . *Everyone.*"

"But—Jassion?"

"The master of Denathere's Scriveners' Guild saved him. He hid Jassion's tiny body with his own." Kaleb shook his head. "My understanding is, old Jeddeg's the only Guildsman of whom Jassion has ever spoken highly.

"Mellorin, your uncle waited in a *pit of corpses,* and he was conscious for every moment of it. He struggled to breathe beneath the weight of the dead, to keep their blood from his eyes and mouth, for *hours,* before anyone found him."

Mellorin had gone white as a corpse herself, her lips trembling. "I had no idea . . ."

"It's not something he shares readily, though anyone who was around in noble circles at the time has heard the tale. Jassion is—*broken.* I don't think he'll ever be an entirely rational person, though we can certainly hope that once he's caught up with your father, his temper might cool a *little.*"

"And you?" There was no mistaking the bitterness that flavored her words. "What's your excuse?"

"My—?"

"The ogre wasn't a threat to us, Kaleb! I know why Jassion killed it anyway. I want to know why *you* didn't stop him!"

"I could tell you it wasn't my place," Kaleb said slowly, "that, appearances aside, I'm the servant in this expedition, not the master. I *could,*" he reiterated, raising a finger as her mouth opened to interject, "but I won't."

"Then why?"

"Do you remember what I told you about my magics? About never really having been afraid?"

She nodded.

"I've also grown accustomed to doing things the, ah, *expedient* way," he admitted. "When you have more power than everyone else, I suppose you start to view people as just problems to be dealt with. I've killed before, Mellorin. Sometimes a lot, and often without much more provocation than your uncle."

"And you're satisfied with this?" she demanded.

He reached across the gap between the horses to rest a hand on her arm. "I used to be," he said. "Now I think I want to do better."

Yes, he thought as Mellorin tried, and failed, to repress a bashful smile. *I believe I am, indeed, doing* so *much better.*

THEY STUMBLED UPON THEIR DESTINATION not long after, cresting a shallow rise into the hollow between a pair of great, grass-clad slopes only just too small to be counted among the proper mountains of the Cadriest range.

The valley sprawled wide, a cupped palm full of lush greens and bright golds, undulating where the edges of the hills failed to conform to even curves. A bucolic cottage hid shyly within the shadow of the leftmost hill, and beyond that stood a primitive but sturdy fence of wooden posts. It formed an enclosure sufficient to pen an enormous herd of barnyard animals, or perhaps one abnormally lackadaisical dragon.

It turned out, thankfully, to be the former. Scores of sheep, goats, and the occasional cow wandered about, on both sides of the fence and through an open gate. And it was only those animals that offered the newcomers any sense of scale for the whole tableau.

"You could hold a masquerade ball in that house!" Mellorin murmured after several moments.

Kaleb shrugged. "That's a guest list I'd love to see."

"Are we certain Davro lives *here*?"

"I'd say so," Jassion answered. "Even if Kaleb *did* bollix up the spell"—the sorcerer bowed sardonically at that—"I can't imagine any *human* hermit needing fifteen-foot ceilings."

"I know," she admitted. "It just doesn't seem very—ogrey."

"Are you sure that's not 'ogrish'?" Kaleb asked her. "Perhaps 'ogresque'?"

Mellorin grinned; Jassion looked about ready to strangle something. "Are you two *quite* finished?"

"Probably not," Kaleb and Mellorin told him in unison.

The baron began marching toward the house, muttering a dozen separate imprecations. With a shared chuckle, the others fell in behind.

"I'm not seeing any smoke from the chimney," Jassion said after allowing himself a moment to overcome his latest snit. "But it's warm enough here that that doesn't prove anything. I'm hoping he's out, so we can catch him unawares, but keep your eyes open."

"I—"

"Shut up, Kaleb."

The rich tang of grasses and turning leaves gave way as they neared, overpowered by the musk of, as Kaleb later put it, "Beef, mutton, wool, and leather in their hoofed larval stage." This close, they could see a few swine as well, rooting in the mud beneath a trough behind the house.

A trough that dripped with the sludgy remnants of a *very* recent feeding.

The trio drew to an abrupt halt as the implications dawned. Hands dropped to hilts, or rose in readiness to cast.

It was Mellorin who, glancing just the right way through sheer happenstance, saw the spear arcing toward them. She screamed something garbled even as she dived to the soil. The weapon planted itself in the earth nearby, vibrating with a dull *thrum*, and Kaleb completely understood when he saw her eyes widen in alarm.

It looked very much like someone had just hurled a sharpened tree at them. The spear was two feet longer, and a third again as thick, as that wielded by the ogre in the swamp.

They turned—Mellorin and Jassion picking themselves up from where they'd thrown themselves aside—and there he was, emerging from the house's shadow. The tip of his horn surely cleared fourteen feet, and Mellorin could damn near have stretched out her saddle on one of his arms. In one fist he clutched a second spear, not quite as large as the first, and a weapon that was less a sword than a row of jagged steel teeth protruded from the other.

"All right." His voice was the cry of the earthquake, the deep echo of the mountain hollows. "I knew someone would find me eventually, so let's get this done with. I have cows to milk. You want to tell me what horrible atrocities you're here to avenge, or should we forgo the formalities and just start ruining each other's outfits?"

"Yep, he's definitely been with your father," Kaleb whispered to Mellorin. Then, more loudly, as Jassion began to slide Talon from over his shoulder, "No! Damn it, no steel!" Then, louder, "Davro, we're not here to hurt you."

"Good," the ogre said, his advance never slowing. "Because I'm pretty certain you *won't.*"

"Look," Kaleb continued, backing slowly away, "we just want to talk to you. Just talk!"

"He's not buying it, Kaleb," Jassion growled.

"He's also no good to us dead," the sorcerer reminded him. "My name is Kaleb," he shouted.

"Never heard of you."

"This is Jassion, Baron of Braetlyn."

That, finally, got a reaction. The ogre halted, nostrils flaring. "You, I've heard a great deal about." He cocked his arm, ready to throw, and Jassion tensed to spring aside.

Mellorin stepped forward, shrugging off Kaleb's hand as he reached to stop her, ignoring his hiss of warning.

"My name," she said, holding sword and dagger out to her sides rather than before her, "is Mellorin Rebaine."

And the ogre finally froze—more out of shock, Kaleb surmised, than anything else.

"Mellorin *Rebaine?*" Perhaps uncertain he'd heard properly, Davro tilted his head, his horn and his shadow making him look very much like a bewildered sundial.

"Yes. I know you've no reason to love my father—"

The ogre unleashed a peculiar barking cough, and the others could only wonder in confusion. It wasn't until he wiped away a tear with the back of his sword-hand that they realized he'd been laughing.

"I see that you've inherited a certain gift for understatement," he said finally.

She nodded. "Among other things. But that's actually why we're here, Davro. Help us, and you might find some measure of retribution."

Davro's brow furrowed, making the great horn quiver. "Perhaps," he said, planting the butt of the spear in the soil beside him, "you'd better come in after all.

"But please use the scraper by the door, would you? I just swept the damn place."

———

"I TAKE IT YOU'RE NO GREAT admirer of your father, then?"

Mellorin sat on the edge of a lumpy mattress that was apparently stuffed with untanned hides and untreated furs, and tried hard to breathe as little as possible. Kaleb perched beside her, offering no sign of his own discomfort save for the occasional flaring of his nostrils, while Jassion stood apart and made no attempt at all to keep the revulsion off his face. Davro himself squatted atop a broad stump that apparently served him as a stool. This close, and undistracted by the rigors of battle, Mellorin noted that each of his hands boasted only four thick fingers, and the deep red of his skin—which she'd previously attributed to sunburn, both on him and the ogre in the swamp—was his normal shade.

Recognizing belatedly that she'd been addressed, she blinked and focused on Davro's face, trying not to gawk at the solitary eye, the towering horn, or the protruding lower tusks. "I, ah, actually know surprisingly few details of my father's life," she admitted. "I didn't even know who he really was until a few years ago, and my mother *still* thinks me ignorant." *Or she did before I ran off with Kaleb and my uncle.* "But no, I'm not happy at all with what I do know. Corvis Rebaine was *not* a good man."

"Again with the understatement," Davro rumbled, accompanied by another bestial chuckle. "So what is this, then? Are you out on a great crusade of justice, to make right your father's wrongs?" The disdain was palpable, thick enough to paint with.

Kaleb frowned. "I'm not certain that her motivations are germane to—"

"No," Mellorin interrupted. "That is, if I *can* make up for some of what he did, I'll certainly take the opportunity. But it's not why I'm here. I want," she elaborated without waiting to be asked, "to find out how he could do what he did . . . why he abandoned his family to pick up where he left off after so many years."

"He wanted to protect you from Audriss," Davro protested, even as his expression twisted in what could only be stunned disbelief that he was *defending* the man.

"Originally, maybe. But he didn't stop there."

"Of course he didn't." The ogre shook his head. "I should have known. You can't believe anything that bastard says. If he told me the sun would rise tomorrow, I'd stock up on torches."

"Right. I want to ask him *why*."

"I see." The ogre chewed the inside of his lip. Then, "And if you pull the other one, my horn lights up like a firefly."

"What—?" Mellorin sounded almost shocked, and Jassion was scowling darkly, but Kaleb's lips curled into a shallow, knowing smile.

"The thing about your father," Davro said, "is that he had a motive for *everything*, be it ulterior or just—uh, 'terior,' I suppose. And I don't believe for a second that your apple, however cute and tiny, fell *that* far from his ugly, ornery tree. Curiosity can make a person do a lot of things, but give up the only life they know? Uh-uh. You don't have a *question*, Little Rebaine, you have a *goal*."

And for the first time in Kaleb's experience, he saw the girl's expression twist—not in fury, not in sorrow, but in *hatred*. "My father," she repeated, "was not a good man. He was a monster. Those lives he didn't destroy . . ." A single tear threatened to spill from her eye, then evaporated in the searing heat of her emotion. ". . . he turned into lies. And he never paid for any of it."

"He lost his family," Kaleb pointed out. "He lost you."

"Another crime, Kaleb. Not a punishment."

"All of which is utterly immaterial," Jassion growled, unable to swallow his rising impatience—and, just perhaps, taken aback by the fervor of his niece's hate. Mellorin leaned back, breathing heavily, and allowed the interruption to go unchallenged. "We need your help *finding* him. Nothing else matters."

"I have no loyalty to Rebaine," Davro said thoughtfully. "And precious little affection for him."

"Then—"

"But I also don't need trouble from the likes of him again, and he knows where I live. I like my solitude; you might've picked up on that. I'm not convinced it's in my best interests to get involved."

"Is that so?" The baron took a single pugnacious step. "Then perhaps, ogre, you might consider what sorts of attention we can call down on your valley! You'd never be left alone again, if you—"

"No!" Kaleb shot to his feet, grasping Jassion's shoulders and spinning him around. "You might try *not* talking for a change, old boy. You *clearly* need the practice."

"What the hell do you think you're—"

"How do you think Rebaine got his help in the first place, you idiot?" he hissed, casting a glance at Davro's rapidly reddening face. Then, to the ogre, "My apologies, Davro. My companion spoke without thinking. We would not, of course, attempt to force your cooperation."

Jassion glowered, but said nothing.

Davro himself nodded in Kaleb's direction, though his lone eye never left Jassion. "Apology accepted."

"Good." Kaleb stepped in front of Jassion, a clear signal that it was he, not the baron, with whom Davro would continue to deal. "We've no intention of interfering with your life here, or of bringing trouble— be it Rebaine or *anyone else*—down on your head. Please, just tell us anything that might help us in our hunt. We'll bother you no more, and you just might acquire some small measure of that justice you earlier mocked."

Inhuman shoulders rose and fell in a heavy shrug. "I'm really not sure what I can tell you. I've neither seen nor heard word of Rebaine

since I left Mecepheum six years ago. He's obviously not with his family, so I have no sodding idea where he might've gone."

"That's *it*?" The words practically quivered as they escaped Jassion's
tightly clenched teeth.

A second shrug. "Seems so." A pause. "Maybe if you've access to a
sorcerer. After the war, Rebaine cast . . ." Broad lips quirked into a
scowl around the two protruding tusks. "We haven't met, have we?" he
asked Kaleb abruptly.

"I think I'd remember. Why?"

"I don't know. Something vaguely familiar about you—but then, all
you two-eyed little dwarfs look the same to me."

"Maybe," Kaleb said, "but I can assure you, we've never met. You
were saying?"

But it was no good. Whatever the ogre had seen in Kaleb—or imagined he'd seen—was apparently too much. "No, I don't think so,"
Davro told him, rising from his stool to tower above them. "I think it's
time for you to go."

"Damn you," Jassion began hotly, "there's no way—!"

"I think there is." Somehow, without the twitch of a single muscle,
the ogre's hand drew their attention to the massive blade at his side.
"Go away. You want answers? Go ask Seilloah, the witch, if Theaghl-
gohlatch doesn't eat you—and if *she* doesn't, for that matter. *I* still have
cows to milk."

Without another word, Kaleb offered a shallow bow, and led both
a puzzled Mellorin and a sputtering Jassion through the cavernous
doorway.

"ALL THIS WAY!" MINUTES AND SOME few hundred yards
later, the baron remained furious enough to chew horseshoes into
nails. "For nothing! Just more wasted time. We ought at least to make
sure that damn monster pays for his *own* crimes before we leave!"

Mellorin scowled but chose, for the moment, not to respond. "I
don't understand," she asked Kaleb instead. "He was about to tell us
something. What happened?"

THE WARLORD'S LEGACY
235

"I don't know," the sorcerer admitted with a much smaller shrug than Davro's. "Maybe he sensed something of my magics? Ogres aren't much taken with sorcery. Or maybe I really did remind him of someone."

"Or maybe he's just a lunatic!" Jassion snapped. "What does it matter?"

"It's just, if we could convince him to finish what he was saying . . ."

"He doesn't have to," Kaleb told her. "I know what he was saying." Then, "If you two keep staring at me like that, your eyes are going to pop out and roll away."

"You *know*?" Jassion squeaked.

"I'm almost certain that's what I just said. It's what I *heard* myself say. Perhaps I need to clean out my ears."

Despite his warning, the others continued to stare.

"During his various campaigns," Kaleb said with a sigh, "Rebaine cast a spell on his lieutenants, so he could find them again if necessary. It's a flimsy, tenuous magic, and no, before you even ask, I *can't* use it to trace him back. If the spell had been cast on me personally, I could probably do it, but as it is, the connection's just too faint."

"Oh," Mellorin said, disappointed. "I guess maybe we *did* come all this way—and kill that ogre," she added deliberately, "—for nothing."

Jassion, however, was frowning, not in his typical disapproving scowl but apparently in thought. "I admit, I know almost nothing about magic . . ."

Kaleb's eyes went comically wide. Jassion ignored him.

"But would such a spell last indefinitely?"

"No," the sorcerer told him. "A long time—decades, potentially, if no other magics interfered with it—but not forever."

"So wouldn't Rebaine have likely cast the spell on Davro again, after his war against the Serpent? In case the old one eventually faded?"

"Quite possibly. Are you going somewhere with this, old boy? Thinking of taking up magic? It's a little late, and I'm not sure you've got the brains for—"

"It just seems to me, in my *ignorance*," Jassion said with a slow smile, "that if the first one hasn't dwindled yet, *two* such spells on the same subject might leave a heavier magical trail than one. Wouldn't they?"

Kaleb's jaw sagged, practically unhinging itself very much like a snake's. "I'm an idiot," he said to Mellorin.

"I just want it noted," Jassion announced smugly, "that I'm not the one who said that."

⸻◗ ◖⸻

THE SUN HAD SETTLED beyond the mountains by the time Davro returned to his house, carrying a bucket of milk large enough for Mellorin to have bathed in. His eye narrowed in a fearsome glower at the sight of her perched on his stoop.

"I told you to leave!"

"We did, Davro. Kaleb and Uncle Jassion aren't here. It's just me."

"Fantastic. That's two-thirds what I asked for, then, isn't it? What are you doing here, Little Rebaine?"

Mellorin rose. "I want . . ." She swallowed once. "I want you to tell me about my father."

"You're joking."

"No, I'm not."

"You're crazy, then. Go away."

"Davro . . ." She rose to her feet, which brought her barely up to the giant's waist. "I don't know what drove you to live out here, apart from your family and your tribe. And I don't *need* to, to know that it can't have been an easy choice.

"But it was a choice *you* got to make. I don't know my father anymore—I suppose I never really did—and that's not something I chose. It's something that was *taken* from me. I know he's not your favorite topic . . ." She smiled. "Understatement, again?" she asked.

Despite himself, Davro grinned back at her.

"Please, Davro, just tell me *something* about him. Then, I promise, I'll go."

The ogre set down the bucket with a deep sigh and dropped into a crouch. "All right," he agreed. "But just a little bit."

"Thank you."

"I suppose," he began, deep in thought, "it makes—" He yawned deeply, his head splitting into a gaping chasm of chipped teeth and jagged tusks. "I'm sorry, it must've been—" Yawn. "—a more tiring day than I—" Yawn. "—realized. It makes most sense—" Yawn, a few blinks. "—to start with—"

The ogre toppled with a crash that set a dozen startled sheep to bleating. His snores, sufficient to shake the earth and shame the thunder, began instantly.

An unwary mind, and a few moments of contact.

Mellorin's body flexed, bulged, and melted like candle wax. A moment of hideous distension and impossible shapes, and then Kaleb stood in her place, blinking rapidly as he acclimated to the change in height. Swiftly, he knelt at Davro's side, casting a second spell to keep the ogre deep in slumber. When he finished, he glanced around and found he remained alone.

"Hey! Are you two just going to leave me standing here with my bugger-stick in my hand, or were you planning on joining me anytime soon?"

A shuffling in the nearby grasses presaged a pair of silhouettes rising into view.

"I think I'm appalled. Must he say things like that?" he heard Mellorin ask plaintively.

"I don't know if he *must*," Jassion replied with unaccustomed humor, "but I've noticed that he very often *does*."

"Keep watch on him," Kaleb said as they neared. "He should be out for hours, but I've never tried anything quite like this. Fiddling with Rebaine's location spell *shouldn't* have any effect on the magics keeping him asleep, but let's not take chances."

And then, despite his insistence in calling them to his side, Jassion and Mellorin could do nothing but wait as Kaleb knelt over the ogre's chest and muttered his incantations.

"So?" Jassion asked as the sorcerer rose, his expression weary, more than an hour later. "Did it work?"

"I'm not . . ." Kaleb shook his head and leaned against the wall of the towering house. "Maybe. A little."

"How could it work *a little*?"

"Even with the two spells layered on each other, the trail's so tenuous I can barely feel it. I'm sensing a *slight* pull, but it's about as precise as pissing into a crosswind. I can tell you that he's somewhere between south and east of here."

"Ah. So we only have to search about a *third* of Imphallion, rather than all of it," Jassion groused. "At this rate, Rebaine will be dead before we ever get near him."

"He may not be the only one," Kaleb said.

"At least it's something," Mellorin interjected, not in the mood for another argument. "It's more than we had before."

Kaleb offered her a gentle smile.

"There's another option, isn't there?" Jassion asked. "As I recall, Rebaine was known to have had *four* lieutenants during the Serpent's War. We've only found three. We could try to find—Ellwyn? Something like that."

"I thought you were getting tired of traipsing all over the map hunting for these people," Mellorin said.

"I am. But I'm not sure how traipsing all over a third of the map looking for Rebaine is any better."

"Ellowaine."

The baron and the warlord's daughter both blinked. "What?"

"Her name," Kaleb said, "is Ellowaine. She's already been dealt with. She can't offer us anything new." And that, no matter how Jassion insisted and Mellorin cajoled, was all he would say.

"Fine!" Jassion, clearly, felt he'd had enough. "Let's conclude our business here, and we can be on our way." He moved toward the slumbering ogre, hand closing about Talon's hilt.

"No!" Mellorin hadn't even realized she'd spoken until the faint echo came back with the sound of her own voice.

"Oh, come *off* it!" her uncle snarled. "You want to snivel for the life of some random ogre, that's your call. I needn't understand it. But this is *Davro*! How many did he slaughter under Rebaine's orders? How many more will he kill if we let him live?"

"He doesn't look like he's all that interested in killing anymore," she noted, gesturing at the surrounding vale.

"This is not up for discussion," Jassion said coldly. "And *you* need to learn to think with your head, rather than your heart."

Gales of uncontrolled laughter burst from Kaleb's throat. He doubled up, clutching his stomach, and only the wall kept him upright. "That, coming from you," he gasped when he could finally breathe, "is hypocrisy that even the gods must envy. I expect that you've carved out a place of honor in Vantares's domain, where the entire pantheon will come to learn at your newly angelic feet."

Even beneath the chain hauberk, in the dim light of the moon and stars, they saw the baron's shoulders tense. His hands, as he raised Talon, vibrated with suppressed emotion.

"You," Kaleb said far more seriously, "are *not* going to kill that ogre. It is, as you said, not open to discussion."

"And why might that be, sorcerer?" Jassion demanded. At least for the moment, he'd stayed his stroke. "Surely not because you're hoping to win more of my niece's misdirected favors?"

Mellorin gasped, and there was no telling whether the spots of crimson across her cheeks were birthed by embarrassment or fury—or perhaps both. Kaleb held out a pacifying hand but otherwise remained focused on the baron.

"Because, m'lord Cretin, if we can't locate Rebaine in any reasonable amount of time, we may have to come back and repeat my efforts to track his spells back from Davro. And for that, he has to be *alive*."

They heard Jassion's ragged breathing as he struggled to decide.

"Look around you," Kaleb continued. "Davro's obviously not going anywhere. Once we've dealt with Rebaine, you can always come back and do whatever you feel needs doing. But for now—think with *your* head."

Jassion, with an audible hiss, slammed Talon back into its sheath. He spoke no word to either of them as he headed toward the horses, leaving his companions to hurry in his wake.

THE DARK NIGHT and mountain trails made for treacherous, nerve-racking travel, but they could not afford to make camp too near Davro's vale. It seemed unlikely that the ogre would come after them once he awoke, but the beast knew this terrain better than they, and it wasn't a risk any of them cared to take. The thought of a single sentry meeting up with him, while the others slumbered unawares, was the stuff of nightmares.

Albeit very *short* nightmares.

Jassion had gone some ways ahead, seeking a hollow or a clearing broad enough for them to bed down, and Kaleb took the opportunity to bring his mount alongside Mellorin's own palfrey.

"Could you really kill him?" he asked gently. She, at least, did him the courtesy of not pretending confusion.

"I don't know," she said with a sigh. "I don't even know if I actually want him *dead*. But I have to see him pay for what he did. I know that you and Jassion are planning to see that that happens, and I want to help—or at least to be there."

"Because of what he did to Imphallion? Or for abandoning you?"

"It's all the same thing," she insisted with a sidelong glare—one that answered the question far more truthfully than her words. Kaleb chose not to pursue it further.

"Thank you for, um, for back there," she said then, with a vague wave back the way they'd come.

Again he smiled at her. "For what? I was just following the most rational course."

"Of course you were," she said stoically, and then she, too, broke into a smile. "But are you sure it wasn't maybe, just a *little bit*, to earn my 'misdirected favors'?"

"Hideously misdirected," he told her. "But for them, I'd have done far more."

Driven by a single shared thought, they leaned over the narrow gap between the horses. Lips pressed tightly together, they drank deeply of each other, and for once, nobody appeared from nearby to interrupt.

Chapter Sixteen

SHE MARCHED THE CITY'S OUTERMOST STREETS, oblivious to the muttering and joking of the men in loose formation behind. She knew she could count on them to watch her back if trouble appeared, and that was all she asked. Beyond that, she cared as little for what they had to say as they did for her.

Nobody who'd ever met or even heard of this woman would have mistaken her, for she looked very much today as she had for over a decade of violence and carnage. Her blond hair was perhaps longer in back than once it was, tied in twin braids that reached to her shoulder blades, but it hung unevenly at the sides. She remained gaunt, almost to the point of appearing ill, yet more than strong enough to outmuscle enemies who outweighed her twice over. A pair of short-handled hatchets hung at her waist, and over her chain hauberk she wore, not the tabard of a true Cephiran soldier, but a simple crimson sash crossing her chest from the left shoulder. Clasped with a cheap tin gryphon, it was the standard "uniform" of all non-Cephiran mercenaries who served the invaders.

The mark of a traitor to Imphallion, some would say—a few *had* said, to her face—but if she cared, it never showed. What had Imphallion done for her?

Emdimir itself, in fact, had changed more in weeks than she herself had in years. The streets, recently so crowded with refugees that the dirt had practically been compacted into stone beneath uncounted feet, now hosted only sporadic traffic. Nowhere in Cephiran-occupied Imphallion did the populace enjoy those freedoms that the invaders had initially permitted their early conquests, such as Rahariem. No longer did citizens go about their business in greater numbers than their occupiers, living daily lives as though little untoward had occurred. No longer did Guildsmen and nobles of the region govern with only occasional nudges and directives from Cephiran officers.

No, the destruction of Rahariem's western gates, and the rise of the abortive insurgency, had shown the occupiers the error of mercy and kindness. Men- and women-at-arms—both Royal Soldiers of the Black Gryphon, and mercenaries of varying nationalities and scruples—patrolled the occupied cities in overwhelming numbers. Gatherings of Imphallian citizens were restricted to five or fewer, with violators immediately relocated to the constantly inflating work gangs, whether or not they were of proper age or health for heavy labor. Shops providing basic goods and services were permitted to remain open, but between the restrictions on public assembly and the fact that Cephiran soldiers took what they needed for whatever price (if any) they felt like paying, most merchants found it more cost-effective to keep their doors shut.

She'd heard rumors that a few stubborn pockets of resistance remained back in Rahariem, but they were little more than outlets for angry youths to hurl waste and scrawl defiant slogans. The fools seemed incapable of understanding, the mercenary mused, that far from doing any good or inspiring others to rise up, they were merely providing the invaders with the excuse and motivation to crack down all the harder.

The people in Emdimir and other more recently conquered communities were more pliable. But still, their movements were restricted, their curfews enforced.

Her patrol route took her along the impoverished and half-ruined neighborhoods, near the outer wall that, when faced by the Black Gryphon, had served as no defense at all. Most of the citizens had been moved away from the gates, either deeper into the city or out into temporary camps meant to ease Emdimir's overcrowding. Those few who remained worked daily, beneath the watchful eyes of Cephiran taskmasters, to reinforce those walls against possible Imphallian counterattack. Choked with the dust and sweat of ongoing construction, this was a particularly unpleasant part of town.

Which was precisely why she'd received this assignment. The Cephirans might *use* Imphallian mercenaries, but they weren't about to trust them with anything *important*. She scowled, swallowing a surge of resentful bile so familiar in flavor that it might have been a favorite meal. *After everything I did for them . . .*

"Captain Ellowaine!"

She spun on her heel, expression neutral. Even in those two simple words, she could hear the man's disdain—none of the Cephiran soldiers appreciated being assigned to a "filthy mercenary"—but at least she'd finally beaten it into their heads that they'd damn well better call her by rank.

"What is it, Corporal?"

Corporal Quinran pointed toward a dilapidated building farther along the packed dirt road, one scheduled to be torn down for raw materials in a week or two. It was a sad, sunken façade, the frowning windows and cracked wood forming the face of a tired old grandfather. She'd passed it any number of times on any number of patrols, and couldn't easily imagine what made it worthy of attention this time.

"What of it?" she asked.

"Just saw a man in rags slip through the front door, Captain."

"And?" Those poor souls still dwelling here were miserable enough; no reason to begrudge one whatever shelter he might find.

"I can't swear to it, Captain, but I think I saw a sword under his cloak. It was certainly jutting out like one, at any rate."

That brought a frown. Traveling under arms was another prohibition the Cephirans had heaped upon their conquered territories. Any citizen caught with a blade larger than an eating utensil was risking far worse than assignment to the work gangs.

"All right," she said. "It could be anything, but we'll check it out." Then, in the probably futile hope of thawing out *some* of their working relationship, "Nicely spotted, Corporal."

"Thanks, Captain."

She and Quinran hit the door shoulders-first, practically ripping the rotting wood from its hinges. Without waiting for their vision to adjust they darted aside, one each way, leaving the doorway clear for the crossbows of the soldiers behind. When they saw no one on whom to loose their bolts, Lieutenant Arkur and Corporal Ischina entered, carefully stowing their arbalests and drawing broadswords in their stead.

Ellowaine appeared briefly in the doorway and raised a hand toward the last man, Corporal Rephiran, still lingering outside. Palm, fingers upright, followed swiftly by a single finger pointing downward, then two pointing directly at him.

Stay here, watch for anyone who gets past us.

He nodded and stepped back, keeping his weapon trained on the doorway.

Rear guard established, vision adjusting to the gloom, Ellowaine took a moment to orient herself. A large entry chamber, coated in paint so faded that she couldn't guess at its original color, offered only a single exit other than the front door and an empty coatroom. What remained of a desk, its legs long since scavenged for firewood, slumped atop rat-eaten carpet. The air was pungent with old dust and older mildew, spiced just a bit by fresh urine.

Ischina sidled up to the far door and peered cautiously around the corner for just an instant before jerking her head back. Spotting no danger, she dropped into a half crouch and darted through for a closer look. Ellowaine moved toward the door, while the others gathered on either side.

"Hallway," Ischina whispered as she reemerged into the chamber. "Lots of doors, staircase at the far end. I'm guessing a cheap hostel, maybe a flophouse."

Ellowaine nodded. She'd seen the like before, and in her experience, it probably hadn't been much nicer *before* being abandoned.

"Whistles," she said simply. Instantly, the others produced, from within pouches or on thongs around their necks, plain tin tubes that produced a surprisingly sharp tone. She drew her own from a pocket on her belt and wrapped the thong around her wrist.

"Two by two. Quinran and I are upstairs. You do not, under *any* circumstances, let your partner out of your sight."

Three quick nods were all the acknowledgment she received, or required.

Slightly more gently—but only slightly—she continued. "Judging by the smell, more than a few vagabonds have been using this place. Try not to kill anyone unless you're certain they're a threat—but don't risk your skins for it."

More nods, and then she was off toward the stairs, Quinran falling into step behind. Even as they reached the steps, she heard the first door being kicked open back down the hall.

The stairs creaked and screeched like a cat under a rocking chair, and the entire structure quivered beneath their weight. Ellowaine, a hatchet now in each hand, winced with every step, but no amount of care could silence the rickety wooden banshees, so she'd little choice but to bear it. Gaps in the dust suggesting that someone else had come this way might have been days or even weeks old, but the broken spiderwebs hanging between the banister and the inner wall had to be more recent. Keeping silent, despite the stairs heralding their approach to all and sundry, she gestured at the webs with a blade. Quinran nodded his understanding and shifted his grip on his broadsword.

Below, Arkur and Ischina kicked in a second door.

The light faded as the captain and the corporal climbed higher. Presumably, most of the second floor's windows were shuttered or boarded. They slowed, hoping to give their eyes time to adjust, and scowled darkly at each other. They were a daytime patrol; none of them carried lamp or torch.

"If this was just some vagrant carrying a stick that you saw," she breathed at him in a voice below even a whisper, "you'll be digging latrine ditches for a week."

"If this is the other option," he whispered back, flinching away as another step screamed in the near darkness, "I might just *volunteer*."

A third door clattered open on the floor beneath them.

And something moved in the shadows above.

It was nothing Ellowaine had seen, or could put a name to. Just a sensation, a touch of breeze without benefit of an open window, a flicker of movement in the dangling cobweb. She froze, listening, halting her companion as he tensed to take another step.

Nothing. Nothing at all . . .

Except, just maybe, the faintest creak. It could have been the building itself, sighing and settling its aching joints. But so, too, could it have been the muffled protest of a floorboard buried beneath old carpet.

Weapons at the ready, Ellowaine and Quinran increased their pace, hoping now not for the stealth that the stairs had rendered impossible, but to reach the top before anyone could intercept them partway.

Nobody tried. They found themselves in a hall very much like the one below. Doors occupied the walls to either side. A few hung open, the wood dangling loosely from the hinges like hanged convicts, but most were firmly shut.

Again they looked at each other, then at the nearest door. Quinran shrugged, and Ellowaine made a flicking motion toward it. Hatchets in hand, she stood back, ready to strike as the corporal kicked.

Rotted wood gave way so easily he stumbled. A cloud of foul splinters wafted into the air, and the stench of mildew grew nigh overpowering, but the room was empty save for a splotched mattress and soiled sheets.

The same across the hall, and again in the room neighboring that. They were just turning toward the fourth door when Ellowaine drew abruptly to a halt.

"What is it, Captain?"

"Listen!"

A moment. "I hear nothing."

"That's just it!" She tilted her head, indicating the stairway, and Quinran understood.

Where were the sounds of Ischina and Arkur opening doors downstairs?

The corporal opened his mouth, but no answer crawled its way onto his tongue. They couldn't be taking a break, not so early in the process. Could they have run into trouble? What could have silenced them *both* before either could sound a whistle?

Ellowaine stood, undecided, but only for a span of heartbeats. Absently spinning her hatchets in small circles beside her, she stepped once more toward the stairs. "Watch my back."

She'd moved only a couple of paces before she realized that no sounds of footsteps followed her. Behind her, the door to a room they'd already searched slammed shut, hiding whatever lay beyond.

Of Quinran, or any life at all, the hallway offered no sign.

Ellowaine hit the door at a full tilt and dropped into a roll as it fragmented. Across the moldy carpet she tumbled, then back to her feet, blades at the ready.

Quinran crouched on the floor, holding one hand to the back of his head. A thin trickle of blood—not enough, Ellowaine noted with no small relief, to suggest a dangerous wound—welled up between his fingers.

For just an instant, she couldn't understand how the room could be empty. *Someone* had grabbed the corporal, struck him across the head to keep him silent, but where—?

To her right, nigh invisible in the artificial twilight, a low hole in the wall provided egress to the next chamber. She listened, but neither the thump of a footfall nor the creak of a board suggested any movement.

"Can you stand?" she asked softly.

"I can bloody do more than that." Quinran rose, lifting his sword from the floor beside him. "Where are the bastards?"

"Later. First, we're checking on the others."

The corporal frowned, but when Ellowaine headed for the stairs, he followed.

They bounded downward, at speeds one notch shy of reckless, and the steps unleashed a chorus of wails. It was easy enough to see where their companions' efforts had ceased: Just look for the last open door. Once they were off the shrieking stairs they slowed, progressing with weapons at the ready.

Only as they neared could they see the crimson smears leading into the nearest open room. They gagged as the swirling dust of neglect pasted the acrid and metallic tang of recent slaughter to their tongues, their teeth, their throats.

Ellowaine darted past the door, crouched low, and rose with her back to the wall. Quinran mirrored her posture on the opposite side.

One . . . two . . .

She spun through the doorway, hatchets whirling, the corporal at her back.

And all but slipped in the puddled gore.

"Good gods . . ."

The mercenary was certainly no stranger to violent death. It was the swiftness of it all, the fact that they'd heard nothing, that gave her pause.

Arkur lay just inside, apparently slain by a single blow that cleaved him cleanly from right shoulder to left hip—a hideous, jagged mirror of Ellowaine's own sash of rank. To judge by the drag marks, he'd been attacked in the passageway and hauled messily into the chamber.

Across the room, Ischina sprawled beside the decomposing mattress. Her blade lay beside her, shattered into steel splinters, and little remained of face and skull save a dripping ruin of mangled flesh. Largely hidden by the carnage, a tiny weed grew through the buckling floorboards. It wore an array of needle-like thorns as a crown, several of which appeared to be missing. Ellowaine knelt and found them protruding through the leather sole of Ischina's left boot.

And Ellowaine damn well knew witchcraft when she saw it.

She opened her mouth to bark an order at Quinran, but froze at the gaping shock on his face. His pupils flickered wildly from side to side, and then he was gone from the doorway.

Ellowaine followed at a run, rounding the corner just in time to see him reach the building's front door. He hauled it open, and she clearly heard his cry of "Get in here!"

"Corporal Quinran!" Then, when he reacted not all, "Gods damn it, Corporal!" She reached his side and hurled him against the wall by his shoulders. "What the hell are you doing?"

"Need help," he wheezed, even as Corporal Rephiran pounded up the steps and into the building, seeking targets for his crossbow.

"*My* call!" Ellowaine growled, shoving him once more into the wall for good measure before releasing him. "Don't you *ever* countermand my orders without checking with me first!"

"Understood," Quinran whimpered.

"Arkur and Ischina are down," she told Rephiran. "Enemies still unknown. We—"

She whirled at the sudden *thump*, watched one of the open doors drifting on its single remaining hinge—and allowed herself to breathe once more. It was just a feral cat, tortoise-haired. It stood in the hall-way, hissing at them, back arched and tail bushy.

From what was now behind her, where the last survivors of her squad waited, came a burbling, stomach-turning crunch. Again she spun, just in time to see Rephiran slide to the floor, brains spilling from his shattered skull. Quinran just shrugged, shook the worst of the gore from his sword, and lunged.

Ellowaine's hatchets rose in a perfect parry, catching the blade be-tween them and shrugging it to one side. With the rightmost she lashed out, and the treacherous corporal sucked in his breath as he leapt back, dodging the hatchet with nothing to spare.

Furious at the loss of her men, shamed that she'd never suspected the traitor in their midst, Ellowaine shrieked, leaping at her foe over Rephiran's mangled body. Her hatchets buzzed from all directions, a swarm of enraged hornets with lethal stings. Quinran backpedaled, and only the unnatural speed of his desperate parries kept his limbs at-tached. His body and face flickered as his concentration lapsed, and Ellowaine realized that poor Quinran, the *real* Quinran, probably lay dead upstairs. Well, she'd see who she fought soon enough . . .

And then she could only scream, leg buckling beneath her. With a strength and accuracy impossible in any normal animal, the alley cat had come up behind and sunk its teeth *through* the leather of her boot, into the flesh and tendon of her ankle.

She toppled, caught herself against the wall, and looked up just in time for the haft of her foe's weapon—revealed, now that the illusion was fading, as an axe, not a sword—to completely fill her vision. She felt the skull at her temple *flex* beneath the impact of the heavy shaft, and then the pain, along with the rest of the world, went away.

———————

The Prurient Pixie had, for Ellowaine, more unpleasant memories and restless ghosts on tap than it had any of the more traditional sorts of spirits. In her mind, overlaid across the sawdust- and dirt-caked floor of the common room, she still saw dozens of men laid out in rows, slowly dying of agonizing poison. Sitting amid the various drinkers, she saw friends long gone; over the din of conversation, she heard Teagan's boisterous laugh. The clink of every coin was a knife-thrust to her soul, a reminder of all she'd been promised, and lost.

And through every open door, she saw, for just an instant, a glimpse of that cursed helm, and the lying bastard who'd worn it.

No, given her druthers, she'd never have come back here, or to the town of Vorringar at all. But this was where he was, so if she would speak with him, here she must come.

He'd arrived at the Pixie first and had, rather predictably, chosen a booth far from, but with a clear view of, the door. (She wondered idly if it had been empty, or if he'd cowed someone into leaving.) He barely fit in the chair, and the mug of ale looked like a child's cup in his meaty fist. The razor-edged shield that made up the lower portion of his left arm rested on the table, doubtless leaving deep scores in the wood.

Their greeting had gone well enough, and they'd passed several pleasant moments in friendly reminiscence and talking shop about weapons and tactics. Unfortunately, when she'd finally steered the conversation around to her current needs, any luck Panaré had bestowed upon her swiftly ran out.

"Losalis, please. You know me. You know damn well I wouldn't ask anything of you—of *anyone*—if I wasn't desperate."

"I know," he told her in his deep baritone. "If it was up to me, Ellowaine, I'd have *already* brought you on. Nobody knows better than I do just how good you are."

"But it's not up to you." It was not a question.

"No. I have to clear any new commissions with the baron, and I can already tell you what he'll say. I'll try anyway, if you want me to, but it'll be a waste of your time to wait around for his answer."

"Why me," she asked him, "and not you?" Her tone was bitter, yes, but not at him. She blamed many for her fate—and one in particular above all others—but she would not make Losalis a scapegoat just because it was a fate he'd managed to escape.

"I've wondered about that, a little," he said. "Partly, I think, it's simply that I've had my reputation longer than you. Also, my company's a *lot* bigger. People are less willing to go without.

"But mostly? I'd have to suggest it's because you were with him inside Mecepheum. Sure, generals and commanders saw me leading his forces, but the nobles and the Guildmasters watched you standing *right beside him*. I don't think they're likely to forget that anytime soon."

Ellowaine nodded sourly. "It always comes back to Rebaine, doesn't it? I think I'd willingly put up with everything that's happened if I could just get my hands on him for a few minutes in exchange."

Losalis nodded noncommittally, and for a few moments they lost themselves in drink.

"Did you know," she said softly, "that I've lost half my men in the last four years? Not on the battlefield, I mean they just left. Loyal as they've always been, they wouldn't stick with a commander who couldn't find them work, and I can't blame them."

The larger mercenary leaned back, ignoring his chair's desperate creaks of protest. He had, indeed, known Ellowaine a long time—and he knew what she was asking, even indirectly, and how hard it must be for her.

"I can take them," he said with a surprising gentleness. "Not all at once—I don't think I can convince the baron I need *that* many new swords. But it'll provide work for some, and the rest are welcome to join my company when we start looking for our next contract."

For the first time in years, Ellowaine smiled and meant it. "Thank you, Losalis." *At least now I'm only failing myself, not them.*

"There might be something else I can offer you," he said, as though reading her thoughts or her future in the swirling suds of his tankard. "Nothing I'm *positive* about, mind you, just some whispers through the usual channels. Someone's putting an operation together, they're looking for Imphallian mercenaries, and

I don't think they're likely to care that you were part of Rebaine's campaign."

Ellowaine tilted her head. "*Imphallian* mercenaries?"

"Yeah, you'd need to do a bit of traveling. How do you feel about the kingdom of Cephira?"

"If they pay, I'll feel any damn way about them they want."

***

IT WAS, DISTRESSINGLY, THE THROBBING in her skull that convinced her she was alive. For long moments she didn't move, even to open her eyes. Mentally she ran through weapons drills and strategic puzzles, carefully examined a few randomly chosen memories, even took the time for some quick addition and multiplication. She found herself a bit slow, occasionally not as accurate as she'd have liked, but eventually the proper answers and images swam to the fore through the churning tide of pain.

Satisfied that she'd likely sustained no permanent damage, she allowed her eyes to open. Although the light was dim, still it was nearly blinding, and she had to swallow hard to keep from vomiting.

But like her thoughts, her vision swiftly cleared.

Moving carefully, she examined what she could of her surroundings. She was inside one of the flophouse rooms—probably on the second floor, to judge by the sound sneaking in through the boarded-up window. Tiny, unseen things crawled beneath the outer layer of the mattress, causing unsightly bulges. She sat in—and, she realized as she attempted to move her arms, was bound to—one of the rickety chairs.

No, wait. Two chairs, back to back, so that she couldn't easily snap the wood. She grinned darkly. Whoever had taken her knew what they were doing.

But then, so do I.

She lifted her face to the ceiling and groaned, as though just waking up. It wasn't hard to fake the pain.

Behind her, the tip of her left braid dipped into her waiting hands. Digging swiftly with thumb and forefinger, she slid a sliver of metal from within the hair. It wasn't much, just a flattened, sharpened needle. But given sufficient time, it would do.

Even as she went to work on the ropes, she glared around the room. *Distract them, whatever it takes . . .*

"I don't know who you are," she began, "but you've made an enormous—"

And then he stepped into sight from the shadows, gently carrying that damn cat, and put the lie to her first words. She knew *exactly* who he was.

"It's not the way I'd have preferred for us to meet again, Ellowaine."

"Speak for yourself, Rebaine. I'll take my shot at you any way I can get it."

———————

UNNOTICED BY EITHER CAPTIVE OR CAPTOR, Seilloah abruptly tensed, her back arching slightly and her tail growing bushy as a squirrel's. Had she felt something, just then? Something in the air, or the ether? If only the pain would stop, if only she could concentrate, she'd be sure, but now . . .

No. Whatever it was, if it had been anything at all, was gone. Forcing herself to calm, she swiveled her ears to focus on the conversation once more.

———————

Ellowaine darted through a forest of wooden targets called simply the Thicket, hatchets carving chunks and splinters as she passed. Some hung limp, some swung side-to-side on creaking pendulums, and some were weighted so that anything but a perfect strike would send them spinning, slamming an arm of wicker painfully into an attacker's back.

Or so she'd been told. So far, she'd not triggered a one of them.

In fact, this wasn't really training so much as it was showing off, proving herself over and over to Cephiran officers she could easily have slain on the battlefield. She'd run through the exercise twice already *today*, and the only difference this time was that they'd removed the canvas ceiling, allowing the snows of winter to filter down and impede her footing.

It didn't slow her much, just made her shiver uncomfortably in those few seconds when she wasn't actively moving.

She came to the end of the Thicket and finished in a swift spin, dropping to one knee in the snow and striking up and back, sinking both hatchets into what would have been the lower backs of two enemy "warriors." And only then did she notice the man standing just beyond the array of posts, watching intently.

He was a burly fellow, wearing a thick black beard. In his youth, he might have resembled a bear clad in armor, but much of his bulk—not all, she could see that immediately, but much—had run to fat as age sank its claws into him. His hands, rough and callused, were crossed over a barrel chest that bore the crimson tabard of the Royal Soldiers of the Black Gryphon. Unlike the others Ellowaine had seen, however, his was trimmed in gold, both around the edges and surrounding the iconic gryphon.

"Good afternoon," he said without preamble. "I'm General Rhykus."

Ellowaine rose, offered a shallow bow, and sheathed the hatchets at her side. "I'm honored." She knew nothing of Rhykus, save that she'd heard the name and that he was one of only three soldiers to carry that rank in the royal Cephiran military.

Which, for the moment, made him her employer.

"Walk with me." He turned away, clearly accustomed to instant obedience.

For the sake of her coin purse, that's what she offered, falling into step beside him, her long legs easily keeping pace. She wasn't certain if he was gathering his thoughts or waiting for her to open the conversation, but after a few moments of crunching through shallow snow toward no apparent destination, she decided to take the initiative.

"I'm assuming you're not here to critique my performance in the Thicket. Sir," she added quickly. *That's going to take some getting used to.*

"Do you feel it needs critiquing?"

Ellowaine swallowed a flash of annoyance. "Not really. And I'm assuming if you did, you'd have said something."

"Just so." A few more steps. "You're the same Ellowaine who served under Rebaine during your nation's so-called Serpent's War?"

Her blood ran cold as the surrounding snows. Surely the Cephirans wouldn't hold that against her?

"I am," she said carefully.

General Rhykus nodded. "I normally have little personal interaction with our mercenaries," he told her.

"Should I be honored again? Or worried?"

The coal-dark beard split in a grin. "I see you're accustomed to speaking your mind. Few of my soldiers will. Not to my face, anyway.

"No, Ellowaine, you needn't worry. In fact, I require your assistance."

They crested a small rise, and Ellowaine saw a great pavilion before them. Even from here, she could feel the radiating warmth of a fire.

"Join me for a meal," the general invited. "There's much I would discuss with you."

"Such as?" she asked, still vaguely suspicious.

"Why, such as everything you can possibly remember about Corvis Rebaine."

"AND OF COURSE, YOU TOLD HIM everything," Corvis said disgustedly.

"Why not?" Despite her bonds, she matched him glare for glare. "You hardly provided me any reason for loyalty or affection."

'She's not wrong, Corvis. When it comes to loyalty, you pretty much

fall somewhere between a scorpion and, well, an even more unfaithful scorpion.'

He shrugged, so far as the cat in his arms permitted. It wasn't as though he was about to argue the point—not with her, and certainly not with himself. He saw Ellowaine's eyes dart past him as Irrial entered the room, saw them widen briefly in recognition. They'd never met, that much he knew, but doubtless the Cephirans had spread her description far and wide.

"Was it necessary," Ellowaine asked abruptly, voice hard, "to kill my men?"

Again, Corvis shrugged. "We needed to ensure that we'd have time alone to talk with you. And anyway, this is war."

"Oh, I see," she scoffed. "*Now* you're a patriot, are you?"

Corvis dropped to one knee so that he could look the bound prisoner in the face. "I've *always* been a patriot, Ellowaine. Don't ever think otherwise."

The cat, perhaps for no better reason than to break the silence, leapt from his arms to the floor between them.

"How did that thing bite through my boot, anyway?" the mercenary demanded.

"Magic," the cat said. Corvis was morbidly amused to see Ellowaine jump, but her shock didn't last.

"Ah, I see. Seilloah?"

"Ellowaine." The witch didn't offer an explanation for her current form, and Ellowaine obviously knew better than to ask.

"So tell me," Corvis began, "why did . . . ?" He paused, watching carefully as the prisoner shifted in the chair. She might have just been repositioning herself after the sudden start, but then again . . .

Scowling, he moved behind her, saw a swift glint of metal that she couldn't *quite* hide in her fist. He reached out and yanked the sharp-edged needle from her fingers, ignoring the profanity she spit his way.

"Where the hell were you hiding *that*?" he demanded. He didn't really expect an answer, which was a good thing, since she clearly wasn't about to offer any. He leaned in, examining the ropes, and decided with a soft grunt that she hadn't cut through enough of the thick hemp to matter. He casually flicked the steel shard into a distant corner and stood before her once more.

She raised her face to the ceiling, chewing on the inside of her cheek and mumbling a few more curses, before looking his way once more.

"Tell me," he said again, "why General Rhykus wanted to know about me. And Ellowaine, please don't waste my time, or yours, by lying."

"If you think you could tell, you're kidding yourself," she said. "But I've no need to lie. The truth is, I really don't know. He obviously had his reasons, given how thoroughly he pressed me on it. He got me to remember details I hadn't even realized I'd ever known. But he never once told me *why*."

"And you didn't ask?" Irrial asked incredulously.

"Wouldn't have mattered. If he'd wanted me to know, he'd have told me. Besides, I'm used to following people without knowing the whole story. It's what I get paid to do." She stopped and glowered at Corvis. "What I *usually* get paid to do."

Corvis turned, first toward Seilloah at his feet, then Irrial behind him. The baroness shrugged, while the cat merely flicked her tail.

You've really got a way with women, haven't you? No wonder you can't seem to keep one.' Corvis would, in that moment, have gladly drilled an awl through his own temple if it meant digging out that *damn voice*.

"So what are we thinking, then?" Irrial asked. "Is the whole thing a Cephiran operation? To what end?"

"Distraction," Seilloah suggested. "Something to keep the Guilds and the nobles from countering their invasion?"

"Maybe." Corvis didn't sound convinced. "It seems awfully convoluted, if that's all it is, though."

Ellowaine leaned forward, so much as the ropes would allow. "You're talking about the murders. It wasn't you, was it?"

Again they glanced at one another, then Corvis nodded.

"I thought so. I couldn't imagine what you'd have to gain. Now I understand."

"And does it bother you?" the baroness demanded. "Knowing that you provided information that led to the murder of innocents?"

"Why would it?" the mercenary asked, her tone philosophical. "I'm a soldier; I kill. The Cephirans offered me work when nobody else would—thanks to *him*." She actually smiled at Irrial. "Whatever he's promised you for your help, lady, I'd suggest you count it in advance."

"No," Corvis said, only half listening. "Think of where the murders occurred, the fact that they targeted so many of the people connected to me."

Seilloah nodded, her whiskered snout wrinkling. "If the Cephirans could get into the Hall of Meeting like that, they wouldn't *need* this sort of deception. They could just take the government down and be done with it."

"They'd have to have Imphallian operatives, then."

"No," Irrial said slowly. "Not operatives. *Co-conspirators*. This feels very much like a political maneuver, albeit a bloody one."

And then she and Corvis turned to each other, the understanding that dawned on their features enough to light up the room.

"Yarrick," they both said at once.

"He wasn't just a collaborator," Corvis continued. "He was a *part* of this—whatever this is."

Even Ellowaine appeared to have gotten sucked into the discussion. "If you're right," she said, "if there is some sort of cross-border conspiracy, it couldn't just be a local Guildsman, no matter how potent. It'd have to go a lot higher."

"So what would the Guilds have to gain," Seilloah mused, "by cooperating with a Cephiran invasion?"

"Not *all* the Guilds," Corvis interjected. "I'm starting to think that's what some of these murders were about: Silence anyone who knows about what's going on but isn't willing to go along with it."

"And in the process," Ellowaine said, "provide a distraction in the form of the vicious 'Terror of the East.' Actually pretty neat, when you think about it." Then, at their expressions, "I know less about this than you do. I'm just speculating."

"And why," Corvis said, dark, suddenly suspicious, "might that be?"

The chair creaked as she shrugged. "Something to do while you've got me stuck here."

"I don't think so." Fists and jaw clenched as one. "You're *stalling*."

Seilloah bounded to the window, peering between the uneven boards. "There's a squad of soldiers clearing people off the street!" she hissed.

Ellowaine smiled brightly beneath their withering glares. "Oops," she said.

"I can see the spell," Seilloah whispered, studying their prisoner, "now that I know to look. Someone's been watching us through her, Corvis. They've known we were here since she opened her eyes. Arhylla damn it all, I *thought* I felt something! I should've made sure . . ."

Corvis nodded bleakly. "Let's get the hell out of here before they've finished assembling, then."

"We're not just going to leave her, are we?" Irrial demanded. Corvis actually flinched, startled at the bloodlust in the baroness's tone—until it struck him just how she must feel about an Imphallian siding with Rahariem's oppressors.

It was, however, a moot point. Even as he considered Ellowaine, still uncertain as to what he'd do with her, she rose from the chair. Shredded ropes fell from about her chafed wrists, and Corvis saw just a glimpse of a second needle clutched in one fist.

And as clearly as if she'd explained it to him, he understood. *Of course. One in each braid.*

He lunged, but she was already moving. Blood welled up beneath the ropes that wrapped her calves, but the chair legs snapped as she twisted. With her captors mere inches behind, she hit the boarded window at a dead sprint. Corvis was certain that some of the snapping he heard must have been bone as well as wood, but it didn't stop her. He watched, his lopsided expression settling somewhere between enraged and impressed, as she landed in a shower of splinters, rolled awkwardly across the street, and limped into the nearest alley, dragging a clearly broken leg behind. Just before vanishing into the shadows, she paused long enough to cast an obscene gesture back at the shattered window.

"Can we go after her?" Irrial asked.

"Not unless you want to face the entire Cephiran invasion force on our way out of here. If we leave now," he added with a sickly grin, "we'll probably only have to dodge about half of it."

"Where are we going?" Seilloah asked, leaping into Corvis's arms as he headed for the flimsy stairs.

"For now, anywhere that's not here. After that?" He shrugged, checking his headlong dash just enough to prevent the stairs from collapsing beneath him. "If this conspiracy really does involve some of the Guilds, we'll have to go to them to find out, won't we?"

"Not Mecepheum again!" Irrial protested.

"Unless we come up with a better idea." He hit the ground floor and began to run, hoping they could clear the street, hoping they could reach the horses, and the gate . . .

Hoping against hope that they could, indeed, come up with a better idea.

Chapter Seventeen

JASSION CROSSED THE ENTRYWAY at a deliberate pace, Talon at the ready. The thick carpeting muffled any incidental sounds he might have made, while the sundry tapestries, drapes, and patterns hanging on every available inch of wall throttled to death any potential echoes. Across the room and perhaps two strides back, Mellorin crept in a low crouch, heavy dagger clutched in her fist, a fearsome anticipation writ large on her face.

And behind them, emitting frustrated sighs like a depressed bellows and making no effort at stealth whatsoever, Kaleb followed.

"I'm telling you," he said, giving Jassion a violent start just as the baron had been reaching for the knob on the room's far door, "he's not here."

Jassion glared, and even Mellorin couldn't help but cast the sorcerer an exasperated look. "Will you *be quiet?*" the baron hissed.

"I rather doubt it. I haven't so far."

"Kaleb . . . ," Mellorin began, then visibly flinched, wilting at the sorcerer's glare.

They'd been passing through Vorringar when they heard the rumors: muttered tales that Rebaine had targeted the Weavers' Guild of Kevrireun for his latest rampage. Not merely the local Guildmistress, but most of her lieutenants, had been slaughtered in a quartet of vicious attacks—three by axe, one when his entire bedchamber was engulfed in roaring flames. And several times, those rumors claimed, passersby had spotted a towering figure in black-and-bone, lurking nearby immediately after the carnage.

It was—Jassion had been utterly convinced—the break they were waiting for. "People wouldn't just make up stories like this," he'd insisted. "*One* murder, perhaps, but *four?*" Even Kaleb's failure to detect Rebaine's presence using Mellorin as a focus for his spell hadn't convinced him otherwise.

"Isn't it possible," the baron had asked, "that he's found a way to block your 'blood divination' even once you've gotten close?"

"With *his* mastery of magic? I seriously doubt it."

"But it can be done?"

"Anything *can* be—"

"Then we go."

So they'd gone, traveling several days to the small and slowly dying city of Kevrireun. Missing stones marred the uneven streets; the buildings peeled and sagged like rotting fruit. Carelessly throwing both money and rank around him, Jassion either bribed or cowed witnesses, guards, even government officials into providing every detail of the murders.

Yes, m'lord, Rebaine had been spotted at two of the scenes.

No, sir, he'd never attacked his victims in large groups.

Yes, the victims were all members of the Weavers' Guild.

Most of the remaining Guildsmen were now barricaded in their homes, protected by Kevrireun's ragtag militia. Embran Laphert, now the highest-ranking survivor, had closed down the Guildhouse and told everyone to go home—or into hiding—until further notice.

Despite Kaleb's continual protestations, Jassion had determined that investigating the Guildhouse itself was their next step. "Perhaps," he'd argued, "we can find some hint as to why Rebaine chose these poor fools as his latest targets." Mellorin, though not so quick to dismiss Kaleb's arguments, was sufficiently swept up in her uncle's enthusiasm. Once she'd agreed to go, the sorcerer had grudgingly followed.

Now they stood within the foyer of the Weavers' Guild Hall, one of the few such institutions left in Kevrireun. Jassion once more reached for the door, hurling it open and dashing into the hallway beyond. Kaleb irritably circled the room, examining the various tapestries— *Mount Derattus doesn't actually look like that*, he noted while passing one particular landscape.

He knew damn well that these murders weren't part of the pattern, no matter *what* the witnesses claimed to have seen. But how to convince the simpleton and the brat without explaining *how* he knew, *that* had so far eluded him. Nor was the summons that had been ringing in the confines of his own skull for the past ten minutes, deafening as any church bell, making it any easier to think.

He expected this sort of nonsense from Jassion, but that Mellorin had gone along with it, had refused to heed his words . . . His fists trembled in frustrated fury, and the nearest tapestry actually began to smolder around the edges. Seething, his thoughts darker than the armor for which they searched, Kaleb moved to catch up with the others.

Their exploration took them through workrooms replete with looms and spinning wheels of every conceivable design, including some that hadn't seen regular use for centuries. Up thickly carpeted stairs they trod, through heavily locked chambers containing a fortune in textiles and rare yarns and intricately woven garb, and finally into a hallway of opulent offices.

It was here that Jassion insisted they split up, each searching an office for anything even remotely useful. The sorcerer welcomed the opportunity for solitude, however brief, partly to avoid speaking with the baron whose obstinacy was driving him inexorably mad . . .

And partly because it finally offered the chance to silence that damn summons, even if it meant turning his attentions toward a *different* idiot.

Kaleb slipped into one of the chambers, garishly decorated with an array of mismatched stitchings, and slumped into the thickly upholstered chair behind the desk. "What?" he rasped under his breath.

"*Gods damn it all, Kaleb! I've been trying to make contact!*"

"I'm very well aware—Master Nenavar," he added quickly, as he felt the first stirrings of pain rack his body.

"*I am not accustomed to being ignored.*"

"We can work on that." Then, before the old coot could grow even more irritated, "I was with the others. Couldn't get away. Jassion's a bit dense, but I think even *he* might notice if I started to talking to myself."

Nenavar remained silent. Kaleb leaned back in the chair and propped his feet up on the desk.

"I assume you had some reason for contacting me other than just wanting to yell at me?"

"We've found him."

Kaleb's feet hit the floor with a resounding *thud;* he was out of the chair before the echo faded. *"What?* Where?"

"He triggered the ward that I ordered placed on Ellowaine. Apparently he finally figured out that she was our initial source of intelligence on him."

"He's in Emdimir, then?"

"No. Nearby, though." Kaleb heard the accustomed exasperation in the old voice, but for once it wasn't directed his way. *"It took the Cephiran sorceress who'd been scrying on Ellowaine over an hour to reach me. Godsdamn incompetents. I told Rhykus to let me cast the spell, but no, it had to be one of his people. Military paranoia at its finest.*

"Anyway, the Cephirans are dogging his heels, and even if he enchants the horses again, there's a limit to how far he can push them. We should be able to maintain at least a general idea of his location. Be ready to move swiftly to intercept; I'll get back to you when we're certain which way he's heading."

Kaleb nodded, though he knew Nenavar couldn't see him. "And what would you like me to tell Baron Tantrum and She-Rebaine?"

But there was no answer. Nenavar's presence was gone from his head.

No worries. He'd find something.

"I'VE FOUND SOMETHING."

Kaleb's voice in the hallway was enough to conjure Jassion and Mellorin from their own offices. They appeared in twin swirls of parchment, and Kaleb could only shake his head at the detritus they were leaving behind. "It's a good thing we weren't trying to be subtle or any-thing," he told them. "It looks like you've been shearing parchment sheep in there."

Mellorin offered a grin that was at least *slightly* embarrassed, but Jassion—as usual—cared little for Kaleb's concerns. "You've found why Rebaine was interested in these people?"

"I've found an *answer*," the sorcerer said, so smugly that even his words seemed to turn up their noses in disdain. He held out a creased sheaf of parchments he'd found (with the aid of a few judicious spells) in the office files. "It appears," Kaleb told them, "that the late Guild-mistress had commissioned a private investigation of her own. You might like to know what she found." The baron and the warlord's daughter leaned in, scanning the cramped writing, and when they spoke once more, they spoke as one.

"Son of a bitch!"

HALF AN HOUR LATER, THEY STOOD gathered in the living room of a modest house on Kevrireun's south end. What had once been a low table was now so much kindling, books and scrolls were scattered about the chamber, and one Embran Laphert—a bald, broad-shouldered fellow who currently led the Weavers' Guild, despite look-ing like the most unlikely weaver imaginable—hung from the wall, held aloft by Kaleb's magics. He was clad only in a nightshirt, and couldn't cease babbling long enough to form coherent speech.

Neither Jassion nor Mellorin currently had a single glance to spare him. They were too busy marveling at what lay beyond the open door to an inner room.

"You have *got* to be joking," Jassion finally said.

A small workbench held a large battle-axe with several simplistic but skillful engravings across the blade. Beside it slouched a fat wineskin that smelled, not of wine at all, but of lantern oil.

And behind that, on a large wooden rack, stood a suit of armor, mod-eled after the most ornate of knightly plate. It had been coated in a black lacquer, the breastplate and spaulders adorned with a few shafts of what appeared, up close, to be iron painted ivory white. To the visor of the helm was bolted the face and jawbone of a human skull.

"It's actually pretty clever," Kaleb said, "in a 'limited intelligence' sort of way." He offered Laphert a friendly smile. "I'm curious: When you were drummed out of the Blacksmiths' Guild, wouldn't it have made more sense, given your talents, to become a jeweler or copper-smith? Weaving seems like a stretch."

It was hard to interpret an answer, given the fellow's blubbering and sobbing, but he *seemed* to be telling them that, in a city as small as Kevrireun, those Guilds fell under the same general oversight as the blacksmiths' did.

The sorcerer nodded. "So when you learned of the report someone had made to the Guildmistress, about you embezzling from your for-mer Guilds, you figured you could protect yourself and take over the local branch of the Guild in one stroke. And you had a perfect candi-date to take the blame."

Not actually all that dissimilar, he mused inwardly, *to some other scheme I could mention.*

"Let's go," Jassion muttered, irritable but subdued. "We've wasted our time."

"I believe," Kaleb told him with a jaunty grin, "that it's actually *you* who have wasted our time."

Jassion swept through the door, slamming it behind him.

"Not," Kaleb continued, his grin faltering as he turned toward his other companion, "that he was the only one." Mellorin blushed and stared at her feet, her hair falling over her face in a flimsy curtain. She mouthed what might have been *I'm sorry*, though he couldn't see well enough to be certain, and went after her fuming uncle—perhaps hop-ing to calm him down before he broke someone, perhaps fleeing from Kaleb's disappointment.

As soon as she was gone, all trace of humor or hurt—all trace of *humanity*—dropped from Kaleb's features. Muttering a spell, he moved with supernatural speed, gathering pieces of the false armor and strap-ping them to the man who struggled and flopped against the wall.

Only when the entire ensemble was complete did Kaleb step away. He cast a second enchantment, ensuring that none of the sounds—or screams—to follow would penetrate the house's walls. And then a final spell, the price of irritating a vengeful sorcerer.

Kaleb headed back toward the hostel in which they'd acquired rooms, leaving the armor—and the man trapped and silently shrieking within—to melt slowly into a puddle of slag.

"WEST."

Kaleb rolled his eyes so hard he could practically *see* the voice inside his head. "Of *course* he's going west," he whispered as he leaned out the window of the austere little room. "You said he was in Emdimir. Unless he's decided to liberate Rahariem on his own—or invade Cephira itself—there's nowhere to go *but* west."

Nenavar's sigh came clear through the psychic link. *"Don't be tiresome, Kaleb. It's all our Cephiran friends have reported to me—and anyway, it's a start. Get moving, and I'll give you more when I have more."*

Kaleb left the room, gathering his possessions with a single swoop of his arm. A second wave of his hand unlatched the door to the chamber beside his, and he slipped inside. For a moment he stood, watching the slumbering figure, scarcely visible in the light of a single candle.

Mellorin moaned softly in her sleep and then, perhaps feeling his attention upon her, sat bolt upright on the lumpy mattress. She gasped, pulling the sheets to her chin—an amusing reaction, thought Kaleb, since her slip was more modest than some formal gowns.

"I'm sorry I startled you," he said softly.

"Kaleb, what's wrong? Is . . ." She glanced through the narrow gap in the shutters. "It's the middle of the night."

"I know, but we have to get moving. I'll explain when I've woken Jassion. You'd better get dressed."

"A-all right."

Nobody moved.

"Um, Kaleb?"

"Damn," he said, weighting the word with as much exaggerated disappointment as he could manage. She smiled, despite herself, and Kaleb could not help but return it—for it seemed unlikely, now, that he would ever need suffer a repeat of her earlier defiance. He turned away, moving toward the third room as Mellorin began to change.

———

JASSION HAD BEEN LESS sanguine about being awakened in the dark and silent hours of the morning, but Kaleb's news mollified him quickly enough.

"How?" the baron demanded as he darted around the room like an angry hummingbird, trying to dress himself for travel and gather up his belongings without so much as a second wasted in hesitation.

"The spell on Davro," Kaleb lied. "The tug's gotten a lot stronger."

"I thought you said it couldn't pinpoint him like that," Mellorin said from the doorway.

The sorcerer shrugged. "I also said I'd never attempted to backtrack a spell like this. Maybe it fluctuates. Maybe he's trying to use it to find Davro, or someone else. Hell, maybe he's picked up on my tampering and he's laying a trap."

Jassion finally paused in his efforts. "And if so?"

"Then we move carefully. It's still taking us where we want to go."

"Keep in mind," he continued as Jassion resumed his efforts, "that I'm not claiming to know *precisely* where he is. I think I can get us close enough to where my other divinations—*our* others," he corrected with a glance at Mellorin, "can pinpoint him." *Actually, Nenavar and the Cephirans can guide me close enough to where the blood-magic can pinpoint him. But you don't need to know that just yet.* "Still, we're talking a lot of ground, and he's not exactly staying put." There was just enough emphasis on those last words to inspire the baron to redouble his efforts, and he stood ready to leave but a few moments later.

"We have to stop on the way out," Kaleb told him, "and acquire blinders for the horses."

Two jaws dropped.

"You just said we had to hurry!" Jassion protested.

"And there aren't any leather-goods shops open at this time of night," Mellorin added.

"Then we break in and steal them. Or leave sufficient coin to pay, if you'd prefer. But trust me, they're necessary, and they'll prove more than worth the time they take to acquire."

And again, as was becoming a habit that irritated Mellorin and drove Jassion up the wall more swiftly than Kaleb's telekinesis, the sorcerer refused to explain any further.

IT WAS AN HOUR, several miles, and three sets of blinders later that they finally got their answer. The road from Kevrireun wasn't a true highway, but was sufficiently maintained that walking the horses in the dark had proved merely inconvenient, rather than dangerous. Owls and crickets called from afar, growing silent as the travelers approached, and the late night hours were just chilly enough to bring a shiver to the skin.

Not long after the lingering lights of Kevrireun had vanished behind them, Kaleb spotted a small knoll up ahead. Handing his reins to Jassion without a backward glance, he jogged ahead to the top of the rise, whispering a spell to enhance his sight. It wasn't much of a vantage point, but it'd do for a start.

There he waited until his companions caught up. Jassion hurled the bridle back at him, and only Kaleb's swift reflexes prevented them from lashing his face like a whip.

"Do I *look* like a servant to you?"

Mellorin snorted. "You should know better than to give Kaleb an opening like that."

The sorcerer ignored both of them as he handed around the blinders. "Put these on," he instructed them. "On the horses," he added to Jassion, as though the baron could possibly have misunderstood. "You're shortsighted enough without them."

Once they were in place, Kaleb moved from animal to animal, adjusting the blinders to block *all* sight, rather than merely peripheral vision. "Hold the reins tight."

With a sickening lurch, they were *elsewhere*. The world dissolved, rather as though a divine painter had wiped a wet cloth across a backdrop of watercolors, and re-formed just as swiftly. Jassion and Mellorin both stumbled as the road vanished from beneath their feet, reappearing before they could fall.

And it was the same road, of that they were certain, but the surrounding trees and shrubs had changed. They stood on a flat stretch, rather than atop the rise, and they heard a chorus of night creatures silence itself mid-song. Mellorin swayed against the saddle of her palfrey while Jassion collapsed to one knee. The horses whickered in confusion, noses raised to sniff at foreign scents, but otherwise remained docile.

"Only a few miles, I'm afraid," Kaleb said casually. "The hills around here aren't really high enough to see any farther."

"What . . . ?" Jassion was clearly having trouble with the concept of syllables. "What did . . . ? What . . . ?"

Mellorin nodded sickly as she extended a hand to her uncle, the other wrapped tight about her saddle horn. "My thoughts exactly." Then, before Kaleb could answer, "You teleported us!"

"I did indeed."

Jassion struggled to his feet, opening his mouth to speak.

"Save your angry sputtering," Kaleb told him. "No, I can't take us to Rebaine, because I can only teleport to someplace I either know well, or I can see. And I didn't do it before because these short-range jumps are exhausting. It wasn't worth it, until now.

"Does that about cover it? Or did you have any other objections you wanted me to shoot down?"

"How long until we need to do that again?" Jassion asked, his face stiff.

"Not for a while. I need a few minutes to reorient myself, and we'll have to find another piece of high ground or I won't be able to see far enough to make it worthwhile." He smiled. "We could stop and boil some tea to calm your stomach, if you'd like."

Jassion yanked the blinders from his horse and began to walk.

"I don't think he likes you very much," Mellorin whispered, only half-joking, as she and Kaleb followed.

"Oh, good. I'd hate to think I'd been wasting my time." Then, at her expression, "I'm sorry, Mellorin. Your uncle just *really* rubs me the wrong way."

"I think a lot of people do."

"True. Not you, though." Kaleb couldn't help himself. "In fact, I'm really hoping for the opportunity for you to rub me the right—"

He choked off as Mellorin deliberately trod on his toes.

Yards of dirt-covered road—and then scores of yards—passed beneath their feet in relative silence, broken only by the scuff of hooves and feet, the rustling of leaves in the breeze.

"What's wrong?" he finally asked. His voice drew her focus from the passing trees.

"Kaleb, I'm not sure I should be here."

"What? Why not?"

She shook her head, gazed morosely down at her feet. "Do I even want to find him? I've told myself for years that I deserved answers, that *he* deserved some measure of justice. But . . . Gods, I can't even imagine . . . What could he possibly say, what could *I* possibly *do*, that would make everything right?"

"Not a thing." Kaleb reached out, took her hand in his. Her skin was cool to the touch, the night air chilling the faint sheen of nervous perspiration. "This isn't about making things 'right.' There *is* no 'right,' not with him. All we can do is ensure he hurts no one else."

"Maybe I don't want to be the one to do it," she whispered, refusing to look up. "Maybe I'm better off with my memories of Cerris untainted by Corvis Rebaine."

"They're the same man, Mellorin. No matter how much you might wish otherwise. And you'd never be able to live with yourself if you decided to spend the rest of your life in ignorance—or if he caused more harm that you could have helped prevent." He paused. "I wish I could promise I'd never let him hurt you—"

Finally, her head came up. "My father would never—"

"Not even if you were trying to kill him?" Then, as her face fell,

"Actually, I really don't think he'd try to *physically* hurt you. But yes, he *would* hurt you. He already has." He reached out, wiped a single tear from Mellorin's cheek. "I can't promise he never will again. But I *can* promise to help you deal with it—and I can promise that you're strong enough to handle it."

"Am I? I'm not so sure anymore."

Kaleb smiled. "I'm a sorcerer. It's my job to know these things."

Mellorin could offer only a shallow smile, but after a moment she shifted closer. For many miles they walked, hand in hand, shoulder-to-shoulder, until the time came to teleport once again.

Chapter Eighteen

GRUNTING WITH THE EFFORT, Corvis yanked Sunder from both the Cephiran body and the rock face beyond in which the demon-forged blade had embedded itself, and made himself ignore the sensation as the weapon gave an almost erotic shudder. Powdered stone and the metallic tang of blood tickled his nostrils, but he lacked even the energy for a proper sneeze. Just moving his head was a struggle as he surveyed the latest in countless scenes of carnage.

Half a dozen bodies, made crimson by both wounds and tabards, sprawled in the dust. A few warhorses stepped carefully between them, awaiting new orders that would never come. Some way back, at the edge of the tree line, the more skittish, less well-trained mounts pranced nervously, disturbed by the scents of death.

For two days now, Corvis and Irrial had sought some compromise between stealth and speed. They chose back roads and even the occasional cross-country gallop rather than the main highways, rode well into the night, and holed up in overgrown copses to placate their fatigue with a few hours' slumber. And still the Cephirans were everywhere, ubiquitous as ants. Every night, they spotted the gleam of campfires in the distance. Every day, they picked their way through fields of dead horses and dead men, littered with broken armor and shattered blades, redolent of old blood and new rot. Irrial's predictions, however cynical, had been spot-on: Torn banners suggested that these were all that remained of the brave forces fielded by those Imphallian nobles desperate enough to take a stand. And to their credit, they'd taken a great many Cephiran soldiers with them, but not nearly enough. A patriotic gesture, the fielding of these tiny armies, but a futile one. There seemed no end to the crimson tabards.

This patrol was the fourth—fifth? Corvis had lost count—that they'd already been forced to battle, and they'd outrun or hidden from half again as many.

Damn it! Scattered as the Cephirans must be, to cover so much terrain and still maintain their hold on the cities, they *had* to be spread thin. If the Guilds had just gotten off their asses and contributed, the Imphallian soldiers might've actually *accomplished* something, instead of just smashing themselves to pulp against the Cephirans like birdshit on cobblestones!

'*My, how poetic. "Birdshit" are they, Corvis? And you always used to think so highly of people . . .*'

He strove, as always, to ignore that voice. Instead he watched Irrial sink exhaustedly to the earth, back pressed to the slope of one of the region's scattered foothills and rock formations, weeds of stone sprouting from Daltheos's garden. Her eyes were dark and sunken, her hair hanging limp, and though she tried to hide it, Corvis could see she favored her left arm where, just yesterday, a Cephiran broadsword had split muscle from bone. Seilloah had done her best to heal the injury, but in her current state, her magics weren't quite up to completing the task.

The witch herself lay slumped over a rock, paws dangling, tongue lolling in an uneven pant. A smattering of open sores beneath mats of fur oozed a constant trickle of yellowed pus and the sickly sweet scent of disease.

And Corvis knew damn well that he was no better off. The face he'd seen that morning, reflected in a small pond at which they'd halted to rest, was hollow, skin grey with fatigue. His neck and back ached as though the horse had been riding him, rather than vice versa, and it took him longer and longer to catch his breath after each engagement.

'*Crybaby. I'm feeling just fine.*'

Axe trailing in the dirt like a child's toy, he staggered over to the others and collapsed, badly scraping his left palm. The pain scarcely registered; just another complaint among many.

"We can't keep this up," he wheezed, gulping for air.

Irrial managed what was probably meant as a shrug. "What choice have we?"

Corvis nodded, frowning. They had no idea what territory was whose around here, how far the invaders had moved beyond Emdimir. Worse, some of the patrols seemed to be hunting them *specifically*; they might even pursue beyond Cephiran lines. Clearly, whoever in the ranks of the Black Gryphon had been studying Corvis Rebaine— General Rhykus, Ellowaine had said—didn't want them escaping with what they'd learned.

On the back roads, it would still be days before they reached any major Imphallian cities, before they could be *certain* they'd moved beyond the reach of the Black Gryphon's claws. On the main highways, it would take less than one—assuming half the invading army wasn't spread out along the way.

Either way, they'd have to fight both enemy forces and their own fatigue for every yard they covered. For long moments, Corvis stared at the rock above Irrial's head, ignoring the squawking crows and buzzing flies bickering over the bodies, ignoring the instincts that ordered him to get up and keep moving before another patrol happened by— ignoring everything but a weariness so heavy it threatened to crush him against the unyielding earth.

They'd still not decided if making for Mecepheum again was truly their best option, and right now the question brought nothing but the sting of bitter laughter to Corvis's throat. The idea that they'd survive to get anywhere *near* Mecepheum seemed about as likely as climbing to safety on beams of moonlight.

Climbing . . . ?

Corvis peered more intently at the rock face, then around at the hill—really just a spur of stone—against which they'd slumped.

"Most people fail to realize," he said didactically, "because they're so far apart from one another, that most of Imphallion's southern mountain ranges are actually all part of the *same* range. They're sort of a smaller mirror to the Terrakas Mountains."

The cat and the baroness looked at each other, then at Corvis. "Yes, that's true," Seilloah told him, using very much the same tone in which one might address a small boy who was proving just a bit slower than the other children. "I've seen the southern mountains, remember? I was with you when ..." She blinked, her back arching and tail growing bushy. "Corvis, what are you thinking?"

He gestured awkwardly with Sunder, first at the stony protrusions around them, then toward the southwest where, after some distance, the rocky hills grew substantially more common. "I was just wondering," he said, "if there's any possibility that these hills here are in any way connected."

"You're not serious!"

'Oh, he's serious. He's just mad as an inbred hatter.'

"If you've got another idea, Seilloah, now would be a great time. Actually, yesterday would be even better."

"Give me a few minutes," the cat growled. "I'll come up with *something*. What in Arhylla's name are you planning to *offer* them, anyway?"

"Whatever I have to," he told her, rising to his feet with a low groan.

"I'm *so* sorry to interrupt," Irrial said peevishly, "but would it be too much to ask that one of you tell me what the hell we're talking about?"

"We're talking," Corvis said, limping over to gather two of the horses, "about finding allies."

"Who very well might save us the trouble of fleeing the Cephirans by killing us themselves," Seilloah added darkly.

EIGHT HOOVES pounded over what had petered out into little more than a game trail, sending twin plumes of dust into the air behind them. They moved with the rumble, not of thunder, but of an earthquake, a constant and unbroken roar—for they ran with a speed unseen in nature, spurred not by their riders' boot heels but by the prod of Corvis's enchantment. Corvis and Irrial hunkered down, squinting against the wind and the sting of the horses' manes in their faces, devoting their attentions entirely to holding on. On occasion, amid the deafening cacophony, Corvis thought he heard a plaintive, feline yowl from the depths of his leftmost saddlebag.

The scrub and dried grass along the road blurred into a thick carpet. The trees were a solid wall, until the riders moved far enough into the rocky terrain that there were none. The occasional battlefields of dead knights and infantry become tiny pools of metal hue, gone almost before they could reflect a single gleam at the passing travelers. More than once they shot past a Cephiran outrider who could only lift his horn and hope to warn his companions up ahead; the soldiers might as well have tried to slap a ballista bolt from the air as to impede the riders' headlong plunge.

From the horizon's edge, the first of Imphallion's southern hills— *true* hills, these, not the rocky lumps through which they'd been riding— drew ever nearer, ships of stone on a sea of cracked earth. From within those hills, barely visible, crimson-clad soldiers rose and lifted longbows toward the sky. Unprepared as they were for the unnatural speeds at which their enemies pounded toward them, the distant horns of their scouts had warned them to stand ready.

Arrows arced up and out, graceful as a flock of raptors, and plunged earthward in a rain of wood and steel.

And Corvis, his body a tangled knot of agonized strands, his head heavy with exhaustion, lifted Sunder from his side and drank from the power of the Kholben Shiar.

Still he did not unleash the *full* might of the demon-forged blade; he never had, and he hoped, swore, even prayed he never would. But he delved now as deep as he ever had, and his mind cringed from the weapon's lustful, sadistic howl. He felt the surging of infernal magics flow through him, until he thought he must scream as the blood threatened to boil within him. A veil of fire shrouded his senses, so that he could see only a handful of yards—but within that distance, his sight was that of the gods. To him, every pebble that lay upon the earth, every blade of grass, even the currents of the wind, were painfully clear. In his ears, he heard the hoofbeats of the horses, not as a constant rumble but as separate and distinct sounds, the steady beat of a slow drum.

When the arrows fell around him, they fell not as a rapid rain but as the light drifting of snow. He rose in his stirrups and it was nothing to him, nothing at all, to reach out with Sunder and sever them from the sky before they could draw so much as a drop of blood.

Without pause they were gone, past the slack-jawed archers and deep into the shallow, winding gorges of the stone-faced hills.

Corvis dropped from his horse and advanced along a narrow pathway, casting about for any sort of hollow, cave, overhang, *any* entrance into the rocky depths. Internally he wrestled with the power flowing through him, struggling to shove it back into the weapon in his fist. Like a slow tide it receded, leaving burns across his soul.

He had just enough time, as his body yielded to the searing pain and he felt himself crumple limply to the earth, to hope that the others would have better luck finding shelter than he had.

———

CONSCIOUSNESS AND VISION RETURNED as one, and Corvis discovered a cat in his face.

"How are you feeling?" she asked.

"Sweet merciful gods aplenty, Seilloah, what the *hell* have you been *eating?*"

The cat nodded and turned away, leaving Corvis to his gagging. "He's all right!" she called out.

A set of footsteps—Irrial's, of course—drew near, and Corvis took a moment to orient himself. He was lying atop his blanket at the rear of what, so far as he could see in the dim light, was a remarkably shallow cave, little more than an impression in the stone sort of like a sideways bowl. He was naked from the waist up, unless one counted Seilloah sitting on his chest. He shifted his weight, and discovered that the blanket beneath him was soaked with sweat.

That realization brought a sudden awareness of a bone-deep ache that covered his body like a shroud, and he couldn't quite repress a groan. "Maybe not *entirely* all right," he admitted to Seilloah through pale, chapped lips.

"You were clinging to life by a single fingertip, Corvis. That damn thing burned you out from the inside. You're lucky I managed to heal you even *this* much."

"I've been lucky to have you do a lot of things for me, Seilloah. Thank you."

The cat smiled—rather a disturbing image in its own right—and then Irrial was kneeling beside them. He craned his head and discovered that the faint light he'd noted earlier was the result of a tiny campfire, barely more than two crossed torches, in the midst of the cave.

"I've never seen anyone move like that," she said, pressing a wet rag to his forehead. "Was that the same spell you used on the horses?"

"No." He waved a finger at Sunder, lying some few feet beside him. "*That.*" Then, blinking, "Where *are* the horses?"

"Gone," Seilloah told him. "They were dying. We pushed them too far under your spell. I thought it best to walk them some ways before they keeled over, lay down some false trail."

"Damn."

"Yeah. Your plan better work."

'*We're reliant on* your *plan? Well, shit. I'm not even* real, *and even* I'm buggered.'

Corvis struggled to sit up. "We don't have much time before they find us. This cave's not that deep, and . . ." His eyes widened as he realized the implications of the fire.

"Relax, Corvis. From the outside, the cave looks just like any other span of rock." She lifted a paw, licked it and ran it over her head. "I *taught* you some of your best illusion spells, remember?"

He smiled and allowed himself to lie back once more. "How long do we . . . ?"

"Long enough. You need to be rested for what's to come. I'll wake you if I think time's getting short."

Corvis's smile widened further, but he was asleep before he could sculpt his gratitude into words.

———

FEELING A LOT MORE RESTED, but only a bit better overall, Corvis moved about the cavern on hands and knees, alternating between scrawling strange sigils on the rock with a lump of charcoal and complaining about what the stooped posture was doing to his back. He was once again fully dressed, and everything the travelers owned was packed and ready to go. "When we move," he'd warned, "we may have to move quickly."

Every now and again Seilloah would rise up from a puddle of fur, totter awkwardly and in obvious pain across the floor, and point out a spot where Corvis had misaligned a design or muddled a rune. (At which point, of course, the echo of Khanda in his mind would mock him unmercifully.) Irrial, still not entirely certain what was going on and a bit put out that they'd not deigned to explain, hovered to one side and occasionally fed another stick into the meager fire.

And then she jumped so violently she nearly swallowed her own eyes as Corvis, in a single swift motion, rose to his feet and drove Sunder into the nearest wall. The crunch reverberated vacantly throughout the cave, but it was the subsequent screech as he worked the enchanted blade from the stone that *really* set hair and teeth on edge, gnawing on the fringes of mind and soul like a maddened beaver.

"Buggering hell, Rebaine! What in the gods' names are you *doing*?"

Corvis froze in mid-swing. "Why, Lady Irrial, wherever did you learn such language?"

"Probably from spending—" She paused, wincing, at the second crash, and then the third. "—spending too much godsdamn time with *you*!" Another crash, a second wince. "Would you *stop that*!"

He glanced at the small chunk he'd carved from the stone, then down at the powdered rock at his feet. "Sure, that's probably enough. I—ow!"

For several moments he hopped on one foot, waiting for the pain to ebb from the other. "What was *that* for?"

Seilloah spat out a few strips of leather. "For not warning me. These ears are *sensitive*."

"Fine! Fine, I'm sorry. I should've told you it was coming."

"I believe I just said that." And, simultaneously, '*I believe she just said that.*'

This was not, Corvis knew without even taking the time to ponder it, an argument he was likely to win. "Irrial," he said instead, "I need a gem."

"What?"

"A gem. Diamond, emerald, doesn't matter, though more valuable is better."

"I don't—"

"I know you took a *few* bits of jewelry from Rahariem."

The baroness frowned. "And you think you're just entitled to them?"

"Consider it fair price for escaping here alive. Unless you don't think it's worth the cost? You're welcome to take your business elsewhere . . ."

Muttering a few more of those words that she must have learned from Corvis, Irrial slipped a glinting blue ring from her finger and handed it over. He took it, flipped it over a time or two, and then snapped the sapphire from its setting and handed the silver band back to her.

"Your change, m'lady."

"Thanks ever so," she grumbled.

He took a few more moments, gathering rocks from around the cave into a circle, for reasons that neither Irrial nor even Seilloah initially understood. Only when he placed the tiny sapphire in the midst of it and raised his axe high overhead did they comprehend: He wanted to ensure the shards and powdered gem didn't get lost throughout the cave.

And it was a good thing he did, too, as he first struck the tiny target only obliquely, sending it skittering across the floor, bouncing and rolling until it fetched up against the edge of his work space. His entire posture daring either of the women to comment, he stomped over to it, put it back in place, and tried once more.

This time it shattered cleanly beneath the Kholben Shiar. Again bending over, and again struggling with the pain in his back, Corvis scooped up the dust and splinters into one palm and sprinkled them into the pile of rock dust he'd already gathered. Then, using an eating knife rather than Sunder, he drew a thin line down the palm of his left hand and squeezed exactly nine drops of blood into the mixture, adding water from a leather skin until the whole thing was a gritty paste.

"What—?" Irrial began, only to have Seilloah look up and shush her.

Corvis moved about the symbols he'd sketched, chanting an atonal, discordant litany as he went, daubing the gunk at various points across the runes. When he was done, he sat cross-legged in the center of it all and, pausing just long enough to draw breath, raised his voice to a shout. Sounds and syllables that were not words echoed across the cave—and then, though Corvis never wavered and his chant continued, those echoes *stopped*, sucked away by the stone.

A minute passed, then two. And then they were *there*, appearing through the shadows and even the rock wall as though stepping between the curtains on a stage.

There were five, or rather there *seemed* to be five; it was impossible to say for certain. They were half Rebaine's height, but there was nothing remotely child-like about them. Filthy, maggot-pale skin covered long and gangly limbs that hung at improper angles and bent in unnatural directions. They did not walk so much as convulse, each twitch carrying them the distance of a single pace. Pink, irritated eyes sat, uneven and far too close together, above a jagged, tooth-rimmed slash.

Corvis thought no less of Irrial when she whimpered and retreated as far as the cave's walls would allow; he'd dealt with the foul things before, but it was all he could do to hold his ground.

He spoke as firmly as a voice made hoarse by his prior incantations would allow. "I offer greetings to the gnomes, true and rightful lords of the earth's inner flesh. I am—"

"He knows." It was the foremost gnome, indistinguishable from any of the others, who interrupted in a voice of grinding stone. They came to a halt, all as one, and the speaker tilted its head to a perfect right angle. "He knows who has come, yes, has climbed into, under, the skin of the earth." He reached an impossibly long arm, sensuously caressed the cave wall with a cluster of irregular fingers. "Who dares again to call, yes, to spit the mountain's voice through flopping human lips. He knows the Rebaine, yes. He never forgets, *none* of him forgets the Rebaine."

"Nor has the Rebaine forgotten him," Corvis replied gravely.

"What . . . ?" Irrial whispered.

"They call themselves 'he,'" Seilloah explained quietly. "I don't know if it's their language, or something about how they think, but they all do it."

"So how do they know which one of them's being addressed?"

"No idea, but they always do."

". . . call to him now?" the gnome was saying. "He has nothing left to say, no, to tell the Rebaine. It risks its life, yes, its flesh, to come here, to his home beneath, below."

"I've come to bargain, as we have in the past."

"So, bargain, yes, deal." The vile creature licked its lips with something that more closely resembled a limp worm than a tongue. "Does it wish the same as before?"

"No, nothing so long term. We require you to guide us through your tunnels, far to the west." Then, at the creature's puzzled blinking, "Ah, in the direction of the sunset. For at least . . ." *Damn it, how do the little creeps measure distance?* ". . . at least, um, thirty-thousand paces. My paces, not yours."

"It wishes to walk, yes, to travel below? Through his paths and corridors? This, he does not like, no, has never allowed. What does it offer?"

Corvis pretended not to hear Irrial's whispered "I don't have a lot more where that first one came from." He gestured vaguely toward the cave mouth, still hidden from outside by Seilloah's phantasm.

"Many men hunt us. I offer you the chance to spill their blood, to avenge the theft of your ancestors and the rape of earthen wombs, as I did before."

The gnomes cocked their heads toward one another, puppets with loosened strings, and whispered in tones that Corvis felt vibrating in his gut and through the floor.

"No," the speaker grumbled finally, "he does not think so, no, does not agree. Before, the Rebaine offered him crowds, yes, homes and cities high above, far above, where normally he cannot go, no, cannot reach. And now it thinks these men here, yes, in the hills above are payment? They are not payment, no. He can take them whenever he wants, anytime, yes."

"And he can take the Rebaine, yes, and its companions."

"That would not be wise of him," Corvis warned, rising to his feet with Sunder in hand. "It would also be inappropriate."

The gnome, which had just begun to step forward, paused. "It thinks so? He wonders why . . ."

"Because I never actually did release you from my service," he said with a smile. "You agreed to serve. It's been some time, but I never ended our agreement."

It was a feeble argument, and he damn well knew it. But he knew, too, that the gnomes did not share humanity's sense of time, and given their peculiar, even alien thought patterns, it just might . . .

No.

The laughter of the gnomes sounded like a man choking on gravel. "It is foolish, yes, pathetic and stupid! He will eat of its flesh, suck the juice of its inner white stones!"

"Don't do this." Corvis wasn't sure if he was still warning, or if he'd crossed the line into pleading. He felt Irrial moving behind him, heard the rasp of steel on leather as she drew. "We've worked well together before. We might again. Don't ruin it now."

"He—"

Every face in the chamber turned as the cat yowled, a wretched, high-pitched squall of pain and terror. Belly pressed to the floor, it fled from beside Irrial's feet and out into the uneven hills. For long seconds, humans and gnomes peered at the illusory wall, as though they could follow the animal's flight.

Even as Corvis directed his bemused attention back to the gnomes, the foremost creature, the one who'd spoken, abruptly twitched. It was faint, scarcely a shiver, and the former warlord wouldn't even have been certain he'd seen it were it not for what came next.

"It is correct," the creature said thoughtfully. Was there, perhaps, just a slight change in its timbre? "He has worked well with the Rebaine in the past, yes, before." The creature twisted its head completely around to address the others behind. "He will guide it, yes, as it has asked."

Every other gnomish jaw dropped in a surprisingly human expression—assuming one allowed for the odd angles and excessive length of those gaping maws. "He is confused," one of them—presumably the one who'd been addressed—began. "Why does he—"

The speaker raised a crooked arm overhead, a motion more comical than threatening. "He is not asking, no! He is telling! He will guide it, yes, will do what he says!"

The pronouns were, at this point, impossible for the bewildered humans to follow, but the gnomes obviously got the message. The one who'd been yelled at actually managed to look a bit hurt. "He will obey," it murmured petulantly.

The speaker nodded, a hideous gesture that took its head so far back it actually touched between its misshapen shoulder blades, and then stepped through a seamless stone wall without another word. Most of the others went their own way as well, leaving the sulking guide along with a very confused Irrial and Corvis. For several long moments, they stood motionless, unsure of what to say.

"It comes," the creature finally snapped at them, "yes, follows swiftly. He will not wait for it, no." With that it stuck its arm elbow-deep in the wall. "Go, pass through, yes."

"What about—?" Irrial began.

"I'm here." From a narrow crevice a strange shape emerged, soft and malleable as though extruded from some digestive orifice within the rock. Only as it hit the ground and scuttled toward them did Corvis recognize the two-foot salamander for what it was.

And it was then, finally, that he realized just what she had done.

Face pale, he knelt down—ignoring the impatient muttering of their reluctant guide—and lifted the creature to perch upon his shoulder. "We're dead if they figure out what you did before we're gone," he whispered.

"They won't," she assured him quietly. "My previous host is, ah, somewhat indisposed. I walked him off a deep ravine down in the caves. It probably didn't kill him, but he won't be talking to anyone else for a good long—"

"Come!" the gnome shrieked at them. "Or he goes alone, yes!"

Steeling himself, Corvis stepped toward the wall. Every sense, every instinct, screamed at him to stop, that he was about to walk face-first into a solid barrier. Though he'd intended to stride casually through, he couldn't keep himself from raising his hands before him, just to be sure.

It was, he decided later when he'd calmed his mind enough for rational thought, rather like pushing through a curtain of beef fat. It failed, for half a heartbeat, to give at all, and then it oozed around his fingers, his arms, his face and chest. It crept over every inch of his body, pressing deep into his nostrils, the hollows of his mouth and ears. No, not over—*through*; he felt it sliding *inside* him, in his throat, his lungs, his gut. He struggled with a panic more primal than any fear he'd ever known, forced his gibbering brain to ignore the sensation of crushing suffocation that threatened to overwhelm him. Despite his efforts to blank his mind, he wondered what would happen if the impatient, spiteful little creature pulled its arm from the rock, allowing the wall to return to its normal state, and he found himself on the edge of hyper-ventilating despite his seeming inability to breathe.

And then he was through, standing in darkness as unrelenting as a demon's heart. Though the viscous stone had felt wet and pasty as it passed over him—*through him,* and he shuddered at the thought—it hadn't clung at all. He was no dirtier than when he'd begun, not the slightest bit damp save for his frightened sweat. For a time he simply stood, breathing deep of the stale but welcome cavern air, listening as the salamander on his shoulder did the same. He heard a horrified gasp beside him and knew that Irrial was through as well.

The air around them was dry, dusty, and very, very still. Wherever they were, it was a *long* way from any proper passage back to the world of light and wind.

"It follows." Corvis jumped at the voice; he'd heard no hint of the gnome's passage. He took a moment to mutter a spell, sending a gentle light emanating from his left hand. The gnome, presumably quite ca-pable of seeing in the dark, glanced back with some irritation, but he felt his own tension ebb somewhat, and sensed some of the stiffness pass from Irrial's shoulders as well.

Though there was, for the moment, nothing to see, nothing around them but an uneven passage of featureless stone. Corvis waved for the gnome to proceed, and the humans fell into step behind.

"I don't understand," Irrial whispered, trusting the echo of their foot-steps to keep her voice from their guide's ears. "I thought you couldn't inhabit anything with a soul." She, too, had clearly pieced together what Seilloah had done to ensure the gnomes' cooperation.

"That's correct," the salamander told her. "I can't."

"But—"

"If you ever hear someone refer to gnomes as 'soulless,'" Corvis said, "they're not just saying the bastards are vicious. It's the gods' honest truth. I have no idea what the little shits really are or where they came from—nobody does, as far as I know—but they're even less human than they look."

Irrial shivered. Then, "So why—?"

It was the witch, this time, who anticipated her question. "Because they have a sense of self, and a will of their own. I can inhabit them, but *control* is another matter entirely. It's *very* difficult. I doubt I could have kept it up for more than a few minutes—not much longer than it took to get them to help us, really."

'And to deal with the only one who knew what she'd done. The witch's teeth are showing.'

It took, at best guess, mere minutes to lose all sense of direction, all track of time. There was nothing but blank stone that had never before been seen by human eyes; narrow, jagged passages that tore at clothes and skin; overhangs that lurked in wait to crack careless skulls. They heard only their own breathing and their own footsteps. Even the echoes were oddly muted, repressed by the weight of the earth overhead.

At times they climbed, hauling themselves hand over fist up steep inclines that threatened to crumble beneath their weight, dropping them back into the shadowed emptiness; or scrambling down slopes on which standing was impossible, tearing hands and knees when they crawled, thighs and buttocks when they slid. And at other times they passed through solid walls, seeping through as the gnome held the way open, praying that the stone would never prove thicker than their lungs could handle. Corvis didn't know for certain what would happen if he took a breath while he and the rock slid obscenely through each other, but he *did* know that he'd rather never find out.

The air grew stale as they traveled ever deeper, and the barriers between them and the outside world thicker. He struggled not to wheeze with every step, heard Irrial gasping at the slightest exertion. And never once did the gnome show any inclination to rest, or even to slow its headlong pace, either unaware of, or unconcerned with, their discomfort. Corvis started to wonder if battling through the Cephiran patrols might not have been the better option after all.

But slowly, so gradually he initially failed to notice, the walls spread outward, the echoes of their footsteps grew louder. Forcing his attention from his exhausted feet, Corvis examined his new surroundings and discovered a far wider passage, replete with forks and little side corridors. From within he heard the occasional scuff of movement, the hiss of a whispered word.

Two humans walked, with faltering steps, through the abode of gnomes.

Bulges protruded into the ever-expanding corridor, and from those solid rocks myriad faces appeared, staring in fascinated hatred at the intruders from above. On two feet and on all fours, across floor and walls and ceiling, the creatures skittered, misshapen limbs pumping and twisting at impossible angles. Air and rock, light and dark, all the same; Corvis, watching as a face slid from a stone to glower at him, realized that these were their actual homes, that the gnomes lived not in the empty spaces beneath the earth, but *inside the rocks themselves*. It was, somehow, even more than their grotesque ability to move through those rocks, a disturbing reminder of their alien nature.

They oozed through yet another solid wall, thicker than any they'd so far passed, and Corvis and Irrial froze, deaf to the impatient cajoling of their guide.

They stood upon a ledge, frighteningly narrow, at the lip of what could only be described as a gulf of darkness. It had, so far as Corvis's light could reach, no floor and no sides save for the one beside them. He had little doubt that were Mecepheum itself somehow transported here, it would have room to grow.

Only the ceiling was visible, casting back reflections of that feeble illumination. Gems, or what Corvis assumed to be gems, gleamed back in every imaginable hue. Most were white or a pale yellow, but there were sporadic glints of rich red and deep green as well. Despite the steady glow of Corvis's spell, the gems glittered, twinkling like the stars of night above.

Gnomes crawled betwixt and between them in defiance of gravity, stopping here and there to perform what Corvis, from his limited vantage, could only describe as a twisted genuflection. In the cavern air, what he'd first taken to be the rush of a distant waterfall resolved itself into a grinding paean, a song produced by inhuman throats. A hundred identical voices wove it together, one picking up where another left off so not even the need for breath ever interrupted the unending, monotonous tone.

Only when the gnome had actually backtracked and reached out to physically drag Irrial along did they begin walking once more, making their way around the impossible, wondrous abyss. Corvis and Irrial kept their right hands on the wall, hoping to ensure that they would not step out over the edge, for they could not tear their attentions from the false firmament above.

At least, not at first. As they progressed, Corvis began to realize that the gems actually *did* match the stars of the night sky. He recognized constellations: here the Scales of Ulan; there Kirrestes the Archer, drawing back his great bow for the shot that, according to myth, passed through all seventeen heads to slay the Ryvrik hydra; farther along the winding coils of the wyrm Anolrach, whose spilled lifeblood made the oceans salty.

Corvis wasn't certain which was worse: the thought that the gnomes had deliberately created this mirror of night, or the possibility that the stones had *naturally* taken such shapes and forms. His mind shied away from the deeper implications of either option.

Nor was this the worst of it. As his vision adjusted even more, Corvis saw other shapes, monstrous, writhing *things* at the edges of his light, moving unlike any natural beast of earth or air or even sea. They strode the empty reaches, the stagnant darkness, at the center of that black gulf, whispering sounds that reached the ear but which the mind fearfully refused to acknowledge. And when they moved, the nearest gnomes genuflected to *them*.

Corvis turned his eyes to the path and refused to look any longer into that abyss.

THEIR SLOG AROUND ONE MINUSCULE FRACTION of that seemingly infinite cavern could have taken hours or even days; their progress through another array of twisting, monotonous corridors, even longer. Corvis's world had become nothing but the beating of an exhausted heart, the slow plod of aching, blistering feet. During those few moments when he could think at all, he began to contemplate the notion that he had died, that this was some horrible torment imposed in one of the darker corners of Vantares's dominion. He even began to welcome the occasional passage through solid walls, for the burning in his chest as he struggled not to breathe was indication that he yet lived.

He only just noticed when the corridors began, ever more frequently, to slope upward, and in his present state he never quite grasped the connotations.

Not, that is, until the gnome informed him "He goes no farther, no," at the same time Corvis felt the faintest brush of a breeze against his face, tentative and soft as a girl's first kiss. It smelled of grass and soil. It was all he could do not to fall to his knees, whether in gratitude or simple exhaustion he could never say.

"Thank you," he rasped, startled at how dry and gritty his voice sounded. *How long have we been down here?* It was only then he realized that not only had they never rested, they'd never stopped to eat or take even a mouthful of water. He looked briefly back the way they'd come, a shiver running down his spine, and wondered how much of it had been real.

"He does not want its thanks, no, its pitiful words of useless gratitude. He does not know what it said to him, why he guided it, took it below, between, the organs of the earth. But he knows that he will not do so again, never again, no. It leaves, yes, swiftly, before he changes his mind."

Corvis nodded. Staggering, holding each other upright, he and Irrial shambled forward, following the siren song of the breeze. They climbed shallow slopes, hands outstretched as though to clutch the diaphanous scents of the world above. The sun, when they found it, was overwhelming, knives of light stabbing at their eyes, but it was the most joyful pain Corvis had ever known.

He pretended, as he wept, that the blinding glare was the sole cause of his tears.

CORVIS LEANED OUT between two uneven shutters, the knuckles of one hand pressed to the windowsill, and gazed morosely over the collection of wooden shacks and winding roads that pretended to form a town. He'd no idea what the place might be called, and couldn't be bothered to care overmuch. It'd been the first dollop of civilization they'd stumbled across after crawling back into the light from the earth's stone womb, and it had boasted rooms for let above the combination tavern/restaurant/general store. That was enough to make it home, at least for tonight.

He felt his head sag, and pressed the thumb and forefinger of his free hand to the bridge of his nose. Much as he might have liked someone to talk to, a part of him was glad that he was alone for the moment—that there was nobody present to witness his weakness. *Or at least*, a faint chuckle in the back of his thoughts reminded him, *nobody real.* Moving from the window, he slumped hard in the nearby chair, unwilling even to expend the effort to reach the thin and lumpy mattress.

Corvis couldn't remember the last time he'd been so weary, so weighted down and oppressed by his own body—although, he admitted with a rueful grin, that might just be due to failing memory. No physical exhaustion, this, easily solved by a day or two of relaxation, a few nights' rejuvenating slumber. Rather, he felt himself sinking, suffocating, in the mire of a mental and emotional fatigue so thick that it bordered on despair. Not since the darkest days of the Serpent's War had he so desperately wanted the world to just go away for a while, to cease its incessant demands. He dreaded the thought of returning to Mecepheum's morass of Guilds and Houses and politics and corruption, and in the deepest recesses of his soul, a voice—his *own* voice—beseeched him to give it all up. *Forget the mystery, forget the conspiracy, forget Imphallion. It's not your responsibility; it never was. So what if someone has murdered in your name? It's a name that cannot possibly be hated any more than it is already. Why continue? Why not find a home somewhere, far from the Cephiran border, and make a life from what years remain?*

He knew his answers, of course: His sense of the greater good, tarnished and frayed though it may have been, so rigid and uncompromising that it had allowed him to murder thousands that he might save millions. His loyalty to companions who had fought and bled at his side. His concern for a family he had lost yet still loved. And, he conceded, his own pride, a towering pillar of fire that refused to be doused.

But for a brief time that evening, had anyone asked Corvis Rebaine if those reasons were sufficient, if they made the struggle worth continuing, he could not truthfully have answered *yes.*

And it was there, at the nadir of his inner pit of exhaustion and desolation, that the gods elected, in their own peculiar way, to yank him out of it.

Corvis was standing up from his chair, mind and muscle groaning with the effort, before it occurred to him that the heavy knock reverberating through the door didn't sound like it came from Irrial's modest fist. He straightened, frowning thoughtfully at the door. No safety there. He hadn't thought to twist the lock as he'd staggered in—not that it really mattered, since both latch and door itself were flimsy enough for an angry rabbit to take down, given a sufficient running start. He thought about keeping silent, but that probably wouldn't put anyone off more than a few moments.

So he stepped, not to the door, but back to the window. *You're being paranoid, Corvis. It's probably just the proprietor.* Still, only once he'd hefted Sunder from where it leaned against the wall below the sill did he call out, inviting whoever it was to enter.

The door drifted open with a melodramatic creak, revealing a looming shape in the flickering lanternlight of the hall beyond. And Corvis, blood pounding in his ears, old agonies coursing through his limbs, could only think to say, "I'm rather stunned that you were able to keep calm enough to refrain from kicking the damn thing in."

"I figured there was no need to rush," said the Baron of Braetlyn. "I've been looking forward to this for *such* a very long time."

Chapter Nineteen

"Are you certain?"

The sorcerer's glare, despite the drooping and exhausted lids that muffled it, could well have flayed the hide from an elephant at fifty paces.

"It's a fair question," Jassion protested. "You've been running on the edge of collapse for days now. We can't afford a mistake at this point."

"Oh? Used up your budget for them, have you?"

"If you're just going to stand there being insulting . . ."

"Not at all, old boy. I can accomplish a great deal *while* being insulting." Then, with a tired sigh, Kaleb rose from where he'd knelt. "Yes, Jassion, I'm quite sure. I was sure yesterday. I was sure the day before that. I was sure the day before—well, I think even you can spot the pattern, yes?"

"Will you—?"

"Yes. It's not an easy spell to cast *once*, let alone on subsequent days like this. But yes, it was worth it, and yes, I'm sure he's quite nearby now—the spell tells me as much—and *yes*, I'll be ready. I recover quickly. Get out there and start asking around. Learn where he's staying, if anyone's with him. I'll be good as new by the time you get back."

"I still think—"

"Don't. You're not good at it. You *will* come back and get me, Jassion." It was clearly an argument they'd had a time or two before. "I don't care what sort of opportunity you think you have. I don't care if you find him unarmored, unconscious, and nailed to a stump, you *will* come get me before you try anything!"

"Fine."

"And don't sulk. It's unattractive."

It was the baron's turn to glare, but his features swiftly softened. "Mellorin?"

"She'll be fine. The spell's a greater strain on the focus than the caster, but she just needs a good long rest."

Jassion frowned. "She doesn't have time for a 'long' rest."

"Sure she does. In fact, I've already cast a second enchantment to ensure that she won't wake up for some time. Not until after we've done what we need to do."

"Oh?" Jassion's brow furrowed. "You think that's wise, Kaleb?"

"I thought you'd be happy keeping her out of harm's way."

"I am. I'm just surprised that *you're* willing to do it. And just how do you plan to explain to her, after she's come all this way and made it possible to find the bastard, that you decided she didn't need to be there for the end of it?"

"Tell me something, old boy: Do you really have any intention of trying to take Rebaine alive? *Really?*"

"Well . . ."

"Exactly. I'm pretty sure I can explain putting her to sleep a *lot* more readily than I could justify anything she'd see in the next few hours."

And I'll need her loyalty when all's said and done, he added silently.

"Good to know your relationship is based on honesty and trust," Jassion grumbled. But he made no further argument, saying instead, "I'm as ready as I'm going to be for this."

Kaleb nodded and spoke the eldritch syllables, reaching out to mold Jassion's face like so much clay, ensuring that the baron could wander the streets and ask his questions without being

recognized should Rebaine spot him. It was a temporary transformation, but given the size of the obnoxious flyspeck of a village, it should more than suffice.

As soon as Jassion was gone, Kaleb began to pace, shedding
all signs of fatigue like a sweaty tunic. His brow furrowed in
contemplation, concentration, as he steeled himself, gathering
magics that even Jassion had never seen, readying himself for a
confrontation six hellish years in the making . . .

⸻⟨⸱⸱⸱⸱⟩ ⟨⸱⸱⸱⸱⟩⸻

THEY GLOWERED ACROSS THE ROOM, each at the other,
two men bound by a chain of loathing that ran the breadth of
Imphallion—and through the wounded heart of a woman whom each,
so far as he was capable, had loved. From the open doorway and between the slats of the floorboards drifted the scents of roasting bird and
beast, the dull susurrus of half-drunk laughter. Hardly appropriate her-
alds of the violence to come.

Corvis felt Sunder quiver in his grasp, like a charger straining at the
reins, and only then did he truly register the massive sword upon which
the man in the doorway so casually leaned. It had been a dagger when
Corvis saw it last, but he knew it instantly for what it was. He could feel
the bloodlust, smelted into the steel and only tentatively leashed, as
clearly as he could sense the smoldering rage, repressed just as feebly,
emanating from its wielder.

He wondered, briefly, how the baron had gotten hold of the vile
weapon, but he'd not provide the satisfaction of asking.

It was Jassion, instead, who broke the brittle silence. "It was a pathetic attempt at misdirection, Rebaine," he said. "Did you really think
that just entering town separately, or checking into different rooms,
would be enough to keep us from spotting your accomplice?"

"Frankly," Corvis said with a shrug, "we were more concerned about
any Cephiran operatives looking for the pair of us traveling together. I
wasn't even thinking of you."

It was a petty sting to the baron's pride, but Corvis could tell from
the twitch of the other man's jaw that it landed. "Be that as it may,"

Jassion growled, "in a village this size, *any* newcomer draws attention. We identified her easily enough." He offered a dismissive wave, and Corvis found his eyes drawn to the green glint on Jassion's finger.

"I'm surprised you're still wearing that ring, Jassion. As I recall, it got you in a bit of hot water during the Serpent's War."

But if he'd hoped to rile the baron further, reminding him of the universal suspicion he'd brought upon himself with his behavior, he was doomed to disappointment. "It's an heirloom, Rebaine. It *should* belong to Tyannon, really, but I understand you gave her another ring to replace it." His lips curled in a vicious, mocking leer. "I also understand she's not wearing it anymore. Maybe I *should* consider giving her mine, at that."

Sunder's blade slowly rotated as the haft twisted in Corvis's trembling fist. "I'll do it for you. Would you like her to have it with or without the finger?"

"Ah. Is that about enough, do you think, Rebaine?" Jassion asked, mockery squirming like weevils through his words. "Have we spent long enough nattering on like bickering fishwives?"

"I certainly hope so," Corvis told him. "I'm looking forward to lancing you like a boil and watching you shrivel." He shoved the room's table aside with a juddering crash. The cramped room made for a poor arena—especially given the oversized weapons each man carried—but it was the best readily available. "What are you waiting for, Baron? Too cowardly to attack when Kaleb's not around to hold your hand?"

Corvis's mention of a name he should have had no way of knowing was apparently lost upon Jassion, washed away in a flood of fury along with whatever satisfaction the baron had hoped to obtain by prolonging the confrontation. He crossed the room in a handful of steps, Talon raised high and gouging a path of splinters from the ceiling above. Nothing but murder remained in his sweating, twisted face, and Corvis could not have said whether it was the pounding of his boots, or his inhuman cry, that made the flimsy chamber tremble.

And then he was upon Corvis, and *through* Corvis. Braced for an impact that never occurred, Jassion slammed hard against the windowsill, arms flailing awkwardly as he tried both to keep hold of Talon with one hand and to keep himself from toppling headfirst through the open window.

Corvis—who had made swift use of Jassion's grandstanding, sidling slowly from the window beneath a cloak of subtle illusion—stepped in from the side, looming behind his startled and unsteady foe. Sunder whirled once, twice, as he neared, then swept through an arc that would have left little but empty air between Jassion's gut and his ribs.

But for all his maddened fury and shock, Jassion had clearly lost neither his speed nor his senses. The narrow window allowed no room to parry or to dodge, but that still left one avenue of escape. Even as Sunder blurred toward him, the baron shifted his weight, letting gravity have its way. He toppled from the window, the Kholben Shiar passing inches above his twisting body, and landed with a bone-jarring thump on the packed earth of the road below.

I guess, Corvis reflected as he leaned outward to study his groaning foe, *that it was too much to hope he'd fall on Talon or break his neck.*

'You want everything just handed to you the easy way, don't you? No wonder I had to do all the hard work myself.'

Corvis vaulted the sill and dropped, twin clouds of dust puffing outward as his boot heels struck the earth. Jassion scrabbled madly backward like a drunken spider and lurched to his feet. The little finger on his left hand protruded at a curious angle, and he winced visibly with every step, but neither the demon-forged sword nor his hate-tempered gaze ever wavered.

They came together, Jassion unslowed by his injuries, and the crash of the Kholben Shiar was the shriek of a thousand tortured angels. Talon's edge pressed hard on Sunder's haft as the warlord and the baron leaned into each other, feet shifting as they circled. Around them, the already sparsely populated street rapidly emptied, men and women fleeing from the gale of violence blowing through their midst. By fits and starts, the din from the restaurant faded as the folk within recognized that something was amiss.

Jassion brought a knee up viciously, driving for his opponent's groin, but Corvis twisted to take the blow on his thigh instead. He staggered, limping for only a step or two, and swept Sunder in a fearsome parry.

Again the demon-forged weapons slammed together, and again after that. Feet sidestepped and bodies twisted with a dancer's skill, even as heavy blades chopped and slashed with a force and a fury more brutish than elegant.

Corvis ducked under a high, arcing swipe, and knew only too late that he'd walked into a trap. Jassion continued his spin, carried by the momentum of his swing, coiling his body low and lashing out in a sweeping kick. Corvis felt his ankles shoot out from under him and toppled like a felled oak. The air escaped his lungs as though fleeing for its life, and the world grew fuzzy as he struggled to breathe.

The moon disappeared from the nighttime clouds as Jassion loomed above, Talon clasped underhanded. The Kholben Shiar plunged earthward as though eager to return to hell, and Corvis could not possibly lift Sunder in time to parry.

Acting on nothing but primal instinct, he slapped desperately at the flat of the blade with a bare hand. And as Talon jerked aside, sinking deep into the dirt mere inches from his ribs, Corvis knew that he owed a dozen prayers to Panaré Luck-Bringer.

Startled and off-balance, his sword sticking more than a foot into the earth, Jassion could not twist aside as Corvis kicked out with both legs. The baron bent double around the impact, hurtling backward to slam against the restaurant's outer wall. Corvis scrambled to his feet, breath coming a little easier, whispering through a hoarse and ragged throat.

The tiny sprouts and sprigs protruding from the soil began to wiggle, desperate to escape the confines of their earthen prison. With a speed seemingly impossible for one so badly beaten, Jassion had risen and crossed half the distance between himself and his foe when the first of the tendrils wrapped around his ankle, yanking him to a halt. A second strand, and then a third—roots and stems, blades of grass and winding weeds—wove themselves over his feet, binding him to the spot until he might as well have been one of those plants himself.

Corvis lunged, but Jassion was already gone. Talon swept downward, severing the plants that held him, and he was twisting aside, all so swiftly that he appeared little more than a blot upon the scenery, a blurred silhouette glimpsed through a thick fog or a filthy pane of glass.

And Corvis, no matter how he hated the thought, knew that he must do the same.

As Jassion had clearly already done—as he himself had dared a few days before—he drank once more from the well of power bubbling in the depths of the Kholben Shiar. And again he recoiled, fighting to keep tight rein on his own emotions lest they be swept aside and lost amid the exultation and bloodlust within the demon-forged blade.

The bulk of the village disappeared, his vision closing in on the street immediately before him. The clouds of dust resolved themselves into individual specks and particles; the stars in the firmament ceased to twinkle. He heard the shouts of distant citizens, too terrified to draw near; the sharp breaths of patrons watching through the restaurant's windows; even the beating of his own heart, and Jassion's as well, now slowed to a casual cadence.

Jassion came at him, falcon-swift and tortoise-slow at once, and Corvis was already parrying before he'd consciously decided to move. Once more the weapons clashed, but they sounded now like slow, ponderous thunder. The baron again kicked one of Corvis's legs from under him, but Sunder swept down and out before he'd toppled more than a dagger's length, propping him upright long enough to catch his balance. Straightening, Corvis drove an uppercut into his enemy's chin, and he saw the tips of each individual hair splaying upward as Jassion's head snapped back. He lashed out with the axe, missing as Jassion ducked with equally inhuman speed. The Kholben Shiar tore instead completely through the nearest wall. The combatants had already exchanged a dozen more blows, moved yards down the street, before the splinters fell to earth.

Jassion's shoulders tensed and Corvis was already dodging away from the expected swing, but the baron jabbed instead, wielding Talon like an awkward spear. Corvis hurled himself aside, heard more than felt the thud as he slammed back-first into another neighboring shop, knew instantly that Jassion would follow with a wide slash that the wall would prevent him from dodging. Hoping the wood was as thin as it had felt, he drove an elbow back with inhuman strength even as his other hand raised Sunder in an awkward one-handed block.

The wall splintered, giving way beneath the impact as the meeting of the blades drove Corvis through the wood. Both men crashed to the floor amid broken shelves and shards of pottery. Clay dust matted itself across Corvis's cheeks and forehead, transformed into paste by rivulets of acrid sweat.

Both hands now locked on Sunder's haft, he strained with all the mundane and mystical might at his command, and it wasn't enough. Jassion crouched atop him, pressing down on Talon with the strength not just of another Kholben Shiar, but of a younger body and a maddened rage Corvis couldn't comprehend, let alone match. Elbows pressed to the floor, arms quivering with strain, he held the axe crosswise, inches above his chest, and with every breath it—and the sword pressed against it—crept nearer. He had no leverage to throw the baron off him, no angle from which to kick, not even sufficient room to bend his neck back for an awkward headbutt.

So Corvis, instead, craned his neck *upward* and bit down with all his strength on Jassion's nose.

He felt cartilage give under the pressure; heard it snap even over the baron's agonized cry; gagged as he tasted blood and mucus sluicing between his teeth. Jassion jerked away, leaving shreds of skin and flesh behind, and Corvis gasped in relief as the pressure against his arms and chest eased. Daring to take one hand from Sunder, he drove the heel of his palm into Jassion's chin, and then, as the baron fell back farther, planted both feet in his chest and shoved. The younger warrior hurtled back through the hole in the wall to sprawl in the street. Corvis spit the vile gobbet from his mouth before rising and following his enemy.

Jassion, with a determination that Corvis could not help but envy, was already standing. Blood formed a mask across his features, dripped down the sides of his neck, and his heaving breaths whistled obscenely through the wreck of his face.

Yet Corvis, though lacking in any such fearsome wound, was gasping no less harshly. His entire body felt bruised and battered, his ribs as though they'd been hammered flat upon Verelian's anvil, his ankles stuffed with ground glass. He had many years on his opponent, and they clung to him now, a weighty chain about his waist.

Both men slowed, now drawing upon the magics of the demon-forged blades just to keep themselves steady.

And Jassion *smiled*, a stomach-churning sight. "You cannot hurt me, Rebaine, not any more than you did when I was a child. And I can keep this up longer than you."

"You probably can," Corvis admitted between gulps of air, allowing Sunder to sink just a bit. "But Jassion? I cheat."

At his best, Jassion would have sensed her coming, been able to dodge or at least lessen the blow. As it was, when Irrial's sword slammed into his hauberk, severing links and splitting skin, it was all he could do to scream and twist aside, preventing her from delivering an immediate second thrust through the rent in the armor.

Rather than follow and risk stepping into range of that monstrous flamberge, the baroness dropped into a defensive stance, the tip of her blade leveled, waiting for him to come to her—and to present his back to Corvis. Jassion, Talon drifting back and forth before him, declined. He stepped slowly backward, trying to gain enough distance to focus on both.

"What took you so long?" Corvis asked breathlessly.

Behind Jassion, the roots and stalks he'd earlier escaped reared like striking serpents, grown to a dozen times their former size. Several whipped outward, drawing bloody welts across his exposed skin, while others curled tight around arms and legs, lifting him bodily from the earth.

From around the restaurant's shattered corner, a mangy hound slunk into the street, crouching at Irrial's feet and scratching idly behind one ear with a back foot.

Corvis allowed himself just a moment to worry for his friend—he'd known the salamander was swiftly dehydrating once they'd left the caves, but he'd not expected her to need a new form so soon—and then focused once again on Jassion. The baron hung helplessly, limbs thrashing, literally spitting as he screamed what sounded like sheer gibberish.

Hesitantly, Corvis opened his mouth, then shut it with an audible click. *No.* No more words, no more taunts, no more *time*. Not for

Jassion. He advanced on the helpless nobleman, no longer a warrior but a headsman. He again felt Sunder quiver in his fist, and for the first time in years he shared the unholy weapon's anticipation.

But the blow would never fall.

The air grew suddenly thick, heavy against their skin, clogging their ears. A horrible shriek split the night as the sky itself screamed, and then the wrath of the heavens, all unseen, struck the earth.

Corvis had little memory of the seconds following the impact, save that entire buildings had crumbled, and that the chunks of wood and stone somehow hurtled *inward*, further battering at his flesh, rather than outward from the center of the blast. He found himself sprawled atop a pyramid of broken rock, with no notion of how he'd gotten there. His ears were filled with an angry buzz. Through bleary eyes, he spotted Irrial lying in a crumpled heap, blood flowing from an ugly gash across her scalp, and his stomach clenched until he saw her pulse flutter in her throat. Of Seilloah—or Jassion, for that matter—he saw no sign.

But there *was* someone else, a thin-faced, brown-haired man standing over him, lips curled in an almost friendly grin. "I've waited," he said, leaning in apparently to ensure that Corvis could see him. "Oh, I've waited for so long."

"Kaleb, I presume?" Corvis offered, then paused to cough up a lungful of dust.

"I'm crushed, old boy. You don't remember me?"

Corvis frowned. He'd never seen this man, of that he was certain, but there was something about that voice . . .

"Well, it's to be expected, I suppose," Kaleb continued, kneeling so his face hovered but a few feet from Corvis's own. "You probably just don't recognize me in this outfit. Here."

Like melting wax, the sorcerer's features began to shift—but the fallen warlord turned away, unwilling to watch. For in that moment, Corvis knew—without question, without doubt—and that knowledge was a blade, slicing holes into his soul that he was certain would never heal. He understood how the murderer had known so much about him and his methods, understood how Jassion had tracked him down across a kingdom, understood how a sorcerer could have so much power.

Understood what it was he faced, and why he could never have won. "Look at me, Corvis. *Look at me.*"

His sight blurred by bitter tears, Corvis looked—looked into a new face, features even more gaunt than before, hair the color of dead straw, and eyes . . .

"Say it just once, Corvis. For old times' sake."

. . . eyes that each boasted a *pair* of pupils side by side, uneven pools of infinite darkness. And beneath their stare, Corvis could scarcely whisper, or even breathe.

"*Khanda* . . ."

Chapter Twenty

HE COULDN'T THINK, couldn't move, couldn't breathe. His mind was swaddled in a rotting shroud, muffling the sights, the sounds, the scents of the world. It took long moments to recognize that the pain in his side was caused by the broken rock on which he lay, that the peculiarly harsh rain drizzling down across his face actually consisted of the splinters of shattered buildings.

But it was, all of it, unreal, diaphanous, a waking dream. Only the flesh-wrapped nightmare gazing gleefully down upon him was real.

"I can't . . ." He had trouble forcing the words to come, his lips and his tongue made numb as the blood drained from his face. "It's not possible. You *can't* be . . ."

"Astonishing." Kaleb—Khanda—shook his head sadly. "I knew you'd counted on me for a lot, old boy, but I'd never realized that included forming coherent sentences. How *have* you gotten by all these years?"

"I *banished* you!" Corvis actually sounded accusing, as though Khanda's reappearance was a personal betrayal. He struggled to sit up, groaning at the aches and bruises that flared anew across his battered body.

"What can I say, Corvis? Hell's not what it used to be. Security's really gone to—well, you know."

But the old soldier's brain was finally catching up with his senses. "Someone had to call you . . . Call you back by name. *That's* what they got from Ellowaine, isn't it? Your godsdamn *name!*"

He rolled aside, as rapidly as the rocks and his own wounds would allow, lifting Sunder in one hand, but it was a pathetic blow, a feeble spit of defiance. Khanda casually backhanded Corvis's forearm and the limb went numb, the Kholben Shiar falling from limp fingers. Corvis curled around himself, clutching his throbbing arm . . .

And from where he lay, he saw a bit of rubble behind the demon, an uneven heap of wooden detritus, begin to shift.

"Why?" he asked, forcing himself to meet Khanda's repulsive eyes. "Why would they summon *you?*"

Khanda grinned, an inhuman rictus from ear to ear. "I don't believe I'm going to tell you that."

"Why not?"

"Because you want to know." That awful grin grew even broader. "And because, ultimately, it doesn't matter. You humans are such petty, insignificant schemers. You think you're *playing* games, but you're all just *pieces.*"

Corvis forced himself to smile. Across the street, Irrial had dizzily crawled through the dirt to the boards, begun laboriously to dig toward whoever lay moving beneath. *Keep his attention . . .* "Are we? It seems to me you wouldn't be here without one of those 'pieces.' And I know a little something about summoning incantations, Khanda. You don't ex- actly have free rein. If you did, you'd have had more than enough power to find me long ago. You're limited here, demon. You're *human.*"

The world briefly vanished behind an array of blinding suns as Khanda struck him across the face. "Why, Corvis, such *language.*" He sighed theatrically and settled himself on the ground, sitting cross- legged as though beside a comfortable campfire. "But you're right, of course. I don't have anywhere near my full might. Even when I was liv- ing inside a pendant and a slave to your every primitive whim, I wasn't at my best. There's never *been* a demon freely unleashed upon your world, not in your recorded history anyway. Even the most maddened conjurers aren't *that* crazy. And that, old boy—not revenge, though I certainly welcome it, and not my orders—is why I've come for you."

"I thought," Corvis grunted, struggling to get his feet under him so he might rise, "that you weren't going to tell me what this is about."

"I'm not going to tell you what *they* want," Khanda corrected casually. "But I want you to understand what *I'm* doing. It's so much more fun if you know enough to be horrified. You see, you have something I need."

He leaned back, waiting, clearly content to let the former warlord ask—or figure it out for himself.

It doesn't make any sense. I don't have anything . . . The demon couldn't use the Kholben Shiar; Khanda knew more or less everything Corvis knew, up until six years ago. There was *nothing*.

Except . . .

"Oh, gods . . ."

Khanda actually clapped like an excited schoolgirl. "I *knew* you'd get there. You really were almost competent at times, for a human." He leaned in, voice marred by excited breathing. "I can't use my own power against him. The summoning and binding spells won't permit it. But someone *else's* magic, an incantation that doesn't draw on my own abilities? That's something else entirely. And I was around you, and your pet witch, more than long enough to learn *human* methods of sorcery.

"Think of it, Corvis! With that spell, I can force 'Master' Nenavar to release me from my bonds, to grant me not only my freedom but my *power*! Enough to make this wretched dung-ball of a world my plaything—to make Selakrian look like a charlatan. You remember what Mecepheum looked like six years ago? That was *nothing*!" A narrow string of spittle dangled from the corner of the demon's mouth. "And you kept the invocation when the rest of the tome burned to ash. *You* made it all possible."

A soft clatter sounded from behind. Wooden planks cascaded away in a small avalanche beneath Irrial's chapped and bleeding hands. Khanda started, began to look around . . .

"It's gone, Khanda!" Corvis shouted triumphantly in his face. "I burned the pages *years* ago. You've wasted your time!"

"Oh, Corvis." A hand shot out, clutching Corvis's chin with bone-bruising strength. Khanda made a soft *tsk, tsk*, wiggling the man's jaw until the joint very nearly separated. "All this time, and you still don't understand me at all. I don't *need* the pages. The words are written down . . ." He released his grip and jabbed a finger into Corvis's forehead hard enough for the nail to break skin. ". . . here. I tried to get what I needed from Audriss first, you know. Would've saved me a *lot* of time. But there wasn't enough essence left in his skull." He shrugged. "What *are* you gonna do?"

It was rhetorical, of course, but Corvis answered anyway. "Stop you," he said simply, his confident tone hiding—or so he hoped—the gaping, empty abyss that had opened in his gut. "We've been through this, Khanda, a long time ago. You don't have the willpower to get into my mind."

The demon leaned even closer, until their noses nearly touched. "That was, as you say, a long time ago. I'm stronger now. I'm a *lot* angrier at you. And," he said, straightening up again, "if you prove too stubborn, I'll just make you watch while I do all *sorts* of unpleasant things to Mellorin."

Corvis's breath slammed into a brick wall at the base of his throat. His face, corpse-pale already, went whiter than the helm he'd once worn.

"Oh, my. Did I not tell you she was here? I'm *so* sorry; how utterly thoughtless of me. Still, perhaps it won't be *too* unpleasant for her," Khanda continued lightly. "She's really very fond of me. She might even enjoy it, as long as I don't tell her you're watching."

He never realized the scream was his, never remembered lunging at the hell-spawned monstrosity. All Corvis knew was that suddenly he hung in the air, feet kicking, Khanda's fist about his throat. The demon was standing now, and a missing lock of hair suggested that Corvis's speed must have surprised even him.

But it was all for naught, all just another dance at the end of Khanda's strings. For in that moment of mindless, bestial rage, Corvis had not been, *could* not be, thinking of anything else.

And with all thought discarded, all effort and concentration gone, Khanda had slipped easily into his mind like a worm eating through an apple.

He felt the obscene presence sliding inside him, a slick and slimy *thing*, a tongue running across his thoughts, tasting his dreams. Images flickered, reflections of the recent past, and all were tainted and rotting at the edges where Khanda had touched them.

/*Really, Corvis.*/ The voice reverberated in his mind, so much worse than the phantom echoes of the past years, eclipsing his thoughts entirely. /*Another* noblewoman? *Since you didn't prove up to conquering, are you trying to fuck your way to the throne now? Or do you just find that the inbreeding makes them more docile?*/

Corvis could only gurgle. Even if he could have forced the words past his tongue, his mind thrashed too violently to form them.

More movement, more images. A nauseating stench began to permeate his memories, corrupting even the most pleasant into something foul, something better forgotten. /*The dog? Seilloah's the* dog?/ Corvis's head felt as though it would burst as it filled with a cruel and hysterical laughter. /*Well, I* always *said she was a bitch, didn't I?*/

On it went, and on, farther and farther back. Through Corvis's recent travels; the life he'd made and the plans he'd pursued as part of Rahariem's Merchants' Guild. And farther still, through his nightmarish experiences in Tharsuul, land of the Dragon Kings, and his all-consuming eldritch studies—not to empower his new plans, as he'd maintained and even believed, but as a means of escaping the pain of Tyannon's rejection.

He would have threatened, demanded, cajoled—even, gods help him, begged for it to stop. But he could not. Khanda hadn't even left him that.

Until . . . /*Ahhh.* There *it is! And just in time. If I had to relive any more of your pathetic existence, I might just vomit. And you call* my home 'hell' . . ./

Corvis saw the words flash across his mind, one at a time, and Khanda peeled them off like scabs. Gradually, inevitably, the entire spell began to form, until the demon was but a single passage from the end.

The scream, when it came, sounded in Corvis's mind and ears both, threatening to shatter hearing and sanity alike. A geyser of pain erupted from his gut even as he fell to the street, a motionless rag doll.

Khanda stood, his body rigid, jaw agape in astonished agony. A mask of blood and ruined, splinter-coated flesh peered over his shoulder from behind, and the wavy blade of a demon-forged flamberge jutted obscenely from his ribs.

"I don't know precisely what you are," Jassion rasped, viciously twisting Talon in the wound. "But I heard enough."

The world held its breath. Corvis gawped up at the two men he hated most in the world; at Irrial standing behind them, her hands raw and bleeding where she'd dug Jassion free; and Seilloah slinking at her feet, one paw twisted at an impossible angle and clutched painfully to her chest.

Slowly, Khanda looked down at the length of hellish steel that had skewered him like a haunch of pork. And then, finally, he spoke.

"Ow."

Though it clearly pained him, he twisted at the waist, widening his own wound as he moved, and jabbed two fingers into the ragged flesh that had once been Jassion's nose.

The baron shrieked, stumbling back with both hands to his face, leaving the sword sticking clear through Khanda's torso. And Khanda himself could only laugh at the stunned consternation in his enemies' eyes.

"I have complete control over my body, Corvis, save for those limitations the summoning spell imposed on me. Why would I *possibly* choose to make myself *mortal*? Don't you understand, you cretins? *You cannot kill me!*" He extended a hand as though tossing a ball, and Jassion staggered farther—but only a few steps. He levitated for but an instant, clearing the earth by only a few inches before he fell once more. And for the first time, Khanda looked genuinely concerned.

"No." He spun, and there was Corvis, standing once more. Sunder slammed hard into Khanda's ribs, cracking bone and sending the demon hurtling aside. "But it looks like we can *hurt* you, doesn't it? Seilloah!"

The dog looked up sharply, peered at the rubble toward which he was pointing. She needed no more than the long years they'd worked and fought side-by-side to figure out what he was asking, and she nodded. Again the stalks burst from the earth, this time lifting the heaviest of the stones and planks.

Beside the road, features now twisted in an agonized rage, Khanda was rising once again.

"Jassion!" Corvis called. "It's the Kholben Shiar! Their magics must interfere with his!" And again he pointed, not at the rubble Seilloah's plants were hefting but at the hard-packed earth below.

Please, gods, make him understand!

And though he twitched visibly, perhaps in frustration at the thought of taking orders from Corvis Rebaine, he obviously did. Jassion leapt the intervening detritus and slammed into Khanda before he could find his balance. The baron grasped Talon's hilt and twisted, forcing demonic blade and demonic body downward. They toppled, the tip of the Kholben Shiar plunging into the earth. Jassion leaned on it, thrusting with all the strength he had left until it slid as far as it would go, the crossbar lying flush with Khanda's skin, staking him to the road.

The plants slackened their grip. Wood and stone rained down to bury Khanda in a makeshift cairn—and would have buried Jassion as well, had he not anticipated what was coming and rolled desperately aside. Obviously, and perhaps understandably, Seilloah held a grudge.

He rose, somehow directing both an infuriated glare at Corvis and a wistful, longing look where his weapon lay interred.

"Is he dead?" Irrial asked shakily.

"You heard him," Corvis said, turning away. "We can't kill him. That probably won't hold him for more than a few minutes." He began to run, but managed only a few paces before his aches and bruises and burning lungs reined him back to an unsteady, stiff-legged walk. The others fell quickly into step behind him.

"Can we possibly get far enough in a few minutes?" Irrial wondered aloud.

"That depends—on him." Corvis halted abruptly, raised Sunder's edge to hover within inches of the startled Jassion's throat.

"*Where's Mellorin?*"

⸺

FOR LONG MINUTES THE STREET WAS STILL, the nighttime silence broken only by the creak of settling rubble and the fearful cries of distant villagers too terrified to leave their homes. Low-hanging clouds began to thin, moon and stars peeking out to see if the chaos had ended.

A peculiar snapping, combining the whistle of a sharp wind with the crackling of a bonfire, sounded a few yards down the road. The dust swirled as though kicked by a giant invisible foot, and a shape—human, feminine, lost in slumber—materialized in the dirt. It would have astonished anyone watching, had there *been* anyone watching, but the street, and the surrounding windows, were empty.

Again, silent moments passed. The debris shifted, stone screeching on stone, wood breaking, and something that had once appeared human rose from the wreckage with a scream to shame the damned. Limbs hung at agonizing angles, splintered bone protruding through rents in the flesh. Blood caked its skin, flowed from a hundred tiny wounds. From its body, unmarred by the impact of the rubble, protruded the Kholben Shiar.

Shattered hands, aquiver not so much with agony as rage, clutched at the blade. He could feel the insatiable hunger within the metal, a power that flowed from the same infernal wellspring as his own. He bit back a hiss of revulsion at its touch, all the while promising Rebaine and Jassion a thousand deaths.

He'd expected that the Kholben Shiar could likely hurt him, even if they could not kill; known that the magics of other demons, no matter what form contained them, would cause him pain. But until he'd felt the weapon sliding through him, piercing mind and body, pinning him to the earth, he'd not truly understood what that meant. Khanda had not worn his human form long enough to comprehend mortal anguish, and nothing—not his various minor wounds, not even the torment of Nenavar's ire—had prepared him for an agony the equal of any found in hell.

Inch by inch, fingers shredding themselves even further against the edge only to form anew, he pressed back upon the blade, driving it out. Finally he felt the pressure and the pain ease, heard Talon clatter to the ground behind him, and he gasped in very human relief.

On legs that bowed like saplings, that should never have supported his weight, the inhuman creature in human form staggered from the cairn. With each stride his body twitched, reshaped by the demon's will. Step, and a leg ceased bending, bones knitting together and kneecap sliding into place. Step, and an arm snapped back into its socket, its fingers straightening with a series of pops. Step, and the blood fell from his face, revealing not the demonic visage that Corvis had recognized, but the more mundane features that had borne the name *Kaleb*.

But though the greatest wound, the mark of Talon itself, had closed, it did not fade entirely. For all his control over his corporeal body, he lacked the inner strength to finish the job. Soon, yes, when he'd had the opportunity to rest, to recover from the unexpected torment. But not now.

Leaving the weapon where it lay—hoping that some villager might be stupid enough to come out and try to claim it, offering him an excuse to tear someone apart—Khanda moved along the road, following the scents of fear and pain and very familiar blood. Past several houses and a smattering of shops he walked, until he came to a large wooden structure with a great hole battered in the side.

Subtle, Corvis. Do you even know *how to use a door?*

He didn't need to enter. The scent wafting from within was more than enough to identify it as a stable. Nor did he need to examine the hoofprints that emerged, for he could literally see the magic rising off them like early-morning mists. Clearly, his prey meant to put as much distance between them as possible. Wise of them, that. Futile, but wise.

With a deliberate, unhurried pace, he returned to the wreckage, drumming two fingertips on his lips as he thought. He'd misjudged Jassion, assumed that the baron's burning hate would blind him to all else. Of course, he hadn't intended that Jassion even *hear* his words to Corvis. He'd thought the baron safely unconscious, if not dead. Still, it was a mistake that had cost him, and—though he'd never have admitted it—shamed him. Once, Khanda had been a far better judge of mortal souls. His long association with, and his smoldering anger at, the Terror of the East had obviously clouded that judgment. Not again. His most important ally remained, and of her he would make absolutely certain.

And there she was. Khanda jerked to a stop, staring at the ground beyond the rocks that had imprisoned him. He'd not seen her when he first emerged, too distracted by his pain and fury, but there she lay, asleep, not half a dozen yards from where he'd been buried.

Ah, Corvis, you big softy. You went after her, didn't you? For that was the *true* nature of the spell he'd cast upon her when she first joined him in his travels. Not to protect her, as he'd allowed both her and Jassion to believe, but to conjure her to his side should her father come too close, ensuring they had no opportunity to reconcile.

Wincing, he knelt and lifted Talon by the hilt. He could feel the weapon squirming, and the skin of his own palm crawled at its touch. It had not been forged for his kind; its shape did not change, for he had no soul to taste. For his own sake, Khanda would have gladly left it behind.

But *Kaleb* would not have, and for a little longer, Kaleb remained essential.

Clutching the Kholben Shiar in one hand, gathering the ragged remnants of his clothes with the other, Kaleb moved to her. He knelt, removing the enchantment that kept her in slumber, and then collapsed to the road beside her, waiting for her to awaken.

"OH, GODS! KALEB, WHAT *HAPPENED* TO YOU?"

Only moments had passed before he felt her hands upon his shoulders, heard the horror in her voice. She didn't even ask how she'd gotten here; she was more alarmed at finding him coated in blood than in finding herself sprawled in the street rather than upon the straw pallet where she'd slept. Feigning exhaustion—well, feigning *part* of it— Kaleb allowed her to help him up, slumped in her arms as he pointed with one shaking hand. "There," he whispered. "I think . . . we'll be safe there."

The restaurant's porch and a portion of its outer wall had collapsed during the battle, but the rest of the squat structure appeared solid— and it had long since emptied itself of fleeing, panicked peasants. Leaning heavily on Mellorin, he limped and staggered inside and up the steps to the first empty room. Talon clattered to the floor by the doorway as he lurched toward the bed, while she darted back downstairs to gather supplies from the kitchen. She was gone only moments.

Forcing himself to remain patient, he allowed her to bathe his face with a wet cloth, cleaning away the last of the dried blood and grime, and to bandage those wounds that still showed in his flesh. At times he groaned, even crying out as he clutched at her. Once or twice he heard her whispered prayers to Sannos the Healer, and had to suppress an instinctive sneer.

Finally she was finished. Kaleb lay flat upon the mattress, stripped to the waist save for various bandages, his entire body damp—and, in a few places, rubbed raw by Mellorin's heartfelt but unskilled ministrations. She sat beside him, eyes clouded by worry and unshed tears, holding his hand in hers. Her hair hung across her face, matted and disheveled from sleep, and flecks of dried blood speckled the tunic and leggings she'd worn ever since collapsing beneath the strain of Kaleb's spells.

"What happened?" she asked him again.

"I . . . I managed to cast one final spell, to call you to me. I didn't want to put you in danger," he said, as though begging her to understand. "But there was nobody else."

"Who did this to you, Kaleb?"

"Your . . . Mellorin, I'm sorry. It was your father."

"What?" Her voice had gone suddenly small.

"I'm sorry," he repeated, sitting up. "I never meant it to go like this. You—you were so exhausted, from my divination spells. We thought we'd let you sleep while we explored the town."

"Without me?" She sounded so terribly hurt, it was all he could do not to burst out laughing.

"Nothing was supposed to *happen*, Mellorin. We just wanted to get the lay of the land, see if we could figure out where he was staying, who might be with him. The idea was to learn everything we could, then come back and make our plans.

"But . . . Your uncle."

She nodded her understanding. "He wouldn't wait."

"He was like a wild animal. As soon as we spotted your father, that was it. I should have known better, should never have let him come . . ."

"It's all right," she told him softly—and then the implications finally struck home. "Where *is* Jassion?"

"Gone." Kaleb looked deep into her eyes. "He went with them. They must have done something to him; he wasn't himself." Carefully, remembering to limp, he rose and moved past her, toward the door. He bent with an audible grunt to lift Talon, extended it hilt-first toward the hesitant young woman.

"No, I couldn't . . ."

"You can give it back to him, if you feel the need, once we've freed him. But it's just the two of us now, Mellorin. And we're stronger with it."

Trembling fingers closed about the hilt, and the Kholben Shiar shifted, folding in on itself. In seconds Mellorin held a brutal, thick-bladed knife with a wide guard, a weapon equally suited for parrying a larger blade or gutting an unsuspecting foe. A street fighter's weapon.

"I guess the formal training didn't take," he joked with a wince.

For several heartbeats she examined the blade, and then resolutely placed it on the floor beside her and stepped forward to take his hands, guiding him back to bed. Allowing her to seat him, he gazed up at her.

"Mellorin . . ." He paused, cleared his throat. "If this is too much, if you want to give up, I couldn't blame—"

"Hush." She placed a finger against his lips. "I won't leave you to do this alone, not now."

He offered her a wide smile, then gently kissed the tip of her finger. Her entire body quivered. Slowly he reached out, pulling her to him.

"Kaleb . . ."

Whatever she might have had to say was lost in a long, impassioned kiss. He pulled back for just a moment, offering her the chance to speak, but there were no words in her quickened, frantic breaths. They fell back, moving as one, and they had no more need for words at all.

But if the soft sounds from beneath him were gasps of passion, even love, in Kaleb's fire-blackened heart there lurked only a horrid exultation.

Chapter Twenty-one

THEY COULD NEVER COMPREHEND IT, of course, but the horses had every reason to be grateful for the sorry state of Corvis and his companions. Had they been able, the riders would likely have ridden the poor beasts to death under the twin pressures of the hastening spell—cast by Seilloah, this time, as Corvis was in no shape to invoke it—and their desperation to put distance between themselves and the manifest demon.

Instead, as they pounded across the open road, every step a jolt of sheer agony, the wind driving dust and grit into open wounds, Corvis knew they would have to stop, and stop soon. If they didn't, the ride itself might well kill them, saving Khanda the trouble.

Well, he noted bitterly, Khanda and the Cephirans.

Khanda, the Cephirans, and the agents of the Guilds.

And possibly the gnomes, if they'd found their missing brother.

And Jassion himself, for that matter.

It was all enough to make a fellow *really* depressed.

For long hours, Corvis didn't see the road before him, or the horse's mane waving in his face. He saw only the farmhouse, less than a mile from the village proper, in which Jassion had *sworn* they'd left Mellorin, and the rented loft in which he'd sworn they would find her.

They hadn't. Indeed, they'd found no sign of *anyone* within the house, be it Mellorin or the homeowners. Corvis would have stayed, torn apart the whole house—the whole *village*—with his bare hands, no matter that it took hours or even days; would have gladly consigned his life to Khanda rather than leave his little girl in the demon's clutches. When his companions had made to drag him from his search, to flee before the creature freed itself, he'd actually reached for Sunder.

It had, astoundingly, been neither Irrial nor Seilloah but *Jassion* who'd gotten through to him. "Rebaine, if that creature finds us, he'll slaughter us. *All* of us. You think it'll matter to him if Mellorin's with us? So long as he can use her, she lives! Would you be the one to change her from ally to enemy in his eyes?"

And so, though Corvis wept with frustration and burned with the need to feel the baron's neck break beneath his squeezing fingers, they had gone. On stolen horses they fled, and swiftly the old warrior learned that he would not easily lose himself in the journey, for each pain he escaped was replaced by another.

Every limb ached. His back screamed in agony where he'd struck the rubble, and each jostle of the horse's steps made it worse. His jaw pounded, the laceration on his forehead itched, his gut ached where the very tip of Talon had stuck him after transfixing Khanda. And thank Kassek and Panaré both that it had *just* been the tip; it didn't take much for the Kholben Shiar to kill. (Corvis hadn't bothered to ask Jassion if he'd *meant* to stab them both, since he was pretty sure he knew the answer.)

But all that, Corvis could have managed. It was the wound to his mind and soul that threatened to lay him low. He couldn't rid himself of the memory of Khanda's foul presence in his head. He felt filthy, violated. He swore something slick and viscous clung inside him, coating his thoughts. He hurt anytime he tried to reason, and the simple act of remembering burned like an infected sore. Even picturing Mellorin, allowing himself the worry and concern that was his right as a father, was almost too painful to bear. Corvis had never been a religious man, but he prayed now beneath his breath, begging the gods to let him heal before the poison in his psyche fermented into true dementia.

At least, if nothing else, the voice that had yammered at him for years, and so much more frequently in recent weeks, seemed to have gone silent. Had it truly been a lingering remnant, now returned to the resurrected demon? Or had it been imagination, the first signs of a fracturing mind, now buried beneath a more severe insipient madness? Corvis dared not even guess, and it hurt too terribly to think about; he knew only that, as silver linings went, trading a phantom of Khanda for the real thing left much to be desired.

He twisted in the saddle, groaning and clutching his stomach, struggling to see the others. The clouds seemed to be following them from town—were they, too, fleeing Khanda's presence?—and they wept a persistent drizzle that hung in the air, forming a glutinous fog. The moon was nothing but a gleaming sliver within those clouds, selfishly hoarding its light, and were it not for the sounds of hooves and the sporadic groan of pained fatigue, Corvis might have thought himself alone.

But then, he didn't need to see, not really. He'd seen his companions well enough when they'd mounted up, and assuredly none of them had gotten *better* over the intervening miles.

He tried to shout, to make himself heard over the horses and the rain, and succeeded only in driving himself into a fit of hacking coughs. Fine, then. They'd just have to follow. Corvis yanked on the reins, driving his horse off the path and across a rocky, scrub-dotted plain.

Here there were insufficient trees in which to hide. But the knolls and rises of stone, while lacking both the height and the sheltering caves of those through which they'd earlier passed, boasted the occasional overhang within the bowl-shaped depressions that feebly masqueraded as valleys. Poor cover indeed, but it would keep *some* of the rain from their heads—and, more important, hide them from casual search. They might even risk a brief fire, if they kept it banked low.

Corvis didn't know if the others realized what he was doing, or followed him purely out of habit, but nobody hesitated or questioned the change in direction.

It was tricky, picking a course through the rocky slopes on horseback. Corvis was forced to gather what little focus he could muster and cast a spell of illumination. He kept it dull, scarcely brighter than a candle. It was feeble, but it was enough, and some moments later they tromped listlessly into a hollow between two hills.

Corvis toppled from the saddle in what couldn't even generously be called "dismounting," landing on his feet through sheer force of will. He watched as the others filed slowly into the meager light upon horses lathered in sweat and rain. Irrial remained in the best shape of them all. Though her skin was pallid, her hands lacerated, her limbs covered in bruises, she displayed no serious injuries and her shoulders remained unbowed. With as much care as she could muster, she hauled Seilloah's canine form from a broad leather saddlebag and laid her gently on the earth. The witch was trembling, whimpering in agonies that resulted only partly from recent travails. Open sores marred her matted fur, and her tongue lolled out in constant panting. Corvis didn't need her to explain that she would need a new body soon—or that she had only a few "mounts" remaining before her magics could no longer sustain her.

That thought, in turn, drew his attention to the final rider, and Corvis found his physical discomfort washed away. Jassion was teetering precariously, one foot in the stirrup as he dismounted, when the older warrior seized him by the shoulders, hauling him bodily from the horse and slamming him against the slope of the nearest hill. Dust erupted around the impact, then fell from the air as the raindrops transfigured it into mud. Corvis loomed over him, fists clenched so hard they trembled. He'd torn open the shallow wound in his belly, making his tunic and trousers run red, but he hardly seemed to notice.

"You *bastard!*" He lurched forward, landing with one hand on the slope, the other grasping at Jassion's neck. "You brought *Mellorin* into this? Does your own godsdamn family mean *nothing* to you?"

Jassion's own hands closed on Corvis's wrist, holding the choking fingers just inches from his throat. He snarled a response, but the words were lost in the steady drizzle and the heavy gasping of two enraged foes.

This close, and with the worst of the blood washed away by the weather, Corvis saw that the injury he'd inflicted to Jassion's face wasn't quite so bad as he'd thought. Only a small chunk of the nose had actually been ripped away. What remained would always be mangled, clearly disfigured, but with proper attention and a skilled healer, the baron would be able to breathe properly, smell the scents of the world around him, speak without impediment.

Except that Corvis didn't plan to give him the time to heal. Or, for that matter, to breathe.

There they remained, locked together by flesh and hatred—for mere seconds, for untold centuries. Until a gleaming length of steel appeared between them, a serpent's tongue flickering between their faces.

"That's enough! Both of you, back off." Startled, Corvis loosened his grip and stepped away, even as Jassion stood upright.

It took Corvis a moment to recognize the voice. Much time had passed since he'd heard Irrial speak as a baroness, but she did so now, her back and her blade held straight, her expression and her voice harder than the surrounding rock. Even battered and bedraggled in the falling rain, Corvis thought she'd never looked so imperial.

And the part of him that could still push some amount of coherent thought through the residue in his soul and the fury burning in his blood believed, without doubt, that she would *use* that blade if they did not heed her command.

"Irrial, what—?"

"No. You first, Rebaine. That—that *thing*. That was the demon you spoke of? That was Khanda?"

"It was," he said, casting a bitter glare at Jassion.

It was nearly invisible, so rigid did the baron hold himself, but his face wilted just a little. "I didn't know. I *couldn't* know."

"Couldn't you?" Corvis demanded. "I don't—"

Again, Irrial cut him off. "Shut it!" She shook her head, sending water spraying in all directions. Then, after a moment, "Baron Jassion?"

"My lady?" he answered reflexively.

"Why did you help us?"

Fingers curled and uncurled, a jaw shifted as teeth ground together. Jassion seemed to wrestle with his emotions more fiercely than he had with Corvis himself.

"Because . . ." He took a deep breath, spat the words as though they burned him. "Because I will not be responsible for setting this Khanda loose upon Imphallion. Because some things"—and his voice dropped in amazement at his own admission—"are more important even than *this.*" His glare left no doubt as to who "this" meant.

"Good. Then you two can damn well put this aside until we've dealt with the bloody *demon*! Afterward, I don't care. Slaughter each other, drown in each other's blood, carve each other into fish bait—I *don't care.* But so help me gods, you'll do it *afterward*, not now!"

Corvis knew that the look he cast at Jassion was petulant, petty—as petulant and petty as the one he received in exchange. But Irrial was right, and no matter how he wanted to deny it, to feel the baron's bones break under his fists, to drive Sunder through that despised face, he *knew* she was right.

It was, for that matter, no more than he'd asked of *her*, from the instant he'd told her his real name.

Lacking the energy even to grumble under his breath, Corvis stalked away to the far side of the tiny vale.

It was only after he'd slumped down, shifted a few times trying (and failing) to find a position where the rocks didn't bite into his aching back, that he noticed the shivering hound beside him. The smell of wet dog was a slap across the face, but he figured it wiser not to comment.

"Yes?" he asked in a coarse rasp.

"You're not just going to leave it like this!" Seilloah demanded.

He would, at least, do her the courtesy of not pretending to ask what she was talking about. "Only for a time, Seilloah. Only until—"

"You said you'd kill him!"

"I will, damn it! But not *now*. Irrial's right. We need him. *Mellorin* needs him! He knows too much about what's going on for us to just throw that—"

"Corvis, he *murdered me!*"

He reached out to take her snout in his hand, but she jerked aside. "And if there's any way for me to make him pay for that, I will," he swore. "But Seilloah, this *has* to come first! This—"

"Of course it does," she spat at him. "Your concerns *always* come first, don't they?"

The witch was gone, limping as fast as three working legs could manage, before Corvis could draw breath to reply.

———————————⊳ ⊲———————————

NIGHTMARES BESIEGED CORVIS'S SLUMBER. Happy memories bubbled like burned stew through his brain, painful and foul. In the shadows of every image, every dream, he saw Khanda, laughing, and from his gnarled, inhuman fingers hung a limp body whose face Corvis didn't dare allow himself to see.

They slept later than they meant to the following morning, bone-deep exhaustion proving more than a match for their need to keep moving. Most of their aches and pains and wounds weren't much improved. Seilloah hadn't returned, and Corvis's own spells of healing were meager, little better than mundane poultices and herbs. But he'd found that, so long as he didn't dwell on anything in particular, the mere act of *remembering* didn't seem quite so agonizing as it had the previous night. He dared hope that the residue of Khanda's violation would fade with time.

Even once they'd awakened, they found themselves unable to get started immediately. The low-hanging sky was thick and grey as dirty cotton, the breeze brushed shivering skin with a thin autumn chill, and the ground had become slick mud, but at least it wasn't raining just then. Hollow stomachs demanded breakfast, fearful minds puzzled over why Khanda had not tracked them down during the night, and Corvis couldn't shake the gnawing feeling in his gut that Seilloah might never be coming back.

It was, blended with his worry for Mellorin, a bitter draught to swallow.

"Perhaps," Jassion proposed as he poked at the remnants of the dried meats that had been breakfast, "we injured him worse than we thought?" His voice, through the bandage that now ran across his face like a scarf, was wretchedly nasal. "Maybe he couldn't even find us."

"How did you find us the *first* time?" Irrial asked.

The baron glanced at Corvis across the charred wood that had recently been a small fire, tensing. "Mellorin."

Corvis could see Irrial and Jassion both holding their breath, and forced himself to remain motionless until he could bring his emotions back under control. "Tell me."

"For what it's worth, Rebaine, *she* followed *us*, and it was Kaleb—that is, Khanda—who decided she would come along. I thought . . . I believed I could protect her.

"In any event," he bulled ahead before Corvis could reply, "Khanda used *her* as a focus of his spells to find you."

Corvis frowned, then nodded. "Blood relation. My spells wouldn't have been strong enough to prevent that."

"No, but they interfered well enough. We had to be pretty close to pinpoint you. I don't *think* we've gotten far enough in one night to escape its range, but maybe, if Khanda's wounded badly enough . . ." He shrugged.

"So, what? You just *happened* to be near enough for the spell to work? When we were staying in the middle of nowhere, in a village roughly the size of a pinecone?"

"Kal—Khanda said he tracked you via the spells you'd cast on the ogre, Davro."

"Wh—Davro? Did you kill *him*, too?"

"No." Jassion shook his head. "Mellorin wouldn't allow it, and Khanda went along with her." It was the baron's turn to scowl. "You'd better know, Rebaine. Her relationship with 'Kaleb' has gotten, uh, complicated. As in, teenage-girl-complicated."

Corvis groaned, head actually slumping into his palms. For several moments, the others decided to let him be, though Jassion—despite his concern for Mellorin—couldn't quite repress a nasty grin at the pain in the older man's tone.

Only when he finally looked up through bloodshot eyes did Irrial ask softly, "Is it possible? Could they have found us through Davro?"

"I couldn't say," Corvis admitted. "Normally, I'd think not. Seilloah barely accomplished it, and the spell was cast directly on her. But I don't know the full extent of Khanda's power in his present form." A thought struck him. "Kaleb mentioned a 'Master Nenavar.' Does that name mean anything to you?"

Jassion's brow furrowed. "I don't believe so. Though it's fairly obvious that I know less of what's happening than I believed."

"I think," Corvis said, steeling himself with another deep breath, "that you'd better tell us everything."

———————

MECEPHEUM. No matter how he tried to avoid it, the answers always seemed to lead him back to bloody godsdamn *Mecepheum!* He was starting to loathe that city as virulently as he did Denathere, but the Guilds were the only answer Jassion could offer. So Mecepheum it would be.

Although the autumn air was cool and the breezes gentle, the ride was hard, the road long. Their days were a frenetic fog of anxiety, pressing the horses as hard as they dared, walking them when flesh threatened to fail beneath the strain. Their nights, save on those rare occasions when they were fortunate enough to stumble upon a convenient roadside inn, were spent tossing and turning on the hard earth. Corvis could not speak for the others, of course, but his own sleep was replete with the most hideous nightmares, growing ever worse even as his *waking* thoughts slowly healed from Khanda's ravages.

Each evening, he cast upon himself those spells that would alert him if someone approached too near at night, and each morning he awoke, head aching, with his wards undisturbed. Jassion had apparently, despite his burning hatred, fully accepted the need for cooperation. For the time being.

Days matured into weeks, and Khanda did not appear. Every waking moment became an exercise in paranoia, the travelers watching over their shoulders, jumping at every sound, hands dropping to weapons if a horse so much as snorted. Wounds refused to heal, thanks to the constant tension in their muscles and the pounding of horseflesh beneath them.

Even worse, Seilloah had never returned to that camp amid the rolling, rocky hills, and after hours spent in searching, they'd been forced to move on. Corvis felt as though he'd left one piece of himself behind in that hollow, and another, even larger, in the lonely farmhouse where he'd all but abandoned his daughter. He wondered, on occasion, if very much of him was left to lose.

Now, only a few days shy of their goal, they'd stopped in yet another small town, taken rooms for the night in yet another small inn. It was bustling without being *too* packed, laborers crowding the benches and tables, barmaids wending their way from one throng to the next. It smelled neither of food nor drink but of autumn leaves. Corvis wondered idly how they managed it, but didn't care enough to ask.

Mellorin had always loved the autumn, as a child.

Jassion sat halfway around the room, uninterested in conversation. He idly examined the blade he'd purchased in Orthessis to replace Talon, checking it for flaws that might somehow have escaped his notice during a dozen prior, similar inspections. Corvis couldn't help but remember another tavern, another common room, another sword, another conversation. He couldn't decide if it felt like yesterday or another lifetime.

Irrial, it seemed, had noticed the same similarities. "It sort of feels like we're running around in circles, doesn't it?" she asked from across the table.

"You've no idea," he told her bitterly. "He's done it to me again, Irrial."

"What are you . . . ?"

"Khanda." Hatred dripped like venom from the name. "Another war. Another threat to my family. And Khanda lurking around its edges, hiding behind whoever started it, drawing me out. Using me for what I have, or what I know. I'm tired enough of battle—I'm bloody *sick* of being led into battle by the nose!" He couldn't hold his hands entirely steady as he took a slug of a drink he'd forgotten he'd ordered; foamy suds sloshed over the tankard's rim, dribbled down his fingers. "I'm tired of seeing the wrong people die."

Irrial furrowed her brow at that, and Corvis was certain some biting comment was on its way, but it never materialized. Instead, "You're really worried about her, aren't you?"

"She's my daughter," he said simply. "I'd die for her."

"I believe you would, at that." She sounded amazed, though whether it was at his assertion, or at herself for *believing* his assertion, Corvis couldn't guess. They sat, each drinking, each contemplating the other.

"I don't understand you, Corvis," she finally told him. "But I think I understand *Tyannon* a little better. There really are two different people inside that soul of yours, aren't there?"

"I'm not sure I follow." *Or maybe you're just going somewhere I don't want to follow.* Postponing her reply, he waved over one of the barmaids, barked an order for another flagon and more bread and cheese. It was gooey, salty stuff, that last, but after weeks of dried meats, it'd do.

Irrial waited, her face blank, until the woman had come and gone, returned with the order and gone once more. She leaned in, so she might make herself heard over the growing crowd without shouting.

"You so *clearly* care about Mellorin—about all your family. I know you're worried sick about Seilloah, I saw your concern for our brethren in the Rahariem resistance. I think . . . I think you even truly care about me, despite the last few months. I know you certainly *used* to."

"Well, gods be—"

"I'm not done."

A pause. "Sorry."

"I've seen all that, Corvis. I've seen that you're not *just* a monster. And I know that you care for the people of Imphallion as a whole—or you think you do, at any rate. You're helping them *now*, even if you also have personal reasons. You told me once that everything you've done, you did for them, and I think part of you really means that."

Corvis swirled his mug until it sloshed. "Um, thank you?"

"And yet," she said, her tone growing hard once more, "you have no trouble at all wading to your goal through rivers of blood. Slaughtering families, hanging body parts like bunting.

"Consorting with demons."

"It wasn't like I *wanted* to—"

"But you did. It doesn't matter if you *wanted* to—you were *willing* to. You know what I think, Corvis?" she asked, gesturing with an empty fork.

"I'm not certain I want to," he confessed.

"Too bad. I think that you're so disdainful of *people* as a whole that you forget—that you *let* yourself forget—that each one is a *person*. You talk about Imphallion like it was a single entity, because that's how you see it; it's the only way you can give a damn about it. You've added it to your list of 'worthwhile individuals,' and everyone else can hang. I think that you're so focused on those few you care about, it's never even occurred to you that everyone else is *just like them*. I think you're so wounded, inside, that you only have so much sympathy, and the more people you're dealing with, the thinner that sympathy is spread.

"You care about people, yes. Deeply, passionately. But only *some* people—because nobody else is a person to you at all. And to pretend that you do what you do for 'the people,' rather than the handful of souls that mean a damn to you, is the biggest lie you've ever told."

Corvis found himself staring into his tankard, clasping it with all ten fingers for fear that he might otherwise lash out. "And even if . . ." He cleared his throat, coughed twice. "If all this is true, why point it out? What difference could it possibly make?"

"Because I also think . . ." It was her turn to pause. Her voice had gone soft, softer than he'd heard since they left Rahariem. He wanted to look up, to see if her face had softened as well, and found he didn't dare. "Because I think Tyannon was right. I think you *could* be Cerris, instead of Corvis Rebaine. I'd like you to be. But I don't think you know how, and I don't think any of us are ever going to be able to show you."

By the time Corvis forced himself to raise his head, she was gone from the table. And for just an instant, as the tavern disappeared beneath the memory of a flower garden behind a dilapidated old church, he couldn't tell if it was Irrial or Tyannon who was walking away.

Chapter Twenty-two

AS THREE DUSTY TRAVELERS MOUNTED the broad stone steps, the guards at the door—and there *were* guards at the door, now, accompanying the ubiquitous clerk—moved to block their path. Jassion marched in the lead, poised, arrogant, and without visible trace of the hideous injury he would sport until the end of his days. Behind him trailed two figures clad in the costly but relatively bland garb of servants. One, the woman, held the arm of the elder man, who took small, hesitant steps as though injured or ill.

He was, in fact, gritting his teeth and straining not in pain, but in concentration, trying to keep three separate images affixed firmly in his mind. It would have been easier had he not still suffered lingering aftereffects of Khanda's attack; had his soul not been wringing its hands inside his body, wracked with fear for Mellorin and Seilloah; had he been at his best.

But only a *little* easier, for all that.

While Jassion spoke in low but commanding tones to the soldiers, Corvis glanced upward, peering intently at the sky through the illusion that masked his features. The uppermost reaches of the Hall of Meeting blended with the overcast skies, dark grey on darker. Only a smattering of windows and, in a few instances, the crows and sparrows perching along the roof's edge, made the looming structure visible against the clouds.

"I'm *really* not comfortable with this, Corvis," Irrial whispered in his ear.

"They can't see our real faces," he reminded her.

"And that worked out so well for us last time?"

He shrugged. "We've just spent weeks in the saddle. I'm not recovered from one of the top five worst experiences in my life. My head feels like a sack of meal left out in the rain, and my body like there's a pair of ogres waltzing up and down my spine. You're lucky I'm lucid; you want *new* ideas, go pester someone else."

"I suppose that's fair." Then, "Only one of the top five?"

"My years have been blessed with an *astonishing* variety of discomfort."

They didn't hear what Jassion said to the guards, but eventually he waved them forward. The soldiers stepped aside, and the trio walked with measured tread into the seat of Imphallion's mercantile government.

"It's disgraceful!" Jassion hissed as they walked, his tone still vaguely nasal. He kept his voice low despite his clear agitation, lest any of the many scurrying pages and couriers overhear. "War with Cephira, attacks by—ah, 'Rebaine'—and for all their added security, the guards just took me at my word and let us in!"

"Well, you *are* who you said you were," Irrial pointed out.

"*They* didn't know that!"

"We're pretty far from the front. And it's not as though they expect You-Know-Who to walk in the front door."

"It's disgraceful," he muttered again. "If a soldier has a job to do, he should *do* it! I'd have these men flogged if they worked for me."

Corvis, feeling that Jassion's sense of propriety was perhaps misplaced at the moment—particularly since *they* were the security breach the guards' negligence permitted—chose not to say anything to get the baron even more riled. He did, however, roll his eyes at Irrial, who rewarded him, oh so briefly, with that amused curl of her lips he'd not seen in far too long.

Through familiar corridors, up familiar stairs—and even, once, past a stain of what was probably familiar blood—they wended their way. It looked much as it had the last time they'd been here, save for the presence of many more guards. Corvis began to have serious doubts about their plan, unsure if they could win free should it go wrong. But as he had no better notions to offer, and as it was already too late even if he had, he kept his misgivings private.

The top floor, and back to that one particular office guarded by half a dozen sentries. Jassion made as if to march right past them, until they steadfastly refused to clear the way. With a full-blown aristocratic glower that Corvis wasn't certain was feigned, he announced, "The Baron Jassion of Braetlyn, and associates, to see Guildmistress Salia Mavere. *Right now.*"

"Have you an appointment?" the guard asked, just as impressed with this strutting noble as he'd been with all the others he'd thrown out.

"No."

"Then—"

"Just announce us. She'll see us."

The guard didn't bother to hide his sigh, and Corvis feared he'd have to physically restrain Jassion from bludgeoning the man to death. After a few deep breaths, however, the baron calmed himself, and the soldier indicated the door with a shallow tilt of his head. One of the other men cracked that door open and stepped inside. They could just hear the voices, here in the hall, and while they couldn't make out a single word, the surprise in one of those voices was more than a little evident.

The guard reappeared, shaking his head in astonishment. "She'll see them," he told his commander, now sounding as surprised as Mavere had.

"She—what? But . . ."

"She said she'll see them."

The officer was visibly crestfallen. "All right," he grumbled. Then, before Jassion took half a step, "but not under arms."

"My companions are *not* armed," he replied. "Search them if you like. As for me . . ." He raised his hand, *slowly* so as not to cause undue alarm, to touch the hilt protruding over his shoulder. "I'll not be relinquishing my sword, no. Ask the Guildmistress. I doubt she'll explain why, but she'll assure you it's all right."

Corvis did his best to look meek, face aimed at the floor so nobody would see him grinding his teeth. Just seeing the blade on Jassion's back was enough to make him want to . . .

The guard returned to the office looking even more dubious, and came out looking even more perplexed. "She says it's all right."

The officer grunted something impolite and stepped aside. Without so much as a nod of acknowledgment, Jassion strode past, Corvis and Irrial following close behind.

"Baron Jassion?" Salia asked, rising from behind her desk. "I have to admit, I'm a bit concerned to learn you're here. Why—?"

It all happened at once, between one breath and the next. Irrial firmly shut the door behind her. Jassion bowed low before the Guild-mistress, far lower than was his wont. And Corvis, allowing his con-centration to lapse and the illusions to drop, sprinted across the room like a starving leopard. His fist closed around Sunder's hilt, yanking it from the scabbard across Jassion's back—and gods, had *that* taken long hours of arguing, and many oaths on Jassion's part, before Irrial con-vinced him to place the weapon, however briefly, in the baron's care. In the heartbeats it took him to vault the desk, sending a flurry of parchment in all directions, the Kholben Shiar had shifted once more from Jassion's two-hander to Corvis's axe, the blade of which now gently kissed the priestess's throat. Corvis wasn't certain whether he, or Salia herself, was more disturbed by the weapon's eager quiver.

"If you so much as raise your voice above a whisper," Corvis warned her, "the Blacksmiths' Guild will be, ah, let's say, looking for a new head."

Her glare was sharper than Sunder itself, her face as pallid as those parchments drifting slowly to the floor, her jaw clenched tight enough to bend raw iron—but she nodded shallowly.

"I'd apologize for the discourtesy," Jassion told her, moving to stand before the desk. The bandage tied across his face, discolored where hu-mors occasionally seeped from his ravaged nose, was now clearly visi-ble. "But in all honesty, I'd prefer to let him kill you."

"Jassion, what . . . ?" Even at a whisper, her fury and her confusion—
and yes, her fear—were palpable.

"I do not," he said harshly, "appreciate being used, Mavere."

"I don't know what you've done to him," she began, eyes flickering
to the man at her side, "what spells you've cast on him, but—"

"No spells, Salia. No tricks, no sorcery. You said that you had knowledge of magic when we last spoke. Take a good look at him."

She shrugged, wincing as the movement scraped the skin of her
throat across the blade. "Wouldn't help. Illusions I can detect; they're
visible. If I could sense spells of the mind, I'd have discovered all your
puppets in Guild ranks long ago." Her voice seemed almost wistful at
that.

Corvis frowned, but it made sense.

"And I cannot," she added, "think of anything *other* than the most
potent magics that would inspire Lord Jassion to cooperate with *you*."

"You should have thought harder then," Irrial interjected, sliding
the latch home on the door and stepping into the center of the room,
"before starting all this."

The Guildmistress looked from one to the other, saw no pity anywhere. Corvis could see in her expression that she was weighing the
odds if she called for the guards.

"You'd be dead before your voice reached them," he warned. Her
shoulders slumped.

"Where's Kaleb?" she demanded.

Jassion smiled shallowly. "I'm sorry, I don't know who you—oh. Perhaps you mean *Khanda*?"

So stiffly did Salia tense that Corvis had to yank Sunder back a hair
to avoid cutting her. "How did—?"

"What were you *thinking*, you stupid bitch?" Irrial and Corvis exchanged worried glances, concerned that Jassion's own temper might
alert the guards, but so far the baron was managing—albeit barely—to
keep his voice low. "How could you use me that way? How could you
unleash something like *that creature* on your own people?"

"I assure you, Khanda is completely under control."

"Not for long," Corvis told her. Then, at her expression, "You asked what could inspire Jassion and me to work together? That'd do it, wouldn't you think?"

"It's not possible. Jassion, whatever Rebaine's told you, it's a lie. He—"

"Is more convincing than you. Especially given what I've seen recently." Then, though it clearly cost him, he forced his voice, his expression, to calm. "Mavere, I only saw the aftermath of the Twins' rampage through Mecepheum, but *you* were present for all of it. You've seen what creatures of such power can do—and you've seen how little we can do to stop them. We know some of what Khanda plans, and I assure you, if he succeeds you'll wish you'd died back then."

"It's a lie," she insisted stubbornly.

"Perhaps you'll want to ask Nenavar about that?" Corvis suggested. Again, standing so close, he couldn't possibly miss the tension that ran across Salia's body like a cold shiver. She knew the name, all right.

"It's he who assured me that the bonds on the summoning were unbreakable. And I've *seen* him put Kaleb—Khanda—in his place. Besides, even if I wanted to, I've no means of just calling him here. I'd have to send a messenger, and I doubt you're willing to sit in this office for the hours it would take for a reply."

"I can be surprisingly patient," Corvis told her. "So can Irrial. Jassion might be a problem, I imagine." He ignored the bandage-wrapped glare. "But that's all moot, since you're not sending a messenger. You're going to take us to him."

Her laugh was a forced and feeble thing. "And why would I do that?"

"Because even walking through the halls or the streets, we can kill you before any help arrives," Jassion snarled at her. "And if you won't help us, there's no reason not to kill you *right now* for what you've done!"

"More to the point," Corvis said, shaking his head in exasperation, "no matter how certain you think you are that we're lying to you, you can *see* Jassion and me standing here, working together, telling you the same thing. And you're worried that we just *might* be telling you the

truth. Tell me, Salia, would Verelian be served by his own priestess un-
leashing a demon in the mortal world? Are you willing to go down in
history as the next Audriss—assuming there even *is* a history after
Khanda gets through with us?

"I don't know what you're trying to accomplish with all of this," he
continued more softly, "though I think I can guess a good chunk of it.
But what I'm *certain* of is that all your plans won't be worth a gnome's
chamber pot if Khanda breaks loose. So you tell us, Salia. Which way
do you want it?"

———————————⟨————⟩ ⟨————⟩———————————

THEY'D NEEDED HER COMPLIANCE, prayed for it, even
counted on it—but that didn't mean they were remotely ready to *trust*
it. Throughout the nerve-racking trek through the corridors and stairs
of the Hall of Meeting, one or the other of them remained at Mavere's
back, ready to act if she even looked askance at a passing guard, the
others equally alert in case any of the passing guards looked askance at
them. Even after they'd gathered their horses, and hers, they walked the
beasts through Mecepheum's streets, the better to ensure the Guildmistress remained within easy reach. Only once they'd passed through
the main gates did they mount up and ride, and even then they took
steps to ensure Salia remained in their midst.

The faint but steady autumn breezes and overcast skies had brought
a certain chill to the roads. Thus, though she'd claimed that the ride
was only a few hours, they'd taken the opportunity—always with careful eyes on Salia, of course—to acquire some traveling cloaks and coats
before leaving the city. It was partly for the sake of their own comfort,
but mostly as an excuse, under the guise of "friendly assistance" while
shopping, for Irrial to search their unwilling guest for concealed
weapons. More than once, Corvis sensed the priestess's gaze upon him
and had looked around to see not merely the anger and the fear that
he'd anticipated—even, he had to admit, reveled in—but also a peculiar *puzzlement*.

He wasn't about to ask her what was wrong, of course. But he did
wonder.

As they traversed a minor highway that was festively garbed in fallen leaves of red and gold, Corvis watched Jassion with idly hostile curiosity. The baron fiddled with the ties around his throat, trying to keep the knot of his bandage from getting caught in the folds of his new midnight-hued cloak. He fidgeted, craned his neck—and somehow, even from the rear, Corvis could tell that he frowned.

Perhaps sensing the older man's questioning gaze, Jassion tugged on the reins, dropping back a few paces. "I'm no great believer in omens," the nobleman told him, "but I have to admit, I'm not pleased at *that*."

Corvis glanced up and noted, despite their growing distance from Mecepheum, a number of crows circling high above. He thought back to the birds perched atop the roof of the Hall of Meeting, and he, too, frowned thoughtfully.

"Keep on going with the others," he said suddenly, wheeling his own horse about. "I'll catch up."

"What? Where are you—?"

"Probably nowhere. You've just got me paranoid now. I want to make sure nobody's following—that Mavere didn't somehow manage to signal anyone."

"Paranoid indeed," Jassion said. "But probably wise," he acknowledged, riding on ahead.

CORVIS DID INDEED CATCH BACK UP a few moments later and fell into step behind the others.

"Anything?" Jassion called over his shoulder.

"No danger," Corvis replied, wrapping his own crimson cloak more tightly against the autumn chill. "As you said, just paranoid."

Irrial might have detected the odd tenor in his voice, or that he sat somewhat straighter in the saddle than before. But Irrial rode at the front, with Salia between her and the others, and Jassion didn't know his hated ally well enough to notice. He simply nodded, and the four rode on.

Above, the crows continued to circle for a few moments more, and then, one by one, they departed for more worthwhile surroundings.

MECEPHEUM, AS BOTH IMPHALLION'S CAPITAL and its richest community, was one of those cities that doesn't seem to know when to stop. Like a noblewoman's skirts, neighborhoods and estates spread from the main walls.

At the edge of what could even *pretend* to be called Mecepheum stood a large estate. A squat stone manor occupied the property's center, surrounded on three sides by gardens and on the rear by a hedge maze that ran across several gentle knolls. A marble wall separated the grounds from the outside, but it wasn't much of an impediment—the iron gate in its center was unbarred, and the wall itself a mere three feet high. Obviously, it had been built not as security, but just an ornate and expensive means of declaring *My territory starts here.*

Save for the lack of guards, footmen, or even a bell-pull at the gate, there was nothing to differentiate it from any of the other rich, aristocratic estates that sprouted sporadically—gilded mushrooms, as Corvis couldn't help but think of them—throughout these long swathes of pseudo-Mecepheum.

"I have to admit," Irrial said as they halted just outside the gate, "it's not what I was expecting."

"Nor I," Jassion said.

"No?" Salia scoffed. "You imagined a bleak tower of black stones? An imposing castle of impossible spires? Or maybe a dank cave somewhere?"

"Well, he *is* a powerful wizard . . . ," Irrial protested mildly.

"And you've been reading too many melodramas. Nenavar earns his wealth by hiring his services out to any who can afford them—a rare and select few, to be sure—and enjoys that wealth as any man would. What *better* place for him to live than here?"

"If we're through critiquing the aesthetics of the nice diabolist," Corvis asked irritably, "do you suppose we might get a move on? I'd like to take steps to prevent it *before* Khanda finally shows up and tries to rip my spine out through my arsehole."

"I don't actually read many melodramas," Irrial informed them as they moved toward the gate. "I prefer to watch them performed on stage. I find it a lot more—"

"Irrial?"

"Yes, Corvis?"

"Let it go."

Jassion pushed the gate wide and led them onto the property. Corvis, who'd half expected it to swing ponderously open on its own, was peculiarly grateful that the wizard hadn't enchanted it to do so. The path led, straight as a lance, through nicely trimmed grasses and well-maintained gardens of tulips and potato blossoms to the manor door. At no point were they approached or harassed, nor did they see any sign of movement, from either the property or the house itself, for which the breeze could not account.

"Are you certain he's here?" Jassion demanded.

Salia shrugged. "How would I know?"

The door, like the manor itself, was thick, solidly built, but relatively unadorned. It boasted a brass knocker in the form of a simple ring, a smaller knob—also brass—and nothing more.

Corvis shrugged and pounded on the heavy wood. They heard the echoes reverberating through the chamber beyond, and a large chamber it must have been, but even after many minutes and several more knocks, they received no response. He clasped the knob, more out of habit than any real hope the door was unlocked, and sure enough it declined to cooperate.

"I refuse to be killed," he told the others without bothering to look back at them, "because one man happened to be out for tea when we showed up on his stoop." He muttered a few words, casting a spell to make obvious any wards or curses Nenavar might have placed upon his door. He spotted only a handful, far fewer than he anticipated, and knew that none could withstand the touch of the Kholben Shiar. Directing his companions to stand back, he hefted Sunder and brought it down beside the knob.

Wood, metal, and magic splintered, the door swung ajar, and beyond it Corvis and the others saw . . .

. . . Nothing. The house was empty. One great hollow chamber, lacking even interior walls.

"I love what he's done with the place," Corvis said blandly.

"I don't understand," Salia muttered, flinching from Jassion's angry glare. "I've sent multiple couriers! This is where he told us to find him, and this is where they've come."

And Corvis abruptly understood. "But he *wanted* them to find him. Us, perhaps less so." He stepped from the door to stare up at the nearest window, idly spinning Sunder at his side. "It's a neat trick, Nenavar!" he shouted, his words carrying to all corners of the property on a voice that had once bellowed across battlefields. "I don't know if it's a teleportation you've cast on the doorway, or an illusion, or even a bubble of an alternative realm inside the house. And I don't care. My companions and I have nowhere to be, so I'm more than happy to take the time to chop through your damn walls! Maybe that'll take us around your little spell, or maybe I'll just have to keep it up until the house collapses. Either way I promise that it'll end with you and me both in a bad mood.

"Or you can assume that, just maybe, Mavere had a good reason for bringing us here, and you can deign to talk to us."

Silence. Until, from behind him, Irrial called out, "Khanda's found a way to free himself from your spells!"

Corvis stared at her. She just shrugged.

The door slammed shut of its own accord, then opened once more. This time it revealed a cozy foyer, replete with burning incense and a cloak rack.

"Come in." The voice was thin, old and on the edge of quavering. It also came from everywhere at once. "Make yourselves at home. But Rebaine, I know what you're capable of, and I know what the Kholben Shiar are capable of, and I assure you I have more than enough power to deal with you both."

"Of course you do." Corvis watched his companions hang their cloaks upon the pegs, ignored their questioning glances when he refrained from doing the same. When they were ready, he led the way into the hall beyond.

Here was all the opulence the manor's exterior eschewed. Fine paintings hung in gilded frames; recessed niches held golden candelabra. More braziers filled the air with a subtle incense, a little cloying for Corvis's tastes but not overwhelming. Even a few of the windows, which had appeared mundane from the outside, showed themselves to be ornate stained glass when viewed from within. Through several of those, Corvis caught glimpses of movement—trees, perhaps, or low-hanging fog—that didn't remotely match the terrain of the estate outside. He wondered where in the world those windows looked. Then he wondered onto *which* world those windows looked, and then he decided to stop wondering.

Assuming that their host would let them know if they chose wrong, Corvis ignored the various closed doors and smaller side passages to either side of the hall, continuing straight until it opened up into a great room. Bookshelves stood like soldiers at attention along one wall, while a large staircase occupied another. The rest of the chamber boasted plush sofas and small reading tables. A balcony loomed above, and the man staring down at them could only have been Nenavar himself.

He looked, to Corvis, like a vulture masquerading as a man.

"I'm sorry, Nenavar," Salia began. "I didn't really have any—"

He waved a hand in arrogant dismissal. "What's this nonsense about Khanda, Rebaine? My creatures cannot harm me, and I'd certainly never release him from his bonds!"

"If you're so certain of that," Jassion murmured, "why did you let us in?"

"He can't harm you with *his* magics," Corvis corrected, ignoring the baron (as usual). "But Khanda's picked up some *human* sorcery along the way. You've no protection from *that*."

"Perhaps," he admitted grudgingly, "but there's no magic he could master potent enough to defeat me before I could cripple him."

Corvis tapped a finger against his own head. "Not even one of Selakrian's own incantations, Nenavar?"

Even from where he stood, he saw the blood drain from the wizard's face, saw his hands clench on the railing. "You kept one?"

"I did."

"Then perhaps the solution, Rebaine, is to kill *you*."

"You could try." The old warlord smiled. "Of course, Khanda's already ripped most of it from my mind. You sure me being dead would stop him from getting the rest out of me?"

Nenavar disappeared from the balcony, whether via teleportation or simply stepping back into the shadows, Corvis couldn't guess. He reappeared a moment later through one of the room's sundry doors.

"We've much work to do," he said simply. "I'll require your help in setting up; it'll go much faster than if I do it myself."

"That's it?" Jassion asked incredulously from behind. "No oaths, no threats of what'll happen if we try to harm you, no safeguards? Just 'we have work to do'?"

Nenavar offered an uneven, sickly smile. "Would you like to have a demon roving about our world unchecked, my lord?"

"Not especially."

"Oddly enough, neither would I. Now be silent and either assist or get out of our way."

For half an hour and more, Corvis and Nenavar mixed powders and herbs, drew ornate sigils across the great stone-floored cellar beneath the house. Irrial, Salia, and Jassion pounded constantly up and down the steps, fetching and carrying at Nenavar's decree—some with greater alacrity than others.

"I think," the old wizard told Corvis as the Guildmistress stomped away once more, "that Mavere still does not entirely believe you are telling the truth."

"Why do *you*?" Corvis couldn't help but ask.

"Because you have not attacked me. Because I do not think you would have revealed that you possess one of Selakrian's invocations just to run a bluff. And because the notion you've raised is horrifying enough that I cannot afford to risk it."

"Perhaps you ought to have considered that before you bloody well summoned Khanda in the first place!"

Nenavar smiled, then winced as he knelt to expand the sigil, his old joints popping loudly in the quiet. "It's what I do, Rebaine. I'm a conjurer. I've never had any difficulties before."

"And you've summoned demons before, have you?"

"A time or two. You've actually encountered my work yourself, you know."

Corvis froze a moment, then continued crushing dried leaves in a small iron pestle. "Have I?"

"Indeed." But he refused to elaborate.

"Why are you even a part of this, Nenavar? What's it all about?"

"Money. A *lot* of money, and a promise of continued employment in the new order."

"Heh. That's never a good phrase. Tell me."

"Nenavar!" It was Mavere, returned to the cellar with an armload of supplies. "Keep silent!"

But the old wizard, perhaps rattled by his guests' revelations and reluctant to alienate those who stood between him and his errant minion, ignored her command. "What do you think, Rebaine? I'm sure you've got most of it puzzled out already."

Corvis nodded and handed over the powder, watching as Nenavar sprinkled it throughout the corners of the room. "I know it involves Cephira and some of Imphallion's Guilds," he said. "And I know you got Khanda's name from Ellowaine."

"Right . . . A bit more of this, if you would."

Returning to the worktable and spilling out more leaves, Corvis continued. "It's a power play, obviously. It always is, where the Guilds are concerned. But I'm tired, I hurt, and I'm just a bit worried about Khanda right now." He mashed down on the leaves with more force than necessary, practically bending the iron in which they lay. "So you tell me."

"Nenavar . . . ," Salia warned. Again, he chose not to listen.

"I know not who first came up with the idea, whether it was General Rhykus or an Imphallian Guildmaster. Cephira would conquer the eastern reaches of Imphallion, and the Guilds wouldn't interfere. Most of the eastern provinces are still strongholds of the nobility, so their power would be substantially weakened. Once done, only then would the Guilds move, fielding their own armies to 'prevent' the invaders from moving any farther, perhaps driving them back—but only partway to the border. Cephira annexes new territories, since the eventual treaty would allow them to keep what they'd taken. The Guilds get to be the heroes who saved the rest of Imphallion from Cephiran conquest. Between their new public support and the further weakening of the noble Houses, they would squelch the political infighting between Guilds and aristocracy once and for all, transforming Imphallion into a true mercantile empire."

Corvis was certain he was driving his teeth back through his gums, so tightly was his jaw clenched, and Salia physically recoiled from his fury. He noticed only then than Irrial and Jassion stood upon the stairs as well, having paused in their errands to hear the wizard's revelations.

"Let me see," Corvis growled darkly, "if I can fill in the rest, then. The Guilds had to eliminate several nobles who weren't based in the east, but were too entrenched to ignore. And they needed an excuse to explain why they didn't react to the invasion sooner. So here comes 'Corvis Rebaine,' whose murders accomplish both right nicely." He took a step toward the stairs, his fists trembling. "I am *so bloody sick of being used!*"

"But it wasn't just nobles," Irrial noted from atop the stairs. "'Rebaine' butchered Guildsmen, too."

"Oh, I can answer that, too," Corvis told her. "Only a few Guild-masters would be in on this scheme—and some of them probably decided it was too treasonous even for *them* to swallow. So they had to go, before they could talk. And that also nicely covered up the fact that most of the *intended* victims were nobles.

"None of which answers my main question: Why Khanda?"

Salia said nothing, her face stiff.

"Because he knew you well enough to make the murders truly convincing," Nenavar answered in her stead. "Because he possessed enough power to reach the targets no matter what precautions they took, and because it put a neutral third party—that would be me, since I was technically working for both sides—in position to force either the Guilds or the Cephirans to abide by the terms of the agreement, should one or the other attempt to renege. Although *any* demon would have done for those latter purposes, of course."

"And me?" Jassion's voice shook, making his words almost unintelligible. "Where do I fit in?"

Perhaps sensing the growing fury mere feet behind her, Salia decided that silence was no longer the prudent course. "We had to look as though we were dealing with the threat of Rebaine, and we had to ensure that he didn't pop up somewhere public and put the lie to what we were doing. And in so doing, we would also punish him for the crimes he committed against Imphallion so long ago. Something else," she added bitterly, "that Khanda was supposed to make happen."

Minutes passed, and nobody spoke. Corvis glared down at Sunder, battling a desperate need to kill something.

"I don't believe it," he said finally, tearing his gaze from the demon-forged blade. "Oh, it makes sense, but . . . Mavere was there, when Audriss summoned the Children of Apocalypse. I saw you," he continued, now turning toward her, "how you reacted. No political scheme would entice you to risk that happening again."

"I was assured there *was* no risk," she muttered, but she could not meet his eyes.

It was, perhaps unsurprisingly, Irrial who figured it out. "She was *afraid.*"

"Shut your mouth, you godsdamned—!"

But nobody was listening to the priestess at that point. "Of me?" Corvis demanded. "More than she was of a *demon*? I was bad, but I wasn't *that*—"

"The demons didn't threaten to take her mind from her, Corvis."

Finally, *finally* he understood. "You thought you might be one of them," he whispered, marveling. "You figured out that I'd charmed many of the Guildmasters, and you were afraid you were among them!"

"Until you had to hold that damn axe to my throat to force me to bring you here, yes," Mavere admitted, her shoulders sagging. "How could I know otherwise? How could I be sure that any choice I made was my own? I had to know I was free of you, you bastard!"

"Well," Corvis said dully. "Congratulations on your success."

Mavere turned away, and again there was silence.

"We should continue," Nenavar said finally. "We're almost ready." Again he began bustling about, while the trio on the stairs descended into the cellar proper.

"What exactly *are* we doing, Rebaine?" Jassion demanded.

"A banishing incantation. An exorcism, if you prefer. Nenavar called Khanda, so Nenavar is best suited to send him back. It's no easy spell, though."

"We can't just kill the old man? Isn't that what you did with Audriss, to banish Maukra and Mimgol?"

"I never did learn if it was killing Audriss or burning the book, actually," Corvis corrected. "But no, not all summoning incantations work that way. This one doesn't, it appears."

"Too bad. It would've made things much simpler."

Corvis nodded his agreement. Only then did they glance at each other, horrified to realize how alike they were thinking. Jassion scowled and moved across the room.

"All right," Nenavar said, standing as straight as his aged back would permit, "I need everyone to move away from the sigil, and to keep silent. Once I've begun, I can afford no—"

Corvis recognized the sound from above, the hideous shrieking of displaced air, but the wide-open cellar offered nowhere to hide. Portions of the ceiling burst in a rain of stone as Khanda's pillar of eldritch force slammed into the earth, hurling people around the chamber, dolls caught up in a child's tantrum. Even as he smashed into the far wall, his head ringing, his lungs burning as the breath rushed from them, Corvis could not help but note that neither Nenavar himself, nor the arcane runes upon the floor, were touched.

The old wizard raised his hands, seeking the source of the attack. "Come out, Khanda!" he cried. "You know you cannot harm me!" He clenched a fist in anger, and from somewhere in the broken house above, a voice shrieked in agony.

But Corvis saw, too, a dark-clad figure slipping through the ruins of the cellar, concealed from the others by piles of rubble—a figure that was most assuredly *not* Khanda.

"Mellorin!" He tried to shout, but his words emerged in only a ragged wheeze. "Mellorin, no! You don't know what he is! You don't—"

For an instant she rounded on him, her eyes blazing. "I know *exactly* who he is! And I know who *you* are, *Father*! I'm just glad I'm here to see you get some sliver of what you deserve."

"No, please . . ."

But she was already moving. Nenavar had only just heard something, only begun to look behind, when she whipped the pommel of a heavy dagger across the back of his head, watched as he tumbled senseless to the debris-strewn floor.

Corvis struggled halfway to his feet, reaching out imploringly for his daughter, when his ears were assaulted by the shriek of another spell from above. He saw only an instant of the second detonation before he tumbled, limp and senseless, to the far corner.

Chapter Twenty-three

ONCE AGAIN, AWARENESS RETURNED to Corvis's body at a slow creep, accompanied by the sharp pain of rocks splayed beneath him and the throbbing ache of bruised, maybe broken, limbs. Despite that pain, his mouth curled in a faint smile. Any human opponent with a shred of sanity would have slain him while he lay helpless, but for once, Khanda's hellish nature was working for them. So deep did the demon's innate cruelty run, he *had* to keep Corvis alive as witness to his ultimate triumph.

Of course, had Khanda known that the old warlord would not long remain as weak as he appeared, he might have acted differently.

Around him, Corvis heard the faint patter of falling dust and settling stones, along with an occasional whimper or moan, and knew he must not have been unconscious long. He heard, as well, Khanda's voice, echoing from all sides. It took him a few moments to recognize, with a dull but growing horror, the familiar syllables.

He struggled to focus, to spur his sluggish thoughts into motion. The demon must have been inside his head once more, extracting the last bits of Selakrian's spell, and Corvis was pathetically grateful that he'd been oblivious during this second violation.

For the decay in his mind, there was little to be done, but his physical hurts could yet be assuaged. Corvis forced his breathing to remain steady as the worst of the pains faded—not entirely or even substantially, but enough to become tolerable. His lips twitched in relief, and he wondered what his companions must be thinking as they felt the same healing touch.

Opening his eyes, he could see clearly into the manor's upper levels. Bits of rock trickled down from what remained of the ceiling, and the cellar's stone floor, except for the area circumscribed by the sigil, had fared little better. Great chunks of it were shattered or missing, revealing pits of clay or soil below, filling the air with a rich, earthen scent.

And there, across the room . . .

Oh, gods. I'm so sorry, I never wanted any of this life to touch yours . . .

She stood straight, her dark hair plastered to the sides of her face with a light sheen of sweat. In each hand she held a brutal, heavy-bladed dagger, one of which was covered in a spidery array of subtly shifting runes. Corvis couldn't help but wonder, albeit briefly, if anyone had ever before, in all recorded history, wielded two of the Kholben Shiar at once.

She'd grown, these past years, into a striking young woman. He saw a touch of his own craggy features, softened and smoothed by her mother's influence. Yet in her eyes he saw neither Tyannon's gentle strength nor his own burning obsession but something else entirely, a deep well of intensity whose nature he could not interpret—in part because it was largely hidden behind a growing spark of fearful confusion as her world spiraled out of control.

And Corvis Rebaine realized, with a muffled sob, that he didn't know his own daughter well enough to know if he should be proud of her—but he knew, beyond the sharpest sliver of doubt, that he *could* be.

/*Ah, there you are, old boy! I was afraid you were going to miss the big finish.*/

It sounded in his mind and soul rather than his ears, just as it had so many years before. He could actually feel his thoughts recoiling from that unholy intrusion like the curling edge of burning parchment. Groaning with only half-feigned effort, Corvis craned around further to glare at the figures beside his apprehensive daughter.

An unconscious Nenavar, bloody head lolling limply on his neck, sat awkwardly before Khanda, propped up by one of the demon's hands. Khanda himself, still wearing Kaleb's shape, knelt upon the floor, chanting Selakrian's invocation without interruption even as his words resounded in Corvis's thoughts.

/Did you know,/ Khanda asked conversationally as the incantation progressed, /that it was Nenavar who helped Audriss awaken Pekatherosh? Small world, isn't it? You ought to be standing in line to kill the old stick, not working with him./

Corvis mumbled something, spat out a mouthful of dirt and sticky, half-dried blood.

/Where is old Pekky, anyway? You didn't send him back to hell—I was waiting—and I know you didn't free him from that silly little jewel./

"Safe," Corvis rasped.

Silence for a moment, and then Khanda began to laugh uproariously—mostly in Corvis's head, but even his physical body convulsed, his mouth bending around a smile that almost, *almost* mangled the next syllables of the spell.

/Oh, Corvis, you really *never* change, do you? You stuck him back in the cave on Mount Molleya, didn't you? "Just in case," yes?/

"It held *you* well enough all those years," Corvis said with a painful shrug.

/So it did, so it did./

Far more quietly, gathering all that remained of his battered will to ensure that none of his words reached Khanda's awareness, Corvis whispered, "Can you do it?"

"Not yet," came the equally quiet reply. "He's far too focused. I need him distracted."

Corvis nodded. "How did you find us?" he asked, raising his voice once more.

/Didn't have to. You've always been predictable, Corvis. As soon as I dropped "Master" Nenavar's name, I knew you'd come here eventually. All I had to do was watch the place./

"I can't believe the idiot didn't have teleportation wards on his own home."

/Oh, he did, more than you'd ever imagine. But he'd attuned them to *admit me. He so enjoyed summoning me to him at every whim, and after all, I couldn't possibly hurt him, could I?/*

Another nod. And of course, he'd have been able to carry Mellorin as well—or at worst, teleport her nearby and then physically open the door from within.

"Khanda, please . . ."

/Eh?/

"Let her go." He hadn't known he was going to say it until the words were out. "She's taken Nenavar out for you, done what you needed her to. This is between us. Let her go."

/Why, Corvis, that's so sweet, I could just cry. Actually, I'd rather make someone else cry. It's so much more fun./

"Khanda . . ." *Just keep talking, you bastard.* With every second, he could feel the pain of his wounds lessening, his strength growing . . .

/I'm keeping her, Corvis. She really wanted to be here for this. Besides, I think I've grown attached to the little lady—rather like a pet. I want her around to see what happens to you, and you to see some of what I'll be doing to her. It's not good for family to have secrets from each other, you know./

Corvis choked, fire roaring in his mind. And as it had before, his concentration wavered.

/Corvis . . . ?/ Not merely the demon's tone, but the set of his shoulders, bespoke a sudden suspicion. */Corvis, what are you doing?/*

"Damn it!" If Khanda had sensed the slow spring of magic flowing through their bodies, mending their hurts, they could wait no longer. "Are you ready?"

"No!" that voice insisted. "Corvis, I need more time!"

"Then I," he growled, tensing muscles that should have been too weak to move, "need the Kholben Shiar."

Beneath Corvis's cloak and tunic—and, too, beneath the soil exposed by the rents in the floor—unseen things began to move . . .

———————————◼▸ ◂◼———————————

"What? Where are you—?"

"Probably nowhere. You've just got me paranoid now. I want

to make sure nobody's following—that Mavere didn't somehow manage to signal anyone."

"Paranoid indeed," Jassion said. "But probably wise," he acknowledged, riding on ahead.

Corvis wheeled his mount in a tight circle and galloped back the way they'd come, straining to keep one eye on the sky, the other on the road. As soon as he was well and truly out of sight of the others he reined the beast to a halt and raised an arm out before him.

Having been waiting for just that, or so it seemed, one of the crows circling above plummeted to alight upon his wrist. It was a bedraggled, sickly-looking thing, with drooping feathers and weeping eyes.

"I see you brought some friends," Corvis said.

Wings rose and fell in what was probably meant as a shrug. "They followed me," the crow told him. "Probably figured I knew something they didn't. Or maybe they were curious about me."

"Or maybe they're just birds, and gods know why they do anything."

"Or that, yes."

Corvis lowered his wrist so she could hop onto the pommel of his saddle. "I was afraid I'd never see you again, Seilloah."

"You almost didn't," she admitted.

"I'm sorry I—"

"No, Corvis, *I'm* sorry. Of *course* finding Mellorin and stopping Khanda take precedence. I don't like it, but I understand it. It's just—it hurts so much, you've no idea how much . . ."

"I understand," he told her softly.

"You don't. Not really."

"No, not really. Seilloah . . ." He swallowed, reached up to wipe away tears he refused to shed. "Seilloah, if you want, I could—I could end it. Make it quick."

Corvis didn't understand how, but he swore he saw the beak flex into a sad smile. "No, dearest. Thank you—I know how much you didn't want to offer that—but it's not necessary. If I want to end it, all I need do is stop fighting. Let the spell lapse. It'll be over in seconds."

"Then why...?"

"I thought about it. More than once, especially in the past few weeks, I very nearly did. But I couldn't, not yet."

"Why not?"

"Khanda. Corvis, I think I know how to beat him..."

CORVIS ROLLED TO HIS FEET, his companions—all save Salia Mavere, whom Seilloah had not thought worth the effort to heal— following only seconds after. A small crow stuck its head out from within Corvis's tunic, and from beneath the exposed soil erupted a squid-like array of roots and tendrils, drawn through the earth from the surrounding gardens and hedge. With uncanny speed they lashed out, some knocking Khanda and Nenavar aside, others wrapping like whips about Mellorin's wrists. She cried out, and the Kholben Shiar plummeted earthward.

Even more tendrils intercepted them, flinging them hilt-first across the room. Seilloah dived from Corvis's clothes and fluttered toward the cracked ceiling as he snagged the weapons in mid-flight. Sunder he clasped in his left fist, spinning it in an upright grip even as it shifted into its familiar shape. But Talon—Talon he whipped back behind his head and hurled back across the chamber. It tumbled end over end, forming into an axe not unlike Sunder itself, and struck...

Not Khanda, for the demon had not been Corvis's target, but Nenavar. The old wizard's body spasmed as his head split under the axe's caress, and then lay forever still.

Everything went silent as death. Slowly, Khanda rose from where the writhing plants had flung him. With an angry grunt, he shoved Nenavar's body off him, small gobbets of his former master's brain and skull clinging to his face. Corvis spun Sunder smoothly through the air before him, ready for any response.

Except, perhaps, for Khanda to simply stand gaping at him, jaw moving silently. In all the years they'd known each other, in all the forms the demon had worn, Corvis had *never* seen him at a loss for words.

"You . . ." Even when he finally spoke, the words seemed almost too much for him. "You *bastard!*"

"Really, Khanda? That's the best you can do?"

"Kaleb?" Mellorin appeared at his side, clutching her lacerated wrists. "Why is he calling you—"

But the demon ignored her, had eyes only for the man he hated most in all the world. "Do you have *any* idea how hard it is for a sorcerer to *take over* another's conjuration? I don't even know if there are any alive who could do it! I'm going to have to search for *years* before I find someone who can usurp Nenavar's spell!"

"And until then, there's no way to free you from the binding's limitations. I know." Corvis shrugged. "Weren't you the one who just told me I ought to be trying to kill Nenavar? You were right. Thanks for the suggestion."

"Kaleb," Mellorin demanded, her tone far more insistent. "What's he talking about?"

"Yes, *Kaleb*." Corvis smiled grimly. "Tell her what I'm talking about."

Khanda growled and shoved Mellorin aside, not hard, just enough to stagger her. "You," the demon hissed, "are now officially more troublesome than you are fun. Good-bye, Corvis."

Flames bridged the chamber. Stone cracked; brimstone-reeking smoke made for the holes above, seeking its own escape. Anticipating just such an attack, Corvis and the others dived aside. He continued rolling, rose and ran as Khanda spun, sweeping his hellfire across the far wall in swift pursuit.

Sweat poured down Corvis's face, his heart pounded in his chest. Over the roaring fire he heard his daughter shouting, but what she said, or whether she addressed him or the man she knew as Kaleb, he couldn't tell. He was nearing the end of the cellar, had nowhere else to dodge . . .

And the flames abruptly angled upward before ceasing entirely. At

Seilloah's urging, the tendrils lashed at Khanda yet again, knocking him backward and disrupting his attack. For the second time in as many minutes, the room went abnormally, impossibly silent.

In that instant of calm, Corvis saw the others staring at him, nightmarish phantoms in the flickering light of the many small fires that illuminated the cellar. And he saw in their faces a growing despair, for what, really, could they do against such a foe?

Struggling to catch his breath, he gestured toward Khanda, who was even now rising once more to his feet. "Wound him! It'll be enough!" He didn't know if they heard, wasn't even certain how loudly he'd spoken, but Jassion and Irrial both nodded all the same. They separated, advancing on the demon from different sides. In her right fist, the baroness clutched her dueling blade—better than nothing against Khanda, albeit only just—but Jassion's hands remained empty.

Khanda stood tall, hands raised, and from above came the first hint of whistling—of the air itself splitting—as he prepared to call down another storm of undiluted eldritch force. Corvis cocked his arm back as though to hurl Sunder like he had Talon, and just as he'd hoped, Khanda flinched, allowing his spell to fade. Immortal the demon might be, but with the aid of the Kholben Shiar, they had taught him to fear *pain*.

The others lunged, taking advantage of that momentary distraction. Irrial's blade sank deep into the meat of Khanda's side; a mere sting, less than an inconvenience, but at least a start. Jassion, however, hurtled *past* his foe; stooped, instead, by Nenavar's corpse and lifted Talon from the human wreckage. Clutching the hilt in both hands as it sculpted itself again into his great two-hander, he took a single step toward Khanda and offered a twisted smile.

The demon waved, and Jassion felt himself lifted from his feet, as had happened thrice before. This time, however, he recognized the gesture and twisted aside while thrusting with the demon-forged blade, as though parrying a corporeal weapon. Perhaps it helped, perhaps he'd simply avoided the worst of the spell, but he tumbled only a few yards before landing in an awkward crouch.

Seilloah's roots and tendrils continued whipping themselves at

Khanda, forcing him to split his attentions, lest he be knocked aside or bound long enough for either Kholben Shiar to deliver up far greater torment.

Mellorin appeared suddenly at his side, her own dagger held before her. "Go!" she insisted, placing herself between her lover and her father's relentless approach. "I can hold them long enough for you to get out!"

Corvis pulled up short just beyond his daughter's reach, his eyes imploring, his soul shivering at the gleam in Khanda's own.

"No . . ." The demon turned away, devoting his attention to Jassion and Irrial. "No, don't keep him off me. Kill him."

"*What?* No! Kaleb, I don't think I'm—"

"*Kill him.*"

Her face gone slack in horrified disbelief, tears beginning to roll along her cheeks, Mellorin advanced on her father, blade held high.

"Mellorin!" Corvis stretched forth a hand, only to yank it back as her blade nearly took off the tips of his fingers. "Mellorin, stop!"

"I'm *trying!*" And he saw, then, the unsteady gait as she approached, the twitching and shuddering that ran through her limbs without slowing her movements one iota. "Oh, gods, what's happening?"

Corvis backpedaled as fast as the loose rubble would permit, Sunder held defensively, casting about desperately for some solution. Time and again Mellorin's blade struck, and each time he parried only to find himself faced with a new angle of attack. She was good, she was fast; better and faster than he'd ever have expected. He felt his chest swell with pride even as he wondered how to stop her. More than once she left herself open, and he felt the tug as Sunder, or perhaps his own instincts, goaded him to strike. But by every god and every damned soul, he *would not!*

Over her shoulder, he saw Khanda hurling himself about like an acrobat, spinning between Seilloah's tendrils, always just beyond reach of Jassion's furiously hacking blade. Now and again, bursts of fire or shrieking levinbolts would hurtle from the demon's fists, pour from his eyes. Thanks to the speed and magics of the Kholben Shiar, the baron avoided or even parried most of them, but burns across his arms and chest showed where a few had found their mark.

Corvis saw, too, the witch fluttering in the corner above, raining feathers and bloody pus as her strength ebbed, the corruption spread through her latest—her last?—body.

And then Corvis's boot came down on a rough chunk of stone, and he found himself flailing. With a cry of infinite despair, Mellorin lunged.

Still he could have stopped her, could have cut her down with Sunder before the dagger fell. Still he would not.

White-hot agony yanked at his entire body like an angry puppeteer as her blade plunged deep into his left side. He coughed twice, felt the slick steel slide from his flesh as he staggered. Groaning, he pressed his left hand to the wound, felt liquid warmth between his fingers.

"Daddy? I'm so sorry, Daddy . . ." Even as she wept, she came at him again, bloody knife poised, and it was all he could do to stay ahead of her.

"*Sorry?*" Khanda's mocking laugh echoed through the cellar. "This is what you *wanted*, Mellorin! Ah, fickle youth . . ."

A shadow fell across Mellorin and the baroness appeared behind, hands outstretched to wrestle the blade away. The girl spun a brutal kick into Irrial's knee and continued on, ignoring the other woman as she collapsed to the floor.

"Corvis . . ." It came from above, the caw of a wounded bird. "Corvis, I can't hold on much longer. If it doesn't happen soon . . ."

"Aw, poor Corvis." Again from Khanda, literally dancing away from Jassion's blade. He wasn't even *trying* to attack anymore, wasn't throwing fire or arcane bolts. He was, Corvis realized with a choking mouthful of bile, enjoying the show. "Did your little plan fall apart? Did you smuggle poor, dying Seilloah here for nothing?"

Corvis snarled something, but the words that crossed the cellar were Mellorin's, not his own. "Kaleb! Gods, Kaleb, don't make me do this! Please . . ."

"I admit," Khanda continued, "it's not as efficient as Selakrian's charm, but it seems to be doing the trick, doesn't it? Of course, it'd be a lot harder if part of her hadn't already wanted to see you dead. Poor abandoned waif. But if it makes you feel better, it's *mostly* me. I told you, I've complete control of my physical form—and I've spent many a night these past weeks leaving tiny parts of that form in sweet little

Mellorin. And now look. Why, the result is almost as much fun as the process!"

Corvis stumbled once more, so violently was he trembling, and only Sunder's unnatural speed enabled him to parry the stroke that followed. Thick blood soaked his trousers, left a trail across the floor, and with every step his wound pumped another spurt of his life.

"Daddy, please! You have to fight back! *Please* don't let me do this!" But he *could not*. Another stroke of the dagger and Sunder went spinning across the room, knocked from a broken and bleeding hand.

"Do you suppose I'm fortunate enough," Khanda asked, slicing one of Seilloah's roots with the edge of his bare hand, "that she might conceive? If so, Corvis, I hope you'll be good enough to let us name the child after you. It was you, after all, who brought us together."

Corvis was screaming unintelligible, bestial sounds. Veins stood out in his neck and across his forehead; spittle hung from the corner of his lips. Irrial was back on her feet, struggling to reach them, to do *something*, but with her limp she had trouble even walking, certainly could not keep up with his constant retreat or Mellorin's relentless advance. Even Salia Mavere, it appeared, was trying now to lend a hand, but she could only crawl and stagger from where she'd been thrown, looking for some way to help.

Mellorin closed, her dagger flashing . . .

THROUGH HIS BURNING FURY, through his constant slashes and thrusts at a target who evaded his every effort with inhuman grace, Jassion still managed to keep track of what was happening to the others. He saw the Terror of the East forced into retreat, saw blood spilling from his side, and in his soul, he rejoiced. No matter what threat Khanda posed, an uncountable array of wrongs would be set right by Rebaine's death; no matter what the warlord and Seilloah had planned, surely he, with Talon, could serve just as well. The time had finally come for retribution for Denathere, for all Imphallion . . .

For Jassion, and for the sister who was ripped from him.

But then, as he swung Talon, he *saw* his sister, saw Tyannon not as the girl he remembered from so long ago, but as he'd seen her months before, for the first time in his adult life. He saw her face, staring, imploring. And he saw, too, Mellorin's eyes, horrified as she'd taken her first unwilling steps toward Rebaine.

He saw, and he knew that neither woman—none of his *family*—could live with what she was about to do.

And Jassion, the Baron of Braetlyn, abandoned his fight with Khanda to save the life of the Terror of the East—and the soul of the Terror's daughter.

———————

"IRRIAL! CATCH!"

Corvis heard the call, saw Jassion sprinting his way, tossing Talon at the limping baroness as he neared. The distance between them was not vast, but broken pebbles shifted beneath his feet, slowing his headlong plunge, and Mellorin's dagger rose ever higher.

Rose . . . and stopped.

Steel glinted, seeming to dance in the flickering firelight. Inches separated father from daughter, and the old warlord knew he should already be dead.

Mellorin's blade, her hand, her entire body shuddered, muscle and flesh warring against each other. Dried lips split and bled, so tightly were they compressed together. She cried out once, in pain or fury Corvis could not tell, and then she was moving again, once more a slave to Khanda's whims. But in that one moment of rebellion, she'd bought Jassion the extra seconds he'd needed. She heard his footsteps, turned to face her charging uncle, thrust with the vicious weapon.

Jassion made no move to stop her. He twisted so that the dagger grated across his chain-armored ribs, winced with pain as several links parted, and then slammed into his niece, carrying them both to the floor. He lay atop her, pinning her with his bulk, fighting to grab at her wrists. He saw hope flare in her features, even as she bucked and thrashed beneath him, struggling to break free.

"Oh, no, this will never do." Flame again roared from Khanda's hands, reducing the intervening tendrils to ash, but it approached slowly, a tide rather than a rushing river. The demon, Corvis realized, wanted to force Jassion to release the young woman, rather than simply char them both to nothing. He struggled to close on Khanda, and found he could scarcely walk. The agony in his side flared, his legs turned to so much paste, and he collapsed to an awkward crouch.

More feathers rained from above and Seilloah landed clumsily on his shoulder. Half her body was bare of feathers, covered in weeping sores, and her beak was *cracked* down the center. "I'm sorry . . . ," she told him in a broken whisper.

No . . . No, it can't *end like this . . .*

Khanda screamed, a high-pitched, inhuman thing.

Irrial lay on the floor before the demon, as near as her limping and crawling would allow. Talon stretched from her hand, a slender-bladed duelist's weapon, its very tip punching neatly into the muscle of Khanda's calf.

No serious wound, this. Even inflicted by the Kholben Shiar, for the demon it was but a momentary hurt.

But for that moment, Khanda was distracted. Khanda was *vulnerable*.

"Corvis . . ."

"Is there no other way?" He felt the words catch in his throat, even though he knew she was already dead.

"None." The crow looked at him, and he wished he could know if she was trying to smile. "Good-bye, my dearest friend."

"Good . . ." He choked, then, and there was no time to say more. The crow squawked once, trembled, and lay still.

Groaning with the effort, Corvis rose once more to his feet, turned his tear-streaked face toward his daughter's struggling form. "Mellorin . . ."

She knew his tone for what it was. "No! No, don't . . ."

"Tell your mother . . . Gods, you know her better than I do now. Figure out what she needs to hear, tell her I said it. I love you, Mellorin. Whether you believe it or not, I always have."

"Daddy, *no!*"

But Corvis was already running, the last of his strength pumping through his legs. He had to be there, had to reach him before it was too late.

Khanda had begun to catch his breath, was leaning down to clutch at the weapon in his leg. Irrial had scurried away, knowing full well she had no way to save herself if the demon turned on her. For a moment, as he crossed the cellar, Corvis thought it hadn't worked, wondered if Seilloah had held on all this time for nothing.

Wondered, and began to despair, until Khanda shuddered. His face went slack, and his entire body fell back against the nearest wall.

No, not *his* body. The body he'd *created* around himself, to wear in the mortal realm. A body over which he had full and absolute control.

A body that, inhabited by a demon, possessed no mortal soul.

<hr />

IT HURT. Oh, Arhylla Earth-Mother, it *hurt*!

The ground beneath her was rough, abrasive against her feet. The scents of thick soil and rock dust and sweat in the air were acrid, scratching at her lungs with ragged claws, until she was certain she must choke on her own blood. Around her, every line, every corner, the edge of every brick, the contours of every stone, were razor-edged, slicing at her even from feet and yards away.

And those lines looked *wrong*. The illumination came, not from above, but from all around her. They burned, the *people* burned; men and women both, and she recognized none of them. She saw no faces, saw no features, for the light emanated from deep inside them, through bone and flesh and fabric and armor.

Every mortal soul, *every* soul, was a light—and that light was terrible. It pierced the eye, no matter how she turned away; cast shadows sharp enough to slit her own flesh; burned against and beneath her skin, inferno and infection intertwined as one, worse than hell's own fire.

A world, a whole world, of torment, distilled impossibly pure.

But not *everywhere*. Not quite.

Amid the awful glow were patches of comforting shade; open

wounds in mortal flesh seeped blood and pain, and from those spots, the light grew dim. She heard hopeless cries, the song of sorrow and fear, and where despair shrouded any soul, the burning abated.

She laughed a cruel, exulting laugh, rejoicing as the agony of those nearby lessened her own, if only just. Laughed, and wept, for she understood that in a world of such perfect torment, the waning of her own pain was the only joy.

Pummeled by agony, weeping ever harder as she sought only to lash out, to inflict more pain to detract from her own, she doubled over, gazing down . . .

The body she wore was not bird, nor beast, nor her familiar feminine form garbed in earthen browns and forest greens, but clad all in black, a thing that was not human in human form.

And Seilloah remembered. Who she was, where she was, what she must do; she remembered.

She also understood now, just a little, what Khanda was. And she almost, *almost* pitied him.

Then Seilloah rose up, gathered her strength for the very last time, and reached out through the body she wore, wrestling it away from the demon it housed . . .

CORVIS CLOSED, AND FOR A SINGLE heartbeat, he saw Khanda's lips curve, not in his own smile, but in Seilloah's. He saw, and his heart exulted.

Khanda had no soul, perhaps, but his will was great. For only seconds, those few heartbeats before the demon understood what had happened and fought back, would the witch have control.

But those few seconds were enough for her to draw upon the demon's own power, to send it flowing through muscle and bone and organ. To reshape his body within, rather than without.

To make him well and truly and *utterly* mortal.

Corvis swept up Talon from where it lay at their feet. He smiled, too, meeting Seilloah's eyes behind Khanda's. And then, both hands clenched upon the brutal Kholben Shiar, he struck.

The axe punched through half the demon's rib cage with a shower of bone and blood, embedding itself deeply in the stone wall beyond. Khanda—and it *was* Khanda, again—stared at him, then down at his mangled body. He raised his head, he opened his lips . . . .

SHE WELCOMED THE PAIN OF THE BLADE, the swift fading of the body she wore. It meant that she'd won, that the far greater torment in which she'd lived for so long would soon fade, that she had not suffered it in vain, that . . .

Her limbs shuddered around her; a wave of fire and rot washed over her thoughts, sweeping them away. In the dark of the cellar, or perhaps in her own mind, a pair of eyes gleamed open, staring at her through four separate pupils.

And just before the world faded away, she heard that terrible voice, one last time, in her own soul.

/Not alone!/

"NOT . . ." KHANDA COUGHED, wet blood spraying his enemy's face. "Not alone . . ."

Then he was gone, just another corpse to fall at the feet of Corvis Rebaine.

Corvis turned toward the others, a smile stretching across his face, and took a single step . . .

The sky screamed, the whistling of the final spell Khanda would ever cast. Corvis heard it coming, tried to dodge aside, but the last of his strength was gone. His entire left side was numb, the floor around his feet a slick pond of blood. He fell back, slumping to the floor against the wall, sinking down to Khanda's side. He reached, grasping at Talon, trying to pull himself up once more, and the Kholben Shiar shifted, grinding even farther into the battered and broken stone of the cellar.

A resounding *crack* echoed as the demon's magic slammed into the splintered ceiling above. Dust choked the air, perhaps an unnatural mist rising to hide the next world from mortal view. Corvis fell prone beneath the weight of the invisible force, felt the first of the stones falling on his shoulders like hail, heard the rumble of shifting masonry, and allowed himself to drift away.

⸺⸺⸺⸺⸺⸺❘⸺▸ ◂⸺❘⸺⸺⸺⸺⸺⸺

NOTHING MOVED but a final handful of rocks, clattering off the heap of stone that now filled a quarter of the cellar. They bounced with hollow clacks and clicks, finally tumbling across the floor and fetching up against the corners. The clouds of grit began, oh so gradually, to sift down from the air, the echoes of the ceiling's collapse to fade from aching ears.

Mellorin attempted to stand and found she could not for the weight atop her. Only then did she remember where she was. "I . . ." She swallowed, trying to clear the dust from her mouth, her throat. "I'm all right, Uncle Jassion."

She felt the suspicion, the tension in his tentative shifting, but he moved. She rose, knees wobbly, abandoning her blood-encrusted dagger on the floor. Her steps hesitant, she staggered toward the heap of broken stone that had buried one man she had thought she'd loved, and another she'd thought she hated. She felt a dampness on her cheeks, but for the moment she wept no more. Her soul was distant, numb; she had no more tears to shed.

Without thought, she reached toward the stones, and blinked in dull confusion at the fingers that clamped around her wrist, halting her.

"Don't," Jassion told her. It took her a moment to recognize the foreign tone in his mangled voice as compassion. "We don't know how precarious that pile is. You could bring it down on you."

"I never . . . I never got to . . ."

"I know. I'm sorry, Mellorin." And damn if it didn't sound like he meant it, too.

She heard shuffling, watched from the corner of her eye as Irrial appeared beside her. Mellorin flinched as the older woman laid a hand upon her shoulder, but did not pull away.

"He loved you, Mellorin. Whatever else you hear about him—and there will be much you'll wish you hadn't—believe that he loved you."

"I think . . . I think I almost do."

With that she crossed back across the chamber, leaving the unsympathetic stone behind, crouching to retrieve the one piece of her father that remained. Again Sunder shifted in her hand, becoming the heavy dagger she already knew so well, already despised, already needed. She glanced about her, saw Jassion, Irrial, and Guildmistress Mavere all watching.

Still on her knees, she ran a finger across the tiny feathered body that lay nearby. It rocked beneath her touch, one wing falling open to reveal mottled patches of bare skin between clinging feathers.

"There's so much I don't understand, so many lies Kaleb—Khanda?—told me. You'll explain it to me?" It seemed directed to the room at large, rather than any one soul. "All of it?"

"We will," Jassion promised.

"Even the parts you don't think I want to hear," she insisted.

"Yes." Irrial, this time, her tone no less sincere.

"Thank you." Mellorin rained dust as she rose, but made no move to brush herself clean.

"For what it's worth," Mavere began, her voice weak from her injuries, "I'm sorry. If we'd known Khanda would try this, we'd never have called him." Her gaze flickered from one to the next, imploring. "But *something* had to be done, don't you see? For the good of Imphallion, we—"

She grunted once, less in pain than surprise, and slid, with a final rattling sigh, to the floor. Her expression blank, Mellorin shook the Guildmistress's blood from Sunder's edge.

Irrial grimaced, Jassion nodded. Neither spoke.

"We should go," the warlord's daughter told them.

Her uncle nodded again. "There's much to be done. We have to try to explain what's happened, and to mount a defense—a *true* defense—against Cephira."

Irrial quirked her lip. "That might've been easier if we had—"

"No." Jassion shook his head. "She'd never have admitted to any of it. It would've been our word against hers. As it is, we've precious little proof, but . . ." He shrugged.

"But we have to try." Irrial took one step, a second, and staggered. "I don't think I can ride. I *certainly* can't climb out of here. Go."

"My lady, we—"

"Take Mellorin back to Mecepheum. You can send someone back for me with a coach. And rope. Lots of rope."

The baron nodded reluctantly and began examining the broken ceiling overhead.

"Jassion? Send a squad of soldiers, too, would you? Just in case."

"Of course."

IT TOOK SOME DOING, especially since they refused to touch the stones that had become a makeshift cairn for Corvis and Khanda both, but eventually they stacked together sufficient rock and timber for Jassion to leap up and clasp the edge of the floor above. After a moment of scrabbling, while the others held their breath and prayed the stone would hold, he vanished over the rim. He reappeared a moment later, one arm reaching downward. It probably wasn't necessary—Mellorin could likely have made the jump herself—but he offered, and she accepted. A bit more scrabbling, Jassion called out once more to ensure Irrial would be all right for the duration, and then they were gone.

For several minutes the baroness waited, until all sounds had ceased above and she was certain the others were on their way. Then, leaning against the wall for support, she inched her way toward the unsteady heap of rock.

And again, for long minutes, made no move at all.

Who had he been, there, at the last? Who had slain Khanda, had risen in the face of a mortal wound and lashed out to save, if not the entire world, then his beloved daughter? Corvis Rebaine, the Terror of the East? Or Cerris of Rahariem, whom Irrial herself had once thought to love, and who—though that love was past—might have been a friend and companion worth having?

Irrial didn't know. But as sure as she was that nobody could have sur-

vived either that dreadful wound or the weight of the crushing stones—
let alone both together—she knew that she must do all she could to be
absolutely certain. No matter how futile the effort.

How many times, after all, had Corvis Rebaine already performed
the impossible?

She could accomplish little enough by herself, perhaps, but at least
she could make a start until the soldiers arrived to aid her. Grunting
with exertion, the baroness of Rahariem leaned down and heaved aside
the first of many stones.

Epilogue

MELLORIN STOOD CALF-DEEP in snow, one hand resting on Sunder's hilt, and struggled to peer through the whirling blizzard at the path before her.

She had indeed learned much about Corvis Rebaine, and as she'd been warned, there was much of it she wished she hadn't. Still she'd sought more—and more she had discovered. From Tyannon and Jassion, from Irrial and even from Davro; from scholars and sages, historians and even oracles. She devoured it all, until there was no more to be learned.

And she'd learned what she must do with that knowledge. She wondered if, in the many months that had come and gone, her mother had begun to forgive her—or if she ever would.

But it didn't matter. Mellorin knew her father, now. She knew why he'd left, and if she couldn't yet forgive him for that, she could at least understand. She knew what he'd hoped to accomplish and the world he'd hoped to build . . . And she knew where he'd gone wrong.

She had no children waiting for her. She could avoid his mistakes. She could do it *right*. But she, like her father before her, needed the power to make it work.

Her guide, scion of a local Terrirpa tribe, reemerged from the wall of snow and beckoned with a fur-clad hand. "We should hurry, good mistress, lest the blizzard grow any worse."

An absent nod was her only response as she gazed upward, as though through sheer force of will she could see into the uppermost reaches of Mount Molleya, or the hidden cave at their peak where her prize awaited, entombed within the ice.

I'll build the world you wanted for us, Father. I'll make you proud.

Plans for the future and memories of the past twining around each other behind her eyes, Mellorin waved her guide forward and began to climb.

About the Author

ARI MARMELL would love to tell you all about the various esoteric jobs he held and the wacky adventures he had on the way to becoming an author, since that's what other authors seem to do in these blurbs. Unfortunately, he doesn't actually have any. In point of fact, Ari decided while at the University of Houston that he wanted to be a writer, graduated with a creative writing degree, and—after holding down a couple of very mundane jobs, in retail positions and as an advertising proofreader—broke into freelance writing. He has an extensive history of writing for role-playing games, but has always worked on improving and publishing his fiction at every opportunity. He has several shared-world novels and short stories in publication—including *Agents of Artifice*, a Magic: The Gathering novel—but *The Conqueror's Shadow* was his first wholly original published book. *The Warlord's Legacy* is the next book in the Corvis Rebaine Saga. He also has a new book, *The Goblin Corps*, coming out soon.

Ari currently lives in an apartment that's almost as cluttered as his subconscious, which he shares (the apartment, not the subconscious) with his wife, George, and two cats who really need some form of volume control installed. You can visit Ari online at www.mouseferatu.com

About the Type

This book was set in Electra, a typeface designed for Linotype by W. A. Dwiggins, the renowned type designer (1880–1956). Electra is a fluid typeface, avoiding the contrasts of thick and thin strokes that are prevalent in most modern typefaces.